# Ghosts
# of
# Orion

Doug L. Hoffman

ISBN 978-0-9884588-8-8

Published by
The Resilient Earth Press
http://resilientearthpress.com

## Books By Doug L. Hoffman

*The T'aafhal Legacy Series*
Ghosts of Orion
The Queen's Daemon

*The T'aafhal Inheritance Trilogy*
Parker's Folly
Peggy Sue
M'tak Ka'fek

*Non-fiction (with Allen Simmons)*
The Resilient Earth
The Energy Gap

# *Preface*

This is the first book in a new series set in the same Universe as my earlier trilogy about Earthlings finding their place in the galaxy, the T'aafhal Inheritance. I'm calling this and forthcoming tales the T'aafhal Legacy series and it is an open ended proposition. I have been storing up a number of adventures involving the crew and characters from the first three Peggy Sue novels—some ideas I have had from the beginning, while others are prompted by questions and suggestions from readers. There is no overall story arc as there was in the trilogy, and the books may not be published in strict chronological order.

This novel, the Ghosts of Orion, follows the further adventures of the crew of the Peggy Sue, this time without the leadership of Jack and Ludmilla. Instead, Billy Ray and Bobby are in the lead, along with their significant others, Beth and Mizuki, respectively. There are other characters from the previous stories as well as some new ones. As always, there will be strange new worlds to explore and even stranger aliens to meet.

As always, I thank my early readers for their many corrections and suggestions: Rik Faith, Stuart White, Bobby Johnson, David Metheny, Clayton Ward, and Jesse Perkins. Mistakes that slip through are all my fault, certainly not theirs. If you like this book please tell your friends. If you really like it consider writing a review online at Amazon.com.

Regards,
Doug L. Hoffman
Conway, Arkansas
July 4, 2014

# Prologue

## *Gliese 667Cc*

The Senior Academician fumbled with the recorder connections. Anxiety made the familiar task frustratingly difficult. With a sigh she looked out the arched side window at the tranquil scene beyond. Puffy white clouds, blushing red at their edges, floated in a cerulean sky. Below, trees adorned in light green leaves brushed fields of red flowers with graceful ground-sweeping branches. Scattered among this verdant display were the flowing white stucco shapes of the city's houses and buildings.

Her city was located well inland, a center of commerce for the large farming region in the heartland of the planet's largest continent. Home to perhaps 150,000 souls, it was not a large city, yet big enough to warrant its own branch of the state University. Years ago she had accepted a position here, to live and raise her daughter in a more natural environment.

It was not like the major cities along the coasts, where graceful spires reached for the sky and people teamed among them in their millions. The glitz and glamor of big city life beckoned to many, but not to her. This lovely little city ran at a slower pace. It was a paradise where one could escape the hustle and bustle of big city life. A paradise soon to be lost.

Returning her attention to the device in front of her, the Senior Academician finished attaching the leads to the recorder. She often came to the Hall of Memories to make archive copies of her thoughts—much more frequently than average citizens were wont to. In fact, the large hall was empty; she was the only person making a deposit into the city's collective memory this day. But then she was, above all things, an historian. It was her obligation to record events for the edification of future generations.

A soft green light glowed on the console, telling her that the recording process had begun. Closing her eyes, she thought back over the events of recent days. Four days ago, it was a day like any other. The red sun rose, accompanied by its two companions, a sliver of the inner planet just visible in the morning light. Several bright streaks marked the passage of meteors out over the middle sea.

Normally, meteors marked the death of the objects that caused them, the objects themselves evaporating into nothingness during their fiery transits. But the objects that morning survived to reach the surface of the sea, completing their transformation from meteoroid to meteor to meteorite. Given the heat generated passing through the planet's atmosphere, it seemed improbable that anything living could survive the journey. Yet something did survive.

Whether that something was actually alive was a matter of debate among the more scientifically oriented academics the historian knew. Not that the debate had much time to develop. A day after the impacts it was noticed that fishing boats and pleasure craft were failing to return to port. The reason for this soon became apparent when something emerged from the coastal waters and began moving inland.

Her colleagues were still unsure just what the invader was: Was it a single organism or several? Was it intelligent or not? Was it plant or animal? Was it even alive at all? Their ignorance was not alleviated as the foul pestilence spread inland consuming everything before it. Scientists sent to analyze the infestation did not last long enough to report back, let alone learn enough about the threat to suggest countermeasures.

From remote cameras, the pestilence itself appeared to be a simple black substance with root-like runners spreading out before it. It advanced like a black tide, pouring over everything in its path. On encountering anything organic, runners shot out of the main mass, racing ahead faster than a person could run. Black tendrils of death that enveloped every living thing—people, plants and animals all were consumed.

The runners quickly wrapped the people they overtook in black cocoons, while exuding some form of acid that rapidly dissolved the hapless victims. Were they being digested to feed the spread of the expanding mass? No one knew for sure. At the trailing edge of the swath of death, the black material soaked into the ground without a trace. All that was left was a barren wasteland where nothing living survived.

The infestation raced inland, destroying cities and towns, farmland and forest. Flying creatures vanished from the air above and aquatic creatures from the waters of sea, lake and river—even diatoms and plankton. Nothing was spared.

Trying to maintain her composure, the Senior Academician thought about these matters, hoping to leave a clear record of her civilization's final days. She had dutifully entered recordings of the destruction of her world into the archives and now it was almost upon her city. Though this was only a minor city, and a minor branch of the University, she had a scholar's pride in her work. If anyone survives, if people come in the future, they will find that she performed her duties properly.

The door to the hall flew open. Standing there in the light was a single young girl—the Senior Academician's daughter.

"Mother!" the girl called, "the black death has invaded the city, everything is dying!"

Glancing sideways out the window, the Senior Academician saw the graceful trees being torn down by whipping black sinews and the bright flowered fields turn to putrescence. *How can something so vile exist?* She looked back at her daughter, her only child.

"I know, daughter."

"But what are we to do?"

"I'm sorry, my precious, there is nothing that we can do but be brave. The pain will last but a moment."

"Mammaaa..."

The girl's final cry became a short strangled scream as black filaments whipped around her body. A hissing, sizzling sound arose as the dark threads sank into her living flesh. Within seconds, all that was left was a crumpled black mound, slowly sinking back into the mat of alien corruption spreading across the floor.

The Senior Academician forced herself to not look away. She was an historian; those who might come in the future deserved an accurate record of the end. The storage array was inorganic, made of metal and glass and doped semiconductors, a vast repository of memories recorded by generations past, all stored as holograms, interference patterns in blocks of impervious crystal.

Once recorded, the information held within needed no energy supply to sustain it. Scholars like herself and everyday people had been storing their life memories in the Hall of Memories for more than a hundred generations. Hopefully it would be impervious to the ravaging alien pestilence that reached for her.

*So this is how our world ends,* she thought, *not bravely shouting defiance at our foe, but each one alone crying for help where there is none.*

As she had promised her daughter, the searing pain lasted only a moment.

*Part One*

# *An Anomaly Without Parallel in the History of the World*

# Chapter 1

### Gliese 667C, Six Months Ago

Under the baleful glare of a small red star the fabric of 3-space rippled and shimmered. Accompanied by a burst of gamma rays and a spray of fundamental particles, a survey drone emerged from alter-space. Around it lay a system rich in rocky planets—three of them within the star's calculated habitable zone. Two other major planets and the usual collection sub-planetary flotsam rounded out the family album, but it was the three super-earths that interested those who sent the probe.

They were a young race who only recently survived their traumatic debut as a spacefaring species. Having fought off those who would have driven them to extinction, *H. sapiens* was actively looking for new planets to inhabit, new worlds to call home. This system, cataloged as Gliese 667C, was known to humans prior to the discovery of alter-space transit, back when traveling to the stars remained the stuff of fiction. Now, having cleared the surrounding 10 parsecs of known hostile species, the surviving natives of the planet called Earth were starting a diaspora on which their future survival could well depend.

The robot probe quickly found its own location within the system: a quarter of an AU from the star and slightly above the planetary orbital plane. There was a large rocky planet very close to the star, with an orbital period of only seven days. That one would not be friendly to Earth life.

A bit farther out, however, were three rocky planets with orbits of 28, 39, and 62 days. They all massed more than humanity's home, the innermost one being the heaviest at 4.5 times Earth. That world had managed to hold on to its atmosphere and was warm enough to support life. Quickly running a remote spectroscopic analysis of the planet's atmosphere showed that it was composed primarily of nitrogen with a significant amount of oxygen. It also showed traces of water vapor—$H_2O$—the single most important substance for terrestrial life.

The probe switched on its gravitonic drive and laid in an intercept course for the planet designated Gliese 667Cc. It would take closer readings, but preliminary indications were that it had found what it sought—a planet that could be colonized by Earthlings.

## *Jesse's Bar, Farside Base, Present Day*

Jesse's bar was the most exclusive drinking hole in the solar system. Not the swankest, or the most expensive. There were no gatekeepers at the entrance passing judgment on who could enter and who should be turned away. It was a more self selecting process —those who didn't belong felt uncomfortable and soon moved on. This was because Jesse's bar was a Navy bar, filled with veterans from the Fleet.

Those veterans were mostly officers, though senior NCOs sometimes gathered to drink the potent tropical concoctions served up by the bar's eponymous owner. Foremost among the proffered libations was the Fantasy, a mixture of tropical fruit juices, strong Island style rum and "secret" herbs and spices. The first Fantasy was often described as creating a sense of warm contentment, the second euphoria, the third mind erasure. There have been those who consumed more than three Fantasies at a single setting. It is rumored that they are confined for their own safety at a special psychiatric facility on one of the outer moons of Saturn.

It's not that imbibers aren't cautioned about over consumption— Jesse and the bar's watch lizard, Freddy, are careful to warn those sailing into dangerously drunken waters. Sadly, some customers, having spent too much time pondering the dark void between the stars, come seeking oblivion. Not everyone is meant to travel the inky vacuum that is space, or the even more mind-bending nothingness of alter-space. Others, however, thrive on it.

At a far table, under one of the big palm trees, was a gathering of four such travelers of the void. Three of the four were dressed in the black jumpsuits of naval officers—one captain and two commanders. Among them, they had held the post of captain aboard a dozen starships. The fourth was dressed in the dark maroon of the government science section, an astrophysicist of some note and an adventurer in her own right.

At other tables and from seats at the bar, other customers cast surreptitious glances at the four. Not because they were high

8

ranking naval officers, but because they were former members of the original crew of the Peggy Sue and known friends of Captain Jack Sutton and Colonel Ludmilla Tropsha. The Peggy Sue was Earth's first starship and as much a legend as its Captain and his lady. Jack and Ludmilla were pretty much credited with saving Earth and all its lifeforms from extinction at the hands—or equivalent appendages—of the Dark Lords' minions.

After the battle for Earth, the couple stuck around only long enough to make sure things were running on a mostly even keel. Then they departed in the M'tak Ka'fek, the four million year old T'aafhal battle cruiser that had accepted Jack as its captain for life. One rumor was that they left to look for the T'aafhal home worlds. Others say they went to hunt the Dark Lords themselves on their rogue planets, drifting in the cold darkness between the stars. Jack and Ludmilla and their small crew of close friends didn't say where they were going, or when they might return. That was over two years ago.

As former associates and friends of the departed saviors of mankind, Capt. William Raymond Vincent, Cdr. Elizabeth Melaku, Cdr. Robert Danner, and Dr. Mizuki Ogawa were the objects of much unwanted attention. They were treated with a mixture of awe and resentment that they all found annoying at best. Most troubling, because of their special status, they found themselves courted by political factions within the Navy's growing ranks. As the waiter departed after serving their first round of drinks, the senior officer, Billy Ray, spoke.

"You sure you two kids are old enough to drink those Fantasies?" The facetious question was directed at Bobby Danner and Mizuki Ogawa, Bobby's significant other.

"Just because you and Beth are a half a foot taller than we are doesn't make us children," Bobby replied. "Besides, we've all fought enough aliens to qualify for a bar pass."

"These drinks are very strong," said Mizuki after taking a sip of the cloudy, apple cider like liquid in the glass in front of her.

"Don't consume them too fast, Mizuki," Beth warned, "or you will end up with a very short evening and a date with the porcelain throne."

"That's true, you have to just sip at a Fantasy," Bobby confirmed. "Jesse should rename them Pan-Galactic Gargle Blasters."

"That would be appropriate, pardner. I think ol' Douglas Adams would have approved if he had ever tasted one. How did he describe the effect of his favorite fictional cocktail?"

"'Rather like having your brains smashed out with a slice of lemon, wrapped around a large gold brick'," Bobby answered his friend, pausing to take a sip of his own drink.

"He never did write down a recipe," said Beth, taking a sip of her Hendrick's martini. "Pity, really."

Beth had grown up on the outskirts of London, though her roots were in Ethiopia. She and Billy Ray were a stunning couple, both near two meters in height and fashion model attractive. Standing next to them Mizuki and Bobby did look like adolescents, though they were contemporaries of the taller couple.

"So how are things going with you two?" Billy Ray asked, "And where are the children?"

This caused Mizuki to look at Billy Ray with a puzzled expression on her face while Bobby suppressed a grin. Beth elbowed her man in the ribs.

"He means the butterflies, Mizuki-chan," Bobby told his love. Several years ago, while on a mission with Capt. Jack, Mizuki was part of a boarding party that had to fight its way across a gigantic alien space station in search of antimatter to refuel their ship. During that action, a semi-sentient flock of alien butterflies became enamored with the katana wielding astrophysicist. They had been with her ever since, following her everywhere she allowed.

"Oh, you were making a joke," Mizuki said with a smile. "We left them at home in our quarters. The last time we brought them with us Freddy the bar lizard tried to eat one of the flock."

"Yeah," Bobby added, "he snagged a butterfly with his tongue and it shocked the shit out of him. He fell off his post and lay on the bar top like he was dead—Jesse had a conniption."

"My goodness!" exclaimed Beth, looking across the bar to find the little green lizard at his normal post. "It looks like he survived the ordeal."

"Yes, but so as not to upset Jesse, we no longer bring the *aoi chō*—the blue butterflies—here with us."

As everyone at the table enjoyed a polite laugh, Billy Ray made a casual scan of the bar's interior and decided that their conversation would be private enough. "Any more thoughts about re-upping with the Fleet?"

Bobby half laughed, half snorted.

"We have not yet decided, Billy Ray," said Mizuki quietly. "I have been offered a position at a research base on Triton. There would be no problem with Bobby signing on as a shuttle pilot with them."

"Triton?" asked Beth, incredulously. "Isn't Neptune a bit far away?"

"About as far as you can go and stay in the solar system proper," Bobby agreed.

"Astrophysically speaking, Triton is a very interesting moon," said Mizuki, a scientist to her core. "It is an irregular satellite—its orbit is retrograde to Neptune's rotation and inclined relative to the planet's equator. It, and Neptune's six other irregular satellites, are probably gravitationally captured objects from the outer solar system."

"Seems like a damned cold, remote place to go to just to study strange moons," commented Billy Ray, swirling the bourbon and ice in his glass. "And flying a shuttle has got to be a comedown after captaining a starship."

There were a few moments of awkward silence as the four friends avoided eye contact by staring at their drinks. Finally, Bobby broke the silence.

"What have you and Beth been thinking, Billy Ray?"

"Maybe pooling our accumulated back pay and buying an asteroid mining ship."

Beth looked at her husband and lay her hand on top of his.

"It's almost as disagreeable an idea as fleeing to the outer solar system," she said, "but there is really no good alternative."

"Yup," Billy Ray added, "the only employers for starship captains are the Fleet and the Colonization Board. The CB is a bureaucracy run by idiots, and both Beth and I have had our fill of the Fleet's internal politics."

"I hear you, brother," said Bobby, nodding in agreement.

Until the first dome of the new Earthside base was completed, Farside's Atrium, with its palm trees and waterfall, was the largest habitable space on the Moon. As the quartet slipped into a morose silence a strange object floated into the bar, past the towering palms.

About the size of a golf ball, the object was polished silver in color and hard to distinguish against the background. It flew a zigzagging course until it hovered above the friends' table.

"What's that thing?" asked Bobby.

"I don't know, pardner."

As the foursome rose, preparing to vacate the area, the hovering sphere hummed and projected an image beneath it. Floating above the table was a man's head and shoulders—like a living bust. Each of the four saw the man face on, regardless of their position around the table. At the same time their view of the rest of the bar darkened and became blurred.

"Good evening, children!" said the apparition. "Don't stop drinkin' on my account."

"TK?" said Beth in an unsure tone.

"Yes Ma'am, in the flesh. Or rather, in the hologram. I was hoping to catch you all together."

TK Parker was a former Texas oil billionaire who had bankrolled the construction of the Peggy Sue and her first voyages into space. He was now a member of the ruling council and rumored to be the richest man in the solar system.

"If you wanted to talk with us you could have just called," Billy Ray replied, settling back into his chair, "why the parlor tricks?"

"The little gizmo in front of you has a remote holographic link over a quantum encrypted comm channel. It also cloaks the conversation on your end so no one can listen in. I don't really trust the public network."

"Isn't that rather paranoid, TK?" asked Beth

"Even paranoids have enemies, darlin'."

"So what's up, sir?" Bobby said, hoping to get to the point so they could go back to drinking in quiet misery.

"I understand that those of you who are currently serving in the Fleet are being pestered to commit to an extended period of service. Once you sign on there's no tellin' where they'll send you. Now I'm not one to tell folks how to live their lives but it seems to me that young people like yourselves would much rather have jobs where you could stay together."

"Please explain, Mr. Parker," Mizuki said.

"Call me TK, no need bein' so formal, girl. Anyway, if you're interested, I would rather explain in my residence later this evening —say around 11:00?"

The friends looked at each other and found almost instant agreement.

"Yes," they said in unison.

"Great! See y'all then." The hologram vanished and the small silver sphere flew off through the surrounding foliage, disappearing into the night.

"So what do we do now?" asked Beth of her companions. "It's only 9:30."

"I think we have another drink," said Billy Ray, motioning to the waiter loitering next to the bar.


### Officer's Quarters, Farside

In a different part of the base, three Fleet officers were holding a clandestine meeting of their own. Each of the three steadfastly believed that things would be much better off for the human race if

13

they were in charge. In a sense, they and others like them were the cause for the friends' complaints.

The Fleet was expanding rapidly, doubling in size since the momentous battle in which the minions of the Dark Lords were defeated and life on Earth saved—at least for the present. New, larger warships were added and the existing frigates upgraded with more effective shields and more powerful weapons. With the expansion came the recruitment of new captains and crews for the added ships. The best berths went to the veterans of the battle for Earth, those with actual experience in space combat.

While this made sense, it created two classes of naval officer: those who had defended the solar system under the command of Captain (now Admiral of the Fleet) Gretchen Curtis, and those who came later. Naturally, the late comers felt unfairly discriminated against. They despised those at the top of the command chain, who held their positions not through merit but because of personal ties to Adm. Curtis and Gen. Rodriguez, the head of the Marine Corps. They only held their positions because they happened to be in the right place at the right time, or so the disaffected officers thought.

Moreover, those not among the higher ranks suspected the top of the command structure was occupied by two women as a ploy by the rich civilians who ran the place. It was not enough that the old billionaires on the ruling council kept the Fleet on a tight leash by controlling the means of production, be it ships, food or ammunition. By keeping officers they could control in charge of the Fleet and the Marines they made sure they remained on top of the political heap.

Those officers not in favor with the powers that be were shunted into non-combat commands—personnel, supply and maintenance. In times of peace, such positions often held more sway than those commanding the sharp end, but that was little recompense for the officers sharing a drink in private quarters that night.

"It looks like the first of the colonization ships will be operational within a month," said the middle ranking of the trio, a commander in procurement. "That means continued delay in building more cruisers to patrol beyond the solar system."

"Yes, the building of the colony ships will slow production of new combat ships," said the senior officer, a Navy captain in personnel. "That means fewer senior slots to fill with new officers."

"It also means that there will be further delay in the launch of the first Planetary Combat Ship," added the third, a Marine major assigned to training. "Until that happens we have no good way of getting more than a few platoons of Marines to an exoplanet."

The PCS was intended to house and support a full battalion of Marines, 800 combat personnel and others to support them, their assault shuttles and transatmospheric fighter craft. The PCS would also mount the shields and offensive weapons of a cruiser, enabling it to operate autonomously in hostile space, though it would normally have at least one frigate as an escort. More PCSs meant more Marine combat battalions, and that meant more slots for more field grade officers to command them.

"All it is going to take is for one of the colonization ships to run into trouble and the priorities will shift back to warship production," said the Commander, "just wait and see."

"I'm surprised that the Fleet has not been tasked with escorting the colonists," said the Major.

"According to the all knowing high command, there are no hostile aliens left within 10 parsecs or so. They were all expended in the last assault on the solar system," said the Captain. "Myself, I think that is just hopeful thinking. The only semi-military personnel on the colonization voyages are going to be a handful of sailors to fly the ships, seconded to the merchant marine from the Navy training schools."

"At least some of them will get to captain starships of their own," groused the Commander.

"I wouldn't want to be in their place—babysitting a pack of civilians, flying into unknown space in a glorified freighter," said the Captain in a supercilious tone. "Better to wait for a real command to open up."

"That's true," agreed the Commander, "remember, we are playing a deeper game."

"Right," said the Marine, "eventually the Fleet and Corps will expand to the point where they will have to promote officers to command positions who have no actual combat experience."

"And eventually, the privileged cabal will find themselves outnumbered and pushed aside," the Captain finished. "Still, we need to stay alert for opportunities to advance our allies whenever and where ever possible."

"Speaking of such things, I have caught wind of an interesting development. It seems that TK Parker is planning to launch a venture to hunt for exoplanets and alien civilizations on his own and is looking for Navy officers he trusts."

"How did you hear of this, Commander?"

"It all started back eight months ago when the Fleet tried to assign the Peggy Sue to a patrol and reconnaissance mission. The ship seemed like an underutilized asset and sending it out with a Navy crew made good sense. Unfortunately, Parker stopped the plan cold."

"Really?" said the Marine. "How did he do that? Through his pet Admiral?"

"Through the council. They let the Navy know in no uncertain terms that the Peggy Sue, along with the interplanetary freighters and local Earth-Moon shuttles, were civilian owned and not Fleet assets."

"Peggy Sue," scoffed the Captain, "damned silly name for a ship if you ask me."

"In any case, since then the rich old geezer has been having his ship refitted in his ship yard. The scuttlebutt is that Parker and several other council members are forming a joint venture to go looking for interesting things—meaning profitable things—out ahead of the colony ships."

"Those old bastards wouldn't want a load of colonists stumbling upon some ancient treasure by accident," the Major said, scorn in his voice. "Or any useful alien technology that they don't control."

"Exactly."

"So what can we do about it?" asked the Captain.

"The word on the street is that Parker has already put out feelers to recruit a crew for some kind of voyage. Fortunately, there's not a big pool of experienced spacers just hanging around Farside waiting for a berth. We have a plan in motion to place an agent of our own in the Peggy Sue's crew."

### 3rd Level Commercial Zone, Farside

Roselito Acuna sat uncomfortably in a corner chair of the nondescript coffee shop as a slow trickle of civilians came and went around her. It was getting late and she would soon have to find a place to stay for the night. Dressed in a civilian tan jumpsuit she felt out-of-place and definitely out of uniform.

*How did things come to this?* She asked herself. *All you ever wanted was to go into space and fight aliens, now here you are lying low. You are supposed to be outbound on a troopship full of recruits, but instead you missed the movement—face it girl, you are now AWOL from the Corps.*

Things had seemed so perfect. Returning with Captain Jack in time to win the battle for Earth, the entire crew were heroes. Most of the Marines on board were bumped a couple of stripes as recognition. Not that the added rank wasn't earned the hard way: She had fought the hairy crickets in the Bug Queen's palace; driven off flying batacudas on an alien space station; and faced a half dozen other horrors in the trek across the planet encircling Ring Station. And that didn't count helping fight the ship in a number of space battles. Life was good. She loved her work, was advancing in rank and had good friends all around—then the wheels started to come off.

Naturally, the problems started with a man, two men actually. She had maintained a casually intimate relationship with two of her Marine squadmates, Ronnie and Jon, across 3,000 light years. Nothing serious, just an occasional tumble when the mood struck her. But when they got back to the solar system there was not much to do—practice assaults and training missions. When you have fought real aliens on worlds circling other stars, maneuvers on Mars or Io just didn't get the old juices flowing.

17

Out of boredom, casual flirtation became more serious, with her two guy friends competing for her attention. At first it was flattering. Rosey knew she was no great beauty, not unattractive but not one to stop conversation when entering a room. Nonetheless, the competition soon spun out of control, ending in a bar fight between her two squadmates—guys who had been close friends.

Both of her suitors lost a stripe and were sent on patrol aboard different ships. Though Rosey was the cause of the fight, she had not been a participant so she didn't face any official disciplinary action. There were, however, many ways of punishing a Marine informally. She was informed that she would be shipping out for Mars to be part of the training cadre at Camp Aries.

Realizing that she was being sent to a backwater to rot she tried to resign, but the Corps was intent on getting its pound of flesh. She was told that her last promotion, to gunnery sergeant, entailed a reenlistment for four more years—something she was not told at the time. After thinking things over for a couple of beer soaked evenings she decided that wasn't fair and fuck the Corps anyway.

Before deciding that she was not interested in going to Mars, Rosey had never considered how difficult it was for someone to drop off the grid on the Moon base. There was no physical currency, all transactions being handled electronically. As a Marine, her comm pip also served as a transponder that allowed her to purchase goods and services. Since all purchases were registered centrally, she couldn't buy anything without the Corps being able to track her movements.

To get around this problem, she hit on a rather devious solution. New refugees were issued temporary cards linked to small government stipends. After locating a few willing newcomers, Rosey made purchases from her funds and resold the goods to the refugees at a discount, taking their cards as payment. Using the cards she could make small purchases—like food and drink—without showing up on the authorities monitoring net. Unfortunately, the scheme didn't solve the problem of where to sleep.

Everyone on the base either had quarters provided by the military or were assigned housing by the government. There were no hotels where an anonymous traveler could stay. There was one hotel off the Atrium for visiting businessmen and dignitaries, but it was far too public and far too expensive for her needs. Instead, she had scouted the maintenance tunnels that honeycombed the base. There she found unlocked storage rooms not under the same surveillance as the public parts of Farside.

For each of the past three nights she had slept in a different room, showering in public facilities on the refugee level and collecting fresh tan jumpsuits each morning. But her funds were running low and it was just a matter of time before they came looking for her.

*No doubt about it, Marine,* she thought, *this was not a well planned operation.*

The waiter began stacking chairs on the tables, getting ready to close for the evening. Picking up the bag that contained all her worldly possessions, Rosey slipped out of the cafe and headed for the Maintenance tunnels, looking for a place to hole up for the night.

## Chapter 2

### Parker Residence, Farside

When the quartet of friends showed up at Parker's residence in the upscale part of the base they were greeted, as usual, by Maria. Maria Lopez had been TK Parker's cook and housekeeper for more than two decades and was one of the few people who TK trusted without reservation. Maria had been widowed long ago when her husband was killed in an accident on one of TK's Texas gas rigs. TK gave her a job so she and her children would not be deported and she had stayed with him ever since.

Maria's family perished in the alien assault on Earth and TK had no family of his own—now they only had each other. After TK, who had been confined to a wheelchair for more than a decade, was miraculously healed by advanced T'aafhal medical technology, the octogenarian billionaire realized that he still had a long and productive life ahead of him. The few who knew them well were unsurprised when Maria traded her maid's apron for a very large engagement ring.

"*Buenas noches*, welcome my friends. Please come in," Maria said, ushering the visitors inside. "TK is in the living room at the bar, as usual."

TK was a man who enjoyed his whiskey, though these days he talked a lot more about drinking than actually imbibing himself. Part of that was Maria's doing, and part the realization that he was not nearing the end of his life. With nanite treatments and the occasional full body tuneup there was no reason a human being would not live to see 200. One tends to treat the equipment better knowing you're going to need it for years to come.

"There they are, my four favorite young people," the old man said. "Mosey up to the bar and grab a drink; I got things to discuss with you."

After helping themselves to TK's well stocked bar, the young officers and scientist were seated in the living room's spacious conversation pit—a recessed area in the floor lined with built in seating. On one side of the pit was a large fireplace where a comforting fire blazed warmly.

21

The fire was a hologram; no one, not even a billionaire, could afford to import wood simply to burn. The oxygen use alone would set off alarms. A fake it might be, but it was a very good fake; slowly burning down over the course of an evening, occasionally throwing a shower of heatless sparks onto the hearth.

"Your fire is ever so lifelike, TK. I marvel every time I see it," said Beth, carefully balancing her third martini of the evening on her knees. "Are you planning to sell copies to the public? I should think it would turn a reasonable profit."

"Sooner or later," replied TK, "right now it's one of a kind. In fact, I'm still tinkerin' with it."

"Here we go," said Maria. "He just loves showing off his toys." TK made a few finger swipes across the face of his wrist watch and the room went away.

It took several moments for their eyes to adjust to the lowered lighting. In place of the walls and ceiling were low dark hills with scattered clumps of scrub; overhead, stars twinkled and a shooting star streaked across the heavens. As the group fell into stunned silence the sound of crickets could be heard, along with the occasional lowing of cattle. The fireplace was now a campfire, illuminating the circle of friends with welcome light—a bucolic nocturne in an open field.

"Wow!" said Bobby, "It's like we're sitting in a field back in Texas cattle country!"

"That's the effect I was shooting for, Bobby," the old man chuckled.

"Except the seating is more comfortable than a bedroll," added Billy Ray. "And I notice that the bar is still there."

"Yeah, I was going to have 'em change the bar into a chuckwagon but decided that was a bit too hokey."

"It is very beautiful," said Mizuki, "very tranquil."

"Humans in our natural habitat," mused Beth. "I wonder if future generations will feel at home in such a setting, after being born and raised inside space stations and on board starships?"

"I sure hope so," said Billy Ray, feeling a bit underdressed without a cowboy hat and boots.

"Yeah, there is just something about looking up at a night sky that gets a feller thinking," said TK, hinting that there was something specific on his mind.

"And what does it make you think of, TK?" asked Beth, taking the bait.

"Fermi's Paradox comes to mind, young lady. Are you familiar with it?"

"Are you referring to the physicist Enrico Fermi?" asked Mizuki.

"The very same, Mizuki, the very same," said TK with a smile as he warmed to his subject. "You see, three quarters of a century ago, Dr. Fermi looked up at the night sky and asked a simple question: 'where is everybody?'"

Those assembled around the fire looked at one another and then back at the old man. TK took a sip of his whiskey and then leaned forward—this was not his first time telling a tale in front of a campfire.

"As Miss Mizuki said, Enrico Fermi was a physicist, and a rather famous one. When he looked at the night sky he looked through a scientist's eyes. What he saw was billions of stars, each possibly harboring a planet like Earth. Moreover, he realized that the Sun was only about five billion years old and that many stars were much older than that. Assuming that the occurrence of life was not unique to our planet, this meant that there should be bunches of older, more advanced aliens running around the galaxy.

"On top of that, given even fairly rudimentary space travel, an advanced civilization should be able to colonize or conquer the entire Milky Way in maybe 10 million years or so—the blink of an eye in terms of the age of the Universe. All this led Enrico to ask why we hadn't seen any aliens. In fact, we hadn't even detected any signals from aliens."

"Well, TK," Billy Ray began, "I think we found out why no one came by for a social call when we found them varmints hidin' here on the Moon."

"Yeah," said Bobby, "any time a civilization got to the radio and rocket ship stage the Dark Lords sent their minions to wipe 'em out."

"I think that probably had a chilling affect on interstellar socializing," add Beth, with a bit of British understatement.

"I suppose you children are right, the Dark Lords put the kibosh on the galaxy's social scene. But that still doesn't mean that many alien civilizations didn't start to develop."

"That is correct, Parker-san. There are estimated to be 200 billion stars in the Milky Way alone. NASA said there might be eight billion Earth-like planets circling Sun like stars. In recent times astronomers began looking for exosolar planets in earnest, which caused the estimate of possible life bearing planets to rise significantly. Include red dwarfs and the estimate rises to 40 billion habitable planets in our galaxy alone."

"Right you are, darlin'. Possibly billions of worlds that might have risen to the level of ancient China or India, or the Roman Empire. Maybe even as advanced as the early Industrial Revolution, yet to be quashed by the Dark Lords. Wouldn't it be nice if we could find some of these civilizations and offer 'em protection?"

"That seems very noble, TK, but you have never struck me as all that altruistic," Beth observed.

"Now, girl, you do me a great disservice," said TK, feigning hurt feelings. "After what we just went through I was thinking it might be a good idea to go looking for some prospective future allies... and maybe some trade opportunities."

"Trade opportunities?" said Billy Ray. "Now that sounds more like the TK Parker we all know and love."

"OK, fine. So I don't see anything wrong with makin' a little something for yourself while helping out some fellow beings. And with the Colonization Board about to start sending ships full of settlers off to the stars, I think it might be a good thing for any undiscovered aliens if we got to them first."

"That is probably true," said Bobby, "given our own species' history of colonization and conquest. It wouldn't take much for a ship full of humans with advanced technology to subjugate a primitive native race."

"So what are you proposing, TK?" asked Beth.

"What I and a couple of partners from the council are proposing is forming a trading company—the Honorable Orion Arm Trading Company. The company would send out agent captains to explore this region of the galaxy, establish trade relationships with alien species and identify worlds available for colonization. The captains, crews, and of course the partners back here, would all share in the profits of the venture."

"Why does this sound familiar?" asked Billy Ray.

"Because of the Honorable East India Company," said Beth, "through which England controlled much of the world during the 18th and 19th centuries. And often not all that benignly."

"Yes indeed," said TK, "at the time it was a radical, unprecedented idea—an empire built on trade and commerce instead of military conquest. As one historian labeled it: 'An anomaly without parallel in the history of the world'. "

"So you say, TK," said Maria. Undoubtedly, TK had been practicing his pitch on his betrothed.

"Come on, *mi corazón*, we don't want to rule a bunch of aliens, we want to make money trading with 'em."

"Assuming we decide to sign on for this little venture, where are you going to get the ships?" Billy Ray asked, his mind already jumping ahead to the planning of such a voyage.

"We will eventually build our own—armed merchant ships that can take care of themselves in a tough situation—but for the first expedition we will have to use resources at hand."

"What resources?" asked Bobby.

"Except for Cdr. Melaku you've all sailed in her," TK said with a large smile, "my yacht, the Peggy Sue."

## Apt 31, Refugee Housing, Farside

Seated on cushions around a low table, three men were having a discussion over brunch. Drinking small cups of tea made from cardamon and eating dates from a shared bowl, each was careful to use only his right hand. Eschewing the free, government issued jumpsuits, they were dressed in the traditional garb of their people.

After the alien bombardment and near annihilation of the human race, it was decided that, in the words of the immortal Robert Heinlein, Earth was just too small and fragile a basket for the human race to keep all its eggs in. As a consequence, the ruling council instituted an aggressive policy of relocating survivors to other human outposts across the solar system. Mars received the largest portion, but the asteroid belt and the moons of Jupiter and Saturn absorbed a goodly number as well—all survivors rescued from the surface of humanity's battered home planet.

Construction of the new Earthside lunar city was well underway, holding the prospect of a new life for hundreds of thousands more, but even that was not considered enough by the council. They would not be satisfied until humanity had successfully planted colonies on planets circling other stars.

For the Fleet, this posed a daunting challenge, for they were expected to defend all humanity. If people eventually spread to planets outside the solar system the Fleet's responsibilities would increase. Currently, the Fleet's policy was to ignore colonists until they successfully settled an exosolar planet. On the other hand, the proposed human diaspora provided plenty of justification for expanding the Fleet's starships and Marines.

A number of interstellar transports were under construction, both in the yards at Farside and at Olympus Mons. Very soon the first settlers would be sent out into the Orion Arm to begin man's colonization of the galaxy. In looking for good prospective colonists, small, close-knit communities that had experience living self sufficient lives under isolated circumstances were given preference. The representatives of three such groups of refugees were meeting to discuss their impending voyage to a new home.

Each of the three groups had been rescued from small agrarian settlements back on Earth. Moreover, each group contained only members of a single religious sect: one Jewish, one Christian and one Islamic. It was felt by those arranging the voyages of colonization that the uniformity within such groups might give them an edge over a group of randomly selected strangers. It was also felt that the religious nature of the three groups might give them better ability to deal with adversity.

There is no doubt that religion has served humans as a positive survival trait in the past. Indeed, nearly every organized group of humans either created or adopted a set of religious beliefs in the past. Religion provides a way to transmit and enforce a set of social values and societal norms among groups larger than extended families. Over the course of human history tribes have had gods, cities have had gods, nations have had gods, even whole empires have had gods. Of course, when different people with different beliefs met it often meant war and strife.

Quite frequently, warriors had ridden out for the expressed purpose of spreading the worship of their god to heathen lands. By comparison, no band of militant atheists ever invaded a bordering nation for the express purpose of bringing non-belief to the god fearing. Modern communists do not count as they substituted their political beliefs for traditional religious ones; in a sense, making worshiping the state its own religion.

Whether religion's net contribution to human development has been positive or negative, whether it has brought more comfort and peace than tension and strife, is still a topic of debate among scholars and theologians. As with other fields of human endeavor, there have been good religious persons and bad. The saintly and compassionate have inspired millions over the ages while scoundrels, madmen and fiends have all used religion as cover for their misdeeds. It was from the latter end of the religious spectrum that the three men in apartment 31 descended.

Rabbi Yitzhak Menaheim was the authoritarian leader of an ultra orthodox Jewish sect branded the Jewish Taliban for its strict interpretation of their faith. An offshoot of Ontario based Rabbi Shlomo Helbrans' *Lev Tahor*, or "Pure Heart," isolationist sect, Rabbi Menaheim's followers also hid themselves from the world, lest they be corrupted. Like the *Lev Tahor*, the sect's men and boys were indistinguishable from other orthodox Jews. The women and girls, however, followed dress restrictions not found in mainstream Jewish orthodoxy.

Rarely seen outside of their homes, they were shrouded head to toe in black robes from the age of three, even their faces hidden behind burqa like veils, behavior more reminiscent of Islam than Judaism. The sect's resemblance to conservative Muslims no doubt helped inspire the "Jewish Taliban" tag. Strangely they did not shy away from the label. It was said that the Rabbi exerted absolute control over his followers lives: telling them when to rise, when to go to sleep, what to eat, who to marry and when to have children.

The second of the three groups was led by Mustafa Al-Ghazali, a self proclaimed Imam and Sufi mystic. Al-Ghazali was thought to have adopted the name of the famous 11th century Muslim theologian Abu Hamid Muhammad ibn Muhammad al-Ghazali. The historic al-Ghazali was of Persian descent, as was this later day cult leader. Imam Mustafa preached strict adherence to the Hadith and Shariah law, the traditional moral code and religious law of Islam.

Like Rabbi Menaheim he forced his followers to adopt traditional patterns of dress, the women covered from head to toe by the hijab. Interestingly, Mustafa's interpretation of the hijab left his women's faces exposed in the Iranian style, unlike the Rabbi's sect. This was not to say that Imam Mustafa was in any way a liberal progressive. In his world women were chattel and totally controlled by their men.

*Salat*, the formal prayer at the heart of Muslim worship, was performed the required five times of day. Beyond the teaching's of The Prophet, the Imam's followers lived under strict discipline, much like in the Jewish sect of Rabbi Menaheim. When not praying or working, his followers were expected to memorize verses from the Qur'an.

While not practicing as severe a dress code as the other two groups, the nominally Christian *Or Hashem*, or "God's Light," were definitely not slaves to fashion. Back on Earth they dressed in simple clothes, made from homespun cloth dyed in blacks and browns. What they thought of the standard issue tan jumpsuits provided by Farside base remained unknown. What was known is that their leader, Abraham Creshe—known as Brother Abraham among his flock—led his followers into the mountains of Montana to avoid being arrested.

It seems that Brother Abraham was an enthusiastic proponent of polygamy and had a penchant for very young girls. He was wanted in several states for transporting minors across state lines for immoral purposes. Within his sect he told members who was to marry whom, though he reserved the right to sleep with any woman among his flock. His theology was a strange amalgam of fundamentalist Christianity and Mormonism, though certainly, neither of those religions would condone his teachings or sexual depravity.

It might seem improbable that three authoritarian, religious fanatics from three different faiths, each harboring messianic delusions, would set down voluntarily to plan a combined trip of emigration to another world. In truth, the three sects had more in common with each other than they had with most residents of the Moon base. As much as the three leaders despised one another, they hated the godless masses and secular leadership of Farside base even more. What they wanted most of all was to lead their followers away from this lunar den of iniquity before the tainted beliefs of the surrounding infidels could poison the minds of the faithful.

"So we are agreed that we will only take food animals with us that are *halal*," said Imam Mustafa. "Nothing *haram* will be allowed on the ship."

"Agreed," said Rabbi Menaheim, "we must keep *kosher* when it comes to diet." The dietary strictures of both Jewish and Islamic faiths were basically the same, being based on the same ancient scriptures.

"Though I believe what Jesus said—it's what comes out of a man's mouth that makes him unclean, not what he puts in it—I will agree," said Brother Abraham with a beneficent smile, "for the sake of harmony." *Though God knows I'll miss bacon.*

"And the ship's passenger compartments are to be split into three sections, only accessible by single entrance ways," added Rabbi Menaheim, thinking, *I do not want my flock mingling with you godless shkotzim.*

29

"Certainly," responded Imam Mustafa, *you kafir dog.*

"That sounds reasonable, my friends," said Brother Abraham, *if that will keep your heathen hands off my women.* "So it is agreed, we shall approach the Colonization Board with a mutual request for a ship so we can depart as soon as possible?"

"*Metzuyan!* The sooner the better!"

"*Tayeb,*" finished the Imam, "*yella,* we go."

With that, the three leaders arose and headed for the administrative offices seeking a meeting with the authorities they despised. They did not even care which star they were sent to—surely God would provide for his faithful. As the door closed behind the trio, women swathed in black robes scurried into the room to remove the coffee cups and straighten the pillows.


## *Atrium Restaurant, Farside*

The morning after TK's campfire discussion, the three officers all resigned their commissions in Earth's Space Navy. On their way to Fleet HQ, the four friends agreed to meet for lunch at the restaurant overlooking the Atrium just before noon.

Mizuki and Bobby already occupied a table when Beth and Billy Ray entered the large, second level restaurant. Being just outside of the base administrative offices, the restaurant was always crowded, even though the food was unremarkable. Mizuki was dressed in her usual science section maroon, but Bobby was wearing the plain tan of a civilian resident of Farside, as were Beth and Billy Ray.

"I guess this makes it official, pardner—we ain't in the Navy any more," Billy Ray said with a grin.

"Yeah, I almost didn't recognize you two in civies. I hope we get better looking clothes from the company."

"You still have your government jumpsuit on, Mizuki," said Beth.

"Yes, I have some things to wrap up in the lab so I gave them until the end of the week. Unlike everyone else, I am not yet free."

"Depends how you look at it, Mizuki," said Beth taking a seat. "You're the only one of us still employed."

"It feels so weird to not be in uniform."

"I know what you mean, Bobby. Beth and I felt like fish out of water inside the HQ wearin' these civilian duds."

"At least we all have off base housing," Beth observed, "so we don't have to move on top of everything else."

"That is good," said Mizuki with a hint of a smile. "It could be hard finding a new place that allows pets."

This time it was Billy Ray's turn to be momentarily confused, until he realized she was referring to her flock of winged admirers.

"Why couldn't you just make do with a dog or cat, Mizuki?"

"The butterflies aren't that bad," answered Bobby, coming to his partner's defense. "At least they don't need a litter box or have to be walked. We do take them out every now and then, kids love 'em."

"That's because, outside of the polar bears, there isn't any wildlife on this rock."

"I suppose that you would want to keep horses, if they let you, Billy Ray," Beth teased.

"Actually, they've brought some horses up from Earth," Billy Ray answered. "They intend on sending them along with the colonists."

"What in heaven's name for?"

Bobby, whose vast knowledge of science fiction made him an expert on colonizing hypothetical alien worlds, jumped in with an explanation. "If you are going to establish a colony dozens of light-years from Earth, where the cost of transporting agricultural equipment would be astronomical, horses make sense."

"Really? How so?"

"They can be fueled locally anywhere you can raise grass. They are not apt to break down and become useless for want of spare parts, like mechanical farm equipment. And if you take both mares and stallions with you they can make more on location."

"I never thought of it that way, Bobby. I guess I'm just not much of a farm girl."

"That's one of the things I love about you, sweetheart," said Billy Ray, giving his wife a peck on the cheek. "One ex-ranch hand per family is enough around here."

"I hope we find out more about the coming voyage when we visit the company offices after lunch," said Mizuki, changing the subject. "We will need to find others to help crew the Peggy Sue for any significant trip."

"You're right, of course. I think that TK is holding back some of the details until we are officially signed up. I wouldn't be surprised if some old friends and acquaintances sign on as well."

"Really? Like who?" asked Bobby.

"I don't know about you, pardner, but I can't imagine a trip on board the Peggy Sue without Chief Zackly."

"We'll need more than just the Chief to run the ship," said Beth

"We will need a number of scientists: a geologist, a chemist, and probably several biologists," said Mizuki, "and we will also need a doctor for the medical section. We have never gone anywhere without needing medical care."

"Right, so let's get something to eat and think about who else we need to take along."

## Chapter 3

### *The Orion Arm Trading Company, Farside*

"Good afternoon, I'm Billy Ray Vincent and we're here to talk with whoever is in charge," Billy Ray said to the receptionist inside the nicely decorated lobby of the Orion Arm Trading Company.

"Yes, Captain Vincent, we have been waiting for you to arrive," the woman said, her distant stare indicating that she was checking the other's identities with her data enabled contact lenses. "Someone will come and collect you all in a moment."

"Thank you," said Mizuki, with a polite bow. Her companions looked around the lobby of their new employer—a tasteful blend of wood veneers, natural rock and brushed metal. Flanking the receptionist's desk were two large potted palms and on the walls hung panoramic holograms of distant star systems.

"Looks like TK isn't skimping on the start-up money," observed Bobby, "the decor is top notch."

"Yes, moon modern," quipped Beth, less impressed by their surroundings. On one side of the lobby a door slid open and a trim young man entered.

"Good afternoon, I am Remi de Voorst, director of personnel for the company. If you will please follow me we will dispose of the formalities of bringing you all on board."

They followed the gentleman down a short hallway and into an office. The office contained a desk to one side and a larger conference table in the middle. De Voorst motioned to four chairs along one side of the table while he sat in the lone chair on the other side.

"Please place either hand on the tabletop in front of you to identify yourself to the company computer net."

As they complied, their pictures appeared with a welcome message on the table's display surface. These were soon replaced by legal looking documents adorned with company letterhead.

"Before you are your employment agreements. Note the base salaries have been communicated to each of you privately and do not include profits from any expeditions you might participate in.

Please sign the form by pressing your right forefinger to the table in the rectangle provided on the form image."

Mizuki hesitated.

"I am not yet released from my old job with the science section. I do not think it proper to sign this form before the end of work on Friday."

"Of course, Dr. Ogawa," said de Voorst, tapping his fingers on the table top in front of him rapidly. "If you will look closely, I have just changed the effective date of your employment to this coming Saturday. If you will sign now confidentiality agreements will be put in place so you can attend today's briefing."

"Thank you, that will be satisfactory." Mizuki signed the document.

"Given that Capt. Vincent has had the most time in grade and has commanded the Peggy Sue on previous voyages the board has named him captain for the upcoming venture."

The four new employees all nodded.

"It should also be noted that this is a civilian vessel, not a Navy ship, and that the command structure is not the same as in the military," the company representative said. "Given that Cdr. Danner has extensive time actually piloting the ship it was thought that he could serve as sailing master and Cdr. Melaku as first officer. Dr. Ogawa would be the head of the mission's science section. Do you all find this agreeable?"

The four looked at each other and replied in the affirmative.

"Very good then, I think we are done here. Welcome aboard," de Voorst stood and shook hands with each one in turn.

"Now that you are officially part of the company we can proceed to the main briefing room for an overview of the star system we have identified as the target for your first mission. The briefer will be our staff astronomer, Dr. Lucrezia Piscopia. I believe that you already know her..."

### Commercial Port, Farside

The in-system freighter *Isaac Asimov* had just docked after a return voyage from Olympus Mons. On the outbound voyage the hold had been stuffed with equipment and the passenger section bulged with 200 refugees headed for a new life on the red planet. That trip took three weeks while the trip home took only two due to changing orbital configurations and lower mass. Combine the shorter trip with the fact that only a half dozen passengers booked passage to the Moon and the trip home was a comparative pleasure cruise. Now, with the passengers disembarked and the scant cargo unloaded, members of the crew were free to go ashore.

Two of the crew were old time spacers, having done time on a number of Navy ships before switching over to the merchant marine. Where once they traveled among the stars, now they traveled local space, hauling people and cargo between the various planets and moons of the solar system.

"Well, Stevie. Looks like we survived yet another death defying voyage through the icy vacuum of space," said Matt Jacobs, as the pair shouldered their sea bags and headed across the docks.

"Matt, the only thing life threatening on that tub is the boredom," his friend, Steve Hitch, replied. With no alter-space drive and barely able to pull 1G when heavily laden, the Asimov couldn't really compare with any Navy vessel.

"Hey, you were the one who was tired of the Navy chicken shit, and the low pay."

"Come on. You can't say that what the Navy had us doing was anymore exciting than this. The only difference was having to take a ration of crap off of the officers and senior chiefs. Admit it, the pay is a lot better and it's not like the Navy was an adventure. Nothing like the old days on the Peggy Sue."

Matt gazed across the huge open space that was Farside's main commercial port and sighted a familiar shape—a beautiful swan nestled among the ugly duckling transports. There was no mistaking that bow, the curving transparent panels framed by sinuous sliver strands, like half of a crystal egg designed by Fabergé with a hint of Gaudí for good measure.

"Speak of the devil, isn't that the Peggy Sue across the way?"

"I think you're right. It looks like the old girl has been getting refitted—I wonder what for?"

"I think we ought to find out, don't you Stevie?"

"Hell yes. Let's stow our gear back at our quarters and go do some investigating."

"By investigating you mean drinking in some of the dockworkers' favorite bars?"

"Damn straight, my friend. No reason gathering a little intelligence can't also be enjoyable."

### *Apt 32, Refugee Housing, Farside*

Among the refugees rescued with Imam Mustafa were a pair of sisters: Shadi, then fourteen years old, and Dorri, eleven. They were not a part of the Imam's terrestrial flock. The sisters' family had lived in Tehran, where their father was an engineer. Engineers were valued, even in the economic basket case that was twenty-first century Iran. The ruling mullahs recognized the need for men who could actually design and build things.

As a result, Shadi and Dorri grew up in an environment as close to middle class as existed in modern day Persia. They attended private schools, enjoyed modern amenities and knew something of the outside world. In a country where many girls were uneducated, they could speak and were literate in Farsi, Arabic and English. Their parents, while Muslims, were not overly religious—attending prayers at their local mosque just frequently enough to avoid suspicion.

Both girls were attractive, their long, raven black hair framing faces with flawless pale skin. Beneath dark brows flashing grey eyes peered mischievously, almost seductively at the world around them. Their blossoming young bodies remained mostly concealed beneath the modest dress demanded by the theocratic state in which they lived, but even the hijab could not hide the truth—these were two very pretty young women. Undoubtedly, they would both grow into stunning beauties like their mother.

Just by chance, the girls had been in the mountains visiting a favorite Aunt when fire rained from the skies and the world was broken. The torrential rains that followed the alien bombardment sent a cascade of mud through their Aunt's village destroying most of the houses. Somehow the sisters managed to survive and months later were swept up by a rescue mission sent from the moon base— the same shuttle that gathered up the Imam and his flock of true believers. With no parents or adult relatives of their own, the refugee officials simply lumped them in with Mustafa's other followers. That was over two years ago.

When Mustafa himself became aware of the girls' addition to his flock he greeted them with kindness, as required by the teachings of the Prophet. He attached them to his own household and treated them like his own daughters. The Imam's first wife, Manijeh, took them under her wing and put them to work. Treated with strict compassion, life for Shadi and Dorri was a far cry from what they had been used to, but as long as they did their chores and attended prayer five times a day with the other women, things were tolerable.

The girls slept on mats next to each other in a room shared with five other girls ranging in ages from six to fourteen. They spoke in English, having discovered that none of the other girls could understand the language of the infidels.

"Do you ever think we will see home again, Shadi?" asked Dorri in a hushed voice.

"No, Dorri," her sister replied, "I think we are never going to see Tehran, or even Earth, again. I overheard the men talking and they say we are to become colonists on some strange new planet."

"That might not be so bad, as long as we are together."

"Yes, little star, as long as we have each other," the older replied. *No need to tell her that we will both be married off to strangers when we arrive at our final destination. No need for her to worry about that until the time comes.*

37

### Briefing Room, Orion Arm Trading Company

"Our first target system is an interesting one—a triple star system located in the constellation Scorpius called 142 G. Scorpii, with a catalog designation Gliese 667," said Dr. Lucrezia Piscopia, known to her friends as Elena. The astronomer summoned a star chart on the wall display.

"The larger two components, 667A and 667B, orbit each other with an average angular separation of 1.81 arcseconds. At the system's estimated distance, this is equivalent to a physical separation of about 12.6 AU, or nearly 13 times the distance between Earth and the Sun. Their eccentric orbit brings the pair as close as 5 AU and as far apart as 20 AU, corresponding to a fairly high eccentricity of 0.6. This orbit takes approximately 42.15 years to complete and the orbital plane is inclined at an angle of 128° to the line of sight from the Earth. Both the A and B stars are K types with 0.73 and 0.69 solar masses respectively. While this is in the sweet spot for habitable planet formation around binary systems, the high eccentricity does not bode well for any stable planetary orbits."

Elena paused to take a sip of water and then continued. "According to work done by Kaib, the stellar orbits of wide binaries are very sensitive to disturbances from other passing stars as well as the tidal field of the Milky Way. This can cause their orbits to constantly change eccentricity, with the system inevitably developing a high eccentricity at some point in its life. As a result, any planets that might have formed would probably have been forced into very distant orbits or ejected from the system all together."

"If there is little chance of finding a habitable planet, why are we going there?" asked Beth.

"Ah, good question," Elena said with a coy smile. It was easy to see why she had been a good TV science presenter—she looked more like a starlet than a professor. The Italian astronomer shook her tawny tresses and moved to gesture at the wall display. "You see, it is the third star in the system that we are interested in."

"Don't keep us in suspense, Elena," said Billy Ray. "What's the story on star number three?"

"Gliese 667C is the smallest stellar component of the system, with only around 31% of the mass of the Sun. It is a red dwarf with a stellar classification of M1.5 that orbits its other two companion stars at a distance of over 230 AU. A small star, it radiates only 1.4% of the Sun's luminosity at a relatively cool effective temperature of 3,700 K, giving it a red-hued glow. Most importantly, it is known to have a planetary system of at least major five planets.

"The second confirmed planet, 667Cc, is a super-Earth that orbits along the Inner edge of the habitable zone with a year of only 28 days. According to a survey probe report, it has a breathable nitrox atmosphere and liquid water. Based on orbital analysis 667Cc would receive 90% of the light Earth does, however much of that electromagnetic radiation would be in the infrared, making the planet warmer than indicated by the raw figure."

"In other words..." began Mizuki.

"In other words, this world could support human life," Elena finished.

"You said it is a super-Earth, what is its mass and diameter?" asked Mizuki. "If the gravity is too high people may not wish to live there."

"The survey drone's best estimates are mass 4.5 and diameter 1.9 times Earth. That works out to a surface gravity of 1.27G."

"Making the surface gravity tolerable."

"Si," Elena confirmed. "What a world it must be! Almost seven times the surface area of Earth. And from its surface, the red star would have a visual area more than five times greater than that of the Sun as viewed from Earth."

"So sunset on 667Cc would go Tatooine one better, having three stars in its sky," said Bobby.

"Depending on the orbital alignment, you could certainly see triple sunsets or sunrises," Elena confirmed.

"Why this particular star system, Elena?" asked Beth, "There have to be any number of good candidates."

"That is true, Beth. I think I had better let TK answer that question." While the briefing occupied everyone's attention, TK had quietly slipped into the back of the room. The others turned to look at their new boss.

"The answer to that is a simple matter of expediency. In about three weeks, the Colonization Board is going to send its first load of settlers to Gliese 667Cc with an eye to claimin' the whole planet. We need to see if there is anything dangerous waiting for them, or anything that we might want to stake a claim to first."

"So it's a race?" asked Bobby. "Given the low mass of the M type the transit is going to take a long time."

"Si, it has been calculated at almost 22 days."

"Three weeks doesn't give us much time to finish gathering a crew, provision the ship and get underway," said Billy Ray. "Not if we need to do a reasonably complete planetary survey before the settlers arrive."

"We might have an ace up our sleeve on that one, Billy Ray. You see, a transit to 667A only takes about 14 days; you can gain a full week on the colonists during transit."

"You said that the smaller star was more than 230AU away from the pair of K types," said Mizuki. "It could take a month traveling in 3-space to get from A to C."

"That's why we retain the services of humanity's greatest experts in alter-space travel, including your mentor, Yuki Saito. They tell me that, given the long distance between the red dwarf and its companions, it should be possible to do a shallow transit through alter-space between 'em."

"Forgive me, TK, but that seems like an extremely short distance for an alter-space transit. Saito-san says this is possible?"

"Both he and Rajiv Gupta have done the calculations. They hadn't thought it possible over so short a distance either, not 'till they learned about those T'aafhal particle cannon that shoot faster than the speed of light."

"Technically they do not exceed the speed of light, they send a particle beam skipping in and out of alter-space," Mizuki corrected. She was, after all, an astrophysicist herself and a former student of Dr. Saito's.

40

"Whatever. In any case, they say that if you carefully calculate the entry point and are really accurate with the approach vector you can do a short hop from one star to another within the system. It's this system's fairly unique geometry that makes it possible."

"Just how long would such a transit take, TK?" asked Billy Ray.

"They said on the order of five or six minutes."

"Wow!" Bobby exclaimed. Alter-space transits usually took days or weeks.

"Right, so you should be able to get there a couple of weeks ahead of the colonists' ship."

"Then I guess we had best start loading the ship. What about the rest of the crew?"

"We'll be sending qualified candidates directly to the ship for you to interview. Chief Zackly has already signed on and can help screen the prospective spacers."

"Will you be coming with us, Elena?" asked Mizuki.

"No, I am very happy right here, thank you. But I will make sure all of the course calculations done by Yuki and Rajiv are downloaded into the Peggy Sue's computer."

"Well people, we had best get on board then," said Captain Vincent, smiling at his officers. "We got a lot to do and a short time to do it in."


### Residence Level 5, Farside

Jimmy Tosh was making his way home from working the lunch shift at Jesse's bar in the Atrium. While primarily a drinking establishment, Jesse's served an assortment of lighter Island type fare—conch salad, grilled redfish with mango chutney, chicken baked in banana leaves, and such. Though some of the customers were more interested in drinking their lunches, the tips never quite rose to the level of the evening crowd. Jimmy would be returning for an evening shift starting at six.

A tall, slender young man with dreadlocks and mocha skin, Jimmy was a native born Jamaican, like Jesse Lowe, his employer.

He professed to be a Rastafarian, as his mother had been. Indeed, his name did honor to two notable reggae musicians: Jimmy Cliff and Peter Tosh. Last name not withstanding, to Jimmy's knowledge he was not related to either. Like most reggae artists, he did have a fondness for the Rastafarian sacrament of choice—ganja.

Strangely, the widely used term for marijuana did not originate in Jamaica; it was actually a Hindi term for hemp resin derived from ancient Sanskrit. But then the islands of the Caribbean had been a veritable multicultural stew, melding cultural influences from all over the world. Right now, Jimmy was looking forward to taking a few tokes and having a nap before returning to work. Rounding the corner to his apartment block, he did not see the two burly men until they were upon him.

"Oof!"

Jimmy exhaled forcefully as one assailant grabbed his left arm and the other put a meaty fist into his solar plexus. Doubling over, the slender Jamaican found he could not inhale. Supporting their victim between them, the thugs swept him into a side alcove with a conveniently disabled surveillance camera.

"Where you going so fast, boy?" asked Vasyl, still supporting Jimmy by his arm.

"We think maybe you not like us anymore," said Ruslan, the thug who had struck the blow, "and after we were nice enough to give you credit."

All that Jimmy could manage as a response were a few gasps.

"You see, boy, you owe us 400 credits and we want it now," Vasyl said, tightening his grip on Jimmy's arm. Vasyl and Ruslan were Ukrainians, part of a gang that ran various illicit enterprises— prostitution, drugs, gambling, etc. Though much of mankind had been destroyed and those on the Moon were comparatively few, there still existed among the survivors a strain of human that found preying on their fellows preferable to productive labor.

Several days ago, Jimmy happened upon one of the Ukrainian gang's floating crap games and proceeded to lose his accumulated savings of several hundred credits. Sensing a mark ripe for the taking, the game's organizers gladly extended credit to the young man. In short order he lost those credits as well, ending the evening more than two weeks' wages in debt.

"You transfer money to account on card," Vasyl said, handing Jimmy a card, which he accepted with trembling fingers. The fact that there was no physical currency on the Moon was no impediment to vice—criminals were infinitely inventive when it came to milking their victims. "If you not pay by Friday, you owe 500 credits,"

"And we come visit again," added Ruslan, "only we not be so nice."

To underscore the threat, Ruslan sent a short jab into Jimmy's back in the area of his kidneys. Again the young man's knees buckled and this time his attackers let him fall to the floor. Their message delivered, the two Ukrainians departed, walking down the hallway, chatting amiably with each other. In the alcove Jimmy remained on his knees, retching.


### Polar Bear Habitat, Farside

Umky gazed up at the dark starry heavens, where uncounted points of light twinkled through the cold air. The temperature was frigid, befitting a cold winter's night, and a constant wind blew traces of snow over the ice ridges. The male polar bear raised his nose to the wind and sniffed... and the illusion was shattered.

Polar bears have the sharpest sense of smell of any Earth animal, capable of detecting prey kilometers away beneath the Arctic pack ice. It was that keen sense that betrayed the simulated environment provided for his kind. No matter how well the filters scrubbed the recycled air there were still smells that could be detected by ursine noses: the smell of far too many bears, crowded into the habitat's small area; the smell of humans outside the simulated environment, living in the surrounding Moon base.

*The humans mean well,* Umky thought, *they tried to make the habitat as natural as possible.*

The temperature, the seasonal change of the day-night cycle, the sky overhead, even the windblown snow, were all there to ease the stress on Farside's polar bear community. But any bear who smelled the air instantly knew that he was not free on the polar ice pack, he was in a cage. A comfortable and elaborate cage, but a cage nonetheless. True, they were free to come and go, free to mingle with the humans on the rest of the base, but there the heat was so sweltering and the monkey smell so overpowering that most bears stayed in the habitat. Many, having served in the Marines, called it their quarters, but at times Umky thought of the habitat by a different name, a despised name among his kind—zoo.

Umky sighed. Things had become so complicated since aliens rained gigantic meteors down upon Earth several years ago. The weather patterns were still greatly disturbed and the planet was trending colder and colder—the human climatologists said that the next glacial cycle was starting and things would get much colder before they got warmer again. It was not the cold that bothered the white bears, it was the lack of food that kept them in their safe-haven on the Moon, and dependent on the humans.

Umky felt trapped. He had fought along side humans against the alien invaders, but now he could not help feeling that the humans would rather their ursine allies stay out of sight. New humans recruited into the Fleet and Marines did not value the presence of polar bears like the old timers. He put in two years with the Marines and was glad to return to the company of his own kind. But things were also changing in polar bear society.

Some bears, mostly females, were saying that they should emulate the humans by forming stable family groups. In the wild, male bears only associated with females during mating season. They then left the females to give birth and raise the cubs on their own. This made good sense in the wild, it was hard enough for a single bear to feed itself without a mate and cubs along. But they were no longer living in the wild.

His own mother and father, Isbjørn and Pihoqahiak, had started the trend toward families, staying together to raise their cubs jointly. Several of the older males said that it was unnatural and that polar bears should not ape, so to speak, their human allies. But then his father, who was known to most humans only as Bear, was a most unconventional and famous polar bear.

He was the first of the talking polar bears to be recruited by the legendary Capt. Jack. Isbjørn and Umky himself were among the first batch of bears that humans brought to the Moon. Now his parents and their latest litter of cubs were off with the Captain somewhere in search of more adventures. Unfortunately, their odd ideas about family commitments lingered on.

Like his father, Umky was a large bear. At six years old he was full grown and an adult in all ways but one—he had yet to become a father himself. That was proving to be a bit of a problem because, given his linage, the young she-bears all assumed that he would be willing to settle down and be mates for life, what the humans called "marriage."

Umky felt the instinctive drive to father cubs, but he was not ready for a lifelong commitment. The available females, however, felt otherwise and without said commitment mating was out of the question. His life had devolved into a morass of temptation and frustration.

*What's a bear to do?* he asked himself. *I need to get out of this place or I will go crazy.*

He recalled that another young bear, Aput, mentioned a group of humans preparing to make an extended space voyage exploring the Orion Arm. A long space voyage might be just the ticket; remove temptation and give him other things to think about. Maybe they could use a bear on the crew.

## Chapter 4

### *Main Lounge, Peggy Sue*

More than 135 meters in length with a beam of 12 meters and massing 8000 metric tons, the Peggy Sue was not a small ship. This was her third major overhaul since her launching from Parker's ranch in Texas, years ago. Her updated armaments received the benefit of the latest technology, gleaned from the M'tak Ka'fek. New shields, based on the T'aafhal battle cruiser's designs, now protected against superluminal weapons of the type used by the Dark Lords. This was a technology shared with the ships of the Fleet.

To make room for a larger complement of drones and remote sensing instruments, the gravitonic torpedo magazines shrank leaving space for only 10 antimatter tipped weapons. To compensate for the loss of firepower two new superluminal particle cannon were mounted, one portside and the other to starboard. This new armament was complemented by sensors that could see massive objects through alter-space, be they stars, planets, or ships with gravitonic drives.

This was technology not shared with the Fleet, and it made the Peggy Sue more than a match for any vessel Earth's Navy possessed. Withholding the advanced technology from the Fleet was not done out of malice. The particle cannon and sensors were still experimental. Peggy Sue's upcoming voyage would be a field test for the copied T'aafhal weaponry.

Other changes had been made to the ship's layout, including expanded laboratory space for analyzing samples from alien worlds. To prevent contamination, several clean-rooms were provided that could be isolated from the ship's environment, even ejected into space in an emergency. To make room for the expanded lab space the armorer's facilities and machine shop moved aft next to the engineering spaces. There also resided the suits of space armor for the crew. Riding on top of the ship's hull were two pinnaces, a larger shuttle for crew and cargo and a fourth armored shuttle modeled on the assault craft used by the Marines. Captain Vincent believed in being prepared.

It was the middle of the afternoon and Beth and Mizuki were drinking tea in the ship's main lounge. The main lounge was a space more like a fancy restaurant and nightclub than a mess hall on a Navy vessel. Spanning the full width of the ship it featured several sizable portholes and one very large, eye shaped observation port on the starboard side. The two women were seated at a table in front of the observation port, with Mizuki's flock of butterflies flitting about the ceiling.

"It looks like we are ready to depart, as far as the science section is concerned," said Mizuki. "Though I wish we had a microbiologist."

"You've got a chemist, a geologist, a climatologist, and a biologist," the First Officer replied. "That's pretty good considering how quickly we have thrown this crew together."

"Yes, but I wish they were more experienced. None of them have ever been outside the solar system."

The flock of butterflies suddenly descended from the ceiling and swarmed around the two officers, flashing green and yellow. Then they darted across the lounge toward the aft doorway. They arrived at the same time a woman dressed in medical white stepped into the lounge. Mizuki almost shouted a warning but paused when the flock began swirling around the newcomer, flashing gayly in a rainbow of colors.

"Well hello," the woman said, "I've missed you little guys too."

Mizuki jumped up and ran across the room to the woman in white. "Betty! It is so good to see you!"

"It's great to see you too, Mizuki," Betty White said, as the women embraced amidst a cloud of fluttering color. Beth walked over to join them and Mizuki barked a command to her pets in Japanese, ordering them to behave.

"Hello, I'm Beth Melaku," said Beth, extending her hand.

"Nice to meet you," replied Betty, shaking the proffered extremity. "I'm Dr. Belinda White, though my friends call me Betty."

"Doctor?" Mizuki said. "You went back and got your medical degree?"

"Yes, Ludmilla insisted."

"Dr. Ludmilla Tropsha?" asked Beth.

"Yes, after we all got back I worked with her for a while on some of the T'aafhal medical technology—they are so far beyond us I felt like a tribal witchdoctor. After a few months Ludmilla arranged for me to go back to school and get my MD."

"Betty was our Navy corpsman on the Peggy Sue and the M'tak Ka'fek," added Mizuki, "she grew me a new set of legs after I was wounded on Ring Station."

"Then I'm doubly happy to meet you, Betty."

"I just got back from a year's residency at the Mars Base hospital. I came in on the *Issac Asimov*, along with a couple other Peggy Sue veterans. I ran into them again a few days ago and they told me you were planing another voyage."

"Yes, we are going to go looking for fame and fortune among the stars," Beth said with a hint of sarcasm. "Emphasis on the fortune according to TK. Who were the others you mentioned?"

"Steve Hitch and Matt Jacobs. I see you have them both working below under the watchful eye of Chief Zackly."

"Yes, we've been fortunate to sign up a number of veterans from previous voyages."

Betty looked down for a moment, as if embarrassed. "Speaking of that, this is more than a social call."

"Oh?" said Beth.

"Yes, I understand that you were looking for a ship's doctor for the upcoming voyage. Has the position been filled?"

A hint of a smile appeared on Beth's face. "If that is why you are here, I think it just has."

"That would be so wonderful!" exclaimed Mizuki.

"You will have to speak with the Captain, of course. But since you know him, and the Sailing Master, I think there should be no problems with you joining our merry band."

"That's fantastic!" Betty said, a huge smile lighting up her face. "I was afraid the position would be taken."

"This will be such fun," Mizuki enthused, hugging her friend again. As she did, the flock of butterflies changed color to reds and oranges, flew a tight circle around the three women, and then exited the lounge headed aft.

"Now what's got into them?" asked Beth.

"Red is usually a danger warning," said Mizuki, "I wonder what is happening?"

"Maybe we should follow them," added Betty.

The three followed the butterflies' trail, heading aft at a run.

## Sick Bay, Peggy Sue

Mizuki and friends found her errant flock of butterflies milling about the door to the medical section. Inside they found one of the crew, Matt Jacobs, supporting a slender man with dreadlocks. Looking on was Jesse Lowe, concern etched on her normally smiling face.

"What's going on here?" asked Beth, the ranking ship's officer present.

"Jesse showed up at the port cargo hatch with this fella in tow, Ma'am," the sailor replied. "He's pretty banged up and Chief Zackly said to bring him to sick bay."

"Set him on the examination table, Matt," said Betty. Regardless of the man's identity, he was hurt and she was a doctor.

"He is the waiter from Jesse's bar," said Mizuki, recognizing the young man.

"Yes, yes," Jesse said fretfully, "dat be Jimmy Tosh. He de waiter and part-time cook at my restaurant."

"What happened to him, Jesse?" asked Beth. "He looks like he was in a fight."

"Yeah," said Betty, easing her patient back on the table with Jacobs' help. "A fight he lost."

"No mon," Jimmy slurred through puffy lips, trying to make light of the situation, "you should see de other guys."

With Jimmy lying down on the table the medical sensors lit up, showing heart rate, blood pressure and respiration. His left eye was swollen almost shut, his lip split and he was favoring his right side. Betty picked up a tablet and used it to examine his limbs and side. Holding the tablet over parts of Jimmy's body its screen revealed the bones and soft tissue beneath his skin and clothing.

"If the other guys are worse than you they'll need an ambulance. You have three fractured ribs and a fractured left ulna." Lowering the tablet viewer, Betty looked directly at the battered man. "I'd say you were on the receiving end of a severe beating."

Jimmy moaned and closed his eyes, unable to reply.

"It was de Ukrainians; dis be de second time," said Jesse. "Dem rude boys is no good, I tell you."

"Why were they picking on your waiter?" asked Mizuki, her butterflies hovering near the door, showing worried shades of dark blue and purple.

"Dis stupid boy! He got de gamblin' sickness. If dey is a card game or someone throwin' dice he has to bet on it, for true. Trouble is he don' ever win, he just lose all his money."

"And now he is over his head in debt to the Ukrainians," said Beth, adding one and one together. Most fleet officers were aware that there was a criminal element on Farside and much of it was controlled by the Ukrainians.

"Dat's right, Miss Elisabeth. He owe dem 500 credits." Jesse wrung her hands and shook her head in disapproval. "I'd pay it, but he would just be back in debt de next time he found a bettin' game."

"And just what do you think we can do about it, Jesse?" asked Beth, sensing that the Jamaican woman was leaving things unsaid.

"I hopin' dat you could take him wit you on de Peggy Sue. I heard you was needin' a cook and he can cook pretty good. He really is a good boy—he don' drink or show up for work late—he just can' resist gamblin'."

"I am going to give him an analgesic and get a cold pack on those ribs and bruising," said Betty. "He needs to stay on his back

51

until the fractures knit. Even with regrowth stimulators, I will need to keep him at least overnight for observation."

"I think that Jesse needs to talk with the Captain about her ward here," added Beth.

"Oh yes, please let me talk wit' Captain Billy Ray. He a good mon, I just know he help Jimmy."

With that Beth and Mizuki led Jesse forward to see the Captain, butterflies in tow. After the women departed Matt looked questioningly at Betty.

"You need me to stick around, Doc?"

"No, you can go back to whatever you were doing. Thanks Matt," Betty said with a smile. "I used to work on wounded Marines; I think I can handle one beat-up Rastaman."

## Port Cargo Hatch, Peggy Sue

Chief Hank Zackly was standing at the top of the short ramp leading from the surrounding dock platform to the large, rectangular door opening on the forward end of Peggy Sue's main cargo hold. He held a tablet in his hand, allowing him to check off late arriving crates of equipment and supplies against the master inventory in the ship's computer. He looked up to see a woman in a tan civilian jumpsuit coming up the ramp.

The woman had short hair and walked with an assertive stride. She was full bodied, but not to the point of being stocky; attractive but not beautiful. Something about her tickled the Chief's memory.

"Permission to come aboard, Sir?" the woman asked, coming to a halt at the top of the cargo ramp.

"Granted," the Chief replied, "come aboard, Ms. Acuna."

Rosey smiled at the wiry little man and stepped over the lower lip of the door and into the ship's interior. The hold was stacked full of crates and equipment strapped to pallets, all secured to the deck with clamps. Despite the use of deck gravity old habits died hard, all the cargo was made fast so it would not shift while underway. The Chief squinted and looked Rosey up and down.

"So what brings you to the Peggy Sue this fine afternoon, Marine?"

"Ex Marine, Chief," Rosey replied, "sort of."

"How can you be 'sort of' a Marine? Yer either a jar head or you ain't."

"They tried to shanghai me into a four year reenlistment so I sort of missed a troop movement," the nervous woman said. "I'm AWOL, Chief."

"I guess this is just my day for collectin' strays. First Jesse brings her waiter, then Bear's cub shows up and now you," the old Chief said, shaking his head. "Let me guess, you would like to talk to the Captain, to see if we have room for one more on the crew? "

"Sorry Chief, I didn't know where else to turn." Rosey stared dejectedly at the deck, avoiding eye contact. The Chief looked at her silently for several moments and then sighed.

"Alright, if yous can find yer way forward I'll tell the Captain yer coming."

"Thank you, Chief," the relieved Marine replied. She quickly turned and hurried forward through the airlock door leading to the crew quarters.

"Captain Vincent, Cargo hold," Zackly called over his collar pip.

"This is the Captain, go ahead Chief."

"I think we just picked up another lost soul from earlier voyages, Sir. I just sent Rosey Acuna forward to talk with you."

"Roger that, Chief. Thanks for the heads up."

### Polar Bear Quarters, Peggy Sue

Given his experience in the Marines and having sailed on the Peggy Sue before, Umky was quickly accepted as a member of the crew by the Captain and, equally important, the Chief. He ambled aft to find the his quarters, a refrigerated compartment with a small pool for bathing and ice shelves for sleeping. As he approached the entrance to the converted reefer he detected a scent, the unmistakable odor of a female polar bear. The door slid open and he was presented with the sight of a furry white rump.

"Who are you?" he asked.

"Huh?" the smaller female exclaimed, turning to face him.

"I said, who are you?" Umky repeated.

"I'm Ahnah. And who the hell are you?"

"I'm Umky, I just signed on for the voyage. Why are you here?"

"I'm going on the voyage as well. You're crew?"

"Sensor operator and combat ops if needed. You?"

"I'm on the science staff," the she-bear replied with just a hint of superiority in her voice.

"Really? Are the humans going to study you during the trip or something?"

Ahnah's eyes narrowed and her ears flattened. In a not so friendly tone of voice she replied, "I'll have you know I have a PhD specializing in developmental biology and chemical ecology."

"Whoa," Umky said, "Didn't mean to raise your hackles, sweetheart."

This reply antagonized the ursine scientist even more. "Listen, you stupid bruin, don't get any amorous ideas about this trip or I will remove your hairy testicles and feed them to you. Understand?"

*Damn it all!* Though Umky, *I signed on for this trip to get away from uppity females, now it looks like I'm bunking with one.* "Look Ahnah, I've got no desire to take a tumble with you. I signed up to get away from romantic entanglements, not for a shipboard romance with a she-bear I've never met. Can we call a truce? I have equipment I need to check out in the Armory."

Ahnah snorted. "You've got the left side of the habitat."

"Port side," Umky replied, "on a ship it's the port side, not left side."

"Whatever. Try to stay on your side in the future." Ahnah pointedly turned her back on the exasperated male and took two bounds, landing in the pool. This effectively ended the conversation.

*Well, talk about getting off on the wrong paw,* Umky thought to himself as he went back into the passageway and headed forward toward the Armory. *No, that didn't go well at all...*

### Main Lounge, Peggy Sue

Rosey finished her interview with the Captain and was headed aft. Her intended path took her through the ship's main lounge and down the companionway at its rear. This would take her to the lower deck and the crew's quarters. Ahead, she spied the ship's First Officer leaning against the lounge's curving mahogany bar, viewing a data tablet.

"Good afternoon, Ma'am," the ex-Marine said.

"Good afternoon, Ms. Acuna," the officer replied. "I take it from your smile that things went well with the Captain?"

"Yes, Ma'am, he said I was welcome to join the crew for the next voyage."

"Good," said Beth, wrestling with a decision in her mind.

*Well, nothing for it,* she thought. Decision reached, she straightened up and laid the tablet on top of the bar. "You know, Ms. Acuna, I talked with Gen. Rodriguez about you."

Rosey swallowed and said, "Yes, Ma'am?"

"The Corps Commandant said she remembered you from the Peggy Sue's second voyage," Beth continued in a neutral tone, "that you were a good Marine; steady under fire. She also said you were well liked by your squad mates and members of the crew."

"Yes, Ma'am."

"I also know why you ended up on the Corps' shit list."

Not knowing what to say, Rosey came to attention—back straight, eyes focused at a spot six inches above the officer's head.

"I am also sure that my husband, the Captain, was too much a gentleman to mention this." Beth paused to let that sink in. "What's past is past, and I have no interest in those events, Ms. Acuna. What I am concerned with is the morale of the crew and the smooth operation of this ship."

A pause followed by silence.

"Any action, any activity that sows discord among the crew or interferes with the safety and operation of the Peggy Sue will not be tolerated. Do I make myself clear?"

"Yes, Ma'am."

"Very well," the First Officer said, closing the subject. "In any case, welcome aboard—it's good to know we have people who have been there before. You can carry on."

"Aye, aye, Ma'am," the ex-Marine acknowledged, then she turned smartly and resumed her journey aft.

*Well that was rather unpleasant*, Beth said to herself. *I had forgotten what a thankless job being XO really is. Still, best to make sure everyone understands the ground rules before the ship gets underway.*

### Cargo Hold, Peggy Sue

Jacobs and Hitch were in the armory, adjoining the aft end of the main cargo hold, checking out their suits of heavy space armor. The suits were identical to the ones they had worn on the trek across the Ring Station, meaning they were more advanced than the ones used by the Fleet Marines.

"I tell you these are the same suits, Matt," said Hitch.

"I can't argue with that, Stevie, this suit fits me like a glove."

"Yeah, even with all the weight you gained on those freighter runs."

"Very funny."

"If you primates are done clowning around, how about breaking out my suit," a new, deep voice rumbled. The two humans turned to find themselves facing a full grown male polar bear.

"Lt. Bear?" asked Hitch.

"No way, Stevie," his friend replied, "Bear shipped out with Captain Jack a couple of years back."

"Well he sure looks like the LT."

"Did you ever think of just asking me who I am?" the bear asked.

"You have to be Umky," Jacobs replied, ignoring the bear's suggestion. "The Chief said you had signed on for the voyage."

"You sure are the spitting image of your daddy," Hitch commented.

"And now you know why I am trying to get off this rock," replied Umky. "He's been gone over two years and I am still living in his shadow."

"Major bummer, Nanook," said Hitch.

"Umky. My name is Umky."

"I thought that Nanook just meant 'bear'?"

"It does, Umky means bear too."

"Wow, great nickname: Bear 2."

"Just forget it," said the annoyed Umky. "How about helping me find my suit? There is supposed to be armor for a full sized male bear stowed here somewhere."

"Yeah sure, just give us a second to get out of our armor and we'll help you look," said Jacobs. "Good to have you aboard, Bear 2."

* * * * *

The Chief was standing where he had been for most of the past several days, just inside the forward cargo door on the port side. His inventory was almost complete and only a few of the crew had not yet reported, science section types mostly. The sound of footsteps on the cargo ramp caused him to look up. There coming up the ramp was half a squad of Marines.

"We're looking for an AWOL Marine, Pops," said the sergeant leading the detachment of four. The Chief bristled.

"Stop right there, you ignorant jar head!"

"Hey, don't get your knickers in a twist, Pops. We need to search your ship for the AWOL Marine, so stand aside."

The Chief spoke into his comm pip in a lowered voice: "Hitch, Jacobs, get yer asses forward, we got a Marine infestation."

Then, placing his hands on his hips, the Chief look the Marine sergeant in the eyes and said, "you listen to me you snot nosed, scupper turd, yous ain't setting a foot on the Peggy Sue..."

\* \* \* \* \*

"What the hell is that all about?" asked Hitch, having received the Chief's somewhat cryptic message.

"I think the Chief is in trouble," said Jacobs, "look at the monitor from the port side cargo door."

"Looks like a squad of Gyrenes trying to come aboard."

"Maybe we should go forward and see what they want," said Umky, standing up in his suit of heavy space armor.

"Good idea, Bear 2," Hitch said, climbing back into his suit of armor. "Come on Matt, shake a leg, we got some jar heads to mess with."

\* \* \* \* \*

The sergeant in charge of the shore patrol detachment had had about enough of the unpleasant little sailor who barred their way. He had his orders and no damned civilian swabby was going to stop him from searching this ship, yet there the diminutive sailor stood at the top of the ramp.

"Listen to me, you little runt. We are going to board your ship and search for the missing Marine, you get me you sawed off asshole?"

The Chief crossed his arms, squinting hard at the Marines. Behind him, footsteps could be heard coming from the hold—heavy footsteps. From the shadows emerged two seven foot gray black monsters which took up positions on either side of the diminutive Chief. Then a third armored figure appeared, this one twelve feet tall. The Marines' eyes went wide.

58

"Oh good!" said the armored bear in the middle. "I love snack food in green wrappers!"

The Marines backed down the ramp, eyes fixed on the three armored figures behind the little sailor. None were even tempted to draw one of the stunners they carried on their belts—they knew what men, and bears, in powered armor could do.

"You'll regret this, asshole!" the sergeant shouted as their retreat turned into a route.

"That's Master Chief Asshole, dickhead!" Chief Zackly shouted in reply, happily waving at the departing Marines. "These fuckin' new Marines can't find their asses with both hands in the shower, not without an officer tellin' 'em which end is which."

## Chapter 5

### *Jimmy's Apartment, Farside*

The day after being brought to the ship, Jimmy Tosh was visited in sickbay by Captain Vincent. After talking with the prospective new cook, Billy Ray decided that Jimmy could join the crew. Jimmy seemed a good man, in spite of his vices, and the Captain had a soft spot for Jesse. He didn't want to disappoint the Jamaican bar keeper.

Since the mobsters were undoubtedly still looking for him, it was decided that Jimmy should not leave the safety of the ship to fetch his belongings. Instead, Mizuki and Bobby volunteered to gather his personal effects from his apartment and bring them back to the Peggy Sue. The couple from the ship were accompanied by Mizuki's flock of butterflies, causing a number of passersby to gawk.

"At least we got new uniforms," Bobby commented.

"Yes, they are very stylish, much nicer that the old jumpsuits."

Their outfits were quite attractive, having a two toned color scheme that was mostly black with a departmental color designation on the upper part. Mizuki's was black and burgundy and Bobby's black and dark blue.

"Yeah, except I sort of feel like we're Star Trek TNG wannabees, attending a convention."

"There is just no pleasing you sometimes, Bobby."

In all, it was a ten minute walk from the docks to Jimmy's apartment. Arriving without incident, they soon had Jimmy's worldly belongings stuffed into a duffel bag and were ready to head back.

"I think that's about it," said Bobby, looking around the small apartment one last time. "Hardly worth the trip."

"Yes, I think we've gotten everything, excluding the recreational drugs," Mizuki replied. "At least we took the *aoi chō* for one last walk before confining them to the ship for many months."

"As long as they're around you they are happy, sweetheart." *About the only thing I have in common with the flying circus.*

61

The couple stepped outside of the apartment and closed the door. As the door slid shut, two burly men confronted them.

"Where is the black boy?" demanded the one on the left, closest to Bobby. "He owes us money."

Bobby and Mizuki were not an imposing couple. Mizuki, though tall for a Japanese woman, was not all that large and Bobby was not much taller than she. At one time Bobby had been a pudgy couch potato and not much for physical conflict. That was before they both spent a year in the company of a group of Marines and SEALS, fighting aliens and being fine tuned by the M'tak Ka'fek's AI. That meddlesome sentient computer viewed its crew as biological systems whose performance needed to be optimized. As a result, both Bobby and Mizuki were strong, well trained in the martial arts, and startlingly quick.

"We have no business with you," said Bobby, as he and Mizuki moved apart slightly. "Stand aside and there will be no trouble."

"I think you already have trouble," said the thug on the right, reaching behind his back. Mizuki's butterflies formed a swirling red and yellow cloud above her head.

The thug nearest Bobby lunged at him, throwing a roundhouse right. At the same time, the thug nearest Mizuki produced a knife from behind his back and stepped toward her.

Bobby seized his assailant's arm, pivoted and used the man's momentum to execute a hip throw. The man landed heavily on his back, his head striking the floor and rebounding. His face was traveling upward from the rebound when it met Bobby's fist descending in a straight armed strike. Bone and cartilage crunched audibly.

Meanwhile, Mizuki reached over her head and drew the bokken she always carried when roaming outside the ship. The heavy wooden stick had the same weight and balance as a katana, the traditional long sword carried by samurai. The wooden practice sword was a blur as she first broke her attacker's wrist and then struck the side of his head. The knife clattered to the floor as the second thug dropped like a felled ox.

Mizuki and Bobby stepped clear of their fallen foes only to see a third Ukrainian holding what looked like a pistol. They jumped in opposite directions, forcing the man to chose between targets. Mizuki ended her roll to the right in a crouch with her weapon held before her, ready to strike. Bobby came up low with a small stunner in his hand. Before either could take out the gun wielding thug he was enveloped by a flock of angry butterflies, flashing reds, oranges and yellows.

The man with the gun cried out as sparks flew from the winged creatures alighting on his person. He crumpled as the smell of ozone and cooked meat permeated the area. The butterflies circled above their victim showing more placid colors. No additional targets appeared.

"I think your pets cooked that guy, Mizuki-chan."

Bobby moved forward and examined the third gangster's dropped weapon. Nudging the pistol with his foot, he grunted.

"Looks like a plastic pistol made in a 3D printer or other low-end fab unit. I don't think it would be very accurate."

"Still a threat of deadly force, as was the knife, Bobby." Mizuki was intent on justifying the actions of her flying pets. Bobby nodded absently and brought his foot down on the plastic pistol, breaking it.

"I think we should head back to the ship," he said. "We can call this in when we are well away from here."

"Hai."

Man, woman and butterflies moved off down the corridor in the direction of the docks, leaving one dead and two badly injured Ukrainian gangsters on the floor behind them.


## Colonization Board Office, Farside

Imam Mustafa, Rabbi Menaheim, and Brother Abraham were seated in front of a bespectacled, balding bureaucrat. The official was telling them of the final arrangements for their upcoming emigration to Gliese 667Cc, a matter of grave importance to all three religious leaders.

"As you can see from the manifest, we are sending six cows, six horses, twenty-seven sheep and thirty chickens with you. All of the quadrupeds will be female and there will be three roosters among the chickens."

"Why no bulls, stallions or rams?" asked Imam Mustafa, "How are we to breed more animals without male stock?"

"All of the large female animals will be impregnated before the voyage. Using gender selection during the insemination process we can ensure that half of the births will result in male livestock. You can keep the best as future breeding stock and use the others as food animals."

"And how long do we have to wait for delivery, so to speak?" asked Bother Abraham.

"The average gestation period of a cow is 285 days, a mare 342 days, and a ewe 152 days. Also note that we are sending frozen sperm for each species, prefiltered by sex, and insemination kits for each group of settlers. Using the provided material should allow you to build flocks with enough genetic diversity to be viable on their own."

"Why no goats? We asked for goats," said Rabbi Menaheim.

"We do not have sufficient breeding stock on hand to send goats with you at this time," the bureaucrat replied. "We will send you goats on a followup visit to your colony some time in the future."

"So you are not just going to dump us off at this gleeza place and forget us?" said Brother Abraham.

"Certainly not, Mr Creche. We will schedule yearly visits for the first five or so years. Such visits will carry medical personnel and supplies, along with any items you find needed to make your colonies viable. The Colonization Bureau is highly invested in your success."

"And the separate travel arrangements for our respective groups?" asked the rabbi.

"Each group will be housed on a different deck of the transport while underway. Only you gentlemen will be allowed outside of your designated areas."

"*Tov*, that will be acceptable."

"And when do we depart?" asked Brother Abraham.

"You will board the ship nine days from today, with departure scheduled for the next morning."

"So, in a little more than a month, *in shā' Allāh*, we will be at our new home."

"That is correct, Imam Mustafa," the official answered. "Are there any more questions?"

The three patriarchs looked to each other and shook their heads. The wait for departure was tiresome but the end was in sight.

"Very Good. I will be contacting you again with instructions prior to the boarding. Good day, gentleman."


### *Captain's Sea Cabin, Peggy Sue*

Billy Ray listened to the Farside police chief's talking image with no apparent reaction. A few years back it was decided that having Marines police Farside gave the place the appearance of an armed camp. To make the civilian population more at ease an independent constabulary was established, manned by former law enforcement officers. Peggy Sue's captain was leaning back in his chair while the head policeman ranted and raved via video link from his headquarters.

"I repeat, Capt. Vincent, it is totally unacceptable for your people to assault and kill civilians in the halls of this base! I have two victims in hospital and one in the morgue—and the coroner tells me that the deceased was electrocuted. Electrocuted! How did your people electrocute a large man in a public hallway with no nearby electrical outlets? Do your people carry some kind of previously unidentified weapon?"

Billy Ray canted his head slightly to the left and said, "I asked my people about the altercation and they told me how many varmints they put down. I didn't ask them how they took care of the problem."

"'Took care of the problem'! We are talking about a homicide here! And two attempted homicides!"

"Hardly, Chief Franklin. If my people intended on killin' them other two they'd be dead."

"You think this is some kind of joke, Captain? The constabulary is going to do a thorough investigation of this indecent. I want your people to turn themselves in for interrogation."

"Nope."

"You refuse a lawful order by a law enforcement officer? You and your whole crew of scofflaws, brigands and cutthroats needs to be locked up! I remind you that I'm recording this conversation."

"You really are a special kind of stupid, aren't you?"

"What?"

"Two of my officers were attacked in public by three men, two of them armed. They defended themselves, as is every citizen's right, yet you sit there and threaten to arrest my people?"

"I, I need to interrogate them to clear this situation up," the policeman began.

"They were attacked without provocation and cleared the situation up on their own, without the dubious assistance of the constabulary. As far as I'm concerned, this matter is closed," Billy Ray leaned forward in his chair and gave the caller a hard eyed look. "Furthermore, you would do a lot better to concentrate on the thugs who attacked these two upstanding citizens on the streets of your town. Two citizens who just happen to be a former Navy commander and a prominent government scientist, both bonafide war heroes. I'm thinkin' the Council might be interested in hearing about this matter."

"But, but..."

"Good day, sir." Billy Ray terminated the call and then said out loud what he was thinking: "This place is turning into an asshole farm."

After a moment's contemplation, he placed a call to TK Parker. Within a few seconds the screen lit up with the billionaire's

66

weathered visage—it was obvious from the background that he was at home.

"Howdy, Billy Ray. What's on yer mind?"

"Just wanted to let you know we are about ready to head on out of here. It seems the longer we wait the more trouble crops up with the authorities."

"You catching grief over that dead Ukrainian? Or is it the AWOL Marine?"

"I see yer keepin' current on the situation."

"I try to stay on top of things," the older man chuckled. "Since I got you on the line, there is one thing I wanted to mention before you weigh anchor."

"Yes?"

"When you're out there, you are the man in charge. You can get advice from Beth and Bobby and the others, but in the end you are the captain—the decisions rest with you."

"I figured as much, TK. Jack taught me that bein' in command ain't the same thing as chairing a committee."

"Good. The other thing to take note of is that you are the representative of Earth and all its species. The Council is investing you with plenipotentiary powers, meaning you can arrange treaties or start wars—it's all up to you, son."

"Wonderful. Any more burdens you'd like to add?"

"Naw, I just wanted to be sure you understood that you are calling the shots. I got all the faith in the world in you, Billy Ray, otherwise I wouldn't have hired you."

"Thanks for the vote of confidence."

"And one last piece of advice—just between me and you, I think leavin' sooner rather than later would be a good thing. I wouldn't put it past those asshats in the Fleet to try and mess with your departure."

"I catch yer drift. As soon as I get everyone on board we're going to boost for the transit point."

"Sounds like a plan," TK replied. "Good luck and Godspeed, Captain."

\* \* \* \* \*

Billy Ray's face disappeared from the wall in TK's study. Maria, who had been standing just out of camera range, stepped closer to her significant other and laid a hand on his shoulder.

"I really hope you know what you are doing, TK. I worry about those *niños* like they were my own."

"Our own, *querida*. I'll feel better when they are away and safe."

"Si, then all they have to dread are hostile aliens and hazardous strange planets. What is happening to the people here in the solar system?"

"What always happens after a war—at least a war we've won. The real warfighters go back to doin' what they want, like Cincinnatus returning to his farm. Meanwhile, the schemers, politicians and other assorted snakes-in-the-grass slither out from beneath the rocks they hid under when the real fighting was goin' on."

"Why can't you stop them, *mi vida?* You and the council run this place."

"We're not dictators, Maria, and thank God for that. No small group of people ought to hold absolute sway over all of humanity. As far as I'm concerned everyone has the right to pursue their own happiness, as long as they don't hurt anyone else. But there's always a group of busybodies that want to tell others what to do and how to live their lives."

"You mean like this junta of bad Navy officers?"

"Yeah, and in time there will be others. We can't really get rid of them all. We need to keep growing the Fleet in case we run into more of the Dark Lords' minions and nothing dampens morale like a purge of the officer corps. So we gotta' counterbalance 'em with another force so they can't take over and really mess things up."

"By that you mean the Company."

"Yes, an association of independent, armed merchantmen roaming the stars, ensurin' that the Fleet doesn't have a monopoly on interstellar travel."

"And it is not just a scheme to make you and your friends richer?"

"Without money we can't compete with the military or the various governments that are sure to come."

"You really don't like governments, do you?"

"A government is a body of people, usually notably ungoverned. Unfortunately we seem to need them and until all of humanity turns into philosopher kings or attains total enlightenment that ain't gonna change. So until that day, we need to take steps to avoid sinkin' into a totalitarian socialist cesspool. To help keep that from happening, Billy Ray and friends are on their way to becoming rich merchants in their own right—assuming they are as smart and as competent as I think they are."

"I hope you are right, TK."

"Life's a gamble, *mi corazón,* and you can't win if you don't play."

### Bridge, Peggy Sue

All hands were aboard and the ship made ready to sail; the Captain was on the bridge and all stations manned. Billy Ray, seated in the captain's chair overlooking the helm and forward weapon stations, spoke through the 1MC, the ship wide PA system.

"Attention all hands, this is the Captain. Prepare for immediate departure. This is not a drill."

He then placed a call to port control, to let them know the Peggy Sue was departing.

"Farside Port Control, Peggy Sue."

"Peggy Sue, Farside. Go ahead."

"Be advised that the Peggy Sue is underway and outbound. Please advise all local traffic, over."

"Peggy Sue, interrogative your destination?"

"Somewhere in the starry firmament, Farside."

There was a pause.

"Peggy Sue, be advised that we have a hold request on your departure from a Capt. Perlmutter at Fleet."

"Perlmutter?" said Bobby. "That tool from BUPERS?"

"That tosser could ruin a piss up at a free bar," said Nigel Lewis, a former Fleet officer and Peggy Sue veteran who was seated at the helm next to Bobby.

"You're not wrong about that, Mr. Lewis," added Beth, who was standing beside the captain's chair.

"Farside, be advised we are underway," Billy Ray replied. "Helm, lift the ship and proceed to the exit portal."

"Aye, aye, Sir," said Bobby.

The raucous call of a klaxon sounded throughout the ship as the Peggy Sue lifted on its repulsors and slid smoothly from its berth. Once free of the dock structure it turned and floated upward, toward the large featureless expanse of metal that was the ceiling of the dock area. While seemingly solid, the overhead was actually a large piece of T'aafhal composite. Selectively permeable, it was capable of holding a gaseous atmosphere inside while letting solid objects, like the Peggy Sue, pass through to the vacuum of space. Green lights around the giant hatch's perimeter indicated that the portal was open.

"Peggy Sue, Fleet is demanding that you return to your berth. Something about an AWOL Marine being on board your vessel."

Another party entered the conversation.

"Peggy Sue, Fleet HQ, this is Capt. Perlmutter. I suspect that there is an AWOL Marine on board your ship. I demand you return your ship for inspection."

"Fleet HQ, there are no active duty Fleet or Marine personnel on board this vessel. Break. Farside, Fleet has no jurisdiction over civilian traffic. We are departing as stated."

"Fleet HQ, Farside, Capt. Vincent confirms no AWOL Fleet personnel on board his vessel. Peggy Sue, you are clear to depart."

"Thank you Farside, Vincent out."

"Helm, take us out and on an immediate vector for our transit point."

"Aye, aye, Captain," Bobby said with a grin.

"You lied to him," observed Beth.

"'One ought always to lie, when one can do good by it'," the Captain replied, clasping his hands across his chest smiling.

"That sounds like another one of your literary quotations."

"Mark Twain," he replied, quite pleased with himself, "from 'On the Decay of the Art of Lying'."

"Clearing the portal now, Captain," Bobby called out from the helm.

The Peggy Sue slipped through the port's seemingly solid cover like a submarine surfacing into another world—a world possessing a jet black sky flecked with pinpricks of light above a monochromatic landscape. The jagged black and gray desolation of the lunar surface became visible through the ship's transparent bow and just as quickly fell away. The first expedition of the Orion Arm Trading Company had begun.

"All ahead one quarter, Bobby. Let's not drag this out."

"Aye, aye, Sir."

\* \* \* \* \*

Five hours later, the Peggy Sue was aligned with the departure vector to Gliese 667A. All unnecessary systems were secured for alter-space transit and the ship's computer was making final adjustments before initiating the transition from 3-space.

"Captain, you're not going to believe this, but there is a Navy Frigate on an intercept vector with our course," reported Umky from the main weapon station. Through that console he had access to the new sensor system, which interfaced directly to the part of his ursine brain that interpreted smells from his exquisitely

71

sensitive nose. Effectively, Umky could smell objects in space just as he could smell a seal under the ice in the Arctic.

"Put the plot on the forward screen."

A graphic representation of the Frigate's course was overlain on the view forward. The Peggy Sue's projected course intercepted that of the Frigate out near the asteroid belt, roughly 2.2 AU from the Sun.

"It would seem that our friends in the Fleet really cannot bear to see us go," Billy Ray said, "and it appears that they have some idea of where we are headed."

"It seems that their information is not all that accurate, Captain," said Mizuki from the navigation station.

"What do you mean?"

"Gliese 667C is much less massive than Gliese 667A, which not only affects the alter-space transit time but the location of the transit point itself," Mizuki said. "It looks like they are on course to intercept, or at least interfere with, an alter-space transit to Gliese 667C, which lies on essentially the same course vector but is half an AU farther from the Sun than the transit point to 667A."

"Captain," the ship's computer said, "we are coming up on transit in 4, 3, 2, 1..."

The Peggy Sue rippled and disappeared like an image on the surface of a pond when a gust of wind blows. Its next stop would be Gliese 667A. Five minutes later, the time required for light from Peggy Sue's disappearance to reach the Navy Frigate, the intercepting warship's captain and crew were left wondering what happened to their intended target.

# *Chapter 6*

### *Peggy Sue, Alter-space Day 7*

A week into the voyage, the various members of the crew had come to know one another well enough to operate the ship smoothly. There was, however, still a divide between those who had sailed on the Peggy Sue before and those on board for the first time. Aside from the officers, the veterans included Chief Zackly, Hitch and Jacobs. A second pool of experience was found in the Marines. Rosey Acuna and Herman "Kato" Kwan had been on board during the earliest voyages. Add to them Umky, Vincent DeSilva, and Dmitry Boskovitch, who had been Marines on the Great Alien Hunt.

Being Marines, they started doing PT—physical training—from the first day out of port. Every morning, they did calisthenics, practiced hand-to-hand combat techniques, and ran in the cargo hold. A number of the officers joined them in this activity, including First Officer Melaku, Sailing Master Danner, Science Officer Ogawa, and, not least of all, Captain Vincent. Participation by the old hands soon shamed most of the new crewmembers and the science staff into joining the daily activity, at least the running.

Among the new crew were a number of sailors and submariners. Fred Smith, Lou Wright, and Tommy Chen came from the American Navy, all having served in submarines. Tamara Wilson, Jay Taylor, and Sam Sheffield served in the navies of Canada, Australia, and the UK, respectively, while Katrin "Kate" Hamm was off a German Antarctic research vessel and Kashimawo Ademola from a Nigerian registered supertanker. Also new were Chief Engineer Arinbjörn Baldursson and the other two engineer's mates, whose quarters were aft by the engineering spaces.

It was tradition aboard the Peggy Sue for the crew to have a small libation at the end of the afternoon watch, before going to the mess for dinner. Except for those on watch on the bridge or in the engine room, the enlisted crew were lounging about the day room, enjoying a beer or a glass of wine, waiting for dinner to be announced.

"So far, this has been less eventful than sailing on the sea," said Kate.

"I told you all, nothing much happens in alter-space except drills," said Steve Hitch, playing the wise veteran.

"It's almost like being on patrol in a boomer," said Fred Smith, "but a damn site more comfortable."

"You got that right, Mate. Even the Aussie Navy didn't have a cocktail hour while underway," added Jay Taylor.

"Trust me," said Matt Jacobs, "things will get much more exciting when we get to where we are going."

"You know something we don't?" asked Kate.

"Just that every other voyage on the Peggy Sue has served up more adventure than you can imagine," said Stevie.

"Or want," added Kato Kwan, to which Rosey just grunted. Rosey had been keeping a low profile since she had been given The Word by the First Officer.

"Is that why everyone on this ship is running around like fitness nuts?" asked Fred. "Sailing the ship doesn't seem like such a demanding pastime to me."

"Just wait," said Kato, "one minute you'll be safe and sound on board ship and the next you'll be fighting plasma shooting cyborgs or sex crazed giant insects with swords and axes who would just love to use your abdomen to incubate their eggs."

"Really?" asked Tamara.

"The man doesn't lie. That's why Matt and I joined the PT sessions from the git go."

"Yeah," said Matt, "and trust me, Stevie is normally one lazy SOB. If he feels it's a wise idea to stay in shape you newbies should take notice."

"What about it, Rosey?" asked Kate, seeking another female's opinion, "you were on the earlier voyages."

Rosey looked at the German woman for a moment, shrugged and said, "I figure it's better to run your ass off on board than to get it blown off by some alien later because you're out of shape."

Rosey got up and went over to the booze locker, the storage unit that held supplies of beer, wine and other potables. Regardless of preference, the daily booze ration was limited to two drinks a day that could not be saved for a later time.

"I notice that even the officers participate, particularly in combat training," Tamara added, "including the First Officer. From what I've heard, she is tough enough without practice."

"Don't know about that," said Kato, "But a buddy of mine was on a cruiser she captained—totally by the book and hard as woodpecker lips, but she knows her business."

The assembled crew all nodded in agreement—gossiping about the ship's officers was a long standing tradition on naval vessels.

"What is with that oriental woman and the flock of insects that follow her around?" asked Kashimawo Ademola.

"Now there in lies a tale, my Nigerian friend," began Stevie.

"That isn't just a flock of butterflies, it's actually an alien creature, Kashi," said Matt, beating his friend to the punch. "Stevie and I were there when she acquired it, er, them."

"Bollocks! I think you two are full of it," said Jay.

"Don't take our word," Stevie replied. "Acuna was there too, weren't you Rosey?"

"Yes," Rosey said, sitting back down after fetching a second beer. "I've seen those cute little butterflies electrocute a man sized alien, and I've seen Dr. O slice through three charging multi-armed maggot creatures with that sword of hers. A word to the wise, do not fuck with the butterflies, or Dr. Ogawa."

"OK, and the other officers?"

"They all have experience handling warships, fighting in space armor and making contact with aliens," Matt answered. "You may not like 'em at first, but they are probably the best bunch of officers you could find—assuming you want to return from this little jaunt."

"I want to know about the bears," said Jay, "I don't much care for being trapped on board a ship with 'em. What if we run out of food? They'll eat us just like a pack of dingos."

"Bullshit," said Kato, "I've fought beside bears on a number of occasions and was damned glad they were on our side."

"I have heard that they even eat each other in the wild," said Kashi.

"How would you know?" Stevie retorted. "You and Jay aren't even from the same hemisphere as polar bears."

"But I am, eh?" said Tamara. Being Canadian, she too had misgivings about being in such close proximity to the large carnivores, and she had some idea of how dangerous polar bears could be.

"Well, speak of the devil and up he jumps," said Matt. Ambling into the day room from the forward passageway was Umky, all 600 kilograms of him.

"What are you primates yammering about?" the white bear said as he headed for the booze locker. Though a polar bear's most acute sense was smell, there was nothing wrong with Umky's hearing.

"What brings you to the day room, Umky?" asked Stevie, "we don't normally see you here."

Umky swung his huge head around to look over his shoulder at the assembled humans. He made a point of sniffing the air twice, black nostrils flaring, as if to register the humans' scents. Before answering he turned back to the locker where he fished out a couple of two liter jugs containing dark liquid. These he clipped to his utility harness—being a quadruped made it difficult to carry things.

"Just passing through," Umky replied, closing the locker, "picking up a couple of blackberry brandies before relaxing in the bear quarters—gotta hurry before Ahnah, she bitch of the Arctic, gets out of the science staff meeting and beats me to the pool."

With the two jugs dangling from his harness, Umky headed toward the cargo hold and the polar bear quarters beyond. "You primates take care," he said in departure, winking as he passed by Matt and Stevie.

"Hey, Umky," said Stevie, picking up on the bear's signal, "some of the new crewmembers were asking about your gastronomical preferences. You wouldn't eat a crewmate would you, even if we ran out of supplies?"

Umky stopped and looked back at the collection of anxious sailors. Again the bear sniffed the air.

"Of course not, I would never eat a crewmate."

Relief could be seen on the faces of Jay, Kashi and Tamara as Umky continued aft. Just as he went through the door he added, "unless I was really hungry."


## *ESS Fortune, Outbound from Farside*

The day finally came when the three disparate flocks of colonists boarded the ship that was to take them to a new home circling a distant star. The name of that ship was Fortune, the name of the second English ship to arrive at Plymouth Colony in the New World, one year after the voyage of the Pilgrim ship Mayflower. She was of utilitarian design, a 200 meter cylinder rounded off at either end. Her cabins had more than enough space for the 173 colonists and her hold accommodated their livestock and supplies with room to spare.

On Fortune's outer hull three sizable shuttles were docked, capable of ferrying a hundred people at a time to a planet's surface, fewer with a mix of cargo and passengers. The ship was manned by a crew of twelve: a captain, a navigator, an engineer, three pilots for the shuttles, and six deckhands. The passengers, having been trained on the ship's galley and laundry facilities, were expected to fend for themselves during the voyage. The crew would remain locked in the forward section until planet fall, baring any emergencies.

Two days out from Farside, the colonists were still settling into their spartan accommodations. Shadi and Dorri were in a room with six other girls, where they would be confined during most of the journey. The sisters would have preferred to be in the shared lounge for their deck, with its large viewing screens, but the lounge was filled with men—women, particularly young single women, were not allowed. They could only venture forth, fully swathed in their hijabs, to cook for the men and then carry their own food back to their rooms.

Fortunately, their single room prison had its own bathroom and each bunk possessed a viewing screen. Most of the girls showed no interest in the screen units, having no idea how to operate them. Shadi and Dorri, however, knew about things like computers and the internet. Shadi was quickly able to bring up a floor plan for the ship and information about the voyage.

"We are going to be stuck on this ship for almost a month," she said to her sister in Farsi.

"Why does it take so long? Even a plane trip halfway around the world only used to take a day."

"Evidently we have already traveled a distance many times that of going around the world and are lining up to go some place called 'alter-space'. It will take 22 days in alter-space to get to our new star, and several days in normal space after that before we can land on the planet."

"Another month of this?" said a girl from the facing bunks. "Why do I feel so heavy? I felt light as a feather before we got on the ship."

"That's because the ship is at standard Earth gravity," replied Shadi. "The Moon's gravity is only one sixth that of home."

"Well I don't like it," the other said petulantly.

"Get use to it, it is only going to get worse. The planet we are going to has a gravity that is a third stronger than this. During the trip the ship's gravity will slowly increase to get us use to our new home."

"How do you know all this? Are you just making this up?"

Shadi considered telling the girl that all that information and more was available through the access screen in her bunk, but then hesitated. If it got back to the Imam he might forbid the use of the devices, so instead she said, "I heard some of the men talking when we were boarding."

Her sister looked at her and raised an eyebrow. In English she said, "smart not to tell the others about the data screens—they probably couldn't use them anyway."

"Yes, don't tell anyone else. If you find things you want to read you better do it now. I doubt there will be any such devices when we get to our destination."

### Peggy Sue, Emergence Gliese 667A

Sam Shepard, Tommy Chen and Jimmy Tosh were unpacking a stellar surveillance satellite from its shipping crate under the watchful eye of Chief Zackly. Deck gravity in the cargo hold was reduced to a tenth of Earth normal to make the 500kg space craft easier to handle.

"Move it slowly, yous deck apes! It may not weigh much but it still has mass."

"Aye, aye, Chief," said Tommy, not really understanding the Chief's point.

"That means, if you get it moving fast, it'll be just as hard to stop as on Earth," Sam added, "so take it easy, mates."

"Yous guys turn this space widget into a broke-dick we'll have to get the bilge rats to fix it before it can be launched," added the Chief. "And if we cause a delay we'll all be on the Captain's shit list."

"What is dis ting for, mon?" asked the Jamaican cook, who had been pressed into service to help ready the probe for launch.

"Dr. Ogawa wants us to put this in orbit around the first star we come to," the old Chief said. "As fer what it does it's PFM."

The crewmen carefully landed the metallic dodecahedron on a hover sled and strapped it down. The satellite needed to be taken to an ejection port on third deck, which meant moving it forward to the cargo lift against the forward cargo hold bulkhead. As they carefully moved the hefty payload the men conversed.

"I understand how most of us got on this mission," Sam said, "but how did you find yourself aboard, Jimmy?"

79

"I still be tryin' to figure that out, mon. I was visitin' some friends in Colorado when all Babylon exploded—fire rained down on Jah's creation and I only lived because I was in de mountains. Bamba yay, I brought to de Moon with a bunch of other survivors a few months later. I went from Rocky Mountain high to I and I Moon base."

"Right, mate. But how did you get on the crew?" Sam repeated. "Most of crew were sailors of one kind or another, but you seem like some tosser who just wandered on board before we cast off."

"Hey mon! I be a good cook and de Captain like Jamaican food," replied Jimmy. "In fact, I was savin' money to open I own restaurant back on de Moon. It was going to serve Italian-Jamaican fusion cuisine."

"Italian-Jamaican?" said Tommy. "I can't even imagine what that would be like."

"It be great, mon! Jerk chicken fettuccine, conch Marsala, all sorts of great combinations—I was going to name de place The Pasta Rasta."

"What?"

"Pasta Rasta. As in pasta with a Rastafari twist."

"The only thing I've seen you twist up is a spliff," said Tommy.

"Ya mon! But only a Jamaican spliff made wit ganja, no jackass rope. True Rastas don' smoke tobacco, only God's plants."

"I thought that Rastafari were also vegetarians; how can you cook meat dishes for the crew?"

"Ital eatin' varies widely from Rasta to Rasta; food only need be pure, clean and natural."

"So why aren't you back at Farside, working on your restaurant?" Sam pressed.

"Well, you see, I had some financial difficulties. I hopin' that de profits from dis trip will pay off I creditors and let I start de restaurant."

"Right," said Tommy and Sam in unison.

"All right, quit yer yappin' and pay attention on the cargo lift," the Chief ordered as the elevator platform rose, headed up to deck three.

*  *  *  *  *

On the bridge all stations reported ready as the Captain and crew prepared for emergence—the transition from alter-space back to normal 3-space. There was really nothing for the crew to do during the transition—the ship's computer handled all necessary adjustments to the engines, shields and deck gravity—but you never know what might greet you when suddenly popping into being in a strange star system.

The klaxon sounded and the computer's voice announced, "transition to 3-space in 5, 4, 3, 2, 1."

The panels in the ship's nose went from opaque to transparent as the normal Universe shimmered into existence outside. Directly ahead was a star, orangish and slightly cooler than the Sun, though it looked as large as the Earthlings' native star. This was because the arrival transfer point was closer to GJ667A than the departure point was from the more massive Sun—linked transfer points have complementary spacetime curvature.

"Mr. Lewis, lay in a course to bring her about," Billy Ray ordered. "Notify the Chief when we are properly positioned to release the stellar observation satellite, then line us up for the jump to 667C."

"Aye, aye, Sir."

"Dr. Ogawa, please reconfirm the transit calculations with the ship's computer. I wish to spend as brief a time around this star as possible, but missing the transit point on the first pass would be even worse."

"Yes, Captain," Mizuki answered. "It will take at least six hours to get properly positioned. I will have refined parameters well before we are on the final vector."

*  *  *  *  *

A little over six hours later the Peggy Sue had altered course and was on an outbound trajectory. That trajectory was a line joining GJ667A and 667C, suitably corrected for the time lag incurred by light from the target star. Though part of the same stellar system, it took light more than thirty hours to travel from A to C. The Earth ship was about to make the same trip in fewer than five minutes.

This transit would be the shortest, and quickest, ever made by an Earth ship. Such a brief excursion into alter-space required the utmost care with its entry parameters; the course and velocity must be spot on or, when the computer tried to trigger the transition to alter-space, nothing would happen. Even worse, they could enter alter-space on a trip to some unintended destination. Mizuki had triple checked the parameters and passed them to Bobby, who was manning the helm himself for this maneuver.

"We are ready for the transit, Captain," Bobby reported.

"We are tracking all parameters accurately?"

"One hundred percent balls on accurate, Sir," Bobby replied with a smile. In years past Bobby and Billy Ray had manned the ship's helm together in many a tight situation. "The computer has the conn for transit."

"Acknowledged, Sailing Master Danner," the ship replied. The warning klaxon sounded.

"Transit in 5, 4, 3, 2, 1."

Space rippled for what seemed a longer than usual time as the Peggy Sue slipped from one reality into another. The normally transparent panels in the ship's nose went opaque. The minutes crept by with glacial slowness as the crew marked the passage of time in silence. None wanted to consider what not emerging after the calculated interval would mean. Just over four interminable minutes later, the computer spoke again.

"Emergence in 5, 4, 3..."

*Part Two*

# *Devils In The Darkness*

## Chapter 7

### Emergence, Gliese 667C

The ship shuddered and the normal Universe returned. The view forward was unexpectedly dark—it should have held a head on view of the red dwarf star that was their destination. Instead the view ahead was a starless black.

"What the bloody hell?" said Nigel.

"Shit!" said Bobby, hands dancing over the controls. "I need emergency power, now!"

The view forward spun to show the backlit limb of a planet. A very large planet that was far too close.

"Captain, we have emerged 2.36 seconds prematurely from alter-space," the ship's computer announced as the collision alarm sounded.

"Not now, Peggy Sue," replied the Captain in a dead calm voice. "Engineering, Bridge, we need emergency power to the engines."

The looming planet continued to grow larger at an alarming rate as the ship's bow swung toward the backlit arc that was the planet's edge. Instruments showed that the emergency antimatter reactor was online and acceleration was edging above 60G.

"It might be a good idea to strengthen the forward and bottom shields," Bobby said, while making small adjustments to the controls. "We are going to kiss the atmosphere."

"Roger that, pardner," replied Billy Ray, Navy protocol forgotten as the two friends struggled to save their ship. Seconds later glowing streaks formed around the bow, dim and flickering at first but rapidly turning into a bright cocoon of fire. The view outside the ship disappeared as the planet's atmosphere registered its outrage at being violated by an object traveling a thousand kilometers a second. Then, as quickly as it had started, the sheath of plasma vanished and the half lit disk of the planet visibly fell away in the ship's wake.

"Negative impact," Bobby said, "the course ahead is clear, Captain."

Across the bridge gasps could be heard as people who had been unconsciously holding their breath began breathing again.

"Very good, Helm," acknowledged Billy Ray. "That entrance was a mite more exciting than I would have liked."

"Sorry, Captain," Bobby said with a smile. "We seem to have skipped off the atmosphere of 667Ce. I hope the science types got some good samples as we passed through."

"Peggy Sue, care to explain how we came out of alter-space into a near collision with a planet?" the Captain asked.

"As I reported, Captain, we seem to have exited alter-space prematurely. I have no explanation for this except that GJ667C must have been in occultation with respect to our departure point by the planet we nearly collided with."

"Captain," interrupted Mizuki, "I think that the explanation lies in the distortion of local spacetime by the planet's mass. Evidently, the local distortion was severe enough to cause displacement of the terminal transit point. As a result, we came out of alter-space a million kilometers short."

"What are the odds of that?" Beth said, still standing next to the Captain's chair.

"Based on the planet's diameter and orbit, the probability of emerging with the planet directly in front of the ship is roughly 5.8 times 10 to the -12," the computer answered.

"That's longer odds than winning the old Powerball lottery," said Bobby.

"It is worse than that," added Mizuki, "667C is in orbit around the AB pair. As it moves the orientation of its ecliptic plane also changes. It is only aligned with a path from A twice every 3100 years or so. Add to that the fact that A and B are in an eccentric orbit around their center of mass every 41 years and the probability of an alignment becomes vanishingly small."

"But evidently not zero," Billy Ray noted.

"Not zero," Mizuki agreed. "The Universe is really big, and it has been around a long time—anything that is possible is bound to happen sooner or later."

"Great," said Billy Ray, "we can all cross colliding with a planet off our bucket lists."

"Perhaps we should have tee shirts made up," Beth remarked dryly.

Billy Ray glanced sideways at his first officer and then said, "Helm, lay in a course for the second planet and let's get back to the business at hand."

"Aye, aye, Captain," replied Bobby, turning back to his controls. Next to him, Nigel leaned over and whispered.

"You were bloody brilliant, mate."


### *Deck Three, Peggy Sue*

On third deck, a party of crewmembers were readying robot probes under the supervision of Will Krenshaw. Dr. Krenshaw had spent time at NASA working on robotic missions to Mars and other prime destinations in the solar system. His specialty was hunting for life on other worlds, a task that had yielded no rewards thus far in his career. The work party was busily running diagnostics on the probes that would survey their destination when the collision alarm sounded.

"What's that?" Will asked, looking up at the viewing screen on the wall. The screen went from black to red to bright yellow in the course of a few seconds, and then back to black.

Matt consulted the display on his jumpsuit sleeve, which was monitoring activity on the bridge. Looking up he said. "Its nothing, Doc. We just bounced off a planet is all."

"What!" the microbiologist exclaimed. "Is that normal?"

"Oh sure," said Steve Hitch, "happens almost every time we arrive in a new system."

Matt Jacobs shot his friend a look and murmured in a low voice, "and so the fun begins."

Two types of survey drone were being sent to the surface of GJ667Cc—one terrestrial and one aquatic. The aquatic robot was more conventional, consisting of a dozen cylindrical metal segments, each ten centimeters in diameter and twenty long, joined by flexible, pleated joints. The head and tail segments tapered, giving the contraption a worm like appearance. Four fins protruded from the otherwise smooth, barrel like body segments at 90° angles. A centimeter tall, they ran the length of each segment, their purpose to give purchase on land and aid in swimming.

Powered by a cold fusion fuel cell modeled on those used in the Marines' battle armor, the robosnake was meant to swim or crawl around in harsh environments, exploring its surroundings with a multitude of sensors and cameras. On land it either used serpentine locomotion, slithering slowly through rough sections, or sidewinding on clearer ground, hitting speeds as high as six km/hr. Swimming in water the same undulating motion translated to 1.5 km/hr. Not fast, but persistent.

The other robot explorer, dubbed a flexibot, did not look much like a robot at all. It was, in fact, a deformable, flexible robotic exoskeleton originally developed by NASA researchers. Based on *tensegrity*—a design principle that employs a discontinuous set of compression elements, balanced by a continuous tensile force that creates internal stress, to stabilize a structure. The term was coined by architect Buckminster Fuller, the inventor of the geodesic dome and other novel structures. As a result, the land roving robot looked more like a kinetic sculpture than a scientific probe.

For shipment, the structure was collapsed into a compact bundle. When deployed, the robot itself was a mostly open, roughly spherical collection of cable and crisscrossing pipe segments around two meters in diameter. Its expanded structure could absorb shocks that would destroy more seemingly solid devices. Possessing no wheels or legs, it had no axles or hinges, no single points of failure that needed strengthening to withstand stress. It moved by shortening and lengthening the cables that connect its rigid components. The cables themselves were similar to the electroreactive "muscles" in the crew's armored space suits. This deformable structure allowed it to roll on smooth surfaces and climb over broken terrain. The force of an impact—whether bouncing down a hill or a fall off a cliff—was absorbed and diffused throughout its structure by multiple paths, protecting the scientific instruments suspended within.

Two robosnakes would be dropped in the planet's seas; three flexibots would be dropped, one each for the three largest continents. In preparation for deployment, the crew were running the robots through their paces.

"And this pile of junk is supposed to explore the mystery planet on its own?" asked a skeptical Hitch.

"It does look like a piece of modern art," said Kate, who was running diagnostics on the robot from her tablet. The flexibot quivered and deformed, assuming a number of distorted shapes.

"Yeah, art creeps me out a lot too."

"It's not as creepy as the robosnakes," said Matt. "I had to take two of them to the bear quarters and have them swim around in the pool. Umky looked at me like I was crazy."

"Hey, I've known you were crazy for years."

"Funny, Stevie. It wasn't me who helped smuggle a live walrus into the polar bear habitat back on Farside."

"He did what?" asked Kate, not sure if the two American sailors were joking.

"Never mind, Katrin, Matt has a tendency to embellish the truth. Don't trust anything he says about me. Besides, that was a great day for human polar bear relations."

"Not so good for the walrus."

"You two have been on the Peggy Sue for a long time, haven't you?" said Kate.

"Since the first voyage," Matt said proudly. "Took a little side trip on the M'tak Ka'fek but Peggy Sue's our ship."

"She's never let us down," added Steve.

"Scheisse!" Kate said.

"No, its true," said Steve, a bit defensively.

"Nein, I was not referring to the ship," she replied. "One of the cables failed to pass the test, we will have to replace it."

"I'm half afraid to take it apart," said Matt. "How can we tell if we put it back together right?"

"The computer will tell us," said Will, looking up from his own tablet. "You two stop flirting with Ms. Hamm and get back to work. We still need to bake the probes in the sterilization oven for a couple of hours."

"There's always one guy who spoils the party," muttered Steve. Kate shot him a sideways glance and then winked, causing his hopes to soar. Matt just shook his head.


### *Peggy Sue, Orbit around GJ667Cc*

It took a half a day to match orbital velocity with 667Cc, which everyone was now just calling "*C*". The officers and science staff were holding a planning meeting in the main lounge, the only comfortable space that could accommodate the crowd present. Out the large eye-shaped porthole on the starboard side their destination could be seen slowly turning.

It was a mostly dun colored planet, with a number of sizable seas, dark in contrast with the land. Tufts of white cloud dotted both water and land, and an impressive cyclonic storm was moving from the largest visible body of water onto an adjacent continent. The survey probe sent from Earth had been orbiting the planet for almost five months and had fully mapped the surface optically and with ground penetrating radar. Geo-neutrinographic images of the planet's magmatic reservoirs and the deep structure of its mantle showed that this was still a geologically active world. The Peggy Sue downloaded that information as a starting point for its investigation.

"This place is screwy, I tell you," proclaimed Joe Rogers, the expedition climatologist. "There doesn't seem to be any biological activity at all yet the atmosphere is mostly nitrogen with about 18% oxygen."

"Isn't that about perfect for humans?" asked Beth.

"Yes, but it shouldn't be there!"

"What Dr. Rogers is trying to say is that oxygen is hard to keep around," said Will Krenshaw, the microbiologist. "It's the third most abundant element in the Universe but it's highly reactive. It will combine with almost every other element on the periodic table."

"You're saying the planet should not have free oxygen in its atmosphere?" asked Captain Vincent.

"Captain, Earth started out without oxygen in its atmosphere. Something like 2.8 billion years ago cyanobacteria, commonly known as blue-green algae, evolved and started polluting the air. It took another billion years to change from a mixture poisonous to animal life to the oxygen rich environment we evolved in."

"Yes," said Joe, trying to finish his explanation. "Because oxygen is so reactive it should not be present in such quantity without some form of life to free it and replenish the supply. Yet the reports from the survey drone show no signs of life, at all!"

"Maybe it's hiding in the oceans?" offered Sami Hosseini. "It is certain, based on observations from orbit, that a number of the geologic formations show signs of uplifted sedimentary limestones. That is a pretty sure sign of microbial life at some point in the planet's past."

"That is what our experience on Earth and Mars indicates," said Gerard Leclerc, a chemist. "Perhaps there is some new geophysical process at work here."

"No way to tell until we can get to the surface and examine the strata more closely," said Sami.

"And take some soil samples," added Joe.

"I wonder," said Ahnah, the only bear in attendance. "If life used to be present, as indicated by the oxygen rich atmosphere, what happened to it? The probe data indicates nothing—no forests, no ground cover, no organisms in the sea—it is like the planet has been sterilized."

"Multispectral scans by the survey drone even revealed a number of sites that could be long abandoned settlements," Mizuki added.

"Not to be a buzz kill here," said Bobby, "but we know there are aliens who take a dim view of our kind of life."

"We cannot know if the Dark Lords or their minions caused this anomaly until we send out probes to the surface or, even better, travel to the surface our selves," Mizuki replied. She was well aware of how much Bobby loved a good alien conspiracy.

"I'm just throwing it out as something to keep in mind," he said.

"Bobby has a good point," said Beth. "Though I'm sure finding natural causes for the state of the planet would be more interesting scientifically, we do have incontrovertible evidence that aliens have meddled with the environments of several planets."

"More than that," added the Captain, "we have no idea what we might find down there so we are going to take it slow."

This remark caused looks of disappointment among the science staff, who were champing at the bit to study the planet up close. Fortunately for all involved, Billy Ray had learned to be careful on previous voyages.

"We will launch probes to survey both land and sea. If they turn up nothing dangerous, we will then send a shuttle to the surface. Those on the shuttle will be in suits—armored suits—just in case."

"Armor! What's going to attack us on a lifeless planet?" said Joe.

"I don't know, Dr. Rogers, but the first surface expedition will be armed and armored," the Captain said. "'The universe is relentlessly, catastrophically dangerous, on scales that menace not just communities, but civilizations and our species as well'."

"Hai, Captain," said Mizuki. Then, turning to her staff, "I believe we all have tasks to accomplish."

Joe and Sami looked like they wished to continue the argument but Mizuki's tone made it clear that the discussion was over. As the meeting broke up Beth privately asked her husband, "who were you quoting about the dangerous Universe?"

"John Tooby, an American anthropologist," he replied. "I have read things other than Chaucer, Shakespeare and the literary canon of dead white men."

"I thought it summed the situation up nicely, love."


### Captain's Sea Cabin, Two Days Later

"So the survey results turned up no sign of life?" Billy Ray asked his science officer.

"The surveybots found nothing, Captain, in the seas or on land," said Mizuki. "The place is a desert, except that even deserts harbor life."

"It seems like a real mystery, Captain," Bobby chimed in, "an otherwise livable planet with no life to be found."

"There are some patches that look like they might be ruins, particularly off the coasts," said Beth.

"Maybe they were an aquatic race?" suggested Billy Ray. "We have encountered aquatic creatures before."

Beth shook her head. "Probing with terahertz radar shows similar, but smaller areas inland."

"Dr. Rogers speculates that the planet's climate has changed in the recent past, melting much of its polar ice caps. This would cause the sea levels to rise, drowning any coastal cities." Mizuki's tone indicated less than enthusiastic agreement with that hypothesis.

"That would explain why the largest ruins seem to be offshore," Bobby agreed.

"What's with this Rogers character?" asked Billy Ray. "He seems to have a chip on his shoulder about something."

"Dr. Rogers used to be a prominent advocate for anthropogenic global warming, Captain," said Mizuki. "After the alien bombardment any chance of proving that theory correct was lost."

"You don't believe in AGW, Mizuki?"

"Science is not about belief, it is about observation and evidence. I did not find the evidence behind the AGW theory compelling."

"Earth's temperature had been going up," said Beth.

"Climate scientists had too short a view of the subject. A century of data is insufficient to predict a planet's climate—a complex system that operates over thousands and millions of years. The temperature variation measured was well within historical norms, and any signal caused by human activity was lost in the noise of that natural variation."

"When it comes to backing a theory with hard evidence, Mizuki is a real stickler," Bobby said, "I can't convince her that aliens helped build the pyramids either."

Beth raised a single eyebrow and Billy Ray suppressed a grin, both imagining private arguments between the strictly rational astrophysicist and the ardent conspiracy theorist. How they fell in love was hard to fathom, but then, love has very little to do with logic.

"All right then, we are agreed that the next step is to visit the surface?" said Billy Ray, changing the subject away from global warming and alien pyramid builders.

"Hai, the entire science staff cannot wait to visit the surface, Captain."

"And I guess that you two," He nodded in the direction of Beth and Bobby, "will be wanting to go as well?"

"It would seem a proper duty for the ship's first officer."

"And I have the most experience in piloting a shuttle," added Bobby.

"Now I know how Captain Jack used to feel, always having to stay with the ship."

"Just part of the burden of command, love," said his wife and first officer.

"Fine. As I said, I want everyone in armor, with no exceptions."

"The science staff will not like that," said Mizuki.

"Part of the burden of exploration," replied the Captain. "And take the Marines with you, in heavy armor. It will be good exercise for them. Besides, you never know what you might run into."

"Shuttle One?" asked Bobby.

"Yup, no sense in half measures."

Shuttle One was a large armored assault craft, capable of carrying a whole platoon of Marines in heavy armor. It also mounted exterior armaments—rail guns and X-ray lasers, as well as stouter shielding. The Captain hoped these would prove apotropaic.

"The local day is just under 37 hours in length," said Mizuki. "If we choose a site where we can arrive just after sunrise we will have 16 or more hours on the surface before returning."

"You don't want to stay the night on the surface?"

"I do not think my colleagues are quite up to sleeping in their suits on their first outing."

"They could take their suits off inside the shuttle," Beth pointed out.

"No. We should risk no chance of contamination, of ourselves or the planet, until we know more. We will vent the shuttle cabin to space before descent and again after we climb back to orbit."

"Full UV decontamination as well?" asked Bobby. "Your colleagues are going to think you're a hypochondriac, or xenophobic at a microscopic level."

Mizuki smiled and said, "I'm just going to blame the Captain for all the precautions."

"May as well," Billy Ray said, "they already think I'm totally paranoid. Anything else?"

The other three shook their heads.

"Alright, let's get this little tourist junket underway."

## Chapter 8

### Shuttle One, Descending

Bobby was at the controls of the large armored shuttle designated Shuttle One. In the copilot's seat was First Officer Melaku. In the passenger compartment, nearest the aft ramp, all five Marines stood stoically in heavy space armor—they would be the first off after landing. Equipped with railguns of various calibers, the small squad was more than a match for anything short of a tank battalion.

Also along was the entire science section, led by Dr. Ogawa. Aside from Mizuki, the others were having trouble getting comfortable in the standard armor the Captain insisted they wear. First among the complainers was Joe Rogers, the American climatologist.

"Damn this suit! It's like clomping around in a deep-sea diving outfit on dry land. Why is the Captain so paranoid?"

"Because we have had people wearing only pressure suits get holes burned right through their bodies by plasma cannon, and others killed by giant crickets with spears," replied Mizuki quietly.

"Really?" said Gerard. "Suddenly the armor does not weigh so much."

"Get with the program, Joe," added Will, the microbiologist. "The Captain knows what he's doing."

The climatologist stopped complaining but, from the look on his face, remained far from convinced of the Captain's wisdom. As the shuttle descended into the planet's atmosphere, thicker and denser than Earth's, display screens along the sides of the cabin showed a view of the approaching surface. The geologist, Sami, began pointing out features of interest as mountain ranges and river valleys slid past beneath the shuttle. On the flight deck, Beth and Bobby discussed where to land.

"To start out I think we should land far inland," said Bobby. "We've had some nasty surprises from things coming out of the water on other worlds."

"I agree. I think someplace flat and dry with a good field of view."

"Right. That way we can see any threats approaching from a distance."

"My thinking exactly."

"We are over this continent's central plane—it's as flat as Kansas down there... hey! Look over there. That looks like some kind of ruin."

"I think you're right," said Beth, looking out of the windscreen as Bobby threw the shuttle into a 45 degree banking turn to circle the site below. "Let's set down a couple of klicks outside whatever that is—I'll tell our passengers we are landing."

"Fine, I'll tell the ship what our plans are..."

\* \* \* \* \*

After making two complete circuits of the site, Bobby brought the shuttle to a hover a little less than two kilometers from the edge of the visible ruins. The heavy craft sank slowly to the surface, its repulsors causing rivulets of sand to flee from beneath it. Stout landing legs emerged from the shuttle's underside just before it touched the surface.

"Another smooth landing on a new alien world," said Bobby.

"Every landing is smooth with deck gravity to compensate for any bumps and shudders," Beth said.

"Spoil sport," he replied. "I've landed with the nose pointing to the northwest, into the prevailing wind. That will help keep all of this sand from blowing in the rear hatch when it's open."

"Good thinking. Well, let's not keep the others waiting."

Emerging from the shuttle after the uneventful landing, the five Marines exited first, fanning out to form a defensive perimeter. They were followed by the science party, who milled about like a bunch of sightseers off a tour bus.

"I don't see anything threatening," said Sami, scanning the horizon.

"So we didn't need this restrictive armor after all," groused Joe, "we could've just worn pressure suits."

"No one knows what hazards may await us," said Mizuki, like a school teacher chiding a particularly backward child. "Besides, in a pressure suit you would have no bio-mechanical assist—under this gravity you would be even more uncomfortable."

"There is no way I could carry all this gear," Will Krenshaw agreed, shifting the webbing of the pack strapped to the back of his suit. "My pack must weigh 200 pounds in this gravity."

Beth grinned a private grin, it was her idea to make the scientists carry their own equipment, instead of breaking out a hover sled. That way they couldn't haul along everything including the kitchen sink.

"Ms. Acuna," she called on the Marines' frequency, "have you spotted anything peculiar or can we head out toward the ruins?"

"Nothing obvious, Ma'am. We are good to go."

"Very well," Beth acknowledged, then changed to the expedition's common frequency. "OK people, let's head towards our objective, we're burning daylight."

A pair of surveillance drones hung in the sky over head. Basketball sized silver spheres, one orbited the shuttle at 200 meters, watching for anything approaching. The second floated ahead of the landing party at 25 meters, scouting for danger and acting as a comm relay back to the ship.

After a bit more milling about the scientists formed a ragged column and headed for the ruins spotted on the flight in. Escorted by the Marines—Umky in the lead and a pair of humans off each flank—the scientists chatted excitedly with each other over suit-to-suit radio. With a range of about five meters, suit-to-suit provided an open voice channel that simulated normal, unencumbered conversation. It even acoustically positioned the voices of communicants to simulate their relative spatial positions. Private conversations could be held at a distance over normal radio channels, but for coordinating the activity of a local group, suit-to-suit was as close to talking without helmets as you could get.

"Interesting how the clouds have a slight red tinge to them, around the edges," said Gerard.

"Red sun, red clouds, red desert," replied Sami, glancing at the readouts on his suit's forearm display. "Temperature is a balmy 27°C, with a light wind out of the northwest, humidity about 23%. Given the conditions we could be walking around in short sleeves and sandals."

"Not until we check for biological threats," said Ahnah, who, despite being encased in a space suit, still reflexively sniffed the air.

"Interesting," said Joe, his breathing slightly labored. "The atmospheric pressure is 170 kilopascals, 70% more than on Earth. Even with only 18% oxygen in the air it should be quite comfortable. The $CO_2$ is pretty high though, it's nearly 800ppm."

"Without any plant life to help sequester it I'm surprised it is not higher," said Sami, "Of course, we didn't see any volcanoes from orbit—vulcanism is the major source of $CO_2$ back home."

"Other than people you mean," said Joe.

"Not people anymore," said Gerard, ending the conversation for the time being. Trudging on in silence, the party crested a slight rise in the terrain and the ruins ahead became clearly visible. The science party and officers stood and stared at the eerie desolation before them.

"'When I drew nigh the nameless city I knew it was accursed,'" recited Bobby, "'afar I saw it protruding uncannily above the sands as parts of a corpse may protrude from an ill-made grave.'"

"Now you are quoting things like Billy Ray," said Mizuki, while staring across the sands at the bones of the alien city.

"Yeah. 'The Nameless City' by H. P. Lovecraft," he replied. "You have to admit it fits."

"'There is no legend so old as to give it a name, or to recall that it was ever alive;'" quoted Beth. "I've read Lovecraft also."

"I wonder how old it is?" said Sami. "Things in the desert have a way of looking equally decrepit whether they are fifty years old or two thousand."

"I don't know," said Gerard, "but it feels really old."

"I once went to Petra, the Rose City in Jordan," Sami continued.

"Wasn't that the place they used in one of the Indiana Jones movies?" asked Bobby.

"Yes, huge monuments carved out of the living sandstone. There was a road there built by the Romans around 100AD, but the Nebataeans had been there for 600 years before the Romans came. Those ruins felt old, but these feel even older for some reason."

"If we can find some organic material maybe we can do radiocarbon dating," said Will. "Of course, without growing plants to provide an isotope ratio baseline, we won't know what the samples started decaying from."

"I guess we should have brought an archaeologist with us as well," said Beth.

"Most of their methods still require organic material of some sort. Maybe we'll get lucky and find something buried. Outside of that it could take years to figure out how old these ruins are."

"There are other radiometric dating methods based on other isotopes," said Sami. "Unfortunately, they work on longer, mostly geologic time scales. On Earth we had all sorts of metrics, all tied back to the strata—the layers of rock found around the world."

"Those measurement methods were the end result of thousands of scientists working over centuries," said Gerard, "here we have none of that."

"It appears that a number of scientific disciplines have become many times more complicated since leaving our home planet," Will said, a hint of sad resignation in his voice.

"Let's concentrate on what we can do and get to work on the preliminary survey," said Mizuki. "Remember, nobody wanders off alone. Stay in pairs."


## The Nameless City

The city was significantly bigger than it looked from the air, or maybe walking across its sandy, undulating surface in spacesuits changed that perspective. Wandering among the badly weathered ruins it was possible to make out a grid where streets ran between the low mounds, all that was left of the city's buildings. Bobby was helping Sami drill core samples; Gerard and Joe were off taking samples on their own; and Ahnah and Will were looking for something, anything, living. In contrast, the Marines were not looking down, they were keeping an eye out for trouble while spreading out around the clump of scientists.

"So what are we looking for, Sergeant?" asked Dmitry Boskovitch.

"Anything unusual, Bosco," Rosey replied. "Let's fan out on compass points with Umky near the middle so he can reinforce anyone who gets in trouble."

"Aye, aye, Gunny," said Kato Kwan.

"I ain't a gunnery sergeant any more, Kato."

"The XO treats you like you are."

"Right. Notice how she doesn't mention rank when she's telling me what to do. She's got some kind of hard on for me so the rest of you would do well to stay out of splatter range."

"I think you are reading more into it than you should, Gunny," said Vinny DeSilva.

"Da. Except for the Captain and Chief Ship Starshina Zackly she addresses no one by rank."

"That's because she's married to the Captain and I think that 'Chief' is Zackly's first name," said Kato.

"She commanded the corvette squadron during the Great Alien Hunt," said Umky. "I got the impression her people really liked her."

"I'm not saying she's a bad officer, just that I'm on her shit list at the moment and you should all keep some distance."

"Hey, she'll come around, Rosey," said Vinny.

"We'll see. In the mean time shut your pie holes and keep an eye pealed for angry aliens."

"Aye, Gunny."

\* \* \* \* \*

The Marines assumed perimeter positions, walking slowly around the group of scientists. The science party was oblivious to anything but their own investigations. This left Beth and Misuki with little to do.

"Not a lot of astrophysics going on around here, Misuki."

"I am afraid not, or starship piloting. Let's go to the top of that big mound and get a feel for how large this city used to be." Toward the center of the site there was one mound that rose a bit higher than the others.

"At least it will give us something to do, other than watch the others work."

"Hai."

The two women trudged up the modest slope of the mound, the electroreactive polymer bundles in their suits compensating for the 27% higher local gravity and the weight of the armor. While not as massive as the heavy suits worn by the Marines, moving about would have soon exhausted the Earthlings without the synthetic muscles. On this planet, even Mizuki weighed more than two hundred kilos in a suit.

Cresting the rounded summit, Mizuki turned to Beth and said, "it seems solid, I wonder if there is anything inside?"

She jumped up and down to test the mound's solidity. On the landing she disappeared from view.


### CIC, Peggy Sue

Aft of the bridge and the Captain's sea cabin was the Combat Information Center, or CIC. In Navy speak, it was a room designed to gather and present processed information for command and control of the near battle space or 'area of operations'. In other words, to observe and direct actions outside the ship.

In this case, the large central 3D holotank display showed a real-time reconstruction of the site the surface expedition was exploring. Built from telemetry gathered from the explorers' suits

103

and the surveillance drones circling overhead, it allowed the Captain to follow the situation planet side with only a few seconds of transmission delay.

Mug of coffee in hand, Billy Ray comfortably watched the progress of his crew as they explored the abandoned city. Small black figures moved about over the lumpy, sand colored surface. Each trailed an identification tag, following like a toy balloon above its owner. The Captain blinked twice at the miniature tableau as the display changed—one of the balloons was now ownerless.

"Surface party, Peggy Sue. Interrogative your status?" he called. "Dr. Ogawa has disappeared from the situation display."

"Wait one, Peggy Sue," came the hurried response from the First Officer.


### The Nameless City

"Ayyiiii!" Mizuki cried as she vanished.

"Mizuki!" yelled Beth, rushing to the edge of the hole that had swallowed her friend.

"Surface party, Peggy Sue. Interrogative your status?" said the Captain's voice over the radio. "Dr. Ogawa has disappeared from the situation display."

"Wait one, Peggy Sue," Beth replied. Staring into the ragged opening's dark interior, Beth switched on her suit's light amplification and near infrared illumination. This revealed Mizuki's suited form three meters below, laying on the floor of the cavern, her upper body propped up by her elbows. "Are you alright?"

"Yes, just startled is all." Mizuki struggled and came to a sitting position. Looking around her she said, "This is not a natural cavern, it is a room. The floor looks like some kind of tile."

"Are you sure you're not injured?"

"I am fine, more embarrassed than hurt... My God! There are racks of equipment against the far wall!"

"Great, let me tell the ship that you're OK." Beth switched back to the ship's frequency. "Peggy Sue, Dr. Ogawa is uninjured. She seems to have made a bit of a... breakthrough."

\* \* \* \* \*

A half hour later the edge of the hole had been excavated and stabilized. A ladder led from the surface into the hole and both Bobby and Beth had joined Mizuki within the buried chamber.

"You're right about the floor, Mizuki," said Beth kneeling down to run a gauntleted hand across the chamber's lower surface. "This is nothing that nature did on her own. It looks like a pattern made from ceramic tile, some kind of mosaic."

"Find some ceramic that has not been exposed to daylight," said Mizuki. "Sami should be able to date it with optically stimulated luminescence."

"You mean we can find out how long this place has been buried?" asked Bobby.

"Yes, from OSL dating we can find out how long it has been out of sunlight. And thermal luminescence can tell when the ceramic was fired. That's assuming this floor is older than about 300 years and younger than 100,000."

"If it's a thousand centuries old it's in damned good shape," Bobby commented, looking at the racks of equipment against the far wall. Even covered with dust, the devices contained there looked like nothing designed by man. "I wonder what this place was?"

"One way to find out is to see what that equipment does," said Beth. "Let's get Dr. Hosseini down here to sample the floor tile while we talk to the ship. We need to see what Chief Engineer Baldursson thinks about disassembling the devices on the wall."

"Arin was looking for an excuse to come down to the surface," Bobby grinned.

"Can't blame him, for most of the crew it's their first alien planet."

"Yes, and my first discovery of a lost alien civilization," said Misuki with a smile. "I literally fell into it."

105

## CIC, *Peggy Sue*

Also present in the CIC was the ship's doctor, Betty White, who was monitoring the vital signs of those on the ground. Given the planet's heavier than Earth standard gravity and the added stress of wearing the unfamiliar armored suits, Doc White was keeping an eye on respiration and heart rates among the explorers.

"Given the gravity, that was quite a fall Mizuki took," the Captain said.

"She's fine, Captain," the doctor replied. "Another benefit of wearing armor—it helped cushion her fall. She might have broken a leg or fractured some vertebra in a simple pressure suit."

"I'll add that to my list of reasons for always sending the crew out wearing armor, Doc."

"I'm not worried about the old timers, Captain. It's those scientists that concern me. They are inexperienced and not in the best of shape. Both Dr. Rogers and Dr. Krenshaw are showing signs of tachypnea—elevated respiration—and rapid heart rates. Rogers is on the edge of hyperventilating."

"Do we need to pull them back? I would really like to get through our first surface mission without any casualties."

"I think if they just took a break, and let things return to normal, they will be OK."

"Right. Expedition leader, Peggy Sue," Billy Ray sent over the command frequency.

"Go Peggy Sue," came Beth's voice, in her BBC news reader accent.

"Dr. White says a number of the science party are over-stressing and would do better if they stopped working for a few minutes."

"Roger that, Peggy Sue. I will tell them to take a break."


## The Nameless City

"Listen up everyone," Beth broadcast to the landing party. "The ship says we are ahead of schedule and should take a few minutes of rest. Stand up in a stable position, lock your suit extremities and relax for a bit."

Beth scanned in all directions and could see members of the science staff standing erect—all except Joe Rogers, who continued to struggle with a core drill.

"Come on, people," she repeated, "let's take a break."

"Yeah, just... a... second..." said Rogers, struggling to extract the drill bit from the ground. With a final tug he managed to lift the heavy piece of equipment free, and topple over backward. Landing on his back, with the core drill on top of him, he began to thrash about, making inarticulate gasping sounds.

"Oh, bollocks," Beth said over suit-to-suit, "the bloody barmpot is acting like a tipped over turtle."

"Bobby! Come," Mizuki called. Both Bobby and Mizuki were within range to hear Beth's exclamation, though a few meters closer to the fallen environmentalist. They immediately headed down the sandy slope and ran toward the still flailing Rogers. From the other direction, Rosey Acuna was also racing to help.

"Dr. Rogers, please be calm," Mizuki shouted. "We are coming."

"He's hyperventilating," came Betty's voice over the ship channel. "He is having a panic attack."

"If he keeps flailing around he's going to hurt himself," Bobby replied. "Can you sedate him?"

"Yes, I can do that remotely, but he'll probably not appreciated it afterward."

"If we try to restrain him physically he might really get injured," said Beth, catch up with Mizuki and Bobby, who were standing helplessly next to the thrashing Rogers. "Better to injure his pride, I should think."

"Roger that, sending the command to his suit now..."

It took a quarter of a minute for the sedative to quiet Rogers' thrashing but finally he lay still. Rosey moved next to the downed scientist and gently removed the core drill that was still balanced on his chest, her powered armor easily lifting the heavy piece of equipment.

"Well this is a fine mess," said Beth.

"Yeah," said Bobby, "get his arms and legs in a comfortable position and I'll lock his suit. Then we can carry him to the shuttle."

"Does this mean we have to cut the mission short?" asked Mizuki. "Sami, Will and Ahnah wanted to take a trip to the river bed we spotted twenty kilometers west of here."

"I think we need to get Rogers to sick bay as soon as possible," Beth replied, "and I don't like the idea of staying on the surface with no transport."

"We've found nothing dangerous so far," Bobby said, "and once we get him secured on board the shuttle I can take him back to the ship without assistance."

"We still have seven hours of daylight, it would be a shame to waste them," said Mizuki.

"Engineer Baldursson and a couple of the crew were going to come down in a small shuttle to work on removing the equipment we found in the ruined building," Beth said, thinking through their options. "If they bring the other large shuttle instead, we could use it to evacuate in an emergency."

"That would work," Bobby said.

"Let me run it by the Captain. Peggy Sue, were you listening to that?"

"Affirmative, Expedition leader. We can have Shuttle Two underway before you get Dr. Rogers to your boat."

"Roger that, Peggy Sue. We are heading for the shuttle now."

"I will walk to the shuttle with Bobby and bring back a hover sled," said Mizuki. "A 40 kilometer hike is probably not a reasonable thing to ask of the other scientists."

"Excuse me, Ma'am," said Rosey. "It would be best if both hover sleds were left. If the river party runs into trouble I'd hate to be twenty klicks away with no transport."

"Good thinking, Acuna," said Beth. "You bring the boffin and I'll come along to fetch the second sled."

"Aye, aye, Ma'am." Rosey gently picked up Rogers' rigid form and headed back to the shuttle, carrying him in her arms like a sleeping child. She didn't see the thoughtful look the First Officer gave her, as she strode purposefully across the sandy wasteland.

## *Chapter 9*

### *Main Mess, Peggy Sue*

"So you're tellin' me, that after almost two weeks of poking around on the surface, we have found absolutely nothing alive on the planet?" asked the Captain.

"That is correct, Billy Ray," said Mizuki. The head scientist, Beth and Bobby were seated at a table, drinking tea and coffee with Billy Ray. On the bridge, the four friends adopted a more formal, almost military form of address. This was mostly from long habit but also because it kept things orderly and efficient. Also following naval tradition first names were used in the mess, giving the meeting an informal air.

"It is so odd," said Beth. "Not only have we failed to uncover any living lifeforms, we haven't even found the remains of any. No organic material in the soil or seabeds, no graves of the creatures that built and inhabited the ruins scattered about the planet. Nothing."

"We have identified banded iron formations, indicating a period of strong environmental oxygenation. Back on Earth, this marked the development of photosynthetic organisms. We also found beds of limestone and other sedimentary formations consistent with the development of indigenous life, at least in the ocean. But Beth is correct, no signs of larger creatures have been found, yet someone built the city where we found the strange equipment."

"But we do know when the city was abandoned?" Billy Ray queried Mizuki.

"Yes, from ceramic samples we have dated the ruins at around 10,000 years old. Fortunately, ceramics were widely used by the missing inhabitants. Samples taken from other sites—including some recovered by the robosnakes from cities sunk beneath the ocean—all give the same result."

"So whatever wiped them out happened all over the planet at the same time," said Bobby. His companions could almost see the conspiracy taking form in the sailing master's imagination.

"The dating methods are not accurate enough to support that conclusion," Mizuki said, trying to keep Bobby grounded in fact. "Whatever ended this planet's civilization could have taken several hundred years to spread across the globe."

"Or it could have happened in a matter of days, or even hours," Bobby persisted.

"Yes, that is possible, but we have no way to prove the timeline one way or the other."

"Have we found out anything from the equipment we discovered in the first ruin?" asked Billy Ray, steering the conversation away from hypothetical doomsdays and back to knowable information.

"Chief Engineer Baldursson has done an analysis of the equipment and found it contains some kind of crystalline storage matrix and circuitry to access it," Beth replied. "The circuits themselves seem to be made from semiconductors and the storage holographic."

"Sounds similar to the T'aafhal memory array in the ship's computer."

"Only in concept, Captain," said the voice of the ship's computer. "I have been working with Engineer Baldursson on reconstructing the circuitry needed to access the array."

"That's good Peggy Sue. If we could read that memory module, it might give us some idea of what happened to these folks."

"Being able to read the data does not mean we will be able to understand it, Captain."

"As things stand, it might be the only way we can find out what happened here 10,000 years ago," Beth said. "We've tested for all sorts of calamities—solar eruptions, asteroid impacts, nearby super novae—nothing is consistent with conditions down below."

"This is true. Any of those events would have left detectable evidence behind—a layer of ejected material, shock formed glass spherules, a spike in certain isotopes," Mizuki said. "Whatever it was, it did not just kill all life on the planet, it destroyed almost every trace of it."

"I still think it was the Dark Lords," said Bobby. "This feels too unnatural, it must have been an intentional act."

"Pardner, if the Dark Lords had something that could wipe a planet clean of life why would they send a ship full of space bugs to pelt Earth with asteroids?"

"I don't know, Billy Ray, but this just feels... sinister."

The voyage's leadership fell quiet, pondering the sad fate of the creatures who had once inhabited the planet below. The silence was interrupted when Billy Ray's comm pip chirped.

"This is the Captain, go ahead."

"Captain, this is Lewis on the bridge. A ship just emerged from alter-space; the transfer point is consistent with a transit from Earth. Sensors say it is probably the colony ship."

"Very well, Mr. Lewis. I'm heading for the bridge."

As the four rose from the table, Beth asked her husband, "what are you going to tell the colonists about the planet?"

"I'm going to offer them a data dump of what we found exploring the surface and wish them luck. After all, we haven't found anything that's actually dangerous down there—whatever exterminated life on this world seems long gone."

### Bridge, ESS Fortune

"Earth ship orbiting the second planet, this is the ESS Fortune, please respond."

"ESS Fortune, this is the Peggy Sue. We read you loud and clear."

"Peggy Sue, this is Captain Siddhartha Chakrabarti of the Earth Colonization Council. With whom am I speaking and might I ask your intentions?"

"Greetings, Captain. This is Capt. Billy Ray Vincent of the Orion Arm Trading Company. We are in this system as part of an exploration and trade mission to scout unknown planets."

"Are you staking a claim to this planet, Captain Vincent?"

"No, Captain Chakrabarti, we have surveyed this planet over the past two weeks and find nothing of interest to the Company."

Capt. Chakrabarti was visibly relieved at Capt. Vincent's response. He had a hold full of colonists and livestock that he needed to offload somewhere. If these self described traders laid claim to the intended colony planet he didn't know what he could do.

"Thank you, Captain. Will you be staying in the area for a while?"

"Yes and no, we plan on taking a look at some of the outer planets but we are done with C. We can send you a dump of all the data we collected during our survey, if you would like."

"Yes, that would be greatly appreciated. Did you find anything hazardous?"

There was a pause.

"No, we found nothing dangerous. The planet seems totally devoid of indigenous lifeforms."

"Thank you again, Capt. Vincent. We will be orbiting the planet in about six hours. At that time we will be launching three weather and communications satellites into geosynchronous orbit."

"Thanks for the heads up. Good luck with your mission, Fortune. Peggy Sue clear."

"And to you, Peggy Sue."

"What a coincidence. We spend nearly a month in alter-space and when we get here we find another Earth ship already orbiting the destination planet. The galaxy just isn't that small," said Raoul Mendez, the ship's navigator.

"The Peggy Sue obviously left before we did. I'm just glad they didn't claim the planet—we would have had to turn around and go back home."

"Could they do that? Could we have run them off by force?"

"Hardly. That ship has at least as much firepower as a frigate, maybe a cruiser. She may be listed as a rich man's yacht in the database, but the Peggy Sue has fought more battles than most of the ships in the Fleet."

"We're getting that data dump from them now, Captain. And it looks like they are breaking orbit."

"Good. Put us on course to orbit the planet. Maybe the data from the Peggy Sue will let us speed up offloading our passengers. The sooner we can select the settlement sites, the sooner we can start ferrying them to the surface."

"Roger that, Captain," replied the Navigator, adding, "though I suppose we will have to sit down with the three lead settlers to discuss the landing sites."

"Unfortunately, yes."

"Those guys give me the willies. Especially that Brother Abraham, you can just smell crazy on that guy."

### *Passenger Deck 3, ESS Fortune*

The two sisters were passing through the main lounge on passenger deck 3, returning from a stint in the hold tending the livestock. As promised, the ship's crew did not fraternize with the colonists during the voyage, staying sequestered in their own area at the front of the ship. This meant that the passengers had to see to the care of their own livestock, located in the cavernous cargo hold aft of the passenger decks. The three sets of prospective settlers alternated days looking after the animals.

The horses, cows, sheep and chickens all needed to be fed and their stalls cleaned out. In the Imam's flock this duty fell to the women and young children. While the youngest played hide and seek among the cargo, Shadi and Dorri joined the other girls in farm chores while Mother Manijeh and the older women kept a watchful eye on everything. They were particularly vigilant in keeping the young women from coming in contact with the young men, who were also in the hold being instructed by computer on how to operate various pieces of equipment provided the colonists: communications gear, base stations for the weather satellites, spray foam applicators for constructing shelters and housing, and other such manly things.

115

The young women had been instructed not to talk with the young men, but girls and boys were the same wherever they came from. Some flirting managed to go on despite their elders' best efforts. Dorri in particular had caught the eye of a young man named Ahmed.

Most days, the men stayed in the lounge, drinking tea and arguing. On the lounge's large view-screen a khaki and blue planet, laced with white clouds, hung in space.

"Look, Shadi! We are back in normal space," said Dorri.

"That must be the planet we are headed for," Shadi replied.

"The Imam says that will be our new home, *al-hamdu lillāh*," said Ahmed, who just happened to be standing nearby. Dashingly handsome at age 17, Ahmed had curly brown hair, flashing dark eyes and the scruffy beginnings of a beard on his cheeks and chin.

"After we land I will build a house and then I can ask the Imam to give me a wife." he said giving Dorri a meaningful look.

"Oh?" Dorri replied, a bit confused by his statement. *He couldn't mean me*, she thought, *I'm only thirteen years old*.

"Be quiet, Dorri!" Said Shadi. "You know speaking to men outside our family is forbidden."

"But..." Dorri protested as her big sister hustled her away from the amorous Ahmed. Shadi shushed her and would not let her speak until they were back in their room with the door safely shut.

"Are you crazy?" Shadi said to her sister. "Do you want to be married off the instant we land on the planet?"

"But I'm only thirteen, he can't be serious about marrying me!"

"You are almost thirteen and a half, and you have gone through menarche. You've been having the monthly visitor, that makes you a woman as far as these religious zealots are concerned," Shadi replied furiously. "It is only a matter of time before we are married off, but there is no reason to hurry the process by attracting attention."

"You mean we will be separated? Forced to marry strangers?" Dorri replied tearfully. "I hate this place!"

"Shush, little star, we must remain calm and not draw undue attention to ourselves. Maybe there will be an opportunity to run away from the others after we land."

"You think so?"

"*In shā' Allāh*, Dorri, if God wills it. "

### Goat Locker, Peggy Sue

The senior enlisted quarters on a navy vessel are known collectively as the goat locker, and it is the domain of the ship's chief petty officers—strictly speaking pay grades E7 and higher. On board the Peggy Sue, Master Chief Zackly and Gunnery Sergeant Acuna both qualified by former military rank. Filling out the space were Steve Hitch and Matt Jacobs, both of whom had risen to Petty Officer First Class (E6) before leaving the Navy.

Between the forward guest cabins, occupied by the ship's officers and scientists, and the senior enlisted quarters was a small lounge known as the passenger day room. Aft of the goat locker was the crew's lounge and then the enlisted quarters. While the chiefs could drink with the enlisted crewmembers in the lounge, on occasion they felt the need to meet only with their peers. This they did by taking over the day room. The four "chiefs" were relaxing with drinks, discussing the recent operations on planet C's surface.

"So how did our FNGs do over the last two weeks?" asked Chief Zackly. As senior noncom he led the discussion.

"I'd say pretty good, Chief," Rosey said, "but to be fair none of them are really cherry."

"Except the Pasta Rasta," said Hitch.

"And he didn't go on any of the surface missions," added Jacobs.

"Our Jamaican stew burner is doing just fine. If we get into a situation where we need him to fight we're all in trouble," the Chief replied. "I'm more concerned with the regular crew and the Marines. We haven't found any trouble so far, but it would be good to know which ones can be counted on if'n we run into a shit storm."

"All the Marines seem steady enough, Chief," Rosey commented. The Marines were primarily her responsibility. "They've all seen the hairy cricket before, Kwan more than once."

Seeing the hairy cricket was space Marine slang for having fought hostile aliens, up close and personal. All the chiefs and all of the ship's officers had been in close combat with aliens on prior voyages. The same was not true of the crew, and certainly not true of the science staff, Science Officer Ogawa excepted.

"They all seem pretty squared away," said Hitch. Jacobs nodded in agreement.

"If I recall correctly, yous two wouldn't know squared away if it bit ya in the ass."

"Come on Chief, that was a long time ago," replied Hitch, sounding hurt.

"Right. So what about the deck apes? Any problems there?"

"We managed to rotate the rest of the crew down to the surface at least once, just to give them real experience in armor in an alien environment," Jacobs said. "They all did OK. Of course, they didn't face any creepy crawlies dirtside—nothing but sand and rocks."

"The ones I worry about are those science types," said Hitch. "I think they'll shit themselves the first time it hits the fan."

"Except for Dr. Ogawa, of course," amended Jacobs, "and the science bear. Ahnah, will probably do alright."

"The only way to tell who has a pair is to actually get into a firefight with some bug nasties," said Rosey, "and we didn't have any of that this time, thank God."

"Aye, Gunny. So I guess it's smooth sailing so far," the Chief concluded, finishing his second beer. "Well next watch they best all turn to."

"So where are we headed, Chief?" Hitch asked.

"The Captain says we're going to have a look at the other planets in the system, since we're already here. Hopefully they will be as empty as the first one."

118

"Not too empty," Jacobs said. "After all, we are looking for treasure, right?"

"We ain't pirates, you knuckleheads. If it was up to yous we'd be running around wearing eye-patches with daggers clenched in our teeth."

"Arr, that be right matey," said Hitch with a big grin. Rosey rolled her eyes and the Chief just shook his head.

### Captain's Cabin, Peggy Sue

With the end of surface exploration, Beth and Billy Ray found themselves together in their quarters for the first time in nearly two weeks. Beth was seated in front of the vanity, wearing a cinnamon colored satin slip, performing pre bed ablutions that totally mystified her husband.

"I cannot believe we finally have a night to ourselves," she said, removing the last traces of face cream from her cheek.

"Sometimes the planets align and we're both off watch at the same time. Don't look a gift horse in the mouth," Billy Ray replied. He was wearing a black silk dressing gown that Beth had given him as a gift.

Despite having traveled the world, holding a graduate degree in English literature, and being a starship captain, Billy Ray was a simple man in many respects. One of his beliefs was that a man was either dressed or not, there was no need for any intermediate states. If left to his own devices he would have happily shed his jumpsuit upon entering their private quarters and lounged around in the buff. Beth found this attitude rather uncivilized, hence the gift of suitable male nightwear.

"Where does that saying even come from? Why would I want to look in a horse's mouth?"

"One way to check the health of a horse is to examine its teeth, honey bunch. It's a way of saying be grateful for a gift as it comes."

"Well, it sounds like a cowboy saying to me."

"Around 400AD, St. Jerome, in *The Letter to the Ephesians*, said *'Noli equi dentes inspicere donati'*. Basically, never inspect the teeth of a given horse," Billy Ray said. "In English, the earliest documented occurrence was by John Heywood in 1546: 'don't look a given horse in the mouth'. So you see it's a thoroughly English adage, not some folksy bit of cowboy wisdom."

"I should know better than to argue with you about such things," she said with a sigh.

Billy Ray walked across the room to stand behind his wife. Still seated, she looked at his reflection in the mirror while brushing her hair. "I hope the equipment from the ruins proves to be useful, otherwise we have wasted our time on this trip so far."

"Hey, Bobby got to show off his flying skills," Billy Ray shrugged, "and the ship's company got some good exercise."

"That's true, everyone except Dr. Richards."

"There's always one stray in every herd."

"Now that is cowboy lingo."

"Yup."

Beth stopped and put the hair brush down.

"I fear that I may have misjudged Gunnery Sergeant Acuna."

"You mean, on account of her being a loose woman and all?"

"Not at all. I was concerned more about possible discord among the crew. We all have to live together, work together and, if it comes to that, fight together. Jealousy breeds mistrust and that can poison a crew."

"You sure it ain't because she has a reputation?"

"No! If you will recall, I had a bit of a reputation myself before we met."

"Yeah, that was part of your allure."

"Really? I thought all men dreamt of finding a virginal princess to settle down with."

"Not if they're smart. That's why I could never figure out those Muslims, wanting to spend eternity with 72 virgins."

"And that doesn't appeal to you at all?"

"I agree with Dennis Miller, six or seven virgins in a man is going to want a woman who knows what she's doin'."

Beth suppressed a grin and Billy Ray bent down to nibble on his wife's right ear.

"Feeling a bit randy tonight, are we?"

"Let's just say I feel this way whenever I see you almost naked."

Beth swiveled to face him and he let his gown fall open.

"My, it appears that my Texas stallion is rampant tonight," she said with a smile. Crossing her arms above her head she reached behind her back and grasped the straps of her slip. Standing up, she removed the silky garment with a fluid motion and let it flutter to the cabin floor. Billy Ray let his nightgown slide from his shoulders and took her in his arms. Bodies pressed together, they exchanged a long, languid kiss.

"Now we both seem to be fully naked, what ever shall we do?"

"Oh, I think we'll come up with somethin' to occupy our time..."

### *Moon Circling GJ667Cg*

The sixth planet circling GJ667C was a gaseous world about the size of Saturn. More than two and a half times farther from its star than Earth is from the Sun, it completed an orbit in just under two terrestrial years. Being far outside the habitable zone of a feeble sun it was a frigid world, with little opportunity for life to establish a hold. At least not life of a type familiar to the Earthlings exploring the inner reaches of the system. But life comes in a variety of forms.

Orbiting the outermost planet was a moon, roughly 300 km in diameter. Its spectrum was reddish, not unexpected with an M class sun, and devoid of large features, although subtle absorption features longer than 0.75 µm and shorter than 0.55 µm were present. This was consistent with a mostly metallic object, an object that would be classified as an M-type asteroid if it circled the local star in its own orbit. The fact that its orbit around the planet was retrograde—in the opposite direction of the planet's own rotation—made it probable that the moon was an asteroid that had been gravitationally captured by its larger parent.

Unlike some M-type asteroids, it showed no sign of water or water-bearing minerals on its surface. Unusually large for a metallic object, it could be the exposed metallic core from a larger body—a protoplanet that lost its rocky outer layers in collisions with other asteroids. But there were other aspects of this small moon that were odd.

Most outstanding among the oddities was its low apparent density—a solid metallic object or even a rubble pile of iron-nickel metal would need about 50% porosity to match the moon's overall density. In point of fact, its surface was pierced by a multitude of holes of different sizes, ranging from a meter in diameter to more than a kilometer. This gave the moon a porous appearance, like a sponge or Swiss cheese. It was from one of these openings that a pair of creatures observed the activity centered around the system's second planet.

"See? I told you I heard another ship arrive. Now there are two of them."

"Yes, Gx!pk, you are right. There are messages emanating from the second planet. I wonder if these newcomers will be staying?"

"Hey, we may have neighbors! That would be something new, wouldn't it?"

"No, not really. There used to be creatures living on that world many cycles ago, but one day they just stopped talking."

"Really, Kq*zt? I didn't know that."

"You are still young, Gx!pk, and have much to learn."

"So you keep telling me. Hey, the first ship—the smaller one that entered the system from the path to the parent stars—has left the second planet and is heading away from the sun. Maybe they will come to visit."

"Hmm, you may be right. This bears watching."

# Chapter 10

## New Mecca

After spending several weeks in orbit, waiting for the settlement to be established, Shadi and Dorri were anxious to set foot on their new world. The trip down to the surface was rather anticlimactic; they sat in front of pallets of freight, in the shuttle's spartan passenger section, for more than an hour and then deplaned down a lowered airstair. A warm breeze greeted them as they stepped onto the sandy ground of their new home for the first time.

A couple of kilometers away was a collection of white domes, houses and other buildings constructed by the men spraying foam concrete over inflated forms. It did look a bit like a typical middle-eastern village from a distance and Imam Mustafa rather grandly named the settlement New Mecca. The area around the burgeoning village had been seeded by robot helicopter drones more than a week ago and warm-season C4 grasses—genetically enhanced blue grama, buffalo grass, and bluestems—were just starting to send up green shoots. Once ground cover was established the area would be over-seeded with C3 grasses, more palatable to livestock.

"Hurry girls, it looks like there is rain coming," shouted Mother Manijeh. "We must herd the sheep to their enclosure on the edge of the village."

Manijeh was right, off to the east was a line of clouds with darkness beneath them, suggesting showers in progress. Reliable rainfall was essential to establishing grasslands where the settlers eventually hoped to graze their live stock. The planet's slight axial tilt did not provide much seasonal variation and its equatorial regions tended more to having two yearly rainy seasons. The location of the settlement had been selected with the local weather pattern in mind. Far to the east lay an inland sea that provided the moisture to drive afternoon showers in both spring and fall.

"Come on, Dorri," Shadi said, heading toward the rear shuttle ramp where the sheep were being offloaded. "If some of the sheep run away we will have to go fetch them."

"I don't think they will run far," her sister answered, "my legs feel like they are made of stone."

"Now you know why I made you exercise on the ship. The other girls made fun of us, sitting on their rears more and more as the shipboard gravity increased. Now they will suffer for being so lazy."

It was true. Several of the other girls were having a hard time walking in the combination of heavy gravity and sandy soil. Mother Manijeh urged them on, shouting: *"Yella habibaati! Imshi!"*

Dorri and Shadi soon had the small flock of sheep headed toward the village as a breeze kicked up the sand and the smell of approaching rain filled the air. Wrapping their head scarfs across their faces they urged their wooly charges toward the paddock that awaited their arrival. Straggling behind the bleating sheep came the rest of the young girls and the scolding Manijeh.

*No doubt about it,* thought Shadi, *this is not going to be an easy life...*

\* \* \* \* \*

That evening, with the new arrivals installed in their living quarters and the livestock watered and bedded down, Shadi and Dorri sat on the low wall surrounding the animal enclosure. Both were exhausted from their labors and they watched the red sun sink slowly in the west without speaking. As the sunset faded to black an uncountable number of stars appeared in the sky, undiminished by city lights or air pollution.

"I am so tired," said Dorri, "I wish we had never come to this place. The days are so long and the gravity pulls at us like it wishes to drag us under."

"Hush, little star," her sister said. "This was our first day—it will get easier with time. Just look at the stars coming out."

"The sunset was pretty and the stars are so clear," Dorri agreed.

"Night hides a world but reveals a Universe," said Shadi in Farsi.

"Mother used to say that," said Dorri, looking at her sister with the beginnings of tears in her eyes.

"Yes, she did. It is an old Persian saying," Shadi agreed, putting her arm around her sister's shoulders and giving her a reassuring hug. "Remember this is a big, empty world and there will be new things to do tomorrow—just be thankful that there doesn't appear to be anything dangerous on our new planet."

Off to the west, the afternoon rainstorm had climbed into the far mountain range, visible on the horizon. Piling up against the escarpment that masked the continent's interior, the storm's clouds expressed their displeasure at being blocked by sending lightning to wreathe the offending peaks. Watching the distant fireworks, Shadi could not shake the feeling that there was more to this strange empty world than met the eye.


### Bridge, *Peggy Sue*

The Peggy Sue spent four leisurely weeks visiting the other two planets orbiting within GJ667C's habitable zone. Nothing of real interest was found: *f* was smaller than *c*, with only twice Earth's mass and a Mars like atmosphere, while *e* was nearly as big as the inner planet but with an unbreathable atmosphere they had already encountered more closely than desired. Now, the Peggy Sue was on course to rendezvous with the planet furthest from the star.

Captain and crew were not expecting to find alien life on the outermost planet, a gas giant close to 100 times the mass of Earth. Billy Ray told everyone that he just wanted to do a thorough job surveying their first star system, but in reality, he was reluctant to abandon the colonists to their fate. While it was true that nothing untoward had happened as the three sets of settlers began raising villages and seeding the virgin ground, the mystery of the empty planet nagged at the Captain's mind.

*There's still no sign of life on the second planet, I guess that's a good sign. I still can't figure out how you can wipe a planet clean of life and leave the surface and atmosphere undamaged. Maybe the inhabitants were robots or something, and there never was any organic life. Yeah, and 10,000 years ago they just decided to pack up and move away—now I'm starting to sound like Bobby.*

"We are entering the planet's gravitational well, Captain," reported Nigel Lewis from the helm, interrupting Billy Ray's thoughts.

125

"Maneuver for a high orbit, Mr. Lewis," the Captain ordered.

"Captain, the planet ahead has a number of satellites," said Mizuki from the navigation station. "None is overly large or interesting, though there are several in retrograde orbits."

"Really? It looks like you have found your retrograde moons without having to go to Triton after all."

"Yes, and radar returns from one of them indicates that it is a sizable metallic object, made mostly of nickle-iron, roughly 300 km in diameter. But it seems to have insufficient mass for its size and composition."

"You mean it's an anomaly?"

"Yes, Captain. Might I suggest we establish a retrograde orbit ourselves and send a shuttle to investigate?"

"I think that's a splendid idea, Dr. Ogawa," Billy Ray replied. "This is the first remotely exciting thing to come along in almost a month."

### Engineering Spaces, Peggy Sue

As the ship maneuvered to enter a retrograde orbit around the gas giant Capt. Vincent decided to pay a visit to the engineering crew in the aft of the ship. Chief Engineer Arin Baldursson and his artificers had their quarters in the rear of the ship, close to the drives and reactors that were in their care. Also located aft of the main cargo hold were cold storage, the polar bear quarters and the ship's machine shop.

In older days, when ships sailed upon the seas and not the vacuum of space, navy vessels had well equipped machine shops, capable of turning out replacement components for onboard equipment. In the age of sail they carried woodworking tools, during the age of steam metalworking was required. On the Peggy Sue the equipment to be maintained was likely to be a muon catalyzed fusion reactor, a segment of deck gravity generation grid or an antimatter containment vessel. And while there was still call for metalwork it was most likely to be handled by a 3D printer or 5-axis CNC milling machine inside a fabrication unit.

More often repairs meant dealing with circuitry: superconducting pathways grown by nanites, holographic storage devices, or quantum computational arrays. Sometimes, even old fashioned semiconductors and electronics were needed, but usually repair work involved advanced technology scavenged from T'aafhal sources. The ancient and alien T'aafhal had fought epic battles against the forces of the Dark Lords four million years ago and then vanished, but not before taking a hand in the evolution of life on Earth.

Those with access to the memory stores found among recovered T'aafhal artifacts knew that both humans and polar bears had been pushed toward sentience by those meddlesome aliens. Human scientists had only scratched the surface of the T'aafhal archives, enough to build starships and advanced weapons, but most T'aafhal technology remained beyond human ken. Most of their technology truly was indistinguishable from magic.

Peggy Sue's engineers were called upon to fabricate and repair the mysterious devices that drove the ship between the stars, slipping in and out of alternate dimensions that human physicists had only guessed existed. Their work was as much art as it was science. Naturally, they were the best people on board to divine the purpose of the alien devices recovered from the strange dead planet.

"Well Captain, this equipment is certainly intriguing," said Chief Engineer Baldursson, motioning to the pile of alien devices spread across the repair shop's main tables. At various places wires and probes connected test equipment to the items being examined. Where some of the wires attached to the alien equipment half melted joins, typical of nanite fusing, could be seen.

"Are you getting any closer to figuring out what this stuff does, Arin?"

"Well, Skipper, we think it's some kind of recording system, capable of capturing both sight and sound. But we don't know what it hooked up to for input. Young Michaels here has managed to cobble up some interface circuitry for it."

"And what have you discovered, Mr. Michaels?"

The engineer's mate practically came to attention when addressed by the ship's captain. The engineering staff pretty much kept to themselves in the aft part of the ship, not mingling with the rest of the crew and certainly not conversing with the Captain on a daily basis.

"Uh, well Sir, it looks like this stuff is made from 3D semiconductors, sort of like the most advanced stuff we were working on before the alien attack on Earth."

"So we could be dealing with a home entertainment system or an alien PlayStation?"

"It's possible, Sir. But the technology isn't based on simple electronics, it uses spintronics," the nervous tech continued. "The circuits use both the electrons' spins and their associated magnetic moments, not just fundamental electronic charge like our semiconductor devices do. The technology is quite advanced, spins are not only manipulated by magnetic fields, but electrical fields as well."

"Yer saying that these critters were more advanced than us?"

"At least in this area they were. Of course they were not anywhere near the level of the T'aafhal." There was a growing trend among human engineers and even scientists to hold the long vanished T'aafhal in almost worshipful reverence. For some reason he couldn't quite identify, this annoyed Billy Ray.

"So this group of aliens was on par with us, if not a little ahead, technology wise."

"Yes, Skipper, I would agree with that statement. But we have been making good progress decoding the data stored inside this memory unit here," Arin interjected, motioning to a large device festooned with thin wires that led to a rack of lab equipment. That equipment was sprinkled with tiny flashing LEDs and several screens displayed dancing green waveforms.

"In fact, Sir, we think we have recovered a snippet of the last thing it recorded," Michaels said, pride in their accomplishment overcoming fear of the Captain.

"Really? That's very impressive. Can I see it?"

"Sure, Captain!" Michaels threw a bunch of switches and then nodded in the direction of a large screen on the lab bulkhead. Swirls of colored light danced across the screen, coalescing into a blurry picture.

It looked like the view out of a large arched window opening. Outside were green trees similar to weeping willows, a field of red flowers and a number of white curved shapes that could have been buildings. The picture dissolved into a shower of pixelated color.

"Hmm," Billy Ray said, "I'm assuming there is more of this stored in the device."

"Yes, Skipper," Arin said, "we've been working on cleaning up the video before dumping the rest of the entry."

Sensing the engineers were a bit disappointed by his reaction, Billy Ray quickly added, "it looks like y'all are doing a bang up job of figuring this stuff out, well done. Carry on, Chief Engineer."

"Aye, aye, Skipper," Arin replied, smiling for the first time since the Captain had invaded his domain.

"You too, Mr. Michaels, keep up the good work." With that Billy Ray exited the lab and headed forward, his mind already lost in thought. *That clip was awfully short but it plainly showed trees and flowers, which verifies that the second planet was once a living world. The big question remains what killed it?*

### Mizuki & Bobby's Quarters

Bobby and Mizuki retired to their quarters to grab some shuteye in anticipation of exploring the strange porous moon the next day. Mizuki had been worn to a frazzle, riding herd on the science section's expeditions planet side and subsequent efforts to analyze the samples they collected. Her significant other had put in even more time ferrying personnel between the ship and the planet, but had been able to catch up on his sleep deficit during the survey passes of the habitable zone's other planets.

Their cabin was not nearly as large as the Captain's, but it was still large and luxurious compared with accommodations on a Navy vessel. Intended as a guest suit when the Peggy Sue was fulfilling

129

her original purpose as a wealthy man's yacht, the room had a king sized bed, rich wood paneling and the ultimate shipboard luxury, a private head and shower. Mizuki and Bobby had availed themselves of that luxury and were now relaxing in kimono-like robes prior to crawling into bed.

To Bobby, the silk man's kimono was just what the Japanese word said—a thing (*mono*) to wear (*ki*). For Mizuki, however, it was a link to her heritage and those she had lost forever when Earth was attacked. Simplified significantly for onboard use, her kimono was a far cry from the traditional Japanese formal garment. A typical woman's kimono often had twelve or more separate pieces, worn in prescribed ways. The cut and style of the various parts all carried meaning to traditional Japanese.

"Well here we are, Mizuki-chan. Just you, me and the kids."

Bobby's reference to "the kids" meant the flock of blue-green alien butterflies that shared their cabin. Since Billy Ray had jokingly referred to the butterflies as their children, both Bobby and Mizuki had taken to calling them that. Mizuki had become emotionally attached to them several years ago and they to her. Not true insects—the body segmentation was wrong as were the number of limbs—the butterfly like creatures seemed to posses a shared consciousness, each member of the flock linked to the others like a bevy of blue tooth devices. Mizuki had permitted enough testing of her pets to show that they were, collectively, more intelligent than a dog and maybe as smart as a dolphin.

She often sang to them in Japanese when they were alone together and on occasion they even beat their wings in synchrony to say a few word back. Several times in the past she had found dead individual butterflies. These she wept over and performed Buddhist funeral rights before cremating the remains. The flock hovered around her during these ceremonies and seemed to understand their meaning. That they sometimes acted as one being and as individuals on other occasions did not vex Mizuki. As a physicist she accepted the wave particle duality of photons; she accepted the alien butterflies on their own terms.

Even though a score of the little aliens had perished over the years the flock had not grown smaller. Obviously they were reproducing, though Mizuki had no idea how the new butterflies were conceived, gestated or delivered. If anything, since the flock accepted Bobby as a part of their world, they seem to have grown in number.

"The children did not like it when we left them to go exploring the dead planet. I suspect they will be upset when we travel to the metal moon as well."

"Yeah, but they get so excited when you return."

"When we return, Bobby. I have seen them flock around you when you come home after a watch. I think they have adopted you as well."

"I guess this is as close to a real family we will have until you decide to marry me."

This last remark caused Mizuki to look away. Bobby had been courting her since the night in Tokyo when he rescued her from the yakuza. They had become a couple and began living together more than two years ago, yet for reasons that Bobby could not understand, Mizuki would not marry him.

"You know I love you, Bobby."

"So why won't you marry me?" His voice carried an almost pleading tone. The butterflies scattered about the cabin began to display darker colors—indigo and purple—a sign of emotional distress.

"We have been over this before. I want to accomplish something important before I become your wife. Something that people will remember me for, other than just being the mother of your children."

"What's wrong with being the mother of our children? That's what people do who fall in love, they get married and have children."

"I know that, Bobby. And there is nothing wrong with being the mother of your children—someday I want to be the mother of your children. But I feel I must first do something memorable, something noteworthy. For my family, and for Japan."

"You have already traveled farther across the Galaxy than all but a few Earthlings. You explored the Ring Station, fought many battles and helped to save our home world from total destruction. Isn't that enough?"

"I was a member of the crew, not the leader. It will not be my name remembered in association with those deeds."

"You want to be famous? Is that it?"

"No! Not like a rock star or an actor. I wish to be remembered for accomplishing something worthwhile. How can I explain? The goal of marriage in Japan is to meet social expectations and raise children. In my culture the woman sacrifices herself for her husband and her children. My family was so disappointed when I didn't come home from college with a husband, and were even more upset when I went to graduate school."

Mizuki was close to tears and the flock of butterflies was flitting about the cabin in a state of high agitation. Bobby sat down on the bed next to her and hugged her. She buried her face in his shoulder.

"Oh Mizuki, it's not that way anymore—you can have a career after we're married. I would never do anything to prevent you from being happy or from becoming the most famous sword fighting astrophysicist in the galaxy, if that is what you want."

"Love and marriage are not the same thing. Most Japanese couples hardly sleep together after they have a child. The men have their careers and the women have their children. For women, their pleasure is supposed to come from raising a family. When they get bored, they just go shopping or do other things that housewives do—or have an affair. I don't want you to stop loving me, Bobby."

"If you are afraid I will grow tired of you and stop wanting you if we get married that won't happen! I will never stop loving you, Mizuki. I want to grow old with you, and if you won't marry me I will take you this way—any way—as long as we are together."

"I'm sorry Bobby. I do want to marry you, I just am not ready yet. Please understand." She looked up with tear streaked cheeks and Bobby's heart broke.

"Hush now, I didn't mean to make you cry. Come, we need to get some sleep; it will be a busy day tomorrow."

Without speaking further, the couple removed their gowns and climbed into bed. Mizuki snuggled inside Bobby's embrace. The emotional storm past, the butterflies settled down, alighting on perches around the room. They remained ever vigilant, however, protecting their goddess and her consort.


### *Armory, Peggy Sue*

"Why are we pulling extra duty, cleaning our armor after hours, Gunny?" asked Vinny DeSilva, as he took a wire brush to the overlapping small bands of metal-ceramic in his suit's left armpit. Though the suits had been decontaminated after use on the dead planet's surface there was still the possibility of fine contaminants in the armor's overlapping bands.

"Because the Chief says we are getting close to rendezvousing with some kind of small moon that the science geeks find interesting. It doesn't take a genius to figure out that the Captain will be sending a shuttle to take a closer look, and that means we'll be going along to keep the nerd squad safe."

"All of us?" asked Dmitry Boskovitch, getting ready to strip and clean his railgun. "Why do we all have to go?"

"Because that's what the Captain wants, Bosco. If you haven't figured it out yet, Capt. Vincent is trying to get us as much training time as possible, just in case we do eventually come across some nastiness. So shut up and keep working."

"Ho ho! It looks like the jar heads have the same idea we do, Matt," Steve Hitch announced as he and Jacobs entered the armory. "Getting everything shipshape so's not to be in a panic tomorrow morning when the Skipper sends us to take a gander at that moon Doc Ogawa is all excited about."

"The swabbies have arrived," commented Kato Kwan, "there goes the neighborhood."

While it has been known for sailors and Marines to not get along, that was really not the case on the Peggy Sue. This was partly because the Chief and the Gunny wouldn't stand for it, but also because Hitch and Jacobs had fought alongside Kwan and Acuna on earlier missions. It didn't matter if you bled Navy blue or Marine green, if you passed the trial by fire you were one of the club.

133

"Good to know you two are thinking ahead, even if a bit slowly." The Gunny grinned at the two petty officers as they began working on their own armored suits. "You hear any scuttlebutt about this moon the science types are so ga-ga over?"

"They way I hear it, the whole thing is like a giant sponge made out of metal," Hitch provided.

"Yeah, Commander Danner thinks that the moon has been mined," added Jacobs. There were few onboard activities sailors enjoyed more than spreading rumors.

"Cmdr. Danner believes a lot of nutty things," scoffed Kato.

"That may be, but sometimes he's right," said the Gunny, "and he's one hell of a pilot. If we are going to take a side trip to a funny moon I want Danner at the controls."

"No argument there, Gunny. Hey Umky, what do you think?"

The squad's only polar bear was quietly working on his suit, listening to the humans babble. Of course he had a bigger job than the other Marines, since a bear's suit was much larger than a man's. Its ammo load was much bigger as well.

"I think all you primates believe in kooky stuff," Umky grunted. "But Danner seems OK to me. After all, Dr. Ogawa seems pretty attached to him, so he can't be totally crazy."

"Right you are, Bear 2," said Hitch. "Say, how are things going with your four-legged honey?"

Umky snorted. "If you are referring to Doctor Ahnah the science bear, let's just say I'm looking forward to floating around an airless metal junk pile for a few days, just to get some peace and quiet."

"I though you two weren't talking?"

"Not at first, Gunny. Now I'd pay to have her shut up."

"Maybe she's succumbing to your he-bear charms," said Hitch, waggling his eyebrows.

"Keep it up, Hitch. I'm feeling a bit peckish."

"That ain't gonna work, Umky. You should have heard all the times your Dad threatened to eat Stevie."

The bear turned to look at Jacobs to see if he was joking. Matt looked back with an innocent expression and Umky made a woofing sound as he went back to cleaning his multi-barreled railgun. "So what's the ammo load for this little outing?"

"I'm thinking some of the DU armor-piercing," Rosey replied. "Explosive stuff doesn't work so well in vacuum and we got a shitload of the solid stuff."

"Handling uranium rounds gives me the willies," said Vinny, "that crap is still radioactive. I heard some guys in Iraq got lung cancer from breathing in dust from expended rounds."

"That's bullshit, Marine," said Jacobs. "It's not the radiation, they even use DU shielding to contain dangerous radioactive materials. Most of the problem with DU is that uranium is a toxic metal. There have been reports of an elevated risk of birth defects with long-term exposure."

"That ain't a problem with Vinny. The woman ain't been born that would have his children."

"Funny, Kato, funny."

"Quit your complaining. After all, you're gonna be inside a space suit. No way to come in contact with any uranium, not unless you shoot yourself in the foot." The Gunny paused in thought before continuing. "Maybe after we check the place out we can do a little live fire."

"That would be great, Gunny," said Umky, hefting his weapon. "I've never seen what full rated fire with DU rounds can do."

"Just make sure I am behind you before you open up, da?" Bosco didn't care what the others said, the Russian Marine was still not totally comfortable arming polar bears with 15mm multi-barreled railguns firing depleted uranium slugs.

## *Chapter 11*

### *Bridge, ESS Fortune*

As usual, Captain Chakrabarti was alone on the bridge, all other members of the crew either making shuttle runs or off watch. Siddhartha, Sid to his friends, didn't mind the time spent alone. It gave him the opportunity to think about his wife, Amita, and their two children, back at the Farside Moon base. Once this mission was over he would be able to spend six months or more at home. Oh how he missed his wife's cooking—and her company.

Frank Hoenig, one of the shuttle pilots, had just entered Fortune's bridge. He was reporting in after a trip dirtside to deliver supplies and equipment to the settlers, in this case Brother Abraham's presumptively named town of Zion.

"Welcome back, Mr. Hoenig," said Capt. Chakrabarti, "I trust you had an uneventful trip."

"Yeah, Captain, another in a series of uneventful trips. The most exciting thing was offloading the cows—they really didn't want to get off the shuttle."

"Can you blame them?"

"Hey, I wouldn't want to be off loaded down there. Of the three groups, Brother Abraham's has got to be the strangest. There were no women or children in sight at all when we dropped off the supplies. We had a number of large bales of alfalfa for the animals and they wouldn't let us take it into their 'town' on float palates. Made us dump it just beyond the shuttle's repulsor field zone, saying they would carry it to the settlement. They have to be nuts to want to haul hay bales by hand in that gravity."

"Perhaps it is best they become use to hard physical labor, they will soon be living like peasants from many centuries ago."

"Yeah, I guess sleeping with farm animals, bathing once a year, and shitting in a bucket is a part of everyone's cultural heritage. I just wouldn't go back to those days voluntarily."

The Captain shook his head. "We are not here to judge them, Mr. Hoenig, just to drop them off and get them started. How many more trips will be required?"

Hoenig scratched the back of his head with his right hand and appeared to concentrate on his answer before replying. "I think that was the last of the cattle, we still have to drop off the horses and another load of fodder. That means one more run to each of the settlements."

"How long?"

"A couple of days to load the bulk items and then put the horses on board. This time I'm taking the Arabs, at least there you can catch a glimpse of a woman's face."

The Captain shrugged. He had requested a mixed crew for the mission but the powers that be decided female crewmembers might cause problems with the settlers.

"Maybe on the next mission we will have a mixed crew."

"Yeah. Well with any luck we'll be home in a month and it won't matter. Tell me again why the first people to migrate to the stars are a bunch of religious fanatics? I mean, shouldn't we be putting our best foot forward here?"

The Captain had often had such thoughts himself, both before and during the voyage. *I think the real answer is twofold,* he thought. *First, these three groups were a problem for the authorities back on Farside and this was an acceptable way of getting rid of them. Second, this was an experiment, which may well fail. The authorities only sent expendables, just in case something goes horribly wrong.* He did not wish to contemplate the implications that last point held for himself and his crew.

"Ours is not to reason why, Mr. Hoenig," he said to the shuttle pilot. "Let's concentrate on finishing our mission and go home."

"I'm with you, Captain. At least the robot seeders have done their job, there's a lot of green showing around the three towns. The animals should have plenty of fresh food inside of a month at this rate."

"We may well return one day to find this planet a garden paradise. In fact, that might be a good name for the place."

"You mean you don't like New Jerusalem, New Mecca, or Zion?"

"If we asked the colonists to name the planet I doubt they would reach agreement. As far as I know, the merchants didn't name the planet either. I think I will put down Paradise as the planet's name in the ship's log, being optimistic."

"Right. That's why I am a pessimist."

"What?"

"Optimists are always setting themselves up to be disappointed. On the other hand, we pessimists always have a chance to be pleasantly surprised."

The shuttle pilot grinned and touched his brow with an informal two fingered salute—there was no way Fortune's crew could be mistaken for Navy personnel. Hoenig turned and headed toward the gangway leading aft to the hold and shuttle bays.

"I prefer no surprises of any kind, Mr. Hoenig," Chakrabarti said softly to the man's back as he walked away. *Only another month, Amita, and I will be back with you and the children.*

### New Mecca, Paradise

Shadi urged the small flock of sheep along using a piece of doweling she had found among the supplies brought from the ship. It was hard to herd sheep without a stick or switch and there were no natural items on this world to do the job. The pasture space available to them was small, too small really. Overgrazing can occur when animals are kept on a pasture too long. That's what the instructional video she had studied during the trip out had said.

With the grass barely taken hold, it was probably too soon to begin grazing the sheep in the fields, but the men had decided it should be done. When livestock clip grass by grazing, the plants are injured. Shoots that have been clipped and eaten are no longer able to perform their function of collecting energy from the sun. The plants must tap into the energy reserves in their roots to stay alive and begin regrowth. Shadi doubted that any of the men had viewed the videos on the way out, or bothered to study any of the materials provided by the Colonization Service. They certainly didn't ask for her opinion.

At least being with the sheep got her out of the village, away from the other settlers and household chores. So far, she had been able to bring Dorri with her as well. She was having trouble keeping her little sister from being pestered by Ahmad. It just wasn't right to force a girl of thirteen to become someone's wife—it wasn't civilized!

Shadi had also seen some of the men watching her, talking to each other in hushed tones. No doubt they were sizing her up for matrimony as well. So far her sharp tongue and obvious intelligence had kept her safe, but sooner or later one of the men was bound to ask the Imam for her hand. Who was she kidding? There was no life on this planet outside the settlements, no chance to run away. At least not if they wanted to stay alive.

"Shadi! Let's move the sheep down toward the river so they can have a drink," shouted Dorri from the other side of the flock.

"All right," she replied. Dorri really liked the animals. Shadi wondered how she would handle things the day the settlers started eating them. That was not supposed to happen anytime soon, since all the animals, the sheep included, were female and had been impregnated before the colonization ship left the Moon. Again, she had learned this from the computer system on the ship.

As close as Shadi could figure, the sheep were due to give birth in about 65 of the long local days—that would be exciting. Of course that was assuming that the longer days and heavier gravity didn't affect the sheep's gestation period. If she and Dorri were given their choice, they would choose pasture lambing when the time came, rather than birth the lambs in the corral or barn. One positive about being on a lifeless planet, there were no predators to make a meal of the newborn lambs.

The sheep raising manual said that the average ewe gives birth to two or three lambs, but sometimes only one and rarely four. If their flock averaged two and a half that would give them more than twenty new sheep to raise. They would only keep the biggest, strongest males, the flock only needed one ram though they would probably keep a backup. The rest of the males would be neutered and fattened up for eating.

During the celebration of *Eid al-Adha*, the Feast of the Sacrifice, which came at the end of the *Hajj*, it was traditional to remember

Abraham's trials by slaughtering a sheep. Shadi had no idea where they were in the months of the Islamic calendar, but she bet that Imam Mustafa was keeping track. The fact that some of their wooly charges would eventually end up on the menu was yet another facet of their new existence she wouldn't explain to Dorri until the time came.

### *Bridge, Peggy Sue*

On the forward display hung a dark, heavily cratered moon. So heavily cratered that it appeared porous, with cavities behind some of the craters joined forming large empty spaces. Along the moon's periphery, it looked like the outer surface was pierced by a multitude of holes through which stars could be seen passing.

"Will you look at that," said Sami Hosseini, "that can't be natural, can it?"

"That structure should be impossible," answered Mizuki. "Any object so heavily cratered should not have retained structural cohesion."

"Meaning it should have been blasted apart by the collisions?" asked Beth. All of the ship's officers had come to the bridge to get a look at Mizuki's anomalous moon.

"It could have formed as an aggregate of nickel-iron debris and ice," Sami theorized, "the ice then sublimating away after formation."

"I don't see how it could have such large voids without collapsing if it is just an aggregated junk pile compacted by its own gravity. And look at those surface craters; they don't have raised rims like normal impact craters."

"It looks like one of those impossible planets that exist only in Bugs Bunny cartoons and at the end of science fiction films made by directors who know nothing about science," said Bobby. As usual, he viewed reality through his own unique filter.

"Beth is right, the holes look like they were bored into the moon, not caused by impacts," Mizuki said. "According to my instruments, it must be fifty percent hollow inside!"

"Hey, even I don't believe in the Hollow Earth theory," said Bobby.

"Hollow Earth theory, Bobby?" echoed the Captain, raising a skeptical eyebrow.

"Yeah. In the early 1800s, an American army officer named John Symmes theorized that a hole at the South Pole led to the hollow interior of the planet. As Symmes put it, Earth was 'hollow, habitable, and widely open about the poles'. His theory was actually taken seriously throughout the nineteenth century."

"Yer joking."

"No, a number of scholars wrote papers on the subject. It made a great premise for subterranean adventure stories like Edgar Allan Poe's *The Narrative of Arthur Gordon Pym of Nantucket*, and Jules Verne's *A Journey to the Center of the Earth*. Sadly, there is no scientific evidence that such things are possible."

"You are correct, Bobby," Mizuki said, smiling approvingly at her significant other for not advocating fringe science nonsense for once. "A solid spherical shape is the best way to minimize the gravitational potential energy of a physical object. Nature prefers solid bodies, even fairly small ones."

"But how could impacts cause that?" asked Billy Ray.

"They couldn't," replied Sami.

"Maybe it has been mined," said Bobby, proving he could still find conclusions to jump to.

"Yer sayin' that this moon has been... excavated?"

"Yeah. And I wonder if the miners are still around?"

"Well, there's only one way to find out fer sure. Mr. Danner, take some of the crew and the Marines and recon that moon. Dr. Ogawa, pick who needs to go along from the science section. Let's see if this system has more puzzles to hand us."

"Aye, aye, Captain," Bobby replied, smiling at Mizuki. Mizuki smiled back with glittering eyes. Together they left the bridge headed aft toward the shuttle ramps.

* * * * *

142

There was a small crowd of armored figures at the base of the boarding ramp to Shuttle One. Two were towering gray hulks, giants in ceramic-metallic armor brandishing multi-barreled railgun rifles linked to ammo magazines on their backs. Two others were small only in comparison with the pair in heavy space armor. They were wearing standard space armor, with lighter protective bands and significantly weaker artificial musculature. One of the smaller pair sported a long sword whose handle stuck up behind her bubble helmet.

The smallest member of the group wasn't wearing armor at all. He was all of five and a half feet tall and dressed in a dark navy blue jumpsuit—Chief Zackly. The Chief was addressing the two smaller armored figures who happened to be the officers in charge of the exploratory mission to the metallic moon.

"Yous two don't go doing anything John Waynish out there," the weathered little sailor admonished. "Ya got all the Gyrenes and these two lunkheads decked out in heavy armor—let them take the lead in case there's any trouble." The last sentence was accompanied by a jerk of his thumb in the direction of Jacob and Hitch, the sailors in the heavy armor.

"Don't worry, Chief. We're going to send out recon bots first and then let the Marines take the initial look around," Bobby replied. "Until they give the all clear, Mizuki and I will stay in the shuttle like timid little mice."

"That goes for Dr. Hosseini and Dr. Leclerc as well," echoed Mizuki. "We will be extra careful, Chief."

The Chief stuck out his elbows, balled fists on hips, like a banty rooster puffing out his wings to make himself look larger. "All right then, we don't want no casualties."

Mizuki and Bobby both nodded and then ascended the gangway into the shuttle. As they did, the Chief rounded on Jacobs and Hitch.

"Listen, yous two monkeys. Marines is, well, Marines, so I'm depending on yous. We don't want to lose any civilians and we sure don't want to lose any officers, so keep both eyes peeled for trouble."

"Don't worry, Chief," said Hitch. "Matt and I got this."

"Just remember what I told ya." The Chief stepped out of the way so the two lumbering sailors could board. As the boarding ramp retracted into the shuttle's hull, Zackly stepped out of the boarding area and secured the airlock door. The airlock depressurization alarm sounded and Peggy Sue's oldest crewmember muttered, "I don't know why, but I got a bad feeling about this."

## The Metal Moon

Kq*zt was lounging at the bottom of one of the larger crater openings when his young friend Gx!pk happened upon him. The moon's inhabitants often spent time in contemplation, sitting like immobile boulders on the surface of their little world. They did this because observation and contemplation were counted among the joys of life by their kind. It also did not expend much energy.

The other major activity for the creatures was browsing for food, which they did by eating their way through the solid material of the moon. This required quite a bit of energy and the reward was often small. In fact, the complexity of the moon's internal structure, an almost fractal like maze of intersecting tunnels of many sizes, was an indication of how slim the opportunities for finding food had become. On occasion, an asteroid or other body would collide with the moon, setting off an unseemly scramble to tear the interloping object apart. Sometimes the objects contained food, sometimes not.

A few individuals had begun giving voice to the nearly unthinkable idea of moving to another moon. The only problem with that idea was that the last time the creatures had migrated was so long ago none remembered how they accomplished the feat. These were among the thoughts that Kq*zt cogitated on while sitting placidly at the bottom of the crater.

"Hey, Kq*zt! What are you doing?" shouted Gx!pk, oozing out of a meter wide tunnel from the interior.

"I have been thinking. You should try it sometime."

"What? Oh, funny. I wish I was as quick witted as you. So really, what are you doing?"

If a silicon rock could sigh Kq*zt would have done so.

"Among other things I have been observing that ship you sighted leaving the second planet. It has entered orbit around our gassy primary and looks to be matching orbits with us."

"Oh?"

Gx!pk pulled up next to his friend and focused on the ship, floating in space a thousand kilometers away. Multispectral active sensors on the ship scanned the moon, using electromagnetic radiation ranging in frequency from long radio waves to terahertz bursts.

"It seems to be quite noisy. Why is it shouting so much?"

"I think that it is trying to see our moon more clearly."

After contemplating Kq*zt's answer for a minute or two, Gx!pk exclaimed: "Hey look! A piece has split off from the main ship. Is it reproducing?"

"Reproducing? Not likely. The ship is probably not a single living being. More than likely there are creatures inside it, and given that they visited the inner planets first they are most likely warm life."

"Warm life? You mean lifeforms that live in the zone where $H_2O$ melts?"

"Yes, they can only live unprotected in an environment where $H_2O$ is a liquid."

"But that is still much colder inside than we are. Why are they called warm life?"

"Because even colder lifeforms exist that live on worlds as cold or colder than our own. But unlike us, they are not molten inside. They are cold life, and often the servants of darkness itself."

"You mean servants of the Dark Lords?"

"Don't use their name! They hate all forms of life that are not like themselves. Warm life and cold life have been at war with each other since the beginning of the Universe."

"And which side are we on?"

"Neither, we just stay quiet and hope not to be noticed—by either side."

145

"Really? Well that might be difficult, because the small ship is heading right for us."

"Hmm, I think you are right. This time we must tell Qz@px and the other elders. If these aliens are coming to take a look around we must all hide in the tunnels."

"But why?"

"Because they might be dangerous, now come..."

Showing considerable grace and agility for a pair of multiton boulders, the two friends slithered over to a nearby opening and disappeared into the moon's tunnel riddled interior.

### *The River near New Mecca, Paradise*

It had taken much longer than either Dorri or Shadi expected to move the flock of sheep down to the river. Once they reached the bank they had to move a considerable distance along the shore until they found a bend in the river that created a still pool. Sheep are naturally skittish animals and refuse to drink from a running stream. Having finally located a site that met with the sheep's approval, the girls sat on a small rise above the flock and rested.

"I didn't think the river was so far away," complained Dorri.

"This is a big world, everything is farther away than it seems. The sheep being so fussy didn't help any either."

"At least they are drinking, and none of them ran away on the trip down here."

"You know what?" asked Shadi, "I can't see the settlement from here."

"You need to go back to the top of the rise to see the buildings. Wouldn't it be nice if the village just went away? It would be just us and the sheep."

"It would be great, until we got hungry. What I meant was that if we can't see the village they can't see us."

"Yes, so?"

"I don't know about you, but I haven't had a decent bath since we left the ship. That's more than two weeks ago and I positively reek."

"Yeah, I stink too, and our clothes are pretty smelly as well."

"So if they can't see what we are doing out here why don't we take off our clothes and take a dip in the river? We can wash off and rinse out our clothes at the same time."

"If someone came up on us we would get in big trouble, Shadi."

"Not if we do it in turns. You go down to the bank and clean up; I will go to the top of the rise and keep a watch for anyone coming from the village. The land is so flat, and we are kilometers from the settlement, we should get plenty of warning if someone decides to come check up on us."

"That's the best idea I've heard in ages," Dorri exclaimed standing up and taking off her headscarf. "Yell if someone comes!"

With that the younger girl raced down the bank and, stripping off her remaining garments, splashed into the river.

"Stay close to the shore, and upstream of the sheep!" Shadi shouted, thinking to herself, *if the men in the village saw you like this, little sister, they would have no doubt that you have become a woman. Sooner or later we will both be given as wives to men from the Imam's band. Until then, let us enjoy what little freedom we have.*

Shadi scanned the horizon in all directions from the top of the rise, paying special attention to the gently rolling grassland leading back to the settlement. She turned around just in time to see Dorri wave from the middle of the river. An instant later, Dorri was pulled beneath the surface and disappeared.

"Dorri!" Shadi screamed, running down the bank to the river. But there was no sign of her sister beneath the swirling eddies of flowing water.

## *Chapter 12*

### *The River near New Mecca, Paradise*

Shadi ran along the river's bank in a blind panic. She had not seen what dragged her sister under the water, but there was no sign of Dorri. The current in the middle of the stream was swift, flowing faster than Shadi could run. She ran down stream anyway and after about a half a kilometer the river widened and the water slowed.

Out in the river there was a splash. And then another, as Dorri fought her way to the surface, coughing water and thrashing with her arms.

On the bank Shadi striped off her headscarf and long outer robe, kicked off her sandals and plunged into the water. Both girls knew how to swim because their home in Teheran had its own swimming pool—being well off did have advantages beyond just nice clothes and jewelry.

With strong overhand strokes, Shadi closed on her sister, who was splashing about in panic. Grabbing Dorri's arm, Shadi quickly maneuvered her into a position where she could get her arm across the younger girl's chest. Doing the side stroke while keeping her sister's head above the water, Shadi headed for the shore.

Sensing that she wasn't drowning, Dorri relaxed and stopped fighting her sister's efforts. As they neared the bank, she shouted rather shakily, "it's OK, I'm OK now!"

Shadi's stroking arm touched the sandy bottom and she realized they were in only a few feet of water. Standing up, she lifted her sister until Dorri stood on her own.

"I said I'm OK," she said, but she still clung to her sister's arm. Together, they helped each other to dry land. Stripping off her remaining undergarments, Shadi spread them on the ground to dry. Sitting on the sandy bank, naked and dripping wet, she began to tremble—an after effect of the panic and adrenalin rush.

"I'm sorry," Dorri said, starting to cry. "I went out too far and got sucked down by an undertow. I'm sorry, I'm sorry!" Now it was her turn to wrap her arms around her sister. Shadi took a deep, shaky breath.

"It's OK, little star, we are both OK."

Holding each other, they sat on the bank. The warm breeze and hot sun soon dried their naked bodies. It took several minutes before they both calmed down enough to talk. Shadi spoke first.

"Come, we have to go find our clothes. There is no way we could explain to the other women if we get sunburned in places the sun is not supposed to shine."

"You're right! I just hope we can find everything."

Dorri laughed as they sprinted back along the shore, looking for their discarded clothes and sandals. As they reached the river bend they saw the sheep, placidly munching grass as though nothing had happened.


### Shuttle One, The Metal Moon

As astronomical objects went, the metal moon was a small one, though it dwarfed the Earthlings' armored shuttle as it approached. After completing a slow circuit around the moon, Bobby brought the craft to a hover over a crater nearly ten kilometers across. Within it were a multitude of other craters of varying sizes, turning the crater floor into a complex topography of holes and spires. Spotlights from the shuttle cast long shadows, further adding to the jumbled confusion.

"Well, I think that this disproves my alternate theory," remarked Bobby, his hands resting lightly on the flight controls while his eyes constantly darted from the cockpit's instruments to the scene outside and back.

"What theory is that, Bobby?" asked Mizuki, who had claimed seniority to secure the copilot's seat for herself. "I thought you were pushing the mined asteroid theory."

"I still am, but there was also the possibility that this was a ship. Maybe a multigeneration ship meant to travel the stars in normal space—a spaceship built out of an asteroid."

"You mean like the alien invaders' ship, only much larger?" The alien ship that had bombarded Earth with giant asteroids was a tube many kilometers long made from rubble that could have come from asteroids.

"From what I read about that ship it came through alter-space. Its interior was a skeleton of pressurized enclosures and support scaffolding, wrapped with a hull of asteroid material to provide some protection. But this baby is much bigger, on a grander scale altogether. You said it's fifty percent hollow?"

"Yes, if it is mostly nickel-iron it would have to be half empty space to have such a low overall density."

"So imagine you are an alien civilization without any knowledge of alter-space, but you want to go explore the galaxy. Maybe you are really long lived, like the triads, or you don't mind committing your offspring to spending many generations trapped aboard a ship. You could hollow out a big metal asteroid and build living space inside. Give the whole thing a modest spin to provide a bit of artificial gravity and stabilize the ship in flight. Add a fusion generator to power ion engines, provide light and heat for the interior, and you could head off across interstellar space. The thick metal hull would protect the ship against most objects, and, hopefully, the ship could maneuver to avoid anything large enough to do real damage."

"But it could take thousands of years to reach another star system without alter-space transit or wormholes."

"Yep, it's life in the slow lane where Einstein rules."

"I never thought of doing something like that. I always expected that we would invent a warp drive like in Star Trek."

"That's why it is important to read the classics! A lot of old time science fiction writers came up with the slow ship idea years ago. I keep telling you to go back and read Heinlein, Aldiss, and Clarke. Unfortunately, this doesn't look like the hull of a space ship from up close. If it is, it's badly damaged and must have been abandoned a long time ago."

"I would agree, it is not spinning to create artificial gravity, it is tidally locked to the gas giant. That means it has been in orbit for a long time. The best way to find out if it has a hollow interior is to send reconnaissance drones down some of the tunnel shafts."

151

"I think you're right. Let me tell the Peggy Sue what we're going to do and then we can send out the probes."

\* \* \* \* \*

In the shuttle's passenger section, the members of the shore party were watching the approach on heads-up displays built into their suits. The concerns of the two armored petty officers and their Marine counterparts were a bit more practical than their officers.

"So do you think this sucker was mined like Cmdr. Danner said?" asked Jacobs.

"Sure looks like it to me," replied Kato. "It's riddled with holes. I never seen an asteroid that dug a tunnel through a moon before."

"So now you're an asteroid expert, Kwan?" teased Vinny.

"I've seen more moons than you, DeSilva."

"Maybe in the shower, astroid-boy."

Hitch ignored the Marines' banter. "If it has been mined, I just hope there's something left for us."

"Why do you say that, Stevie?"

"The first trillionaire will be the person who mines an asteroid, Matt."

"Is that your opinion or did someone who counts come up with it?" asked Rosey.

"Neil deGrasse Tyson, that astronomy guy from TV," replied Hitch.

"The guy who did the remake of Cosmos?"

"Yeah, he was a student of that Sagan guy and even ran his own planetarium."

"So what do you think we will find, other than a lot of metal?" asked Bosco. "I do not think hauling iron from distant star systems makes a lot of economic sense."

"So says our communist economist," retorted Hitch.

"I was never a communist, I have always been capitalist. Why else would I sign up for this voyage?"

"We are all in this for the money, but Bosco's right, we ain't getting rich on iron," said DeSilva.

"Well maybe they were after rarer metals, Vinny. Like gold or platinum."

"That actually makes sense, Stevie. If they were after iron they could have slagged the whole moon, instead of turning it into Swiss cheese."

"Look, there go the recon bots," said Rosey. "Look alive, Marines; if they don't run into trouble we'll be next."

"And if they do run into trouble?" asked Bosco.

"We'll be next sooner."


### CIC, *Peggy Sue*

The display table in the center of the CIC traced the tracks of the recon drones in three dimensions, a growing map of the metal moon's interior. On the forward bulkhead, side-by-side displays showed video of the bots' descent. There were twists and turns, and enough intersecting passageways to make the live feeds look like an amusement park ride or video from a computer game. Colorful annotations helped mark the path ahead as the drones flew deeper into the maze. Then the center probe emerged into a large void and paused.

"OK, I see no way that an asteroid strike could create large interior spaces in a body like that," Billy Ray commented. The chamber's walls looked like they had been scooped out with a large ice cream dipper; intersecting concaved furrows and individual hollows dimpled the surrounding metal.

"I'm beginning to think that Bobby was right," added Beth, "this place does look like it was mined, or home to a colony of space-termites."

"Now that would be really exciting," said Will Krenshaw. The biologists were left on the ship for this mission, since their skills were unlikely to be needed on site. From the corner of the CIC Ahnah snorted. The she-bear, though only half the size of Umky, was still sizable and was trying to stay out of the smaller humans' way.

"Metal eating termites that can live in vacuum would certainly be a notable find," the ursine biologist agreed. The drone drifted across the sizable open space and started down another tunnel on the far wall. As it exited the chamber there was a chirp from its motion detector.

"What was that?"

"Something moving behind the probe in the big chamber," Billy Ray replied. "Shuttle One, Peggy Sue. Did you catch the motion sensor alarm on probe two?"

"Roger that, Peggy Sue. I just told it to reverse course and re-enter the chamber slowly."

As they watched, the view from the drone spun wildly and came to rest pointing back the way it had come. It eased ahead slowly, reemerging from the tunnel. The drone's camera panned from left to right, then up and down, but there was no further indication of movement from its sensors.

"I wonder if that drone has a wonky motion sensor?" said Beth.

"I don't know, but there's nothing moving in there now," replied Billy Ray.

"I think maybe we are all a bit jumpy," said Will, as the recon drone once again reversed its course and resumed its journey toward the moon's center. As it disappeared into the tunnel, a pair of boulders that hadn't been in the chamber on the drone's first visit silently moved off through a different side tunnel.


### Interior, The Metal Moon

The spherical, basketball sized drones possessed enough machine intelligence to navigate autonomously, requiring only general direction from their human masters. They were propelled by gravitonic repulsors on all three axes, making them highly maneuverable and well suited to flying down the twisty, maze like tunnels that riddled the moon's interior. On the front of each drone were a number of lenses and protruding sensors, lending the drones a comical, clown-like look.

Even when not careening down enclosed metal tunnels, the drones had a habit of weaving about when they moved. Given their staggering movement and mirth inducing appearance, the human crew had taken to calling them clown bots, or just clowns for short. The inhabitants of the moon saw them a bit differently.

"That was close, it almost saw us," Gx!pk said.

"Saw you, you mean," Kq*zt replied, following behind the younger creature.

"Come on! It's like playing hide and seek, or tag, when I was younger. There's no thrill if you don't take some chances."

"I'm beginning to think I do not understand the younger generation."

"You're closer to my age than to Qz@px's," Gx!pk said in a peevish tone.

"Qz@px said we were to keep track of the stranger, not play games with it. Like I said before, it might be dangerous, particularly if you startle it."

"Do you really think that is one of the aliens from the ship?"

"We both saw it and two others emerge from the small ship that entered the crater on the planet facing side. They seem to be heading toward the center of our moon, while shouting loudly to each other and their ship."

"I don't know, it doesn't seem very smart. If they can build starships you'd think they'd be smarter."

"Maybe they use young, expendable individuals as scouts. People nobody would miss if something went wrong."

"You mean like the elders sending us to keep watch on the aliens?"

"Now you are wising up. You don't see any of the old ones running through tunnels hither and yon, chasing after interloping aliens, do you?"

"No, but that may be because the elders aren't as spry as they used to be, and some of them have trouble remembering where all the tunnels intersect."

155

The two friends laughed loudly at that remark and almost burst into the next chamber where the alien they were following was floating motionless, evidently trying to decide on which tunnel to take next.

### Shuttle One

"Which way now?" asked Bobby.

"I don't know," Mizuki replied, glancing at the other two drones' live feeds. They were still descending along the tunnels they were sent into. "Take the biggest tunnel that heads down."

"Down isn't much around here, there is almost no gravity."

"0.00017 m/sec$^2$," the astrophysicist responded automatically. "Roughly two thousandths of a percent of Earth normal."

"Like I said, almost no gravity. I bet you could jump right off the thing and drift away into space."

"Yes, escape velocity is about 26 kph. But then you would go into orbit around the gas planet. It would probably be a lonely way to die."

"Remind me not to jump." A flashing light on the overhead instrument panel caught Bobby's attention. "Did you see that? There was a burst of RF radiation just before the drone exited the chamber."

"Just reflected signals from the drone or its repeaters?"

"Frequency is all wrong and it registered as pink noise."

"That's weird."

On the center display panel, recon drone two resumed its twisting journey to the moon's core. It had gone about ten kilometers into the moon when it emerged into a third, even larger open space. Slowing to a hover, the drone's camera panned around the chamber. Just as the camera's motion detection software triggered an alarm, something that looked like a large boulder collided with the drone and its video transmission abruptly ended.

### Large Chamber, The Metal Moon

"Oh no!" exclaimed Kq*zt. "Did you see that? Zz#tx just squished the alien!"

"Worse, I think he's going to eat it," Gx!pk replied, "the senile old fool!"

The two friends popped out of the tunnel opening they were hiding in and moved toward the third creature. The one called Zz#tx had pinned the much smaller probe against the hard metallic wall of the chamber and oozed around it on all sides. As he moved, cracks formed in his dark stoney exterior revealing the deep red glow of molten rock within. Before Kq*zt or Gx!pk could intervene, Zz#tx finished ingesting the probe.

"You silly old coot!" yelled Gx!pk. "Didn't you hear Qz@px say not to have contact with the aliens!"

Zz#tx floated away from the wall and noticed the presence of the youngsters for the first time.

"What? Why are you shouting at me, you impertinent young pebble. No respect for your elders."

"You just ate a visitor from an alien ship that's come snooping around our moon," yelled Kq*zt. Zz#tx was known to be hard of hearing, though many thought it was just an excuse to ignore those he didn't want to listen to.

"There was a little metal asteroid here in the chamber so I ate it. You're just mad because I didn't give you any."

"No, no, no," Kq*zt muttered.

"It wasn't very good, though," the old lava creature continued. "Mostly lighter elements; no nutritional value whatsoever."

To reinforce that statement he out-gassed a plume of incandescent vapor. The others just floated and stared at the oldster.

"Don't you understand, Zz#tx? You killed an alien, and there's no telling what they might do if they find out."

"Egh? Alien you say? Well it had a lot of useless metals in it. I'll probably be constipated for a dozen orbits."

"Crap!," Gx!pk said in frustration.

"Exactly!" said Zz#tx, "I won't be able to crap!"

"Come on, Gx!pk. We need to go and tell the elders what happened."

"Yeah, I wonder how long it will take the aliens to figure out what happened."

"Uh-huh, and what they will do then."

As the pair departed, heading back toward the surface, Zz#tx belched again and wandered off into the chamber.


### CIC, Peggy Sue

"Shuttle One, what just happened to recon drone two?" Billy Ray had been idly monitoring the drones' progress when the video feed from drone two suddenly went black.

"Peggy Sue, we aren't sure what happened to the drone. The last we saw it was scanning the chamber when something collided with it. Its telemetry signal dropped but just before it quit the onboard temperature sensor went off the chart—it registered more than 1,000 degrees."

"That's what we saw as well, Shuttle One. Interrogative the status of the other two recon drones?"

"We've halted the others in place."

"Roger that."

"There's something weird going on inside this metal ant heap. We are picking up a lot of electromagnetic radiation, some RF and some microwave. Trouble is, the damn moon is made of metal and it blocks most transmissions." As he spoke, the video feed from drone three went dark.

*Now what?* Bobby thought. *What's taking out my drones?* Before he could take any action telemetry from the remaining drone quit.

"Shuttle One, we just lost the video from the other two drones."

"Roger, Peggy Sue, so did we. This time it looks like the telemetry links were broken." The drones scattered small sensor relays behind them as they descended into the metal maze so they could stay in touch with the shuttle. Otherwise the solid metal of the moon would have soon rendered them incommunicado.

"Understood. You're the commander in place, Mr. Danner. How do you suggest we proceed?"

"I think we should find out what took out our drones. If there are other living creatures in this system—possibly hostile creatures— we need to know."

"Affirmative, if we have hostiles in system we need to warn the colonists."

"Roger, Peggy Sue. I think we need to send the Marines on a reconnaissance patrol."

### *Marine Squad*

"All right, listen up Marines," the Gunny sent over the squad frequency. "Our objective is to find out what happened to the recon drones. We will form three groups and follow the same tracks as the drones until we either find the clown bots or some sign of what happened to them. Hopefully clown bots one and three only lost comm and are still functional.

"Hitch and Jacobs, you will take the port track; Kato and Bosco the starboard track; Umky, Vinny and myself will take the center track which should lead to where bot two went dark. The clown bots dropped sensor relays along their paths as they descended so comm signals could get back out of this metal rat's nest. I want you to scatter extra ones as you go to make sure we don't lose contact. And get your mini-bots out in front and behind you. Questions?"

"What if we get lost, Gunny?" asked Vinny.

"Your suit's inertial tracking will tell you where you are and how you got there, plus we got the bots' track telemetry. Besides, DeSilva, you're with me, which means by definition you are not lost."

The squad chuckled, easing the tension that darkened their mood. They were, after all, about to enter a gigantic maze made out of solid metal that even their weaponry couldn't blast through. Splitting into three teams meant they would be even more isolated once they entered tunnels, but it made sense. The tunnels, spacious for the drones, were only wide enough to let the armored Marines advance single file. Even if they were attacked from both front and rear simultaneously, at most two of them would be able to engage the enemy at a time.

"Hey, I bet we find our clown bot before you Navy jerk offs," said Kato, trying to get a rise out of the two petty officers.

"No way Jar Head, you guys got no sense of direction," replied Hitch.

"Why do you think the Navy always has to transport you Gyrenes to the battle zone?" added Jacobs. "Try not to get lost in the drain pipes."

Vinny made a rude hand signal and Rosey shook her head, a gesture concealed by her suit's full coverage helmet.

"Enough! OK, Jacobs, your call sign is now Drainpipe One; Kato, you're Drainpipe Two; and I am Drainpipe Leader. Got that?"

"Aye, aye, Gunny," replied those named.

"All right people, head out and stay in contact. Break. Shuttle One, Drainpipe Leader."

"Drainpipe Leader, Shuttle One. I read you five by five."

"Be advised we are heading out."

"Roger that, Drainpipe Leader. Good hunting."

The two teams of Marines quickly moved into their assigned tunnels. Hitch and Jacobs peered into the pitch black darkness of their entranceway a bit more hesitantly. With a last look back at the shuttle, they too disappeared into the maze.

# *Chapter 13*

## *Shuttle One*

On the flight deck, Bobby and Mizuki watched the Marines' progress on the same screens they had monitored video from the recon bots. The remaining crew and scientists were looped in via the comm net and watched the teams moving down the almost featureless tunnels on the forward passenger compartment display. All were quiet, listening to the Marines chat with each other until Mizuki could stand it no longer.

"Why did Rosey call herself 'Drainpipe Leader'?"

"What?" replied Bobby, startled by the question amid the tense silence. "I guess it's Marine humor, sweetheart."

"Drainpipe?"

"Yeah, a drainpipe leads down into a sewer or cesspool. Marines make fun of what they are facing to relieve tension before a battle."

"Are we expecting a battle?"

"God I hope not. It would be like a shootout in a... well, a drainpipe. I'm just hoping that we find the missing drones and a rational explanation for why they all went off line."

"Hostile action by unknown aliens is a perfectly rational explanation."

"You know, you are too pretty to be so damned logical."

Mizuki looked at him and smiled, her dark eyes glistening. For reasons Bobby did not fully understand, his beloved came alive when facing danger. She was not the shy and frightened young woman he had saved from the yakuza years ago—this Mizuki would have taken her katana and turned those mobsters into shashimi. She was no longer a damsel in distress but he loved her even more, his Japanese warrior princess.

"Too bad we could not bring the *aoi chō*, I think they would have enjoyed exploring the tunnels."

"I'm sure they would love to explore the tunnels, but I don't think they would do well in hard vacuum. Maybe we will find

161

another planet or space station where they can accompany us, Mizuki-chan."

On the leftmost screen, the one showing video from Matt Jacob's suit camera, progress came to a halt. Matt's voice called over the squad's frequency.

"Drainpipe Leader, Drainpipe One."

Rosey's voice replied immediately. "Go, Drainpipe One."

"We have a bit of a problem here, Drainpipe Leader. The tunnel has narrowed to the point that we can't fit through."

"Roger that. Shuttle One, did you copy?"

*Crap*, thought Bobby, *I knew things were going too smoothly*. He keyed the radio. "Affirmative, Drainpipe Leader. Can they find an alternate route around the constriction?"

"There were a couple of cross tunnels back about twenty meters. We can try one of those."

"It's your call, Drainpipe Leader," Bobby replied.

"Roger, Shuttle One. Break. Drainpipe One, backtrack and try to find another way forward."


### Drainpipe One

"Roger, Drainpipe Leader. We are moving back to find another passageway." Matt switched back to suit-to-suit in time to hear Hitch complaining.

"Balls! Kato and Bosco are going to find their clown bot before we do at this rate."

"Have a little faith, Stevie. It ain't over till the clown bot sings. So turn your ass around and find us an off ramp."

With considerable effort, the two sailors managed to reverse their direction of travel in the cramped tunnel and float back the way they came. A short distance up the tunnel they found two side tunnels, one that headed east and turned up, and one that headed west and turned down.

"What do you say, Bro. West and down?"

"Works for me," Matt replied, throwing a couple of sensor relays down the eastern side tunnel, just in case. The Marines' relays not only passed on communication signals but provided heat and motion detection as well. If something tried to sneak up behind them, or otherwise use the path they had come by, they would know about it.

Inside the moon there was no light, visible or other wise—just what they brought with them. The near infrared light sources built into their suits illuminated the path ahead throwing the melted, almost smooth tunnel walls into stark relief. The suits could also generate visible and UV illumination on demand but IR mode had the added bonus of picking up living creatures from their body temperature. The view was displayed holographically on Matt and Stevie's heads up displays, along with thermal background readings and added depth ques.

After gliding along for several minutes, the tunnel curved, flattening out to the west. Matt sent his small recon bot around the bend before navigating the corner himself. Unlike the bigger recon drones, the mini-bots had limited autonomous capability and, being about the size of a softball, mounted fewer sensors as well. Each suit of heavy armor came with a mini-bot integrated with its sensor suite.

"Hey, Stevie. It looks like the tunnel intersects with a vertical shaft about ten meters ahead."

"Great. All I got is a view of your armored ass."

Matt drifted forward without comment. The moon was essentially a zero-gee environment, which allowed movement using the suit's built in repulsors. The repulsors were meant as an active defense against armor-piercing shaped charge rounds, causing them to detonate prematurely. They did this by creating a sharp but highly localized negative gravity gradient just prior to impact. They were not intended for continuous use nor strong enough to allow flight under any respectable gravity. Fortunately, this excursion was more of a spacewalk than a hike.

"The vertical shaft ahead looks like a big one, and this tunnel widens out to form a bit of a platform."

"Great, Matt. Move over and let me see too."

Jacobs edged right and Hitch maneuvered to his left. Soon they lay side by side, both staring across the larger tunnel.

"How wide do you make that?" asked Hitch.

"My laser rangefinder says 7.2 meters, almost 24 feet."

"It looks like it goes all the way up to the surface," he observed by rolling onto his back and sticking his head out of the side tunnel.

"Get back in here, Stevie! If there are hostiles out there they could take a shot at you!"

"Matt, there ain't nothing moving around out there," Hitch replied as he rolled back onto his stomach. "Have your bot shine a light down the shaft and see if it attracts any attention."

"Right, let's kick over the hornet's nest," he muttered as he ordered the mini-bot to do as Hitch asked. A brilliant white light slashed into the shaft, casting a bright ellipse on the far side tunnel wall. The illuminated ellipse grew more distorted as it ran down the wall until it became a circle on the shaft's floor. As the spotlight traversed the bottom of the shaft, roughly twenty meters below, flashes of color winked back at the two explorers—red, green, blue and white.

"What's that sparkly stuff?" asked Hitch.

"I don't know, but I think we need to find out."

"And just how do we do that, Bro?"

"First we send my bot to take a closer look. If nothing takes it out then we go down ourselves."

"Just for shits and giggles?"

"Right, Stevie. Just for shits and giggles."


### Drainpipe Two

Kwan and Boskovitch were making better time toward their objective than Hitch and Jacobs, not having encountered any obstacles or distractions. As they drifted downward, Bosco, in the trailing position, had little to look at but the tunnel wall—smooth, dark, and rippled like a giant's intestine. There he noticed something out of place.

"Kato, stop! There is something here on the wall of the tunnel."

"What is it, Bosco? I haven't noticed anything unusual."

Bosco moved in for a closer look. Under light from his suit, a silver smear was visible against the dark metal of the tunnel wall.

"It looks like the remains of a telemetry relay."

"The remains of a relay? What happened to it?"

"It looks like something smashed it against the tunnel wall."

"Well that would explain why we lost track of the clown bot. And it also means that there's something down here other than us."

"Da, something big and heavy and strong."

Kato keyed the comm. "Drainpipe Leader, Drainpipe Two."

"Go Drainpipe Two."

"Gunny, Bosco found one of the drone's telemetry relays smashed against the tunnel wall."

"Smashed? How did that happen?"

"It looks like something crushed it on purpose. I don't think we're alone down here."

"Roger, Drainpipe Two. Wait one. Shuttle One, did you copy that last?"

"Roger, Drainpipe Leader. There's no way the relay could have been destroyed by accident?"

"Shuttle One, Drainpipe Two. It was ground into the tunnel wall with considerable force. Something smashed it, either by accident or on purpose—something not us."

"Roger that, wait one."

There was a pause while the officers on the shuttle undoubtedly conferred with the Captain back on the Peggy Sue. The Marines waited quietly, awaiting further orders.

"Drainpipe Leader, have Drainpipe Two leave additional relays and continue toward the drone's last known position. Carefully."

165

"Roger that, Shuttle One. OK, listen up people. This situation is starting to become real. Keep your eyes open and your mini-bots out on point. Report any more smashed relays or contact immediately."

"Aye, aye, Gunny," replied Kato. As the ensuing silence lengthened there came no response from Drainpipe One.

* * * * *

*Now what?* Rosey thought. "Drainpipe One, Drainpipe Leader. Did you copy that last?"

Silence.

*Shit! Leave it to the fuckin' Navy. Can't let 'em off the ship without adult supervision.* "Drainpipe One, Drainpipe Leader. Over."

More silence.

"Shuttle One, Drainpipe Leader. Can you raise Drainpipe One?"

"Negative, Drainpipe leader. We have lost telemetry from both Hitch and Jacobs. There were no threat indications, this is like the telemetry loss on the last two recon drones."

"Roger, Shuttle One. What do you advise?"

Another pause while officers conferred.

"Drainpipe Leader, we show you a half a klick from the chamber where recon two was lost. Proceed to your objective and hold in position."

"Roger, Shuttle One. Proceeding to the objective. Drainpipe Leader out."


## Shuttle One

"This is not good," Bobby said out loud, though mostly to himself. "We have lost three recon drones and now a pair of sailors."

"It just looks like the telemetry link was lost," Mizuki replied. "There was no indication that they were attacked."

"But cutting the communications link could be a prelude to an attack."

Before Mizuki could respond, indicators on the control panel associated with recon drone three came back to life. Then video reception was restored.

"What's going on now? This is getting weirder by the minute."

Mizuki interrogated the control panel indicators and sent self diagnostic requests to the re-acquired drone. After a few seconds, waiting for the self-check results to come back, she smiled and looked up.

"The drone is OK, Bobby. Everything checks out fine."

"Did it see anything while it was out of contact?"

"No, I uploaded the event log and it shows nothing—no contact of any kind. It simply followed its programming and waited for communications to be restored."

"This is getting too freaky for me, I'm going to call the ship." He switched to the inter-ship channel. "Peggy Sue, Shuttle One."

"Shuttle One, this is Peggy Sue. I see you have restored telemetry from recon three."

"Roger, Peggy Sue. I think it must have been Drainpipe Two laying extra relays. They filled the gap created when the drone's relay was smashed."

"We concur, Shuttle One. How do you propose to proceed?"

Bobby paused a moment for thought. Just speaking to the ship helped suppress the growing dread he had been feeling. There was still no indication that they had lost anyone, other than that first drone, and reestablishing control over drone three was a hopeful sign.

"Peggy Sue, be advised I am going to bring recon drone three and Drainpipe Two back to the surface. Then we can send them down the same path as Drainpipe One. If they are having a telemetry problem for the same reason as the drone we should be able to reestablish contact without any problem."

"Roger that, Shuttle One. We will continue to monitor from here."

"Roger, Peggy Sue. Break, break. Drainpipe Leader, Shuttle One. We are going to order recon drone three to return to the surface. Have Drainpipe Two reverse course and come back to the shuttle."

"Roger, Shuttle One. Understood."

### Elder's Chamber

In a side chamber, several passageways away from the recon drones and their would be rescuers, an assemblage of sentient boulders were holding a conference. By acclamation, Qz@px was the leader of the older lava creatures. The collection of elders was as close as the creatures came to a government, being highly evolved they had little time for such tomfoolery. The topic of discussion was what, if anything, to do about the visitors currently making their way through the interior of the metal moon.

"I find these new creatures very annoying," said one of the eldest present. "It's bad enough they are constantly squawking, they leave small noisemakers behind them that constantly squawk back."

"I find that if you crush one of the little noisemakers the others fall silent," said another.

While many of the lava creatures were very old, tens of thousands of years old, most spent their time in solitary contemplation. Qz@px was a bit of an anomaly among them, for he paid attention to things happening throughout the star system they inhabited, not just the little moon on which they lived. Over the millennia he had seen other visitors come and go, usually seeking out the inner planets and seldom calling on the gas giant his home orbited. As a result, his level of knowledge regarding aliens was far superior to that of his peers.

"I do not believe the things that entered the tunnels were creatures at all," he said, causing several side conversations to cease.

"What do you mean, they aren't creatures?" demanded the relay crusher.

"Other visitors have brought devices with them, automata that can explore on their masters behest," Qz@px explained. "Such devices often constantly babble to each other and their masters, who stay comfortably out of harm's way."

"Is that why they make so much noise?"

"Probably. And since it would be hard for the three initial automata to hear one another or the small ship they arrived in once the were inside the tunnels, I suspect the little noise makers are simple repeaters. They pass messages among the explorers and their ship."

"So they are not really living creatures at all."

"And Zz#tx didn't kill an alien, he just ate one of the aliens' machines," said Kq*zt. He and Gx!pk had come to the elders chamber to report what they had witnessed, shadowing the aliens.

"That is correct," replied Qz@px, "though I doubt that the real aliens will be pleased with providing Zz#tx a meal."

"He didn't like it much, if that's any consolation," added Gx!pk. "But I think that smashing the repeaters might also upset the aliens, if it means they can no longer talk with their machines."

"Yes, Gx!pk, you are correct. We need to spread the word that none of the alien devices should be destroyed, no matter how annoying they are. Unless I miss my guess, there will be more visitors entering the tunnels to see what happened to the first ones."

"More of the little metal balls like the one that was eaten?"

"Possibly, or some of the aliens themselves. And beware, the aliens may be dangerous in ways you have never seen. Creatures that build starships have a tendency to also build things called weapons, which can inflict pain, damage and even death on other beings."

The chamber was suddenly very quiet as Qz@px's words sank in. Creating devices was a strange enough concept for most of the creatures present. Creating devices that inflicted harm on other sentient beings was almost beyond belief.

Mortality was seldom if ever a matter of daily contemplation for the sentient boulders. Nor was death a common occurrence among the lava creatures. They had no natural enemies and suffered from no fatal diseases. On rare occasion, one of the very old would simply tire of existence and expire. They would be found one day in a side tunnel or on the surface, cold and rock hard through and through.

"So what would you suggest we do, Qz@px?" asked one of the other elders.

"I would suggest we send some of the youngsters to keep an eye on the visitors, to see what they do next. The rest of us need to stay out of their way—and no more smashing or eating the aliens' devices, it might annoy them."

"Well they have annoyed me by just coming here," one of the senior elders griped.

"Be that as it may, we need to treat them with care. There is no telling what they might do if provoked. We will keep watch on them. Perhaps they will try to make contact with us, or maybe they will simply go back to where they came from if they find nothing of interest on our little moon."

There was a murmur of general agreement among the elders as the youngsters present headed out to spy on the aliens and their strange devices. Among the cadre of spies were Gx!pk and Kq*zt, both excited by the prospect of more adventures.

"I think this is just super, we should have visiting aliens every day," enthused Gx!pk.

"Let's see how this encounter goes before we ask for more tourists," his friend replied, as they disappeared into the maze of tunnels.

# Chapter 14

### Shuttle One

"Recon drone three just emerged from the tunnel, Bobby," Mizuki reported from her position at the copilot's controls. The starboard telemetry display showed a view of the shuttle itself from the drone's perspective. "It must have passed the Marines on the way back up the tunnel."

"Great. I think we should send it down the tunnel Drainpipe Leader went down. It can keep an eye on what's going on in their rear."

"OK." Mizuki sent a string of commands to the bot, causing it to rotate and head swiftly for the central tunnel that the Gunny and her companions took.

"Look. Here come Bosco and Kato."

Mizuki looked up and saw the dark forms of the armored Marines drift out of the tunnel mouth to float above the moon's uneven surface. After taking a few moments to orient themselves Kato's voice came over the comm.

"Shuttle One, Drainpipe Two. We have you in sight."

"Roger that, Drainpipe Two. Proceed to the tunnel used by Drainpipe One and advance until you make contact with Hitch and Jacobs."

"Understood, Shuttle One. We are to go find Drainpipe One."

"Affirmative, Drainpipe Two. Be advised that we have lost communications with Drainpipe One. It may be the same situation as your drone, something destroying a relay or two."

"Roger that."

"Interrogative your relay supply?"

"We both have about a dozen left apiece. Over."

"Good. Let us know as soon as you make contact."

"Roger, Shuttle One."

From the cockpit, one of the Marines could be seen waving at the shuttle before heading off in the direction of the specified tunnel entrance. Bobby raised a hand in reply, though it was doubtful that the gesture could be seen through the shuttle's windscreen. The two Marines drifted gracefully across the spiky, dimpled metallic surface, like balloons in a holiday parade.

"How long will it take for them to find the others?"

"I don't know, Mizuki. The others have been gone for a couple of hours. I hope they can reestablish communications with Drainpipe One quicker than that by restoring the telemetry repeater chain."

"We don't know where the break is; it could take minutes or hours to reach."

"Yeah. You know, years ago I always wanted to be in command. I didn't realize then that command often means waiting and worrying while others go in harm's way. I learned that lesson later and had thankfully forgotten it until today."

"Think of Billy Ray and Beth back in the ship. They are twice removed from the action."

"Let's just hope that the only 'action' we encounter is smashed sensor relays. Combat of any kind inside those tunnels would be a nightmare."

Mizuki reached over and placed her left hand over Bobby's right hand and gave it a squeeze. Silently they exchange glances and then turned back to the telemetry readouts.


### *Drainpipe Leader*

Rosey, Umky, and Vinny drifted along the tunnel leading to the chamber where recon drone two disappeared under possibly violent circumstances. Over suit-to-suit they chatted amongst themselves.

"Gunny, did I mention that I'm claustrophobic?" said Vinny.

"You're not approved for claustrophobia, DeSilva. So suck it up, Marine."

172

Umky chuckled—a low resonating rumble that sounded nothing like amusement. "How do you think I feel? I'm six times your size, primate."

"Yuck it up, furball," Vinny quipped. "You're not finding this a bit confining?"

"I'm finding it rather peaceful, drifting through dark passages encased in my own suit. Temperature set to something reasonable, no monkey smell and no Ahnah."

"Don't tell me you are having romantic problems with the only other polar bear on the mission?" asked Rosey.

"Not at the moment," Umky said, evading the question.

"Hey, what monkey smell?" asked Vinny.

"You humans have practically no sense of smell compared to us bears. I can smell a single human kilometers away. Imagine what it's like being stuck in a metal tube with dozens of you for months at a time."

"And you can pick Ahnah out of that background odor?" asked Rosey, still looking for the inside story on the relationship between the expedition's two polar bears.

"Hell, every time she's fertile her scent permeates the whole ship. And even when she's not I still know she's there. This mating instinct crap is a pain in the rump."

*Yeah, tell me about it,* Rosy thought, *If I hadn't gotten frisky with my squadmates I wouldn't be drifting down a solid metal sewer pipe, headed for where a clown bot got snuffed by parties unknown.* Out loud she simply said, "That must be a distraction."

"That ain't the half of it. We both live in the same habitat on the ship so I can't just avoid her. I'm afraid that one night I'll have a couple of brandies and things will get amorous—I do not want a couple of little white furballs running around calling me 'daddy'."

"I though you bears only mated at one time of year?"

"We smart bears are a bit different than your garden variety polar bear. Our females are fertile in the spring and cycle in and out of heat every few weeks until they get pregnant. If we ever find the T'aafhal I have a bone to pick with them about that."

173

"So you're saying that Ahnah is going to be fertile until she gets pregnant?"

"In the wild it passes with the onset of winter. On board ship I've got no idea how long it will last. Worst thing about it is it makes her kind of flirty."

*Yeah, me too*, Rosey thought, *biology is a real bitch*.

Rosey's little recon drone chirped an alarm as it halted at the end of the tunnel, where it beamed back an infrared view of the large cavern beyond.

"OK, Marines, we have arrived at our destination. Time to look sharp. Break. Shuttle One, Drainpipe Leader, do you copy?"

"Go, Drainpipe Leader."

"We are about to enter the chamber where contact was lost with the recon drone."

"Roger that. Exercise extreme caution, Drainpipe Leader."

Without further conversation the three Marines entered the large chamber and spread out around the tunnel opening. Rosey's mini-bot moved into the open space and illuminated the cavern. Along the walls were boulders of many sizes, ranging from one to two meters in diameter.

"Gunny, did the missing clown bot report boulders?"

"No, DeSilva, it didn't. I think we are about to meet what crushed the recon drone."

Across the chamber a particularly large boulder began moving toward the Earthlings.

### Drainpipe One

Hitch and Jacobs hung inverted above the floor of the shaft. Above them their mini-bots hovered, illuminating the bottom of the pit. The floor itself was hidden by a carpet of loose crystals of unknown depth. The crystals came in many shapes and sizes, ranging from the size of grapes to the size of eggplants.

174

Many of the crystals were rounded octahedra, but others displayed multiple facets that could have belonged to a cube, hexahedron or dodecahedron. Sometimes they were grown together forming double crystals, while still others were long octagonal rods or spiky clumps. They came in colors including yellow, brown, blue, and colorless. Less prevalent were green, pink, violet, orange, purple and red. The colorless ones split white light into spectral colors, sending festive rainbows shimmering up the shaft walls.

"What is this stuff?" asked Hitch.

"It looks like a big pile of gemstones," replied Jacobs, reaching down to pickup one of the larger crystals. "I'm going to do a spectroscopic analysis on one of them."

The suits of heavy armor worn by the two sailors were the same as those worn by the Marines. Their gauntleted hands were definitely not meant for delicate or precision work. Instead of designing an array of custom tools for use by the clumsy mitts of those suited up for combat, a number of devices were built into the the suit gloves themselves. One of those tools was a laser torch that could vaporize small material samples and feed them into a miniaturized mass spectrometer. Holding the large crystal in his right hand, Matt extended the index finger on his left glove and touched it to the stone.

A beep sounded in his helmet to indicate that the sample had been gathered and analysis was underway. A quarter of a minute later the computer in Matt's suit indicated the analysis was complete.

"So what does it say?" asked Hitch.

"It says it's almost pure carbon with some trace elements."

"And what does that mean?"

"It means that this is a diamond," said Jacobs, "a very big diamond."

"What!" Hitch was gobsmacked. "What about all these others, test more of them!"

"Hey, you have a tester too. Lend a hand."

Hitch picked up a blue gem and gave it the mass spectrometer finger. "Hey, what is $\alpha\text{-}Al_2O_3$?"

"Am I a chemist? Ask your computer."

"Oh, yeah. It says it's an aluminum oxide called corundum."

"That makes what you're holding a sapphire. Depending on the presence of other elements they can come in all sorts of colors. For instance, chromium turns them red. You know, red as in rubies?"

"Are they worth anything?"

"Big ones can be worth more than diamonds, depending on color and purity."

"Damn, this is like stumbling across Ali Baba's treasure cave!"

Together, the two friends began feverishly testing crystal of all sizes, shapes and colors. With each new sample their excitement grew until they were consumed by wealth induced giddiness. Hitch scooped up a handful of stones and flung them at Jacobs.

Jacobs returned the favor and soon they were both laughing and throwing gemstones at each other like boys on a dirt pile. Standing on the mound of glittering crystals, behaving like madmen, Jacobs and Hitch were oblivious to things happening around them.

### Platform Above The Gem Pit

Kq*zt and Gx!pk had found their way to another platform on the shaft wall above the gem pit. Peering over the edge, the two friends spotted strange dark shapes at the bottom of the shaft.

"What in the world are they?" asked Gx!pk. "They aren't at all like the small spherical thing that Zz#tx ate."

"They are either a different type of automata, or maybe they are the aliens themselves," replied Kq*zt. Both were operating with a severe deficit of experience—neither had ever seen any type of space alien before. "Why would they be at the bottom of a privy?"

"Look!" Gx!pk hissed. "Look at what they're doing!"

The two dark figures below were hopping about, throwing handfuls of crystals at each other. They were yelling as well, though their utterances were unintelligible.

"I cannot believe it," said the astonished Kq*zt.

"They are throwing poo at each other!" Gx!pk's voice was laden with disgust. "They are standing in a latrine playing with poo!"

"They do seem rather odd. Maybe they are a race of coprophilic monsters?"

"You mean they are all like that?" Gx!pk paused. "Oh no."

"Now what?"

"All this running around, and now watching the aliens in the toilet, I have a sudden need to take a dump."

"You are kidding, right?"

"No, I'm not. I haven't gone in quite a while, and all this excitement has started things... moving."


### Drainpipe Two

Drainpipe Two arrived at the platform previously occupied by Drainpipe One. Cautiously looking over the edge into the pit, the Marines spied the two sailors hopping about. Over their suit radios they could hear the two men yelling back and forth, though their words made no sense.

"What are they doing?" asked Bosco. "And why are they throwing rocks at each other?"

"I don't know, man. Sailors are all a bit crazy if you ask me."

"Da, and those two are crazier than most."

"You're not wrong, Bosco. I'd better call the ship." Moving back from the ledge, Kato switched frequencies. "Shuttle One, Drainpipe Two. We have found Drainpipe One. They seem to have gone down a shaft without spreading enough relays to maintain the telemetry link."

"Roger, Drainpipe Two. We are starting to get readouts from their suits now. Telemetry indicates a high level of physical exertion, what are they doing?"

"They seem to be standing on a large pile of rocks and they are throwing them at each other. Over."

"Are you in verbal contact with the other team?"

"Yes and no. We can hear them shouting and yelling, but they aren't making any sense. They keep saying things like 'mansions', 'champagne', 'women', and 'yachts'.."

"Women?"

"Well, actually 'hookers', sir."

"Anything else?"

"Yeah, the phrase 'rich, rich, rich' keeps coming up."

There was a pause.

"Drainpipe Two, try to get their attention, but be careful. Doc White says they might be suffering hallucinations caused by claustrophobia or some contaminant in their suits' air supplies."

"How did something get into both their suits?"

"We don't know, Drainpipe Two, but they might harm themselves or you if you get too close."

"Roger that, Shuttle One. We will approach with caution."


*Platform Above The Gem Pit*

"I'm telling you I have to take a dump!" There was desperation and a hint of panic in Gx!pk's voice. "When ya gotta go ya gotta go!" For the lava creatures that was literally true—once the process of eliminating bodily waste began it could not be denied.

"Well don't go in here," Kq*zt said. "If you crap in the tunnel you will have to clean it out."

"What would you suggest?" Gx!pk's body had begun rhythmic pulsations and he was bouncing from floor to ceiling.

178

"This is a latrine, isn't it? And the aliens seem overjoyed with its contents—why don't you give them some more poo to play with?"

"Arrgh!" came the inarticulate reply.

Gx!pk hung part of his not inconsiderable mass over the edge of the platform, angling toward the bottom of the shaft and let fly. A stream of red hot crystalline objects emerged from his distended body, showering down on the aliens below.

\* \* \* \* \*

"*Bozhe moy*, what was that!" shouted Bosco, pulling back from the ledge as a fiery barrage streaked past their position headed for the bottom of the vertical shaft.

"Incoming!" Kato yelled over the Marine's common frequency while raising his railgun.

"Can you see where it's coming from?"

"Yeah, there is another ledge like this one about ten meters farther up the shaft," Kato replied. "Somebody is shooting at the Navy guys."

Together, the two Marines did what Marines are taught to do when unknown hostiles shoot at your buddies—they fired several bursts of depleted uranium tracer rounds at the platform where the incoming fire originated.

\* \* \* \* \*

Jacobs and Hitch were still engaged in flinging gemstones at each other and yelling back and forth when the fiery rain of additional stones arrived at the bottom of the shaft.

"We're rich! Richer than Croesus!" yelled Matt.

"Richer than TK Parker!" Stevie yelled back.

"Richer than the entire Council of billionaires!"

It took the impact of several, still glowing gemstones to penetrate their euphoria. A particularly sizable, red hot diamond bounced off Hitch's banded cuirass.

"What the hell was that?" he asked as more glowing gems rained down around the pair.

"It's raining hot rocks!" exclaimed Matt, looking up the shaft for the source of the incoming objects.

"Can you see where they're coming from, Bro?"

"Somewhere up the shaft... aw shit! That looked like tracer fire."

Twenty meters above them several bursts of green fire flew upward in reply to the glowing rain of gemstones. Both men drew their railguns and moved back to stand against the metal walls. Euphoria over finding the treasure evaporated as they found themselves trapped at the bottom of the shaft with no cover.

* * * * *

"Oooow!" yelled Gx!pk, pulling back from the edge as several small objects sparked and ricocheted off the tunnel's ceiling. Kq*zt didn't notice the angry red pock marks that marred his friend's backside.

"What's wrong?" Kq*zt asked, leaning out from the ledge to look down the shaft. He jerked back as a burst of solid 15mm projectiles stitch a line of red splotches up his featureless black outer covering.

### Shuttle One

The officers on both the Peggy Sue and the shuttle were distracted by activity in the large cavern, which seemed the more perilous situation.

"Peggy Sue, are you seeing this?" asked Bobby, watching the slow movement of the boulders toward the three Marines.

"Roger that, Shuttle One. Has Drainpipe Two made contact with the others?"

"Negative. Drainpipe Two has eyes on them but has not made physical contact with Drainpipe One yet."

"Shuttle One, Drainpipe Two. We have hostile contact. Shots exchanged!"

"Drainpipe Two, say again your last."

"I said we have engaged hostiles who fired on Drainpipe One. The hostiles didn't know we were here and just opened up on Hitch and Jacobs. I'm pretty sure we hit a couple of them."

*Fan-fucking-tastic*, Bobby cursed silently, *it's like a contest to see who can start a war first.*

"Give me a sitrep, any casualties on our side?"

"Shuttle One, Drainpipe One. Stevie and me are OK. They shot red hot crystals at us but they bounced off our armor."

"Good to finally hear from you, Drainpipe One. Why have you been off the comm net for so long?"

Pause.

"Er, we sort of made a discovery, Sir, and in the excitement we forgot to call in."

"Your telemetry went dead as well."

"We sent our mini-bots down the shaft and forgot to set relays when we started down the shaft too. Sorry, Sir. We didn't realize we were out of telemetry range."

"Drainpipe One, you are to rendezvouses with Drainpipe Two at their current position and then proceed back the way you came. I want all four of you back on the surface ASAP. Do you read me?"

"Copy that, Shuttle One. We are on our way."

"Bobby," Mizuki said with urgency in her voice, "I think the Gunny is in trouble."

On the middle monitor, the crowd of boulders surrounding Rosy and her Marines became very agitated. Radio frequency static became so intense the shuttle could not talk to Drainpipe Leader. Then that telemetry feed went dead.

"Shuttle One, Peggy Sue. Interrogative, WTFO?"

## Chapter 15

### CIC, Peggy Sue

All idle conversion ceased in the CIC. Those present had relaxed a bit when the Marines of Drainpipe Two reestablished contact with Drainpipe One. Drainpipe Leader was surrounded but not cutoff from retreating back the way they came. Then came word of an attack by parties unknown and an ensuing firefight; then another communication's failure. Now, Billy Ray and Beth were nervously scanning the darkened displays from Drainpipe Leader for any sign of what was happening to them.

"This keeps goin' from bad to worse," Billy Ray muttered.

"I should say so," replied Beth. "If nothing else, this shows that we don't have nearly enough Marines on board."

"No argument there, next trip we're takin' at least a dozen. But that doesn't fix our current tactical muddle. There were more of those moving boulder things in that chamber than mites on a chicken's butt."

"I've no point of comparison for that, Captain, but our people did seem rather outnumbered," Beth said dryly. "Plus, as you said, the hostiles appeared to be rocks."

"Telemetry readings indicate that the aliens are composed primarily of silicon, Commander," The voice of the ship's computer confirmed Beth's assessment. "They have a well masked but significant internal heat signature. If the readings are accurate, I suspect they are molten inside."

"Yer saying the natives are living blobs of lava?" Billy Ray asked the ship's not quite sentient computer.

"Since they seem to communicate using radio frequency EM radiation and act in cooperative ways, sentience of some form is indicated. This would require a more complex internal structure than just blobs of lava—but your overall description seems accurate enough, Captain."

"How are the Marines supposed to fight mobile lava filled boulders?" Beth asked.

"I don't know, but we need to come up with something soon." Billy Ray grimaced and keyed the comm link to the shuttle. "Shuttle One, Peggy Sue. You got a next course of action, pardner?"

* * * * *

Billy Ray's voice on the radio failed to snap Bobby out of the mental paralysis that gripped him. His mind raced with competing thoughts: *What can I do now? Should I pull out those that I can? The other Marines are almost two hours from relieving the Gunny if they head back to the surface now. Hell, we're an hour away if we head down the tunnel ourselves.*

Mizuki's soft voice worked where the Captain's had failed.

"Bobby, did the Marines at the shaft say they shot the aliens that attacked them?"

"What? Uh, yeah. Kato said they hit at least one of the hostiles, why?"

"And did other rounds ricochet off the metal walls surrounding the attackers?"

"I would assume so, let's ask them." Bobby didn't know where this was leading but he had learned to trust Mizuki when she started working a problem, particularly if it included physics. "Drainpipe Two, Shuttle One. Interrogative, were there ricocheted rounds in the vicinity of the hostiles?"

"Shuttle One, that's affirmative. We could see the sparks from here."

Mizuki smiled. "I heard Rosey say that they were going to use depleted uranium rounds in their weapons for this mission. When using DU rounds, the uranium in them can vaporize if they strike an armored vehicle—or metal tunnel walls. This produces fine dusts of uranium and uranium compounds."

"And?" Bobby asked.

"And so the aliens are now coated with radioactive dust."

It took a couple of seconds for the implications of Mizuki's revelation to sink in but Bobby was starting to see the light.

"And?" he said again, this time with a smile on his face.

"The sensors in the Marines' suits and mini-bots should be able to track the aliens through the tunnels, following the radioactivity of the uranium."

"Drainpipe One and Two are down almost as deep as the chamber Drainpipe Leader was located in. If the aliens were scouts, and other aliens are occupied surrounding the Gunny's squad, the scouts would want to get back to the main body to report their run-in at the shaft."

Mizuki nodded encouragingly.

"So if One and Two follow the alien scouts they could lead them to the large chamber."

"It is not a sure thing, but I think the probability is better than fifty-fifty."

"Let's see if they can pick up a trail before we bounce this off the Captain." Indecision swept away, Bobby sprung into action. "Drainpipe One and Two, Shuttle One. Listen closely..."

* * * * *

"You want to send Drainpipe One and Two in pursuit of Drainpipe Leader by having them follow the aliens they shot at?"

"Affirmative, Peggy Sue. We have verified that they can pick up the aliens' trail from the radiation caused by the DU rounds. If they can find the other Marines we can save several hours."

"Roger, Shuttle One. And you think the chance the aliens will lead to the others is good?"

"Roger that, they are down about as deep as the big chamber already and within a kilometer or so of where we last had contact with Drainpipe Leader. We can use inertial tracking and spatial positioning to make sure they aren't going off on a wild goose chase. If it doesn't look like this will pan out we can have them come back to the surface as we originally planned."

There was a pause as the Captain and First Officer conversed back on the ship.

"Shuttle One, we concur with your plan. Go ahead and have One and Two follow the aliens. But tell them they are to reverse course and come to the surface if they lose radio contact."

185

"Roger, Peggy Sue. We will have them go chase the boulders."

### Large Chamber, Metal Moon

"What are they doing, Gunny?" asked a nervous Vinny DeSilva. Scores of boulders seemed to be jostling for position, attempting to edge closer to the three Marines.

"Don't know. But that one seems to be in charge. It's transmitting a whole bunch of RF gobbledygook."

"Can't the Peggy Sue's computer make anything understandable out of it?" asked Umky. Like the other Marines, he was wondering how many rounds of 15mm DU it would take to kill a boulder.

"Something cut the telemetry to the surface again, so the computer can't help us and our suit translators ain't quite up to the job."

Everyone, Earthling and lava creature alike, was startled when a recon drone popped out of the tunnel so recently exited by the Marines. It slowed to a hover and spun around, getting a full scan of the chamber.

"Hey, that's not clown bot two," DeSilva exclaimed. "IFF says it's clown bot three."

Rosey only glanced at the drone, keeping her eyes on the moving boulder creatures. "Looks like it managed to make it down here from the surface before the telemetry link got cut."

"I wonder what chased the clown bot out of the tunnel?" DeSilva asked.

"Probably another one of these mobile boulders," the Gunny replied. "Probably why we lost comm, too. Tell the clown bot to chill out and maintain station, DeSilva."

"Aye, aye, Gunny."

\* \* \* \* \*

"Look! Another one of the little spherical aliens," remarked Kq*zt, as he and Gx!pk entered the chamber from a side tunnel.

Both were moving a bit tentatively, still smarting from the rounds taken from the Marines' return fire.

"Yeah, and more of the big, oddly shaped aliens like the ones that pelted us with food."

"What? Who pelted you with what food?" asked Qz@px, his attention drawn away from the aliens by the boisterous arrival of the two scouts.

"We found a couple of big aliens, like those over there, at the latrine nearby. You won't believe what they were doing."

"Gx!pk just couldn't help himself, he had to go so he sort of took a dump on the aliens."

"That's because they were at the bottom of the privy playing with poo! I figured that if they liked it so much they wouldn't mind a bit of fresh."

"You defecated on the aliens?" asked the dumbfounded Qz@px.

"They were throwing it at each other," said Gx!pk defensively.

"And what's this about them throwing food at you?"

"Well I was sticking half off the platform when something hit me —hard. I mean it stung like getting hit by a small asteroid."

"There were several other aliens on the next lower platform we hadn't noticed," Kq*zt explained, "they were the ones who hit us with the food."

"You got hit too?"

"Yes, when Gx!pk began bouncing around and moaning I looked over the edge. I got hit by six or seven pellets myself."

"And you say these pellets were made of food? What type of food?"

"Mostly U-238."

"The aliens gave you U-238? For free?"

"I don't think 'give' is the right word, Qz@px. They threw it at us really hard," sniffed Gx!pk.

"It did sting a lot," his friend agreed. "I think the food pellets came out of the long things they are holding with their appendages."

All the lava creatures present looked more closely at the three aliens huddled around the tunnel entrance at the top of the chamber. They had never heard of such a thing, pelting people with food pellets so hard they stung!

"Those things they are holding must be some form of weapon," Qz@px mused, "but why would they throw food? These aliens are the strangest creatures I have ever heard of."

* * * * *

In the tunnel recently vacated by the wounded aliens, the two Marines and two sailors of the putative rescue party carefully crept closer to the chamber. Since the aliens seemed to communicate using radio signals, all four Earthlings were linked by thin strands of fiber optic cable, allowing them to maintain radio silence.

Sergeant Kwan was on point. He had assumed the leadership of the combined Drainpipe units and was now using Drainpipe One as his call sign. When he noticed a dim glow from the tunnel ahead, Kato held up a fist to signal those following to stop. Over the secured comm link he spoke to his fellows in a hushed voice.

"Look like there is light in the chamber ahead. I don't want to send my mini-bot forward, the aliens might notice."

"Why are you whispering? We're inside space suits in a vacuum, talking over optical fiber," observed Hitch.

"Force of habit," Kato confessed.

"Why not use a camera snake?" suggested Bosco. A camera snake was a lens mounted on a flexible length of black-clad glass fiber. It was used to snoop around corners without exposing its owner to enemy observation or, more importantly, weapons fire.

"I'm already working a snake forward. I'll patch the signal to you over the optic link." The men were quiet as Kato wrestled the tip of the snake to the edge of the tunnel opening where its hemispherical lens could capture the entire chamber. Software in their suits allowed each to select a point of view, removing the distortion of the half-ball lens.

188

"Look! There's the Gunny and the rest, over by that tunnel."

"Yeah, and there's a clown bot too." added Jacobs. He was bringing up the tail end of the four man formation and was happy to finally see what was going on at the front.

"Man, there's a shitpot of those boulder creatures in there," observed Hitch, "just look at 'em all!"

"Yeah, and it looks like the boulder creatures have the others surrounded." Kato fiddled with the comm hookup until he could call the outside world, passing the signal back through the fiber cables and then the chain of relays. "Shuttle One, Drainpipe One, over."

"Go Drainpipe One." The voice was Cmdr. Danner's.

"We have eyes on Drainpipe Leader. They are pinned down next to a tunnel opening at the upper end of the large chamber. They all appear to be unharmed. There is a recon drone with them as well."

"Roger. What is your position with respect to the others?"

"We are in a side tunnel about one third of the way down the chamber wall, maybe 90 meters from the others. We are observing the chamber using a fiber-optic probe to avoid being seen by the creatures. I am patching the video feed through to you now."

"Roger that, Drainpipe. Wait one."


### Shuttle One

Bobby and Mizuki stared at the scene from the boulder filled chamber, kilometers below the surface of the moon. The motile rock creatures hemmed the Gunny's party in on all sides, though they were keeping their distance, particularly from Umky.

"I don't see how the three trapped in the chamber can make it to the tunnel where Drainpipe One is hiding, do you Mizuki?"

"There are so many of the creatures, I do not think the Marines could all cross the chamber to the other tunnel without being intercepted. Peggy Sue says the creatures are probably molten inside?"

"Yeah, moving blobs of lava with a hard rock cover—I wonder how much they weigh?"

"A one meter boulder would mass approximately 10,000 kilograms," Mizuki replied, doing a quick calculation in her head.

"Ten tons? And that's for the small ones! The Marines' armor is tough but I don't think they want to try dodging a living landslide."

"I would be more concerned about being enveloped by the molten rock inside of the creatures. From the sensor data it looks like the recon drone we lost was surrounded by lava and melted."

"Let's see if the Captain or Beth have any ideas. Peggy Sue, Shuttle one, over."

"Go, Shuttle One," came the immediate reply.

"We've found our missing Marines, but the situation is still precarious. Our people are surrounded by moving, multiton boulders. We think their way out is blocked and there is little hope of them making it to the tunnel Drainpipe One is hiding in without getting mobbed by the lava creatures. If you have any ideas, we'd love to hear them."

"We understand. Beth and I have been looking at the tactical displays and haven't come up with anything ourselves."

"Roger that, Peggy Sue."

"The only possible bright spot is that the computer is making progress decoding the creatures' speech. It looks like they use a kind of spread spectrum RF to talk and microwaves to see with, based on readings from the encounter at the gem pit."

"Can we communicate with them?"

"That's still a negative, Shuttle One. We need more sample signals and the ability to interact with the creatures so we can more quickly nail down the translation algorithm."

"Roger, Peggy Sue. Wait one." Bobby muted the comm. "Mizuki, I have an idea."

"Yes, Bobby?" She gazed at him, her eyes wide, a serious look on her face.

"Somebody needs to go down to reestablish broadband communication to the computer and try to talk with the boulder creatures."

"But that will take an hour or more."

"Not with what I have in mind."

"So we are going to go and rescue the Marines?"

Bobby looked into his beloved's eyes and realized that there was no way he could make Mizuki stay behind if he was going to go in harm's way. In fact, telling her he was going to go alone might be more dangerous than facing the lava creatures themselves. Surrendering to inevitability, he smiled and said, "Let me tell you what I have in mind."

### CIC, *Peggy Sue*

"You want to do what?" demanded the Captain.

"Mizuki and I are going to take one of the hover sleds down the tunnel that Drainpipe Leader went down, until we make contact."

"Is he daft? We already have most of our expeditionary force trapped inside that metal rabbit warren," Beth hissed at her husband.

Billy Ray held up his hand, forestalling further commentary, and said, "Let's hear him out."

"Tell us what you have in mind, Shuttle One."

"Roger. I went over the telemetry from the two drones and Drainpipe Leader's descent into the central tunnel. It is big enough for a hover sled all the way to the chamber. I figure we can reach the chamber in about eight minutes."

"Why do I have visions of you smeared all over the tunnel wall, pardner?"

"Naw, it's all good. I ran simulations on the flight deck computer three times. We just use the sled's attitude to keep its bottom repulsors in opposition to the G forces. It'll be just like a theme park ride. In fact, the sled could probably make the run on its own. Let me send you the simulation runs."

"Roger, Shuttle One. Receiving now."

Beth and Billy Ray fell silent as they watched the computer simulation of the proposed descent on the CIC monitors. Beth shook her head and marveled.

"He's insane, totally barking mad."

"Well, darlin', if it was anyone but Bobby I would have my doubts, but he is the best pilot I've ever known."

"Why is he taking Mizuki with him?"

"Do you honestly think she would let him go on a dangerous mission without her? Hell, he's the less adventurous of the two."

"I just don't want to lose half our crew and our two best friends down some alien death trap."

"Right." Billy Ray took the comm off mute. "Shuttle One. Tell me again why it has to be you two who make this little foray?"

"Peggy Sue, I am the only one qualified to fly the sled, particularly in tight quarters. And Mizuki and I are the only experienced, combat trained personnel left down here. Captain, I sent them into that maze; I have to try and get them back out."

Muting the comm the Captain turned to his First Officer. "Well, he's not wrong about that. You know if our positions were reversed we'd try something to get our people back."

"Something not quite this dangerous, I should hope," said Beth, resignation in her voice. "At this point I don't think we could stop them anyway."

Billy Ray nodded.

"Shuttle One, Peggy Sue. Yer a go on this sled thing. Do not make me regret it, pardner."

"Roger that, Peggy Sue. We'll be careful."

"In a pig's eye," Beth said under her breath.

### *Surface, Metal Moon*

It took only a few minutes for Mizuki and Bobby to don their suits of standard armor and unship the hover sled. The sled was a simple open platform with low sides and repulsors mounted on its bottom, enabling it to fly over rough terrain. Other repulsors were mounted fore and aft and along the sides to allow maneuvering in tight quarters.

On the back of the sled, Taylor and Wilson, the two sailors who rounded out the shuttle's crew, mounted a hatbox shaped container that held within it a coil of thin wire, similar to the guidance wire on naval torpedoes. The idea was that the wire would provide a harder to detect, and hence less likely to be disrupted, communications channel back to the surface.

"You're good to go, Mr. Danner," reported Tamara Wilson. "Are you sure you don't want us to go with you, Sir?"

"We've been over that," Bobby replied. "I want you two on the shuttle's flight deck ready to provide covering fire if we come back out hot. Or to get the shuttle out of here if we screw the pooch. We still have a couple of science section types on board and they didn't really sign up to fight lava filled boulders inside a metal termite mound."

"Aye, aye, Sir."

"So you two are clear on your orders? Wait for us to come back to the surface as long as we remain in contact. If you lose comm head back to the Peggy Sue to regroup."

"Aye, Commander, she'll be right," said Jay Taylor, "it's a box of birds."

"A box of what?" asked Mizuki.

"Sorry, Ma'am, my gran was a Kiwi and that was one of her sayings. It means it's all good."

"Ah," Mizuki replied with a smile. "We used to have an Australian pilot named Sandy, and she had all sorts of colorful sayings."

"Yeah," added Bobby, "but she did it on purpose to mess with us Yanks, at least until everyone on board was speaking in Aussie slang. Damn good pilot though. All right, Dr. Ogawa, your carriage awaits."

Bobby followed Mizuki onto the floating sled and worked his way to the front. Once they were both aboard they laid down on the floor of the open conveyance, hoping for some minimal protection from the sled's low sides.

"Peggy Sue, Slider is ready to depart."

"Roger, Slider. God speed.

As the two sailors reboarded the shuttle, Tamara spoke to Jay on suit-to-suit. "I hope nothing bad happens to them, or the others."

"Too right, Tamara. God help 'em if they get into an argy-bargy with a bunch of rocks."

# Chapter 16

## *Slider Descending*

The tunnel raced toward them like a bobsled run covered in black ice. Bobby's gloved hands rested lightly on the sled's controls, only occasionally making a correction, letting the guidance program he had downloaded into their transport's autopilot do most of the work. Mizuki was snatching occasional peeks over Bobby's horizontal form, mostly keeping her head down as the speeding sled twisted its way deeper into the metal moon.

"I told you this would work, Mizuki-chan. We are making close to a hundred kilometers an hour."

"Great, Bobby. Just don't run into anything."

"I'm trying not to, sweetheart."

The sled rolled right, then left and then right again, as Bobby kept the skittish craft's bottom repulsors in opposition to the G forces caused by the turns. The forces came on suddenly, rapidly building to three or four Earth gravities and then just as suddenly dropping back to zero. Another sequence of turns threw the sled into a corkscrew eliciting a protest from Mizuki.

"*Teishi! Watashi wa byōki ni nari-sōda.*"

As the racing craft entered another welcome straight stretch Bobby replied, "what was that?"

"I said I'm going to throw up if this keeps up much longer."

"Sorry, I'll throttle back a bit, but I can't change the shape of the tunnel."

Mizuki's response was a muffled whimper. She was not overly susceptible to motion-sickness but this was like a carnival ride gone amok. Being thrown from side to side by the cornering forces was not as bad as the transitions to and from zero G. Making matters worse, there was no point of reference, no horizon in the dark tunnel to fix on. Mizuki swallowed hard and squeezed her eyes shut.

None of this bothered Bobby a bit—he was in his element flying a wildly gyrating craft right up to the edge of controllability. If

Mizuki had not complained he would have gone even faster. As it was, his face muscles were starting to hurt from grinning so widely.

"Slider, Peggy Sue. You don't need to set any speed records to impress us, pardner." Billy Ray, who had known Bobby for years and had shared the helm of the Peggy Sue with him in many tense situations, knew his friend's love of speed and inability to resist flying like a madman.

"Just pushing the envelope a bit, Peggy Sue."

"The problem with pushing the envelope is that sometimes the envelope pushes back. Remember we got nobody to come scrape you off the tunnel wall if you discover the limit by steppin' over it."

"Roger that, we are almost to the chamber anyway."

The sled rolled sharply to starboard and then leveled out, headed for the tunnel's end fifty meters ahead. It took Bobby a fraction of a second to interpret the view forward on his helmet's display. LIDAR readings showed that there was something blocking the tunnel, just shy of the large chamber that was their destination.

"Aw shit!" Bobby said under his breath before shouting to Mizuki over suit-to-suit. "Hang on to something, we're going to hit!"

Bobby threw the sled into full reverse, but this type of utility craft was not intended for use in zero G and not known for its braking capability under any circumstances. Their forward velocity dropped to thirty kilometers per hour prior to impact and the forward facing repulsors helped cushion the blow, but Newton's Laws cannot be denied.


### *Arrival, The Chamber*

A boulder creature over a meter in diameter came flying out of the tunnel, careening into another who was hanging in space fifteen meters from the Gunny and her companions. This set off a chain reaction as the initial boulder veered off to the right and the boulder it struck flew to the left. Both collided with more of their kind, initiating a wave of contact that rippled outward, spreading toward the far end of the chamber.

"This is like three dimensional lawn bowling," said Rosey, as the Marines looked on helplessly.

Closely following the living boulder out of the tunnel was the speeding sled. Having struck the boulder a bit low and off center, the sled toppled forward as it emerged, its nose dropping down while flinging Mizuki and Bobby from their mount.

"Jump, Mizuki!" Bobby cried, but she was already airborne, flying toward the gathering of boulders. Bobby himself did a slow tumble, turning head over heels on a collision course with the head alien.

"Those officers must be batshit crazy to ride a hover sled down that tunnel," Vinny marveled.

"If Hitch and Jacobs had done it, it would be crazy," said the Gunny, "Since those two officers did it, it must be a clever tactical maneuver."

"Speaking of the Navy's two trouble magnets," rumbled Umky, pointing across the chamber with the barrel of his railgun, "it looks like Kato and Bosco found them and brought them to the party."

Rosy glanced in the direction indicated in time to see the last of four armored humans emerge from a side tunnel into the chamber. Their appearance added to the confusion among the ranks of boulders as the creatures shied away from the new arrivals. Meanwhile, Misuki had drawn her katana and was about to collide with a large boulder.

"She ain't gonna attack that rock with a sword, is she?"

Mizuki tucked and tumbled forward while waving the katana in a complex pattern. This altered her attitude so that she landed feet first on the boulder. The boulder, out massing the scientist a hundred fold, was barely moved. Kicking off, the sword wielding physicist reversed course and headed back for the Marines deployed around the tunnel opening the sled had just entered from.

"Dr. Ogawa is one of the smartest humans around, DeSilva. She's using the sword like a tightrope walker uses a pole, for balance."

"You're right, Umky," added the Gunny, as Mizuki landed with a particularly theatrical sweep of her katana.

"I think the jury is still out on Cmdr. Danner," DeSilva retorted.

Bobby continued his slow somersaulting trajectory until he collided face first with the lead boulder. Bobby rebounded and slowly drifted backwards, opening a gap between himself and the lava creature. The collision stopped his rotation and allowed him to come to a halt using his suit's repulsors.

"We come in peace," Bobby broadcast using the computer's best attempt at translation. While trying to communicate, he smiled and held both hands up, palms outward.

\* \* \* \* \*

"What are these insane aliens trying to do?" Asked one of the elder lava creatures. Others were busy apologizing to each other and trying to sort out the spontaneous reordering caused by the new arrivals to the chamber.

"Hey," exclaimed Gx!pk, "there are the poo jugglers!"

"And the two who pelted us with uranium!" added Kq*zt.

"You think if I jumped around a bit the aliens would throw food at me?" asked Zz#tx, peering intently at the four oddly shaped aliens. "These are a lot bigger than the one I ate."

This caused a ripple of conversation among those nearby, followed by a tentative advance on the aliens. In response the aliens raised the devices that Qz@px had called 'weapons'.

"Everyone just stop!" yelled Qz@px. "Let's not do anything spectacularly stupid until we can find out what these creatures want!"

\* \* \* \* \*

"OK people, let's not do anything spectacularly stupid until I can establish a rapport with the head boulder here," said Bobby over the squad frequency.

The large alien floating in space in front of Bobby shuddered, waves traveling across the surface of its body. Rhythmic pulsations deformed the alien's dark exterior, sending a web of cracks spreading across its skin. Showing through the cracks was the hot red-orange glow of molten rock.

The alien's entire body deformed as two protuberances formed. One to either side, separated by an angle of around 120 degrees. As Bobby watched spellbound, they grew longer and thinner.

"What's that thing doing, Commander," asked a nervous Gunny, fingering the trigger guard on her railgun. Mizuki, who had landed gracefully on the chamber wall next to Umky, resheathed her katana.

"I do not think it is menacing Cmdr. Danner, Gunny, I think it is mimicking his movements," the always observant Mizuki answered. "Bobby, it looks like the creature is trying to imitate your arm gestures."

"I think you're right, Mizuki," he replied. "Everyone maintain position and don't make any threatening moves or gestures."

"How do you threaten a rock, Sir?" asked Hitch from his position on the side of the chamber.

"Don't point your weapons at them for a starter. You already shot a couple of them." All the while Bobby was smiling for all he was worth and waving his open hands back and forth in what he sincerely hoped was a friendly manner. As he watched, the big alien's new "arms" grew fingers and waved back clumsily.

* * * * *

"I think these creatures are trying to communicate with us," Qz@px announced to his fellows. "Everyone be quiet while I try to talk to them."

"Ask them if they have more food," said Zz#tx. He was immediately hushed by others around him.

"Welcome to our home, visitor," Qz@px said to the alien.

"We... come... gently," came the broken reply. Every lava creature in the chamber stopped talking and focused on the odd creature making silly gestures at Qz@px.

### CIC, Peggy Sue

Doc White and most of the members of the science staff joined the Captain and First Officer in the CIC. They came to witness the voyage's historic first contact with an alien species. Other species had been encountered in the past and some were actually friendly, or at least not homicidal, but this was the first time for the Orion Arm Trading Company.

It was also the first discovery of a non-carbon based lifeform. True, creatures from Earth had encountered non-carbon life before, but they never actually met them, unless you count exchanging gravitonic torpedoes and particle cannon blasts as a form of introduction.

"Well I'll be," marveled Will Krenshaw. "Some of my colleagues used to speculate about silicon based life forms but none of them ever dreamed up mobile, intelligent, lava filled rocks."

"I guess that nature is just more inventive than us humans," said Doc White. The fancy holographic displays of the CIC had lured her out of her domain in the medical section.

"Speaking for us polar bears," added Ahnah, "we never came up with anything like this either."

"I always fought to preserve life—the plants and animals—now it looks like I need to consider the rocks as well," said Joe Rogers, the climate scientist.

"There are more things in heaven and earth, Dr. Rogers, than are dreamt of in your philosophy," Billy Ray recited.

"I just knew you'd work a Shakespeare quotation into the conversation somewhere," Beth said, giving her husband a sideways look.

Ignoring his significant other, Billy Ray addressed the computer: "Peggy Sue, how is the translation algorithm coming?"

"We are making great progress, Captain. Another hour or two and we should be able to converse with the lava creatures with little fear of being misunderstood. Commander Danner is quite adept at pantomime."

"He is a man of many talents, our Sailing Master."

"Yes, dear. Let's listen to what he and the head boulder are talking about..."

### The Chamber

"I am now capable of translating most ordinary conversation with the lava creatures, Cmdr. Danner," Peggy Sue's computer informed Bobby. "As usual, I will automatically translate units of time and distance into familiar terms. Also note that the creature's names are basically untranslatable so I am given them letter designations—the senior alien you are talking to will be called 'Q'."

"Thanks, Peggy Sue. I'll attempt some diplomatic small talk with Q here." Bobby loaded the software changes the computer had sent for his suit's radio, hopefully making his local transmissions sound like one of the sentient boulders. "Greetings, Q. I am Bobby Danner, leader of this small party of creatures from the planet Earth."

There was a short pause while Qz@px mulled that over. Finally he replied. "Welcome Bobby Danner of earth. I greet you on behalf of the people of the moon metal."

"I think that was too literal a translation in both directions, Peggy Sue," Bobby told the computer, before returning to the conversation with the alien leader. "We have come to this system on a voyage of exploration, looking for new worlds and new friends among the stars."

"These worlds are all fairly old, I am afraid," came the reply.

*Again with the literal translation,* Bobby sighed. "When I said new worlds I should have said worlds we had not known about previously."

"I see. Do you often say one thing when you actually mean something else?"

"I apologize. It was a figure of speech, which our translation algorithm handled poorly. As things progress my words should be translated more accurately."

"Apology accepted, Bobby Danner. Now that you have seen our world, why would we want to be friends with you? In the past, we have never had any friends other than our own kind, and that has seemed quite sufficient."

"We have voyaged from our home system seeking other forms of life, with trade our primary interest. We wish to explore the

Doug L. Hoffman

exchange of ideas and technology, though we would also like to form a coalition of species—an association for mutual aid and protection."

"I see. Is the largest member of your group from a different species?" Qz@px was obviously referring to Umky, who towered over the humans.

"Yes, that is Umky. He is of a different species than the rest of us, but his kind and ours come from the same world."

"More than one form of life from a single world? That is interesting. There are no others on the metal moon but our kind. Tell me, why did you pelt several of us with food?"

"I believe that was just a misunderstanding, Q. Several of our people were down in a pit filled with gemstones when a pair of your folks threw a shower of red hot stones on top of them. Our people thought they were under attack and responded with the, er, shower of food. If you thought we were trying to steal your gemstones we apologize."

There was a pause in the translation while the room erupted in a symphony of pink noise.

"What's happening, Peggy Sue? Did I say something wrong?"

"I'm not sure, Commander. The noise transmissions seem to be the local equivalent of laughter."

\* \* \* \* \*

As the leaders on both sides carried out more weighty discussions, the constantly improving translation algorithm was distributed to the other Earthlings' suit computers. This allowed them to talk with the lava creatures around them. Naturally, Gx!pk and Kq*zt sidled up to the four members of Drainpipe One, who happened to be close by.

"Hi! I'm G and this is my friend K. We were at the latrine when you threw food at us," said Gx!pk without preamble. The lava creatures were on a whole plain spoken and to the point.

"Wow, G and K. This is like Men In Black or something," Hitch said to the other humans, causing the Marines to shush him and Jacobs to give him a swat.

202

"Er, hi there G. I'm Kato and these are my friends: Bosco, Steve and Matt. Did you say 'latrine'?"

"Hey," said Kq*zt, "You two are the ones on the ledge, the ones who shot us with the uranium!"

"Uh, no hard feelings," stammered Kato, "we thought you were trying to hurt our friends, Steve and Matt."

"Yeah, those are the two who were in the bottom of the middens, playing with the poo," Gx!pk said, recognizing Jacobs and Hitch from the previous encounter.

"Why did you throw food at us?" asked a puzzled Kq*zt. "And why were two of you messing around at the bottom of a latrine?"

"Is that word getting translated wrong?" Hitch asked the other Earthlings. "It's like he keeps calling the gem pit a 'latrine'."

"You see, G and K, we two," Kato began, motioning to himself and Bosco, "are Marines. We protect the other explorers from our crew."

"Yes," said Bosco, "Matt and Stevie are sailors, so we have to take care of them."

"OK," Gx!pk replied. "You two protect the others, what do 'sailors' do?"

"They help run our ship," Kato explained. "And when we are in port they move things on and off the ship: cargo, supplies and such."

"Right," added Kq*zt, "so these two are poo haulers."

"What!" Jacobs and Hitch exclaimed in unison.

The Marines literally laughed so hard they cried. It was several minutes before Kato and Bosco recovered enough to continue the conversation with the puzzled lava creatures.

* * * * *

Eventually, the wrinkles in communication were smoothed out and Earthlings' *faux pas* regarding the gem pit was corrected. The crew of the Peggy Sue spent four more days getting to know their new found friends, the lava creatures. An understanding was reached with the inhabitants of the metal moon and promises were made regarding future visits by ships of the Orion Arm Trading Company. Finally, with everyone secure on board the shuttle, preparations were complete to return to the Peggy Sue.

When the Earthlings departed the metal moon, Gx!pk and Kq*zt were on the surface to bid them farewell. Both had morphed into large humanoid doll shapes, like basalt Pillsbury Doughboys. In their blob like heads openings formed—two eyes and a mouth, glowing bright red-orange from the living lava within.

Hitch and Jacobs were at one of the shuttle's viewports, getting a last look at the little world that definitely had been more than they expected.

"Look at that, Matt. G and K came to say good bye."

"Yeah, Stevie. They look like a pair of jack-o'-lanterns."

"You know, I think I'm actually going to miss them."

## Chapter 17

### *Main Lounge, Peggy Sue*

The shuttle had returned, its crew and cargo of scientific samples safely secured aboard the Peggy Sue. In the main lounge, the Captain and First Officer were sitting at the big table in front of the large viewport. They were enjoying a well deserved drink, in celebration of a job well done, when Bobby and Mizuki came into the lounge.

"It looks like we are just in time," said Bobby, as the couple approached the table, "before these two drink the bar out of the good stuff."

"Pull up a chair, pardner, and have a little Chateau de Gobbler on me," replied Billy Ray, raising a glass with a half inch of amber fluid sloshing about its bottom.

"Beth, I can't believe you are drinking whiskey," added Mizuki, taking a seat at the table. Beth's usual was a hard to find gin named Hendrick's that was infused with the essence of roses and cucumber.

"Yes, the Captain prevailed on me to join him in a traditional toast to a successful enterprise. According to him, this requires a proper spirit—like straight Kentucky bourbon—not a 'foreign' inebriant such as gin."

Billy Ray waved to Jimmy Tosh, who was behind the bar. "Bring a couple more whiskey glasses and a bottle of 101, if you please Mr. Tosh."

"I comin' right over, Captain," the Jamaican barkeep replied, assembling the required supplies. Bobby could not resist teasing his friend about his drinking preferences.

"Ah yes, a taste of the Kickin' Chicken, the Dirty Bird. The only way to celebrate!"

Though a well respected potable, Wild Turkey was not considered a particularly upper class drink. It was, however, fabled in literature, music and film as the drink of the working man.

"How can you disparage Jimmy Russell's masterpiece? It's been described as a big bodacious bourbon; complex, languorous, rich, elegant and powerful; the Clint Eastwood of whiskeys."

"How many of those has he had, Beth?" asked Bobby. "He's starting to wax poetic about booze."

Beth raised a single eyebrow and shook her head slowly. Jimmy sat two squat glasses on the table and poured several fingers worth of golden liquid into each. Mizuki sniffed at her's tentatively.

"It smells of honeysuckle and old leather," she said looking at the Captain, raised brows bespeaking more than a modicum of doubt.

"Don't let it lull you into a false sense of security, Mizuki," Beth cautioned. "It starts out with sweet berries and vanilla overtones but quickly moves to a peppery wallop."

Jimmy looked at the Captain, who nodded, signaling him to refill Beth's glass and his own.

"Go ahead and pour one for yourself, Mr. Tosh, we are celebrating a number of firsts. Our first new species, our first new allies, our first successful trade."

"Thank you, no, Captain. I a Rastafarian, and we only partake of natural things. Alcohol is a fermented chemical that does not belong in de temple of I body. Better to smoke the holy herb marijuana, which is natural, opens de mind and assists in reasoning."

"Well, it's yer loss, Jimmy. Just leave the bottle."

"Right, Captain. Just signal if you need more." The Rastaman departed with a big smile on his face. As far as he was concerned, a happy Captain meant a happy ship.

Mizuki hazarded a sip. The whiskey's complex bouquet exploded on her tongue as the smokey liquid burned its way down her throat. Not accustom to drinking whiskey neat, Mizuki's eyes began to water—she tended more to fruity drinks adorned with little paper parasols. Blinking, she sat the glass back on the table and gasped.

"Smooth."

This remark caused Bobby to snort, sending some of the 101 proof liquid fire up his nose. The Sailing Master coughed while the others laughed.

"Watch it, Bobby. Yer feelin' that Wild Turkey's bite."

206

"Right," Bobby croaked.

"Now that wasn't a quote from Shakespeare."

"No Ma'am. That would be ZZ Top's *Arrested For Drivin' While Blind*." Billy Ray leaned back contentedly and took another sip of his whiskey.

"I didn't think you liked country music, Billy Ray," said Mizuki, now recovered from her first sip and cautiously attempting a second.

"I wouldn't call ZZ Top 'country' but they are from Texas. In fact, that song is off their fifth album, *Tejas*." Billy Ray's taste in music tended more toward progressive rock than blues or rock & roll. Oddly, it was Beth, a Londoner of Ethiopian extraction, who liked country music, particularly the older stuff by Merle Haggard, Buck Owens, Charlie Pride and Willie Nelson.

"So what's the final analysis of our new rocky friends, Mizuki?"

"According to Ahnah and Will, with some help from Sami, the lava creatures are a true silicon based life form. Exactly what their internal structure is like, what functions as genetic material or even how they move is a total mystery. We do know that they feed by melting their way through the moon itself."

"That must be where all those passageways came from."

"Correct, Bobby. They melt and absorb the material, incorporating some elements into their bodies while storing and eventually excreting others."

"That would be the source of Hitch and Jacobs' mother load of gemstones."

The men suppressed chuckles; Beth rolled her eyes as Mizuki continued.

"Yes, their gem pit was, indeed, the lava creatures' latrine."

"You know, we should find a better name for them than 'lava creatures'. It doesn't seem proper." Beth was big on propriety, particularly after a few drinks.

"They just call themselves 'people', but I think we should call them 'Horta'," said Bobby without hesitation.

"Why 'Horta' for heavens sake?"

"The Horta were a silicon-based lifeform from Janus VI in the original Star Trek TV series. They also dug tunnels through the planet they lived on, though their physiology was nothing like our new friends."

"Hey, I remember that episode! It was called *The Devil in the Dark*. Sounds like a great idea to me, Bobby."

Bobby raised his glass in enthusiastic agreement. The two women looked at each other as if to say "Men!" in the way that women do when confronted with inexplicable male behavior. Mizuki pressed on with the Science Section's findings.

"It would be fascinating to have a better understanding of their metabolism. The only thing we are sure of is that they are kept in a partially molten state by heat from internal nuclear reactions."

"Yer joking? Those boulders, sorry, I mean Horta are little mobile nuclear reactors? If that don't beat all."

"Natural fusion reactors are all around us but natural fission reactors are much rarer, though they do exist. The natural reactors at Oklo in Gabon, Africa, for example."

"That's why they referred to the depleted uranium rounds fired by the Marines as 'food'," Bobby noted.

"And that's why they were happy to take us on tours of the moon and to talk about their history in exchange for a few thousand rounds of 15mm railgun slugs," added Beth.

"I guess ol' Jack Haldane was right: 'Reality is not only stranger than we suppose but stranger than we can suppose'."

"*Hai*, as long as we remember the words of Max Plank: 'One must be careful when using the word, *real*'."

"What?" asked the puzzled Captain.

"Never get into an epistemological discussion with a physicist," said Bobby by way of explanation. Mizuki smiled and Beth started to giggle.

"I think I need another shot, pardner."

"Amen, brother."

### Crew Lounge, Lower Deck

In the crew's lounge there was also drinking going on. In celebration of finishing their visit to the metal moon and its strange inhabitants, the Captain had expanded the quotidian booze ration. All the participants in the initial exploration of the moon were present. Even Umky was having a drink with the human members of the crew.

"It's about time we had a bit of grog," said Jay Taylor. "I was stuck on the shuttle for four days and I'm as dry as a dead dingo's donger."

"You should have been with us, primate. Playing tag with moving boulders." Umky raised a two liter bottle of blackberry brandy above his head in a two pawed grip, sucking enthusiastic on its protruding straw.

"You should have seen Cmdr. Danner knock that boulder out of the tunnel with the hover sled," said Vinny, illustrating the collision with his hands. "That rock popped out and into another, and another, like a break shot in pool."

"You should have seen Cmdr. Danner and Dr. Ogawa fly across the chamber and bounce off the boulders themselves," replied Umky, lowering the brandy bottle, now half empty. "The Doc whipped out that sword of hers, swung it around and made a perfect landing, just like in a Jackie Chan movie."

"Jackie Chan was Chinese," observed a slightly tipsy Tamara, "Dr. Ogawa is Japanese."

"Haven't I told you? All you humans look alike to us."

"Huh?"

Tamara's puzzlement allowed Hitch an opening to join the conversation. "Hey, you should have seen the front end of the hover sled—totally stove-in, smashed the controls and everything."

"Yeah, the engineering gnomes will love that," added Kato.

"What's this about you and Jacobs discovering a sacred alien site and almost causing an inter-species incident?" asked Kate innocently. She had been prepped by the Marines before the two petty officers arrived.

"What we found was fantastic!" said Hitch.

"What you found was a latrine," said Bosco.

"Yeah, we found these two at the bottom of the aliens' dump station playing in lava creature excrement," added Kato.

"Da, gives new meaning to the phrase, 'in deep shit'!"

Those assembled found this hilarious.

"OK, OK," said Matt, trying to maintain some dignity. Reaching into his back pocked, Jacobs pulled out a cloth bag closed with a drawstring.

"Just so you know, here is some of the alien 'poo' as they called it."

As he moved to dump the contents onto the table the others moved back hastily, some covering their drinks. What came out of the bag was a collection of exquisite gemstones—rubies, diamonds, emeralds, and sapphires. The sailor, who had been an amateur gemologist in his youth, had cut and polished the stones to enhance their brightness and beauty. The assembled crewmembers were awestruck.

"*Oh. Mine. Gott.*" said Kate. Vinny emitted a low whistle.

Matt was wearing a Cheshire cat grin and Stevie, his partner in crime, could not resist.

"I guess, if you are all so offended by the stuff we excavated from the latrine, you really don't need to take your share at the end of the voyage."

"Now don't be hasty there, Mate," said Jay.

"I don't care what you had to crawl through to get them," Tommy Chen enthused. "How much of this alien poo did you collect?"

Jacobs could not keep the smugness out of his voice. "A bit over eight metric tonnes."

"That's got to be worth..." began Kashi Ademola.

"About a fortune," finished Hitch.

"Not a bad day's work for a couple of alien turd wranglers," said Umky, summing up the situation. Everyone laughed again, this time including Matt and Stevie.

### Science Lab, Deck Two

Betty White secured the sick bay and headed forward to have a drink in the main lounge. Fortunately, no one had been injured during the exploits on the metal moon. Still, Betty was finding things a bit boring on board the ship at present. In the passageway she ran into Joe Rogers.

The American climatologist was headed for the science labs across from the Medical Section. Aft of the lounge and equipment spaces the Medical section took up the starboard side of deck two, while the Science Section occupied the portside. He smiled and nodded to the ship's doctor, but seemed a bit distracted.

"Aren't you coming to the lounge for a drink, Joe?"

"I don't think so, Betty. There are still some tests I want to run on those core samples we collected back on the dead planet."

"Those samples aren't going anywhere, you should take a break. There will be other, hopefully more alive worlds to analyze in the future."

"Yeah, I suppose so, but I can't help thinking that there has to be some part of the planet's ecosystem that survived. And now we have introduced Earth lifeforms which will eventually overwhelm and erase any vestige of native life."

"Don't take it so hard, Dr. Rogers. There are billions of worlds in this galaxy alone, and life dies whenever its star does, or a nearby star goes nova."

"Your probably right, Doc, but I didn't get a chance to save all those species that were killed off on Earth because of the alien bombardment. I feel like I have a duty to try and rescue a small part of planet *C's* ecology if I can."

"All right, but remember, all work and no play makes Joe a dull boy. And that is medical advice." Betty smiled at the scientist and continued on toward the lounge.

Joe entered the Science Section and went to the middle, bio-hazard isolated lab module. The isolated labs were hermetically sealed with airlock doors, preventing anything from escaping into the ship's interior. The lab module itself was totally separate from the ship, an airtight chamber within the hull that could be ejected if something contaminated it.

No hazardous alien contaminants had been found so far during the Peggy Sue's voyages to the stars, but there is always a first time. Thoughts of such possible danger did not occur to the climate scientist as he sealed himself into the lab. His mind was on doing a bioassay on the deepest part of his last core sample. Given projected deposition rates, it should have captured the surface layer at the time life disappeared from the unfortunate world 10,000 years ago.

He selected the section of core sample from the storage locker and sat it on the bench. Near the very bottom was a layer discolored by a dark substance. It looked almost like charcoal though chemical analysis indicated it was not. All other analytical tests having failed, Dr. Rogers' next step would be to prepare a living solution to test the sample with.

A bioassay determines the physical effects of a substance on a test organism and the relative strength of the reaction in a standard preparation. Whether traces of alien life would interact with Earthly microbes was unknown but, since nothing else had worked, it was a gamble he was willing to take.


*Engineering Spaces, Aft*

One person overjoyed by Hitch and Jacob's discovery of alien "poo" was Chief Engineer Arin Baldursson. He had appropriated several of the largest sapphires to use in device fabrication. Slicing off thin layers of crystal, the ship's engineers were using it to make image sensor arrays, temperature and pressure sensors, and other devices. A major attraction of SOS, silicon on sapphire, integrated circuit construction was that such devices were highly resistant to radiation. It was also great for RF circuits and making white light LEDs.

Earth technology had used SOS devices in satellites and spaceships for decades. The fabrication was straight forward but growing large crystals of sufficient purity was a problem aboard ship. Baldursson now had a ready made supply of large crystals to play with. A new batch of devices was in one of the fab units, components to rebuild the front end of the hover sled that Cmdr. Danner had smashed.

"At least they brought back some useful materials to help fix the things they broke," the engineer muttered as he checked the fab's progress. Nearby, Engineer's Mate James Michaels was still working on decoding the alien memory device that had been found on the first planet the expedition had visited.

"Hey Chief, you need to have a look at this. I think I have finally got the bugs out of the video signal decoder."

On an adjacent wall, a picture appeared on a holographic display. Unlike previous attempts to playback the alien recording, this time the images were sharp and in focus. The display showed a view of the alien world unlike any the Earthlings had seen—a world of trees and flowers, of buildings and living creatures.

"What the... ?" said James.

"*Djöfulsins helvíti!*" the Icelandic Engineer swore. "What is that?"

Everyone in the engineering department stood in stunned silence as the recording played out. When the display finally went dark, Baldursson spoke in a harsh, almost choked voice.

"Start the computer on translating the voice track and catalog this so only the ship's officers can access it from the main datastore."

"Aye, aye, Chief," James replied.

The Chief Engineer turned and headed out of the room, yelling over his shoulder, "No one talks about this until I say, understand? I'm going forward. The Captain needs to see this as soon as possible!"

## *Main Lounge*

Chief Engineer Baldursson strode into the lounge like a man on a mission. He hurried to the Captain's table and halted, coming almost to attention.

"Excuse me, Captain, but might I have a moment of your time. There is something you need to see."

Billy Ray was about to tell the engineer to sit down and have a drink but there was something about the man's deportment that rang alarm bells in the Captain's head. He squinted at Baldursson and saw fear in the man's eyes.

"Certainly, Arin. Let's go to the CIC."

"You might want to have the other officers accompany us, Sir. Dr. White too."

Billy Ray nodded and, rising from his chair, motioned for the others at the table to follow. As the engineer, four officers, and ship's doctor went forward, low whispers spread throughout the room.

Arriving at the CIC, Bobby closed the door behind the party. They gathered around the large holotank in the middle of the room and looked expectantly to the Chief Engineer.

"So what's this about, Arin?" Billy Ray asked.

"I can call spirits from the vasty deep," Baldursson intoned, typing a code on the forward touchscreen display. As he stepped back a holographic recording began to play.

A view of trees with green sweeping branches, and fields of red flowers dotted with white flowing buildings appeared. Accompanying the video a voice, obviously synthesized, started a narration.

"I am Senior Academician [untranslatable], an historian at the local university. I am making this recording for any of you who may survive the calamity that has befallen our world..."

### Science Lab

As was his habit, Chief Zackly was making his rounds of the ship, checking to see that everything was squared away and ship shape. He noticed the presence of someone in the Science Section and entered to see what was going on—most everyone on the ship who was not on watch was in one of the lounges celebrating the end of the expedition to the metal moon.

Inside, he found Joe Rogers, locked inside one of the isolation labs doing something on the bench. The Chief used the intercom on the lab's outer airlock door to talk to the scientist.

"Excuse me, Doc. Is everything alright in there?"

Rogers was startled to hear the chief's voice in the silence of the lab module. He looked around and spied the Chief looking in through the large transparent panels the separated the isolation pod from the rest of the Science Section.

"Oh, it's you Chief. You almost gave me a heart attack."

"Sorry, I didn't mean to make ya jump. Just checking to see that things are squared away. What are you doin' working when everyone else is celebrating?"

"I've just got a few more test to run on some of the samples we collected on the dead planet. Besides, I didn't have anything to do with the mission to the metal moon."

"Any reason to have a free drink on the Captain is a good reason, Doc."

"I suppose. I won't be much longer and then I'll join the others in the lounge." Looking back at the Petri dish on the laboratory bench he noticed that there was motion in the solution—small bubbles seemed to be forming on its surface.

"Hey, it looks like I've got a reaction of some sort..."

### CIC

"That was... horrible!" Beth finally managed. She was the first one to speak after the holographic recording finished.

They had witnessed scenes of destruction unlike any they had ever imagined. Cities demolished, vast open spaces stripped bare, a civilization destroyed, an entire world laid waste. Worst of all, they had seen the narrator's last minutes, as her city was desecrated outside her window. They watched as the Academician's own daughter was brutally killed and consumed in front of her. They listened to the dying scholar's last strangled cry as death took her.

"Those, those creatures were the inhabitants of the dead planet?" managed Betty White.

"Yes, we think so, Betty," answered Arin.

"What in God's name happened to them?"

Though this was the Engineer's second time seeing the recording it still had a chilling affect on him. "It looks like some kind of alien lifeform was set loose on their world—something that consumed every living thing on the planet."

"That poor mother, having to watch her child die in front of her and not being able to do anything." Mizuki was near tears, empathizing with the plight of the mother even though she was not even remotely human.

In fact, the now deceased inhabitants looked like large flatworms, or perhaps snails without shells on their backs. They had two eyes mounted on stalks above their heads and on their sides were frilly membranes that they used to manipulate objects and equipment. The Academician's appearance was definitely not human, yet her last words held emotions that any human mother might feel. What had happened to these creatures was a tragedy so foul, so evil that those present could hardly comprehend the enormity of it.

"I thought that the alien bombardment of Earth was about the worst way for a species to die. That weren't nothin' compared with that black stuff, it killed everything. Do we have any idea what it is?"

"Some form of virulent fungus or other growth," speculated Dr. White. "But I have never seen something spread like that, so quickly, like it was seeking out all living things."

216

"I think we need to call the other scientists in to view this video, Captain," Mizuki said. "Perhaps they can shed some light on what this noxious organism is."

Before the Captain could respond a loud alarm sounded throughout the ship.

"WARNING! Imminent danger of lethal biological contamination in the Science Section, Deck 2..."

# Part Three

# *That Is Not Dead Which Can Eternal Lie*

# Chapter 18

### Science Section, Peggy Sue

The Chief was trying to make sense of what he had just witnessed through the transparent walls of the lab module. Inside, Dr. Rogers reached out with one gloved hand and touched the contents of a Petri dish setting on the bench. Immediately he jerked it back. Rogers staggered backward from the lab bench, holding his hand up in front of him.

A look of terror overcame the scientist as his gloved appendage ballooned and then collapsed. It was as though the hand inside had melted away. Filaments of black—sinuous and questing—reached out from the shriveling stump, wrapping themselves around the scientist's arm, quickly reaching his face. Rogers screamed.

His outcry was cut short as the rapidly expanding mass of black fibers encased his head and torso. Between the inky strands, flesh bubbled and popped. The man collapsed in on himself, like the wicked witch melting in the *Wizard of Oz*. In seconds the only thing moving in the lab module was a mound of pitch-black goo on the bottom of the room. From that noxious heap, tendrils ran across the floor and up the transparent walls, working their way around the airlock door.

As the airlock seals began to bubble, being eaten away in much the same way as the dead researcher's flesh, the bio-hazard alarm sounded. All this had transpired in less than a quarter of a minute.

"Sweet merciful Christ!" the Chief exclaimed. He activated his comm link on the emergency command channel and called the Captain.


### CIC

Barely heard over the sound of the bio-hazard warning, Billy Ray's comm pip chirped.

"Captain, Chief Zackly. We got a situation here in the Science Section."

"Go ahead, Chief."

"Some kind of black crap just dissolved Dr. Rogers, I ain't never seen anything like it. Now it's tryin' to eat through the airlock seals. Whatcha want me to do, Sir?"

Beth called up live video from the lab while the men conversed. The Chief could be seen standing outside the airlock for isolation lab two, staring in horror at the black tendrils attempting the eat their way through the containment barriers.

"Shee-it," Billy Ray swore under his breath.

"If that gets out into the ship we're all dead," said Betty.

"Dump it!" cried Beth.

"Right," said the Captain. "Chief, dump the module."

"Sir?" came the unsure reply.

"Eject the module into space. Get it off the ship before that black stuff can eat through the seals."

"Aye, aye, Captain!"

Over the video link, the Chief could be seen opening the protective cover over the emergency ejection control. With the palm of his right hand, the sailor struck the large red button. If anyone other than an officer tried to eject one of the lab modules, the computer would normally ask for authorization, but the ship's computer was smart enough to interpret the Captain's order to the Chief as *a priori* authorization.

Over the comm link came a thunk, followed by a whooshing sound as the lab module pulled away from the interior wall. From the Chief's perspective the lab flew away into the distance, leaving a large rectangular hole in the ship's hull.

"Initiating level one decontamination of Lab Bay Two," the computer calmly reported. This entailed illuminating the entire bay with high levels of UV radiation. The transparent bay walls turned opaque and the Chief backed away, out of view.

"Good job, Chief," the Captain transmitted, visibly relieved. After a moment's thought he addressed the ship's computer. "Peggy Sue, show us the video recording from the lab."

"Yes, Captain. On the forward screen."

Those present witnessed the death of Joe Rogers as the Chief had witnessed it—sudden, gruesome, and inescapable. Without being asked, the computer played the video again at a slower speed, but the movements of the black pestilence were still breathtakingly quick. The Captain looked around the room at the ashen faces.

"I don't think there is much doubt that what just killed Dr. Rogers was the same thing that wiped out life on planet C. An infestation, a pestilence, a contagion that infects and kills entire planetary ecosystems."

Deciding on a course of action, Billy Ray turned to his officers. "Arin, head down to the Science Section and check for damage from the ejection."

"Aye, aye, Captain." The Chief Engineer hurried from the room.

"Beth, Bobby, I want the crew at battle stations. Plot a trajectory for that module and bring the X-ray laser batteries on line."

"Aye, aye, Sir," the two replied, with Beth adding, "Your intentions, Captain?"

"We are going to vaporize the ejected lab module. I don't think we want that stuff landing anywhere else by accident."

Both officers nodded in agreement and departed for the bridge. Turning to Mizuki he issued more orders. "Dr. Ogawa, please have the other scientists come to the CIC and view the recording—both recordings. I want you to analyze the video record from the lab module. I want to know what Dr. Rogers did to awaken the monster."

"Hai."

"After your people have an appreciation of the severity of the threat I want them to identify any remaining samples from the dead planet and destroy them. I want them turned to plasma, Doctor."

"Understood, Captain."

Billy Ray nodded once, turned and headed toward the bridge in pursuit of his officers. Mizuki headed back to the lounge to collect the rest of her scientists.

## Crew Lounge, Lower Deck

The wailing sound of the bio-hazard warning caused everyone in the crew lounge to sit up and look about. It was not an alarm that required them to report to action stations, just to remain at their current positions or in quarters. Then there was a thump.

"What the hell was that?" demanded Steve Hitch, jumping to his feet in reaction to the accompanying shudder that passed through the ship.

"Did we hit something?" asked Tamara, an edge of fear in her voice. Outside of transitioning to and from alter-space, ships with deck gravity did not shudder or shake unless something was desperately wrong.

While the others were still wondering what caused the disturbance, the raucous call of a klaxon replaced the higher pitch yowl of the bio-hazard alarm. The crew knew precisely what to do when that call sounded. Most were already in motion when the First Officer's voice announced:

"All hands, man your Battle Stations. This is not a drill!"

"Are we under attack?" Kato shouted to the Gunny, who emerged from her quarters in the goat locker only to dive out of Umky's way. His action station was on the bridge at the main fire control console and he was headed there at a run.

"Move your ass, Marine!" was all the Gunny said as she picked herself up off the deck and headed for the port side torpedo station. The Marines, less Umky, crewed that position when the ship was rigged for combat.

A mad scramble ensued as the Peggy Sue prepared for battle with foes unknown.


## Bridge, Peggy Sue

"All stations manned and ready, Sir," the First Officer reported.

"Very good," the Captain replied. "Under a minute and a half, not bad considering they were probably hoisting a few when the klaxon sounded."

224

Beth made a non-committal sound. She had drilled the crew on the passage out until they could assume their action stations in under a minute, even when roused from a sound sleep.

"Mr. Umky, have you a track on the ejected lab module?"

"Aye, Captain. It is ten kilometers off the port bow, 15 degrees above the ship's horizontal plane. It is moving away at roughly fifty kph."

"Helm, roll the ship to starboard until all portside lasers can come to bear on the target."

"Aye, aye, Sir," Bobby replied.

"Fire Control, target the module with all portside X-ray lasers, maximum power, continuous fire."

Along the sides of the sleek silver ship teardrop shapes emerged, the color of obsidian—the business ends of the ship's secondary battery of X-ray lasers.

"Sir! The target is acquired."

"You may fire when ready, Umky."

"All portside lasers firing on the target, Captain."

There was no visible indication that the ship's weapons were firing until the torrent of X-ray energy reached their intended target. Then the twenty ton lab module became incandescent, ablaze with white-hot heat. Molecular bonds were broken, crystal latices shattered, and electrons stripped from their nuclei. In under ten seconds the ejected lab module was turned into a dispersing cloud of plasma—no non-elemental substance survived intact.

"The target is destroyed, Captain," reported Umky.

"Very good. Secure the secondary battery, Mr. Umky."

"All done and well done, Sir," commented Beth, finally allowing herself a hint of a smile. The crew had done their job, smartly and with no drama.

"You may secure from general quarters, Number One." Peggy Sue's previous captain had avoided using that term for the ship's first officer, deeming it too British and too TV SciFi, but Billy Ray had no such qualms regarding his first officer—after all, Beth was British.

"Aye, aye, Captain."

"Your orders, Captain?" the Sailing Master asked from the helm.

"Set a course back to the dead planet, maximum acceleration, Mr. Danner." Billy Ray sat back in the commander's chair, tension from the brief engagement lifting.

"Course set, Sir. It will take us three days and twenty-one hours to enter orbit around GJ667Cc."

"Very good, Mr. Danner. All ahead full, if you please. As soon as Dr. Ogawa and her savants finish analyzing the recordings we will send a message to the Fortune. It appears that planet *C* may be more deadly than dead."


### New Mecca, Paradise

Shadi stared off into space, seeking a glimmer of horizon in the antelucan gloom. She was waiting on her sister to join her so they could take the sheep out to pasture, but Dorri had not yet appeared. The younger girl had finally managed to drop off into fitful sleep sometime past midnight, while Shadi had not slept at all.

The sisters were both unsettled because they had finally learned their fates. Imam Mustafa had summoned them after the evening meal. Standing before them as head of the household, mother Manijeh by his side, he told them who they were to marry—Ahmed as expected for Dorri and Mohamed al Madi, an older man with several wives, for Shadi.

They were to be married the next day until Shadi spoke up and said they were both menstruating. Given popular notions of menstrual synchrony in close female friends this coincidence was not questioned. And since women were considered unclean during their menstrual period the weddings were postponed by a week, allowing the girls to take the sheep out to the fields one last time. They planned on being gone for several days, sleeping under the stars with their wooly charges.

"Good morning," mumbled Dorri, arriving as the first sliver of light limned the eastern horizon. They would be heading west, away from the rising sun, up into the foot hills. The robot quadcopters that seeded the surrounding land had done their job well. A green carpet spread from the river in the east to the stony rise of the hills leading up to the mountains. The sisters' trek would take them miles from New Mecca, into shared solitude.

"Let's get the sheep moving, little star. I want to be clear of town before the others awaken, before the morning call to prayer."

"Yes, I wish we never had to see anyone here again." The bitterness that marked Dorri's comment caused Shadi to glance around nervously.

"Shush. No complaining until we are well out of ear shot. These will be our last few days together, our last taste of freedom, and I want to enjoy them as much as possible."

"But we can still see each other after we are married, right?"

"On occasion, but not like now. We will have to synchronize fetching water and other chores so we can meet. Though settling into our new households will probably take up most of our time once we are married."

There, she had said it, the dreaded word—married. Given to men they did not know in the middle of their adolescence, yet another cruel twist of fate. Shadi had once dreamed of going on a grand adventure, like something in the movies or literature, but this was not an adventure, it was a trip into hell. An empty planet, married to an old man, her sister taken from her. *How could things get any worse,* she wondered.

### Bridge, ESS Fortune

The image of Peggy Sue's captain appeared on the large forward screen. As was usually the case, only Capt. Chakrabarti was on the bridge of the Fortune. The other members of his crew were busy hauling things to the planet's surface or occupied elsewhere within the ship. The message delivered in the other captain's recorded transmission made no sense to him.

"Captain Chakrabarti, I urge you to get the settlers back on your ship and head for home. Or at least wait in orbit until a team of scientists can check more deeply into the conditions of GJ667Cc," Capt. Vincent's image said. "I repeat, we have reason to believe that the colonists on the surface of the planet are in grave and immediate danger."

Sid paused the recording. He wished he could ask questions of Capt. Vincent, but there was a twenty minute transmission delay between their ships. *What danger was he talking about? The planet was under observation for half a year. No life, threatening or otherwise, had been found. Even the Peggy Sue had reported the planet lifeless!*

He resumed the playback.

"If what we suspect is true, the planet is a ticking time bomb. There is a virulent contagion hidden in the soil that can be triggered by the presence of carbon based life."

*What does he mean? The settlers have been on the surface for more than a month. The settlements have been established, the surrounding fields have been seeded and their livestock put out to pasture. Nothing dangerous has been triggered by the presence of life.*

The Captain's thoughts were interrupted by the sound of a doorway sliding open—one of the crew entering the bridge from below. Sid swiveled his chair around.

"Oh, it's you Mr. Hoenig. Back from the surface so soon?"

"Yes, Captain. Not like there's much down there to keep a man's interest. All the horses have been delivered and, with the exception of some odds and ends, we are done offloading."

"Good, another week and we may be able to head for home."

"Sounds like a great idea to me, Captain." The shuttle pilot sat down in one of the bridge chairs without invitation. "You know, these folks may do alright here. As we were leaving New Mecca, I spied a flock of sheep with a couple of herders heading toward the mountains."

"Really? It sounds like the modified prairie grass has spread like weeds."

228

"Yeah, it's tenacious stuff. The flock of sheep was kilometers from the settlement with green fields all around. Hey, who's that on the screen?"

"What?" Then Sid realized he had not removed Capt. Vincent's paused image from the forward display. "Just a message from the captain of the merchant ship. I think they are headed back this way."

"Did they find any trouble on the outer planets?"

"No," Sid said, clearing the display, "no, not really."

"I wonder if they have women on their ship?"

"It hardly matters, as we will never meet them in person. You said there were a few more items to be ferried to the surface?"

"Yeah," said Hoenig, taking the hint. "I'm gonna grab some rack time and then finish hauling the supplies to the surface. Catch you later, Captain."

Sid just smiled. *Impertinent lout. Still, no reason to spread panic among the crew or settlers. When the Peggy Sue gets close enough to have a real conversation, perhaps I can find out what its captain is so upset about.*

The Captain turned back to his console. Picking up his pad he resumed reading the adventure novel he had started a few days ago, his thoughts drifting far away from his ship and the empty planet below.

## Chapter 19

### New Mecca, Paradise

Dorri and Shadi urged their flock onward, up the gently rising slope to where new grass grew. The sheep poked along, but the girls didn't mind, one patch of grass was much the same as any other. They merely wished to put enough distance between themselves and the settlement so that no one would be tempted to come and check up on them.

It was a warm day, with white fluffy clouds dotting the cerulean blue sky. The red sun smiled brightly overhead, giving the world a rosy tint. She had overheard one of the men from the ship call the planet "Paradise." *Under different circumstances*, Shadi thought, *it could well be a paradise.* Her thoughts were interrupted by Dorri's shout.

"Look over there! There is something moving."

Shielding her eyes with the palm of her hand, Shadi looked in the direction Dorri was pointing. There did seem to be something moving through the grass. It was as though sticks kept popping up, flipping end over end through the air, and disappearing again into the tall grass.

"What is it?" She yelled to her sister.

"I don't know. It seems to be a collection of black rods, sort of tumbling along the ground."

Shadi hurried over to where her sister was standing, closer to the strange object.

"Funny, the sticks don't seem to actually touch each other," Dorri commented, as Shadi drew near. "And there seems to be some kind of box or container in the middle of them."

As they watched, the collection of sticks stopped rolling and the entire assemblage deformed, lifting the central box higher into the air. After standing in that position for almost a minute it shrank back down and rolled off in a different direction, parallel to the flock's path toward the hills. It swayed and tumbled up the hill at a speed faster than a walking pace.

"Do you think it's alive?" asked Dorri.

"I don't know, it sure doesn't look like any animal from back home. But it's traveling up hill against the wind so something is making it move. "

"True. And it is keeping its distance from us and the sheep. You don't think it's dangerous, do you?" Concern crept into Dorri's voice for the first time since the odd apparition was sighted.

"I don't know. Wolves looking for strays might track a flock, moving in parallel with it." For the first time since coming to this world, Shadi felt uneasy about being exposed far from the settlement. "Let's stay between it and the sheep, just in case. "

"It's upwind but the sheep don't seem to notice it. If it was a predator you'd think they would react, wouldn't you?"

"It doesn't look like any predator I've ever seen. But you are right, predators always try to stay downwind of their prey."

"What ever it is, it seems to be going away."

Sure enough, the strange collections of sticks was receding, moving away from the flock and its two shepherds. A few minutes later the enigmatic visitor rolled over the next rise and disappeared from sight. Shadi felt the little knot of fear that had formed in her stomach ease.

"Let's move the sheep off that direction, away from that thing's path. And keep an eye out for more of them, or for that one to come back."

"Sure," Dorri agreed, still staring after the departed object. "Maybe this planet isn't as empty as they told us."

"Maybe indeed, little star. A planet is a big place, with a lot of places to hide. I don't care what they told us, I cannot believe they learned everything there is to know about this world in such a short time."

The sheep continued to placidly chew on the green shoots of grass while the sisters contemplated the meaning of what they had just witnessed. On the other side of the rise, the flexibot continued its survey. Having recognized the handful of creatures it discovered as Earth life, and therefore of little interest, the robot headed up slope toward the edge of the prairie grass.

*Armory, Peggy Sue*

"So let me get this straight," said Kato, "the alert yesterday was all because someone ejected a Science Lab module?"

"That's the scuttlebutt," replied Jacobs.

The Marines and the two petty officers were in the armory working on their suits. The time they spent on the metal moon was time spent in vacuum, which was actually less stressful on their armor than trudging around through grit and grime on a planet's surface. Regardless, when your suit is often the only thing keeping you alive, you learn not to scrimp on preventative maintenance.

"More than that," added Hitch, in a conspiratorial tone, "I heard from one of the snipes that Rogers, the climate guy from the science section, got himself killed by some contamination from the dead planet. The Chief saw the whole thing."

"The Chief was the one who ejected the Lab Module, Stevie!" exclaimed Jacobs.

"You are kidding, da?" asked Bosco, looking up from his partly disassembled railgun.

"Hell no. That's why the Captain had the module vaporized by the X-ray laser battery."

"He did, indeed," rumbled Umky. "I was the one who did the targeting. I didn't know that Dr. Rogers had died inside at the time, though."

"What's the straight skinny on what happened to the science guy?" asked the Gunny. "I heard the Science Section types and the officers are the only ones who know what really happened in the Lab."

"Yeah, Umky. What does your girl friend have to say about it?"

Umky gave Vinny a predatory look, but answered anyway. "According to Ahnah, Rogers managed to awaken some kind of killer goo that was hibernating under the planet's surface. He messed with it until it came back to life and ate him."

"Holy crap! We were all down on the surface, running around for a week!"

"Right, well Ahnah said this 'black goo' is triggered by the presence of life. We were safe down there because the Captain made us all wear armor."

"Yeah," added the Gunny, "that's one lesson we learned the hard way—always go in heavy to start with because there's no telling what type of shit you're stepping into."

Those assembled took a moment to contemplate their good fortune in having officers that knew their asses from holes in the ground. This, they knew from experience, was not always the case. Then a thought occurred to Vinny.

"Hey, what about all those settlers? They're all down there running around without armor or even pressure suits. Why ain't the black goo got to them? "

"I think that's why we are accelerating at 60G for the inner system, DeSilva. I expect we'll be briefed soon enough."

"Right, Gunny. You think we'll be safe in armor?"

"I'm hoping we don't have to find out, Kato. But it might be wise to go over your armor twice."

Umky snorted. "It would be really humiliating to be eaten by something without claws or teeth."

"No kidding, Nanook," quipped Kato. Nanook—polar bear in Inuit —was widely used by Marines to refer to any white bear in a casual way. Umky had given up on fighting its use. After all, it was better than being referred to as 'man' or 'dude'.

"We may not have to go back to the surface, but I wouldn't count on it. The only way I can see to get those civilians out of harm's way is to evacuate them." The Gunny gave her fellow warriors a meaningful look and went back to cleaning her armor.

She didn't want to spook her squad, but she couldn't help thinking, *I sure hope the Captain knows how to fight black goo, because I doubt that railguns are going to be very effective.*

### Captain's Sea Cabin, Peggy Sue

The ship's officers just managed to fit in the Captain's sea cabin with the addition of Doc White, Chief Zackly and Gunny Acuna. Even Chief Engineer Baldursson had made his way forward from snipe country to attend in person. The topic of discussion was what to do when the ship arrived at planet C in another day and a half.

"Are you saying that Fortune's captain did not take the warning message seriously?" asked Beth.

"I'm afraid so," the Captain replied. "Seems that Capt. Chakrabarti has a skeptical streak. His reply was more-or-less, 'tell me another good one'."

"I'm not sure I blame him," said Bobby. "If a bunch of treasure hunters—who had given the place a clean bill of health a month ago —suddenly came charging back from the outer planets yelling about dire threats to the colonists I had just finished off loading, I'd be a bit skeptical myself."

"Did you send him the videos?" asked Arin.

"No, I didn't want to shock him or come on too strong. I was half afraid that sending the doomsday video might make him even more suspicious of our motives."

"Why would you say that, Billy Ray?" asked Doc White. For some reason, starship medical officers tended to call their captains by their given name—a tradition going back to Bones and Captain Kirk on the original Star Trek.

"Think about it, Betty. In our report to the Fortune we purposefully omitted the existence of alien technology in the ruins, just in case we found something of commercial value worth claiming there. If what we are sayin' is true, then the ruins on Paradise do contain alien technology, technology that we must have gotten working. Maybe we just realized that there was treasure to be had on the planet, and maybe we came up with a tall tale to scare off the settlers. After all, discovering a video showing the death of a civilization 10,000 years ago seems a mite... convenient."

"I guess you're right, the timing does seem a bit coincidental."

"Paradise?" the Gunny said in a questioning tone.

235

"Yeah, evidently the Colonization Board types decided to name the planet Paradise."

"Sort of like a real estate developer naming a subdivision 'sunny acres' or something similar," observed Bobby.

"What about the accident in the Lab Module?" asked Mizuki. "That does not require the viewer to believe a catastrophe from the past. What happened to Dr. Rogers should be horrible enough to capture Capt. Chakrabarti's attention."

"I'm going to try sending that next. We all may be wrong—in fact I pray we are—but I'm afraid that there's trouble a-brewin' in Paradise."

### Cargo Hold, ESS Fortune

"Come on, Manuel, we gotta get these goats on board the shuttle before anyone else sees 'em," the shuttle pilot known as Mason said to his partner in crime.

"Hey man, I ain't no goat herder."

Months ago, when the Fortune was still in its slip at the Farside Moon base, Mason and Manuel, in collusion with the purser, managed to slip six goats aboard and hide them in one of the cargo hold's many nooks and crannies. They did this not because they were animals lovers, but because one of the lead settlers, Rabbi Menaheim, had made a fuss over there being no goats among the livestock being shipped with the colonists.

The three goat smugglers were not risking their careers out of kindness toward the prickly old Rabbi either. Mason had managed to make contact with Menaheim before the settlers were boarded and negotiated a transport fee for the critters. With all the other animals in the hold, a few more didn't noticeably add to the noise and mess, and there was plenty of fodder to go around. This last part of the scheme was the trickiest, getting the goats to the surface unseen by the rest of the transport ship's crew.

They had to wait until the last load for the Jewish settlers as well. If they transported the goats on an earlier trip, crew from one of the other shuttles might have spotted them in the settlers' compound. As it was the scheme was risky enough, but it was worth it. Mason, Manuel and the purser stood to double their earnings for the voyage.

The smugglers had been concerned about how the payment would be made, given that Rabbi Menaheim would be several light-years away when the Fortune returned to the Moon. If he double crossed them they could hardly return to Paradise to demand their money. In the end it was the Rabbi who came up with a solution. He placed the payment—the accumulated savings of his entire flock—into an account at the First Lunar Bank. That account required the signatures of all three co-conspirators and a code from the Rabbi to open.

Moreover, there was a time delay on any withdrawals until after the ship departed. The smugglers could verify that the funds were in the bank just prior to departure but could not remove the credits. The Rabbi would not give them the secret code until the goats were delivered dirtside—if they didn't come through with the goats, the money would stay locked in the bank forever. Mason and party didn't think that the Rabbi would stiff them on the password. With his entire group on the planet below, he had no further need for Earth credits.

"Here, try waving one of these in front of 'em." Mason produced a hand full of carrots from his coverall pocket.

"Wow, man, you do know a lot about goats," said Manuel as the recalcitrant goats caught the scent of the carrots and followed the two men up the ramp into the shuttle.

"I know even more about makin' money, my friend. Stick with me, this colonial transport business could turn into a goldmine."

With the last of the goats lured aboard, the ramp was raised and Manuel scattered a bail of alfalfa around to keep the goats busy during the descent. Mason started the undocking procedure.

"Fortune, Shuttle Charlie. We are ready for departure." The Fortune's three shuttles were designated A, B, and C, which translated phonetically to Alpha, Bravo, and Charlie for radio communication.

"Shuttle Charlie, this is Capt. Chakrabarti. What is your cargo and where are you bound?"

Mason grinned a smuggler's grin and replied.

"We are bound for New Jerusalem with a partial load of animal fodder and basic farm tools. There are also a few odds and ends like a repair kit for solar panels and replacement parts for the radio."

"And this is the last trip you need to make to the surface?"

"Affirmative, Captain. I think we've pretty much cleaned out the cargo hold. Nothing left but stray manure from the farm animals. I'm sending you the bill of lading now."

"Roger, Shuttle Charlie. Have a good trip."

The shuttle's repulsors pushed it away from the larger bulk of the transport and the two crewmen began their last trip to the surface of Paradise. On the planet below, the local sun was directly overhead on the continent where New Jerusalem lay. It would be nearly nightfall by the time the shuttle landed its cargo of odds and ends, and clandestine goats.

# Chapter 20

## New Mecca, Paradise

Shadi and Dorri began their day with a breakfast of flat bread and *foul mudammas*, a fava bean porridge made with garlic and olive oil. Called *ful* for short, the mixture had been prepared before they departed the morning before. In Muslim countries ful was often eaten for breakfast during Ramadan, the filling dish allowing people to fast more comfortably during the daylight hours. Using pieces of bread to scoop up the savory mashed beans, the girls were quickly sated and ready for another day herding sheep.

After rolling up their sleeping mats and securing their few possessions in bundles on their backs, the sisters resumed their uphill trek, heading toward the rocky foothills beyond the edge of the prairie grass. It was another beautiful day on Paradise, with fluffy white clouds drifting over grassy plains that stretched seemingly to the horizon. The advantage of higher elevation gave the girls a clear view of New Mecca in the distance, its white buildings taking on a slightly rosy tint in GJ667C's redder than Sol light.

Looking back at the settlement, for the second time Shadi saw something moving where nothing should. Shading her eyes with her hand she squinted at the moving figure that was headed their way, wishing she had thought to bring a pair of binoculars from the ship. As the figure drew nearer it resolved to horse and rider.

"Dorri, it looks like we are having company." Shadi pointed with one arm at the figure in the distance.

Dorri looked at her sister quizzically and then followed her outstretched arm.

"It looks like someone on a horse," she said.

"Your eyes are better than mine, little star. It will still take whoever it is a while to get here, but stay close."

"Sure. I hope they haven't been sent to make us come back early."

"We will see."

\* \* \* \* \*

An hour and a half later the horse and rider approached the flock at a canter. Atop the big roan mare was a man in flowing white robes with a red checkered gutra on his head. Both girls recognized the man immediately—Ahmed, Dorri's husband to be.

Ahmed reined his mount to a stop five meters from the sisters. Sweat glistened on the horse's neck and flanks. The mare blew and snorted, tossing her head up and down. After almost a month in a stall on board the ship, being asked to canter up hill under Paradise's heavier gravity had winded her.

"*As-salaam alaikumā,*" Ahmed greeted the sisters with the traditional Arab phrase, *Peace be upon you.*

"*Wa alaikum as-salaam,*" replied Shadi, a*nd upon you be peace.* Traditional pleasantries disposed of she continued in that language. "What brings you so far from the settlement, Ahmed? You know you should not be here with us without a male from our household present."

"Maybe I just couldn't wait until the wedding to see my new bride." He smiled a toothy smile at Dorri, who had the good sense to modestly cover her lower face with the tail of her headscarf.

"What? You would risk you new wife's reputation as a chaste woman because you can't control your lustful yearnings? Be gone!" Shadi made shooing motions with both hands.

Ahmed was taken aback, unconsciously jerking on the reigns, causing his mount to step sideways away from the sisters and their sheep.

"I mean no harm, my soon to be sister-in-law. Besides, there is no one around to see us," Ahmed replied after regaining his momentarily lost composure.

"People in the settlement can certainly see that you have ridden up to the flock of sheep, so stay on your horse and depart."

Ahmed looked nervously over his shoulder at the distant New Mecca. Turning back he had a half snarl on his normally smiling face.

"Have it your way, Shadi, but in a few days you will no longer have a say in things. Dorri will belong to me and she won't be taking anymore nature walks with you and the sheep. And I doubt your new husband will let you wander about, not until he's ridden you bowlegged!"

With that he pulled on the reigns and headed his mount back down hill, angling to the east and the river. As he rode away Dorri let go of her headscarf and stared after him.

"I used to think that I was the lucky one, sister. That I was at least getting a decent young man for a husband. But it appears that Ahmed is a self centered pig."

Shadi shook her head sadly. "He is like all other men, spoiled brats who treat their women like possessions. I hope he falls in the river."

"I just hope he doesn't harm the poor horse."

The sisters looked at each other with brave smiles on their faces, but there was sorrow in their eyes.


### *Mizuki & Bobby's Quarters, Peggy Sue*

The run back to the inner planets was routine to the point of boredom. That boredom did not diminish the constant stream of questions from other members of the crew regarding what they were headed for back on planet *C*, now universally referred to as Paradise. To escape the queries, Mizuki and Bobby had retreated to the privacy of their cabin following the evening meal. The couple was relaxing, sitting on their couch in front of a low table, sipping tea.

Billy Ray was the captain, and one did not cross examine a man who could clap you in the brig or have you thrown overboard. For different reasons, Beth was not considered easily approachable by the crew either. She had not served with members of the enlisted crew before and her stiff, formal deportment, instilled by her previous career in the Royal Navy, made her seem an imposing figure. That left Bobby, the sailing master, as the most approachable officer aboard.

"The whole crew is on edge about returning to Paradise," Bobby said. Having lived with Mizuki for several years he was used to the presence of her pets, the *aoi chō*. They were always about in their apartment at Farside, but since moving aboard the Peggy Sue their personal space had shrunk considerably. Their cabin now resembled a butterfly conservatory at a zoo, with the winged creatures flitting about everywhere.

"I can imagine, the other scientists are anxious as well. I don't really know what we can do when we get there, except try to convince the other ship's captain to transport the settlers back to his vessel."

"That's only part of the battle, sweetheart. We have to convince the colonists to abandon their settlements as well. The satellite recon pictures show that they have really moved fast on constructing their new villages, and the grass that was planted has spread for kilometers in all directions. It's hard to believe that anything could just rise up and erase all of that."

"I know, but you have seen the alien recordings as have I. If what Dr. Rogers awoke was the blight that scoured Paradise clean of life, and it is still present in locations other than the ruined city where we took our samples, disaster could strike at any time."

"Like I said, we have to get those people off of the planet, and we can't do that by ourselves, there isn't enough space for two hundred passengers on board the Peggy Sue."

"You and Billy Ray and Beth will figure something out once we get there." Mizuki took his hand. "Have I told you how proud I was of you on the metal moon?"

"Well, yeah. I mean I was the senior officer present, I had to do something." Bobby blushed. As much as he longed for Mizuki's praise he didn't really handle it well when he got it.

"You figured out how to get there in time to save the mission, and made first contact with the Horta when we got there."

"But you helped a lot. You figured out tracking the aliens using the DU dust. And when we did get to the big chamber you helped calm the Marines down while I tried to talk with the head rock."

"That is because we make a great team, Bobby." Mizuki smiled and stood up. Taking Bobby's other had, she pulled him up from the couch. The air was filled with brightly colored butterflies as the walked together to the bed.

## The River, South East of New Mecca

After his cold reception from Dorri and her sister, Ahmed rode east, heading for the river that lay beyond the settlement. When he arrived on the banks of the river he paused and allowed his horse to cool off and drink. He was not a cruel man by nature and had some experience caring for horses. It was that experience that convinced Imam Mustafa to let him take the big mare out for some exercise.

Once his mount recovered from the trip down to the river, they headed south along its bank. They traveled for kilometers until a shallow oxbow presented a convenient crossing place. Fording the river, Ahmed continued south along the far bank until he was beyond the reach of the grass planted by the settlers' drones.

In his traditional flowing white robes and red checked head cover, Ahmed looked like an Arab sheik from an old Hollywood movie, a solitary figure riding across the vast desert wastes. As he rode, he mulled his encounter with Dorri and her sister over in his mind. It had not been his intention to upset the two young women. In fact, he thought they would enjoy a visit as a break from the boredom of watching sheep turn grass into dung. After seventeen years of life, women remained a total mystery to Ahmed.

*Walah, I am glad I am not marrying the older sister,* he thought, *what a bitch!*

Ahmed held the reins loosely in his left hand and worked the beads of a *misbaha* through the fingers of his right. A misbaha is a string of prayer beads, often used to perform *dhikr*, the personal remembrance of God. His string contained thirty three amber beads, which he would pass through his fingers three times while reciting the Ninety-Nine Names of Allah. Currently he recited no names, but fingered the smooth beads out of habit.

*I just hope that Dorri doesn't sour like her sister over time. This is what happens when you allow women to get an education. Cooking and raising children, what else does a woman need to know?*

The sun was sinking low in the western sky, twilight would be coming soon. Time to start back to the settlement if he was not going to end up riding in the dark. This planet had no large moon to guide the steps of those traveling at night.

He was barely paying attention to where the mare was taking him, lost in his thoughts. The big roan paused and snorted, tossing her head. Then she moved forward with a start.

"What is it, girl?" Ahmed asked.

The horse whinnied and stumbled. The string of beads flew from his hand as he grabbed the reins. The horse whinnied loudly and fell sideways. That was when he noticed black strands emerging from the sandy soil, wrapping themselves around his mount's legs.

Ahmed tried to throw himself off the horse but the black sinews wrapped around his legs, pinning him in place. Searing pain lanced up his thighs and torso as the black sinews whipped around him. He tried to cry out but was paralyzed by the strands that encased both rider and mount in a shared cocoon of agony. His last thought was, *Allah be merciful.*

Down sank their remains as flesh and bone dissolved. Ahmed's clothes and the mare's tack and saddle were also absorbed by the voracious blackness. The corruption that had taken them roiled and quivered and slowly sank back into the sandy river bank. In the failing light it was almost as though they had never existed.

All that remained of the man and his horse was a curved dagger, badly pitted as if from strong acid, its handle and leather sheath eaten off, and the badly corroded metal bit from the horse's mouth. Higher up the bank were several scattered pebbles, the beads from Ahmed's misbaha.


## New Jerusalem, Paradise

Mason and Manuel trudged back to their shuttle after completing the business transaction they had come for—exchanging goats for a slip of paper. That paper contained a string of numbers that would unlock their payoff back on Farside. As with previous visits to New Jerusalem, there were no women or children visible, only men in somber black outfits. The boxes of spare parts and supplies had been unloaded and now a number young men were herding the goats toward town. The smugglers suggested that the four legged contraband be kept under cover whenever one of the

244

observation satellites was over head—at least until the Fortune broke orbit for Earth.

"Looks like our work here is done, Manuel," quipped Mason, touching the pocket in which the slip of paper resided.

"You got that right, amigo. If I never set foot on this rock again it will be too soon."

"At least there is grass on the ground this time," the pilot observed. "The first couple of runs it was just sand. Someday you might regret not buying a homestead somewhere nearby."

"With this gravity? No thanks. Why do you think that old geezer wanted those goats so bad?"

"I don't know. Maybe they want them for a goat grab on some holy day," Mason replied. "Or maybe he's just queer for goats."

"Yeah, I guess it doesn't matter as long as we get paid."

"You got it. You know we should probably hose out the cargo bay before we lift off. I noticed there were some goat pies on the rear ramp."

"Why do I get the impression that 'we' means me?"

Mason grinned at his companion, but said nothing more. Neither man noticed the darkness on the far horizon, like a cloud was casting a shadow on the prairie grass below. Problem was, there wasn't a cloud in the early evening sky. As the men joked and ambled toward the forward crew airstair the darkness crept closer to the settlement.

\* \* \* \* \*

On the far side of the settlement, hidden from the shuttle crew's view by New Jerusalem's buildings, there were women and young children about. They were bent over, working in a large garden, tending the young plants that would eventually help feed the community. Busy at their labors, the gardeners also took no notice of the strange dark stain approaching them across the prairie.

With no warning except a slight rustling sound the black pestilence arrived. The first victim it claimed was a four year old boy. He was kneeling down, playing in the dirt when the malignant

245

sinews enveloped him. So quickly did the dark threads move, and so intense the pain they inflicted on the child, that the boy did not even cry out.

The next victim was a young woman, caught in the act of standing up. The threads emerged from the ground she was working, wrapping themselves up her legs beneath her ankle length skirt. She managed a scream before succumbing.

Hearing the young woman's anguished cry the other gardeners looked around, but it was too late. Sinuous black tendrils reached out for them, racing down the rows of young plants, consuming gardener and plant alike. Some tried to run toward the settlement, but were ensnared after only a few steps. One young mother grabbed her child, trying to carry her to safety—instead they died together, becoming part of the growing mass of black death.

With each ingested victim the volume of blackness swelled. It raced on into the village proper. There was no glazing in the windows or doors to keep out the curious—life on a planet with no insects or other pests made for an open, breezy building style. Black threads flowed over walls, in through windows and out through doors, as death swept from dwelling to dwelling.

The goats never reached their pen, dieing in the dusty street along with their herdsmen. Moments later the threads invaded the stables and the screams of sheep and horses were added to those of the settlers.

* * * * *

In one of the public buildings that fronted on the town's open square, Rabbi Menaheim and several of the more technically educated members of his congregation were looking over the latest satellite pictures of their local region. From them they were planing where next to expand their fields and pastures.

Rabbi Menaheim and his followers may have practiced that old time religion but they fully appreciated the benefits of modern technology. The Rabbi was giving instructions to the young man sitting next to the satellite radio used to communicate with the ship and other settlements.

"Yani, please thank Captain Chakrabarti for sending the spares and repair kits for the solar panels, but no mention of the new livestock, eh?"

"Yes, Rabbi." The young man initiated a call to the colony ship. Currently, Fortune was orbiting high above the planet on the far side of the world. The call was routed through the network of dual purpose weather and communication satellites that had been placed in geosynchronous orbit to aid the colonists.

"ESS Fortune, New Jerusalem, do you read me over?"

After a few moments a reply came from the starship.

"New Jerusalem, this is ESS Fortune, we read you five by five. What can we do for you today?"

"We would just like to thank you for the final delivery of supplies and equipment. Rabbi Menaheim says that the Colonization Board has been most kind and that he will pray for your safe voyage home."

"Thank you, New Jerusalem. We wish you the best of luck with your settlement," came the reply, but no one was paying any attention to the radio.

"Look!" cried a man near the open window, pointing across the square. From the buildings on the far side of the town's central plaza fibrous blackness erupted. From the buildings' windows and doorways, and over the low walls between them, a wave of black sinews poured like a tsunami inundating a fishing village built on an ocean shore. Fed by most of the settlement's inhabitants and their livestock, the infestation had grown into a surging torrent that swept all before it.

"Ahhh!" screamed the man at the window. "It is *malakh ha-mavet*, the angel of death!"

The Rabbi sank to his knees in front of the open door way. Clasping his hands before him like an Old Testament prophet, he beseeched God to spare them. He began reciting a prayer for the dead.

"*El maley rachamim shochen bam'romim hamtzey menuchah nechonah al kanfey haschechinah...*" God full of mercy who dwells on high, Grant perfect rest on the wings of Your Divine Presence...

247

Blackness took him before he could finish. At the radio, Yani tried to tell the ship what was happening, but only managed a single phrase before he too was wrapped in voracious black and his flesh and bones melted into putrescence.

* * * * *

Mason and Manuel were unaware of the slaughter taking place less than half a kilometer away in the settlement. They had almost reached the airstair leading up to the forward crew entrance when Mason noticed a spreading black stain moving through the grass in their direction.

"What do you think that is, Manuel?" the pilot asked, turning to his companion.

"Mrgff!" came Manuel's strangled cry as the threads wrapped him in a bundle of black.

Mason opened his mouth to shout but black sinews cracked around his body like the lashes of a hundred whips. His entire body screamed in pain as he too was consumed. The last image he saw was the black lump that had been Manuel sinking slowly to the ground. Then came blackness; then nothingness.

The black tide raced on, beyond the shuttle, spreading out to consume the entirety of the recently planted prairie. In New Jerusalem not a single soul or animal drew breath. Even plants and inanimate objects made of organic material were absorbed.

Wooden dressers full of clothing, furniture, rugs and curtains, all were gone. In one storage shed there was a large pile of salt spreading out across the floor, freed from the cloth sacks it had been contained in. Other supplies—spices, tea, coffee, beans and rice—had all vanished.

Scattered on the shuttle's sloping rear ramp were droppings from the goats, along with strands of alfalfa and hay that had escaped their bails during unloading. Thin black tendrils felt their way up the metal surface, traveling from one patch of organic material to the next. They progressed up the ramp and into the cargo hold, where they found more material to gorge on.

248

## Chapter 21

### Bridge, ESS Fortune

Captain Chakrabarti paced back and forth on the bridge, a data pad in one hand open to the same page he had been reading an hour before. One of the shuttles was overdue, the one that was making a final drop off at New Jerusalem. The pilot and crewman had disembarked to help the colonists offload and move the cargo, leaving the shuttle's forward passenger door and rear ramp open—after all, there was nothing alive down there that they hadn't hauled to the surface themselves.

Now, hours later, remote status signals indicated that the shuttle was just sitting there, hatches open and no one on board. More disturbing, there had been a call from the settlement of New Jerusalem. It seemed a routine call when shouting and screams could be heard in the background. Then the transmission went dead, the last word sent from the planet was "*malakh ha-mavet.*" The ship's computer informed the Captain that it was Hebrew for "angel of death."

Darkness had fallen on New Jerusalem and the surveillance satellite's last pass only detected some strange heat signatures. The weather satellite in geosynchronous orbit was too high to make out details but light was seen coming from the settlement. A better view would have to wait until morning on that continent.

*Maybe the crew went native and joined the settlers*, Sid thought, grasping at straws. *Maybe they have been incapacitated and cannot reply. No matter, those shuttles are each worth a hundred million credits and I will not leave an abandoned shuttle setting on the planet's surface. They would probably dock my pay if I left it behind.*

Decision made, Sid instructed the ship's computer to initiate a remote takeoff procedure and return the grounded shuttle to the Fortune. In many ways, the shuttle pilots were a redundant system, only backup to the shuttles' onboard computers. The craft were fully capable of making trips to and from the surface on their own.

Sid felt a spark of malice, *If those two are partying with the settlers, let them call in the morning and beg for a ride back to the ship.* The thought shamed him and he was immediately remorseful, *I do hope nothing has happened to the shuttle crew, or the settlers.*

With Shuttle C on its way back all the shuttles were accounted for. Shuttle A was safely aboard, but Shuttle B was on approach to Zion with the final delivery to Brother Abraham's flock. Sid's cautious nature reasserted itself. *Best tell the crew of Shuttle B to be alert for anything strange.*

This was not at all how the mission was supposed to go. Laying down his novel, he reached for the comm panel. Before he could call the shuttle crew a tone announced an incoming call.

### Bridge, *Peggy Sue*

"Capt. Chakrabarti, I cannot stress more strongly the danger that those on the surface of the planet are in," said Billy Ray to the holographic image of Fortune's captain that floated in front of his chair on the bridge. "Did you view the video I transmitted to you?"

"Yes, yes. A tragic accident to be sure, but not proof that a horrid fate will befall those on the surface of Paradise," replied Capt. Chakrabarti, following several seconds of round trip transmission delay. The tardiness of light made conversation awkward but possible as Peggy Sue approached the planet.

Billy Ray sighed. "There is more to this planet than is obvious to the casual observer, Captain. There were certain omissions in the survey report we sent you when Fortune emerged in the system."

"Oh really?" Chakrabarti's voice dripped with sarcasm.

"Yes," replied Billy Ray, pressing forward. "We told you we found indications of an ancient alien civilization and we had examined several sites that appeared to be ruins."

"Yes?"

"What we failed to tell you was that we recovered some alien devices from one of the ruins—I'm sending you the coordinates. That site was the same one where the contaminated sample was collected; the sample that killed Dr. Rogers in our Science Lab."

"This is all very interesting, Captain, but is there a point hidden in here somewhere?"

"It has taken more than a month to decode the data stored in the alien equipment. I'm transmitting a part of that recording to you now. What it shows is the destruction of the entire planetary ecosystem by a malevolent black contagion—the same contagion that took my scientist's life."

"You expect me to believe that this 'black contagion' is just waiting to spring up and engulf the unsuspecting colonists? How long ago did this civilization ending calamity occur?"

"Roughly 10,000 years ago."

"And you are suggesting that this black death has lain quiescent for one hundred centuries, waiting to devour my colonists? You said that your scientist had to prod the dangerous organism back to life, why should we expect its spontaneous regeneration on the surface?"

"The presence of organic material seems to awaken it from a state of hibernation, as seen in the Lab video."

"After 10,000 years!"

"That is well within the limits for known life. My science staff tells me bacteria discovered on Earth's Arctic sea floor have a hibernation period of up to 100 million years."

"Maybe there was some contamination left in the ruins you defiled, but none of the settlements are within a thousand kilometers of that site. I think you simply want the colonists off the planet because you overlooked something valuable, Captain."

Contempt laced Chakrabarti's last reply. Billy Ray's eyes narrowed and his jaw muscles could be seen clenching, a sure sign of his displeasure.

"Captain, all I ask is that you look over the recordings I just sent you. Then tell me there is no cause for worry."

"Fine, I will let you know my decision after I watch your video. Fortune out."

The hologram image vanished, but the tension between the two captains lingered. Around the bridge, crew members concentrated on their instruments, avoiding eye contact with their commanding officer.

"Well, that didn't go quite as well as we hoped," Beth commented dryly. She had been standing near the Captain, just out of video pickup range, during the call. She knew her husband well and had learned that dry sarcasm appealed to his better nature, even when beset by disappointment.

"That man is as stubborn as a mule," Billy Ray finally said, silent rage dissipating. "Mr. Lewis, what is our ETA for Paradise orbit?"

"A bit over four hours, Sir."

"Very well. You have the Conn, Mr. Lewis. The First Officer and I will be in the CIC."

"Aye, aye, Sir. I have the Conn."


### Bridge, ESS *Fortune*

Sid was in a funk, brought on by indecision. On one hand, he was outraged at the highhanded actions of the merchant captain, practically ordering him to evacuate the settlements that had taken several months to establish. On the other hand, he had watched the second video recording Capt. Vincent had sent him and it scared the devil out of him.

If the video was to be believed, this planet used to have a civilization as advanced as Earth's before the alien bombardment. Cities and towns and farms spread across all the major continents. That civilization was destroyed in the matter of a few days, assuming that the video was not a deception concocted by the merchants to have Paradise to themselves.

*Why didn't they just tell us to bugger off when we arrived?* Sid asked himself. *Surely that would have been easier than trying to uproot the settlers now.*

Maybe Vincent was telling the truth. Maybe they didn't know the danger existed, or maybe they needed more time to manufacture evidence of a threat. Regardless, Sid doubted that the colonists would voluntarily return to the ship. He could just take Fortune and run for home, letting the merchants handle the situation—but that would be the coward's way out. He had a responsibility toward the settlers, even if they were no longer on board his ship.

No matter, his options were limited. The Peggy Sue was rapidly approaching orbit around Paradise. The rumors about that ship were undeniably true. It was slowing at over 60Gs and had been for several days. Nothing short of a Navy warship could maintain that sort of acceleration. This made it easy to believe the other rumors, which said the Peggy Sue mounted enough offensive weaponry to go toe to toe with a cruiser. That ship, far from being a merchant vessel or a rich man's play toy, was actually a pocket battle ship.

Since Fortune mounted no offensive weapons and only enough shielding to protect against random space debris, there was no possibility of armed resistance to the merchant captain's will. The best Sid could do was threaten to report his actions to the authorities back at Farside. Of course, the people behind the Orion Arm Trading Company pretty much were the authorities back home.

*Earth was almost destroyed, humanity was almost eradicated by hostile aliens, and now we are rebuilding our civilization,* Sid thought. *Yet the rich are still in charge and the poor have to be happy with the scraps from their tables. They give these poor colonists a new planet and then decide to snatch it back on a merchant captain's whim. Everything has changed but everything still remains the same.*

The injustice of life gnawed at Sid, but in the back of his mind a small voice kept nagging him: *What if Vincent is telling the truth?* If he was anything, Sid was over cautious. That was one of the reasons he had been chosen to captain this first colonization mission. He placed the delayed warning call to Frank Hoenig aboard Shuttle B, on its way to Zion.

### *Shuttle B, Inbound to Zion*

The three settlements were spaced nearly equidistant around Paradise, each on its own continent. It was the wee hours of the morning in New Mecca and the sun had set in New Jerusalem. The day was half spent in Zion, the settlement belonging to Brother Abraham and his flock of fundamentalists. Shuttle B was flying out of the night, descending into the new dawn with ten thousand kilometers yet to go.

"Shuttle Bravo, Fortune, come in please."

"Now what?" mumbled Frank, seated in the pilot's chair. Keying the talk button he replied, "Fortune, this is Shuttle Bravo on approach to Zion, I read you five by five, over."

"Shuttle Bravo, please be advised that we have received warnings regarding possible hostile native life on Paradise. Please keep a lookout for any suspicious activity when you are on the planet."

"Really? We've been messing around on the surface for two months now and haven't seen anything in the way of indigenous life. I thought the OATC types said the planet was totally dead."

"The captain of the Peggy Sue has informed me that the soil harbors some kind of inimical life form that manifests as a moving mass of black threads."

"Say again, Fortune. Did you say a mass of black threads?"

"Roger, Shuttle Bravo. I have been assured by the merchants that the threat is capable of rapid movement and is deadly to unprotected life. If you see anything remotely fitting that description you are to take off immediately. Do you copy?"

"Roger that, Fortune."

"Furthermore, I want you to stay on board while you are on the ground. I don't want both of you off the shuttle at the same time."

"Affirmative, Fortune. I am to stay with the shuttle at all times." *Good*, thought Frank, *Leon will have to manage the unloading all by himself*. Another thought occurred to the pilot.

"Interrogative, should we inform the colonists of the threat?"

There was a pause.

"Negative, Shuttle Bravo. There may be no actual threat, so let's not start a panic. Still, we need to err on the side of caution so keep an eye pealed."

"Roger, Fortune. We will call in when we are on the ground. Shuttle Bravo out."

"What was that all about?" asked the crewman named Leon, leaning in the doorway from the passenger compartment.

"Just the Captain with some wild assed rumor that there is a dangerous outbreak of black threads down on the planet."

"What?"

"Hey, I'm not making this stuff up. You ask me, the Old Man is going space happy, stuck up there on the ship."

"Jeez, I hope he stays sane enough to get us back to Earth."

"Trust me, the return course is already programmed into the main computer. Even if the Captain goes around the bend we can still order the computer to take us home. Now get ready for atmospheric entry in ten minutes."

### The Hills Above New Mecca

Shadi spent a restless night, laying out beneath the stars with her sister and their sheep. Though she was loath to admit it, Ahmed's visit the previous afternoon had unnerved her. With every stirring of the sheep, every rustle of breeze through the grass, she awoke, fearing strangers were approaching their resting place. As a result, she was sore and unrested after the long dark night.

Dorri had no such problem—after a tiring day walking with the herd in the sun and wind she slept soundly. Her sister admired the way she could ignore problems that loomed in the future and simply enjoy the moment. Now, with the first glimmer of sunrise gilding the horizon, the girls arose as the faint cry of the muezzin came to them across the grassland.

After landing on Paradise, there had been a lot of discussion as to which direction the faithful should face to pray. Eventually the Imam decreed that they would place their copy of the Holy Koran in the east wall of the new mosque and the congregation would face east while praying. Those outside of the mosque were to face the mosque itself at the appointed times for prayer.

The girls oriented their sleeping pads toward the settlement and performed their morning *salat*. Though their upbringing had not been particularly religious, prayer was a familiar and comforting ritual that reminded both girls of home. Other than each other, it was one of the last links to their life on Earth, a life that seemed more and more like a dream as the days passed.

Prayer complete, looking down slope toward the settlement offered Shadi a view that would remain in her memory forever. The rising sun painted the buildings of New Mecca rose red, while they cast long shadows to the west. Stray breezes caused ripples in the green fields that tumbled gently down the slope to the village and the river beyond.

"I don't see Ahmed on his horse this morning, coming to check up on us again," said Dorri with a crooked smile.

"Hopefully he is back in town, nursing saddle sores," sniffed Shadi, causing Dorri to giggle. *Oh sister! Stay a young girl the next few days, before we both have to become women and take up a wife's burdens. How can this be the will of Allah?*

"Why the serious look, sister?" asked Dorri.

"Just considering how far we must drive the sheep to get them back to the sheepfold, little star."

"We don't have to start back today, do we?" There was an edge of panic in Dorri's voice.

"No, no. We can wait until tomorrow to head back down the slope. Today we can move along the edge of the grass, just below the rocky hills."

"Good, I want this trip to last as long as possible, forever even. I don't ever want to go back."

"Look out over the grasslands, Dorri, and hold this picture in your heart. In the future, when things seem darkest, think back to the two of us standing on this hillside watching the sun rise."

Dorri said nothing, but a single tear ran down her cheek. She took her sister's hand and the two of them stood silently until the bleating of the flock broke the trance.

* * * * *

Kilometers to the south and east of New Mecca, near where Ahmed and the roan mare met their demise, there was a stirring along the river bank. Hardly noticeable at first, a few sparse strands of grass that had encroached on the river's meandering path, withered and died.

Having lain dormant for centuries, the black spores, all that was left of the contagion that had killed this world, were awakened by the presence of life itself. It was the runoff from the grassland, carried down stream by the nearly daily rains, which summoned the blackness from underground.

Mindless. Voracious. It existed only to destroy all living things. Trace molecules in the water called it back, to feed once more. Only after the planet was barren would it again go dormant, again fall into deathless sleep.

# Chapter 22

### Captain's Sea Cabin, Peggy Sue

The ship's officers and senior NCOs were crowded into the Captain's sea cabin just off the bridge. The purpose of the gathering was to lay out a plan of action for when the Peggy Sue made orbit around Paradise. Whatever the Captain decided, the Gunny and Chief Zackly would pass the word to the Marines and crew once the meeting broke up. Looking up from the surface display in his desk, Billy Ray made eye contact with the others, bringing an anxious quiet to the room.

"Captain Chakrabarti still isn't buyin' our warning about the black goo and refuses to order an evacuation of the surface."

"That seems most unwise, Captain," said Mizuki.

"Agreed, Dr. Ogawa. According to Chakrabarti, one of Fortune's shuttles is on its way to Zion and another is on the ground at New Jerusalem. Somewhat ominously, the New Jerusalem boat has been out of radio contact for almost ten hours."

"Do you think that they have already been attacked?" asked Bobby.

"I don't know, pardner. We'll know once a surveillance satellite passes overhead after local dawn. Since Chakrabarti refuses to send another shuttle to the surface, I'm going to have First Officer Melaku and some of the Marines take Shuttle One down to the third settlement, New Mecca."

"Do you want the whole squad, Captain?" asked the Gunny.

"No, I want Umky to stay here to man the central fire control station. But take the rest of the squad, in full armor."

"Aye, aye, Sir."

"Captain, Beth shouldn't pilot the shuttle," said Bobby.

Beth turned her head to glare at Bobby, thinking he was insulting her piloting skills. Billy Ray raised his eyebrows questioningly.

"The First Officer is going to be busy when the shuttle gets to the surface, handling the refugees or whatever. Given how fast this black stuff seems to move there needs to be a pilot at the controls the entire time the shuttle is on the ground, ready to lift off at the first sign of a threat."

Beth relaxed and Billy Ray nodded slowly in agreement.

"The Sailing Master makes a good case, Captain," Beth conceded.

"I take it you have an opinion as to who that pilot should be, Bobby?"

"Yes, Sir. I'm thinking I should be at the controls, since I have more left seat time in that type of shuttle than anyone else on board. Mr. Lewis is perfectly competent to handle the Peggy Sue under these conditions. After all the only possible hostile craft in the system is that bloated colony transport."

It was Beth's turn to nod in agreement, while Mizuki looked at Bobby without expression. Whatever her opinion of her significant other's volunteering for the shuttle mission, it remained unspoken.

"Chief, we will go to General Quarters when we enter orbit. I don't anticipate any actual combat but I want the ship rigged for action."

"Aye, aye, Captain. The crew will be at their stations, bright eyed and bushy tailed."

"Dr. Ogawa, I would like you, and whichever members of your science team you deem useful, to be in the CIC. You will monitor all activity on the planet's surface. I want to know if that black crud erupts anywhere down there."

"Hai, Captain."

"Beth, Bobby, I want you ready to launch when we enter orbit. I'm still hoping I can get Captain Chakrabarti on board for this evacuation. I'd rather we use his shuttles than ours."

"Aye, Aye, Captain," the two senior officers answered in unison.

"Any questions?"

Billy Ray glanced about the room at his people. Even if they were supposed to be merchants, the looks of grim professionalism on their faces befit a crew of combat hardened veterans, which is exactly what they were.

"Very well. Dismissed."

### Shuttle B, Zion

The red sun was well past its zenith as Shuttle B made a banking turn to circle the settlement. The grass was green and lush, and some industrious souls were taking cattle and sheep out to pasture. An idyllic scene that would have made a great recruiting poster for the Colonization Board.

"Looks pretty enticing down there, eh Frank," said Leon.

"Yeah, if you like tilling dirt and herding animals," the pilot replied. "Next trip let's bring a fusion reactor, and the stuff to build a hotel cassino. Then the place might be tolerable."

"Only if the passenger manifest includes a bunch of single women," Leon replied, grinning. The radio crackled.

"Aircraft above Zion, come in."

"They haven't quite gotten the hang of radio procedure, have they?" Frank reached for the radio frequency setting. "Zion, this is Shuttle Bravo. We are about to land west of the settlement in the usual place."

"Uh, good Shuttle Bravo. Brother Abraham and a work party will meet you on arrival."

"Roger, Zion. Shuttle Bravo, out."

Turning to his crew of one, Frank said, "I'm supposed to stay at the controls while we are on the surface so you are going to have to keep an eye on the offloading by yourself."

"Yeah, I figured that was coming. It'll take these jokers the rest of the day to unload all this stuff by hand. I'll let you know if I spot any rampaging black thread."

"Hey, this is the last trip, focus on that. We'll be on the ground in thirty minutes."

The landing was uneventful, as always. Brother Abraham came out himself to supervise the unloading—perhaps he wanted to make sure none of the faithful had a moment of weakness and tried to return to the ship. Leon soon had the group of young men organized and hauling the contents of the cargo hold to the settlement a half kilometer away.

### *Bridge, ESS Fortune*

Captain Chakrabarti was viewing the video of the fall of Paradise's native civilization for the third time. If it was a fake it was a very well done fake, with some highly imaginative touches. The natives appeared to be some form of flattened, snail like creatures, sans shells, that slid across the mosaic floors and brick lined streets of their cities. If someone on board the Peggy Sue had created this on a computer they were in the wrong business—they should be turning out SciFi horror films back on Farside.

There was still no word from the missing shuttle crew. No word at all from New Jerusalem for that matter. Shuttle B had arrived at Zion without incident and the crew reported nothing out of the ordinary. Another hour or so and the offloading would be complete and they would be on their way back to the ship. The ship's computer interrupted Sid's thoughts.

"Captain, Shuttle C has docked in its berth on the hull and is secured."

"Fine, leave the access hatches closed for now. I will send some of the crew to inspect the interior in a bit."

"As you wish, Captain."

*At least the computer is properly respectful.* Sid's mood was rapidly deteriorating faced with growing uncertainty regarding the settlers' safety. He placed a call to the crew of Shuttle A, who were on board doing something.

"Mr. Chu, Mr. Bell, this is the Captain."

"Yes, Captain, this is Chu."

"I want you two to go to the number three shuttle bay and check out the interior of Shuttle C. See if there is any damage, or signs of why the crew abandoned the boat."

"Sure, we'll get right on that." The call went dead.

*When I get back, the efficiency reports I will write on all of these insubordinate louts will get them dismissed from the service!* The thought of revenge soothed Sid's unsettled mind, providing something pleasant to look forward to. *Oh why didn't I take that job hauling researchers back and forth to Neptune?*

### *Zion, Paradise*

The settlements were rudimentary places to live. None had running water or a municipal sewage system. Zion was no exception. For water, the residents of Zion dug a well in the middle of their town. The water-saturated depth of the local aquifer ranged from a few meters to more than three hundred. Fortunately for the settlers the water table was on the shallow end of that range under Zion.

The other side of the utility equation was fulfilled by a set of municipal privies, located at the edge of town. They were on the down slope side of the settlement, in hopes that the ground water flow followed the modest elevation gradient. There were two facilities for the men and two for the women, each a five-holer that would have done any 18th century frontier settlement proud.

Perched upon a wooden throne, Brother Isaiah was making his daily deposit to the growing collection of human waste at the bottom of the latrine. Isaiah was not the name he was born with; Brother Abraham insisted they all take "Christian" names from the Bible. Isaiah considered the name change to be a small price to pay for having survived the destruction of Earthly civilization and the opportunity to colonize a new world.

Alone in the tranquil silence, Isaiah thought about Rebecca, the girl he hoped to marry one day. She was a little on the plump side, and thus not favored by Brother Abraham, who like his women slender like young boys. Brother Isaiah was not precisely svelte himself, his buttocks making a fleshy seal atop the wooden seat.

Absently, he noticed that the fragrance of the privy was not too bad this evening.

That was because the accumulated night soil from two months of human habitation had been consumed, turned into more fundamental chemical components, by that which lurked in the depths of Paradise's sandy soil. The cache of organic material absorbed, black threads sought more fodder to feed their voracious appetite. Up the pressed particle board sides of the dung pit they swarmed.

Reaching the top, the contagion was faced with a fleshy plug, capping the one open toilet. The black swarm took the path of least resistance and entered the single proffered orifice. Brother Isaiah never new what hit him.

Isaiah reflexively tried to stand but he was dead before he reached his feet. Black sinews emerged from his mouth and nose as death ate him from the inside out. A black trunk slammed his body through the privy door, wearing his eviscerated corpse like a meat puppet. As tatters of his skin dropped off and fell into the surging black torrent, the other latrines erupted with their own fountains of death.

As the threads swept into the settlement proper, the screams began.

* * * * *

At the bottom of the Shuttle's cargo ramp Leon was conversing with Brother Abraham as two young men struggled with the last container of supplies. Leon was anxious to depart, having had enough of both Paradise and Brother Abraham, but the cult leader had a proposition.

"So, brother, I was wondering if you might be returning to Zion on a future voyage?" Brother Abraham had a habit of calling everyone brother or sister.

"Maybe, I can't say for sure," Leon answered brusquely.

"As you may know, when we made arrangements for this enterprise we agreed to forgo some supplies that the other colonists considered forbidden in the eyes of their gods."

"Yeah, and your point is?"

"Both the Jews and Muslims demanded that we bring no food animals their heathen religions declared 'unclean'. Only mammals that chew the cud and part the hoof."

"What?" Leon was now thoroughly confused.

"One of the things we had to leave behind was swine. No pigs means no pork, no ham, and no bacon! I miss them already, and our time in our new home has barely begun." The look on Brother Abraham's face was one of terrible sadness.

"Listen, we don't have any pigs stashed on board the ship or I'd bring you some. What do you expect us to do?"

"I was thinking that, if you were to return to this world on a future voyage, and could convince the powers that be to send along a small herd of swine, I would be in your debt."

This piqued Leon's interest. "And just how would you repay that debt?"

"I think we could come to some arrangement, something to ease the hardships of a man far from home with no female companionship?" Brother Abraham's eyebrows rose in an expression of understanding between men of the world.

*Damn!* Though Leon. *If I knew I could exchange pigs for pussy I would have smuggled some porkers on this voyage.* "Now that is an interesting proposition, Brother Abraham. And I will be sure..."

Shouting and screams from the settlement interrupted Leon's negotiation with the preacher.

"Look!" cried one of the young men, dropping his end of the shipping container. "What in heaven's name is that?"

A tidal wave of black thread poured out of the town and spread across the grassy field. A number of people ran from the settlement toward the shuttle—they were over taken and pulled under.

"Holy shit!" Leon exclaimed. "Get on the god damned shuttle if you want to live, preacher!"

Leon jumped onto the ramp and ran into the cargo hold. After standing for a second, mouth agape, Brother Abraham scrambled on board with his young followers close behind.

"Frank! Get this bird in the air," Leon yelled into the intercom while hitting the emergency ramp closure button. "That black thread shit is for real and its coming right at us!"

The young settlers were still on the ramp as it raised into its closed position, dumping them onto the cargo bay floor. A shudder went through the shuttle as Frank engaged the bottom repulsors.

\* \* \* \* \*

On the shuttle's flight deck Frank had been idly staring off into space, dreaming of what he would do when the Fortune made port at Farside. Leon's cry caused him to look out the cockpit's side window, just in time to see another running settler consumed by rampaging black sinews.

"Shit!"

Though Frank had many shortcomings his saving grace was that he was a good shuttle pilot. His hands flew across the controls as he engaged the bottom repulsors and threw the massive shuttle into the air. Belatedly engaging the deck gravity, he raised the nose and applied the thrusters. The questing black threads fell short of the departing shuttle by a matter of a few meters.

"Leon, are you OK back there?"

"Yeah, man. Tell me we are off this fucking planet."

"The gear is up and we are in the air at about 800 meters and climbing. Did anyone else get on with you?"

"Yeah, the head preacher and a couple of acolytes. They were a bit shook up by the liftoff."

"Tell 'em to complain to the management. I'm going to circle the area and see what is happening on the ground. Check for any sign of survivors."

"Go right ahead, but I don't think you are going to find dick. I'm going to get our passengers strapped in and come forward."

"Right. I gotta call the ship."

### Bridge, ESS Fortune

"ESS Fortune, this is Shuttle Bravo. Come in."

"Go, Shuttle Bravo," Sid replied.

"Fortune, we have a problem." Regardless of what they fly, pilots are pilots—the terse Chuck Yeager, test-pilot speech pattern was seemingly ingrained during flight training.

"What kind of problem, Shuttle Bravo?"

"You know that black shit you warned us to look out for? Well it just ate Zion."

"Ate Zion? What do you mean, 'ate Zion'?"

"Ate as in devoured. Black crap came flowing out of the town, faster than a man can run, and almost got to us before we could lift off."

"Are you sure? Where are you now? I mean what is your position?" The Captain was clearly flustered.

"I'm orbiting the settlement at a thousand meters, scanning for survivors."

"Are there any survivors?"

"Just Brother Abraham and two lucky bastards who were standing near the cargo hatch when the shit hit the fan."

"Roger, Shuttle Bravo. Can you send me video of the scene?"

"Roger that. Patching it through now..."

# Chapter 23

*CIC, Peggy Sue*

The picture in the main 3D holotank showed a miniature diorama of a ruin in the desert. Disheveled white buildings stood forlornly in an endless sea of tan. Here and there the blue-black glint of sunlight reflected off a solar panel flashed. A few hours ago that ruin had been a settlement with over sixty souls living in it, along with growing gardens, grazing livestock, and surrounding fields of prairie grass. The satellite view showed no sign of survivors, no sign of life.

"That is just wrong," said Billy Ray. "Nothing that can do that to a living world should exist in this Universe."

"I am afraid that the organism, whatever it is, has been reawakened, Captain," said Will Krenshaw.

"You think it's some form of life, Doctor?"

"It acts like a biological organism—a voracious, ravaging organism to be sure—but an organism nonetheless."

"Hmm," Ahnah rumbled. "It's more like anti-life than life. Organisms are not supposed to evolve that eat their food supply into extinction—that just doesn't make sense. Predators are supposed to cull the herd, not eradicate it."

"Agreed, Ahnah," said Mizuki, "but there is no reason to assume that it evolved naturally."

"You suspect meddling, Dr. Ogawa?"

"All of us are proof that it does happen, Captain."

"But why create something that wipes a planet clean of life and then dies off itself?" asked Will.

"That is not dead which can eternal lie, Doctor."

"An appropriate quotation from somewhere," Will replied.

"Abdul Alhazred the mad poet," came Bobby's voice over the comm circuit. He and Beth were monitoring events from on board the shuttle, ready to deploy.

"Actually Lovecraft quoting him in 'The Nameless City'." Billy Ray smiled. "You were the one who started spouting Lovecraft when you visited those first ruins, pardner."

"I guess the reference was a better fit than I imagined, Captain."

"Mizuki, can we get a satellite pass over New Mecca? With Zion wiped out, and probably New Jerusalem as well, we need to know if there is anyone left down there to rescue."

"Hai, Captain, there is a pass coming up. I'll display it in the holotank."

The room fell silent as the desolation of Zion was replaced by a pastoral scene, centered on New Mecca. The green prairie was still intact and tiny figures could be seen moving between the low white buildings.

"They seem to be untouched, for now."

"Then there is no time to lose. Peggy Sue, open a channel to the Fortune—I need to talk to Captain Chakrabarti."

"Yes, Captain. Establishing the link now..."

### Bridge, ESS Fortune

"I have told you before, Captain Vincent. I will not jeopardize any more personnel or a shuttle in a vain attempt to rescue hypothetical surviving colonists. You brought this curse down upon us, you deal with it!"

Captain Chakrabarti was fortunate to not be physically confronting Billy Ray. Peggy Sue's captain was exasperated enough to wring his counterpart's neck.

"So yer just going to standby in orbit and wait for the last seventy settlers to become a meal for the infestation? You didn't, by any chance, leave yer balls back at Farside, did you?"

Sid's face turned dark with anger. He broke the connection without saying another word. Sitting at the bridge console, fists clenched in impotent rage, Fortune's captain cursed the other man, and his own wretched luck. In a matter of a few days the mission had gone from complete success to utter failure—the sweet taste of triumph turned to ashes in his mouth. Logic fled as Sid's thoughts became increasingly irrational.

*Why do these meddling merchants have to bedevil me? If they hadn't raised the alarm the settlers may never have been attacked. Captain Vincent is so concerned about the Muslim rabble in the last settlement? Let him risk his crew and equipment trying to rescue them!*

The ship's computer interrupted his dark thoughts.

"Captain, Shuttle B has achieved orbit and is on course for rendezvous in approximately 90 minutes."

"Yes, yes. That's wonderful. Have them come to the bridge when they dock. Have Chu and Bell checked out Shuttle C yet?"

"I believe they are on their way to shuttle bay three as we speak, Captain."

"Good, good. Let me know if they find anything out-of-place." That the Captain was communicating with his crew through the ship's computer was not a good sign. Not a good sign at all.

### CIC, Peggy Sue

The ship was manned and ready for action. On the bridge, Umky was connected to the main tracking and fire control system. It turned out that the structure of a polar bear's brain was perfectly suited to interface with the T'aafhal devices that enabled tracking of ships and large objects in alter-space. Stars, planets and anything running a gravitonic drive impinged on the higher dimensions of alter-space, where effective distances were much shorter than in 3-space. Targets can be detected much more rapidly in alter-space; faster than the propagation of signals at the speed of light allowed in normal space.

Some humans could use the direct mind interface of the tracking system—Dr. Ogawa for instance—but bears were much better at it. This was because the interface operated on a different part of the human brain than it did on bears. A human being's most developed sense is vision, so the interface used the visual cortex to

271

transfer data into the operator's mind. It took much uncomfortable training and a lot of throwing up before the strange multidimensional images made sense to a human.

Bears, on the other hand, had the most exquisite sense of smell of all Earth's creatures. When interfacing with a polar bear, the link was through the olfactory parts of the ursine brain. In effect, Umky could smell the presence of ships and stars and planets. Why they should be such natural operators for this type of equipment remained a mystery, but the few who knew about such things suspected that it was due to evolutionary meddling by the T'aafhal.

"Captain, Fire Control," Umky called over the bridge circuit.

In the CIC, Billy Ray answered.

"Go, Fire Control."

"I'm tracking a shuttle on an intercept trajectory with the colony ship. It should rendezvous in seventy minutes."

"Very good, keep me informed of their activity."

"Sir? I also have a visual on the Fortune. It looks like there are already two docked shuttles aboard her. The inbound shuttle would be the third."

"I see. Thank you, Mr. Umky." Billy Ray muted the link to the bridge. "Damn it all! That miserable little sidewinder has been holding out on me."

"Captain?" asked Mizuki. In good times the Captain had a tendency to quote Shakespeare or Chaucer. When annoyed he reverted to cowboy argot that some found almost comical. That was a mistake people made only once, because when angered he became as cold blooded as a gunfighter.

"That Colonization Board varmint didn't bother to tell me that his missing shuttle had returned to the fold. They must know what happened to New Jerusalem."

"Captain, we have been scanning the New Jerusalem site from orbit and there are no signs of life. While we cannot be 100% sure that settlement was attacked until we get a visual, I am 99% sure the colonists were destroyed."

"That may be, Dr. Ogawa, but if someone escaped they may be able to give us some useful information. Peggy Sue, try to raise the Fortune again."

"I have done so, Captain, and they refuse our call."

Sid swore under his breath and called the waiting shuttle. "Beth, cast off and head for the remaining settlement. We'll get no help from the Fortune."

"Aye, aye, Captain."

"Damn that little pissant, there are people's lives at stake here. Maybe he'll get the message if I send a railgun slug through his hull!"

With that, Billy Ray left the CIC, headed forward to the bridge.


### Flight Deck, Shuttle One

"Peggy Sue, Shuttle One. We have undocked and are starting a minimum time descent to New Mecca." As he spoke, Bobby guided the shuttle clear of the ship. Looking at Beth, seated in the copilot's seat, he said, "You'd better tell the Jar Heads that we are a go."

"Right, Bobby." Switching to the crew frequency the First Officer told those in the cargo hold to prepare themselves. "We are beginning our descent to the planet's surface, people. It would appear that we can expect no assistance from the Fortune so this will all be on us. We should be on the surface in just under two hours."

The heavily armored shuttle did a graceful pirouette combined with a back flip, putting it on a trajectory for the planet below.

"Show off," Beth sniped.

"Gotta make the most of any opportunity," Bobby grinned. Both of them being pilots, he and Beth shared a brother-sister type of rivalry when it came to flying. Turning serious he asked the mission's commander what her plans were. "How are we going to handle this when we get down there?"

"I don't really know, Bobby. If there is no sign of hostile activity I think we should land as close to the town as possible—in the town if we can find an open space big enough."

"That would get their attention."

"Yes. And that is going to be the problem. How to convince the settlers they should abandon their new homes and get on board a shuttle they've never seen. I can talk to them in Arabic, but with no sign of a threat they have little reason to believe me."

"The bitch of it is, If they do see the threat it's probably already too late."

\* \* \* \* \*

All those on board were wearing armored spacesuits: the crew and officers standard armor, the Marines heavy combat armor. In the cargo hold the four Marines were clustered near the rear ramp, discussing the mission. Closer to the front of the cargo space two of the crew, Kate Hamm and Kashi Ademola, were sitting on jump seats, eavesdropping on the squad of hulking armored giants.

"So what's the plan, Gunny?" asked Kato.

"We are going to follow the First Officer's lead. Our job is to keep things orderly, and the boat safe."

"And if a wave of black, flesh dissolving alien crap heads our way?"

"We get back on the ship ASAP and ask Cmdr. Danner to get us the hell outta there."

"Da, this seems well planned."

"If your job was thinking you'd be an officer, Bosco. Just shut up and follow orders. I want everyone to remember that this is a high gravity planet. You are all used to wearing armor under low G and no G conditions. Dirtside these suits weigh the equivalent of seven hundred kilos, more than three quarters of a ton, so do not try to bounce around like a comic book superhero down there."

"We were all down to the surface before, Gunny," chided Kato.

"Yeah, and you have the memory span of a goldfish."

"If we're picking up a bunch of people why aren't there any chairs set up?" asked Vinny. The cargo hold was generally reconfigured for a mission before leaving the ship.

"There's supposed to be something like seventy civilians, so it's going to be a full house. The Chief figured it would be faster just to cram 'em in standing up than have them fumble about trying to find a seat."

"So the plan is to land, pack in the settlers like a bunch of sardines and then get the hell outta Dodge?"

"You got it, Vinny. We send them up the ramp and the two swabbies get to do the packing."

"Great plan, Gunny."

"Nobody likes a smart ass, Vinny."


### Shuttle B, ESS Fortune

"Fortune, Shuttle Bravo. We are maneuvering for docking capture," Frank reported to the ship. The Captain had stopped responding to his calls an hour ago. Instead, the voice of the ship's computer acknowledged the pilot's call.

"Shuttle Bravo, you are cleared to dock in bay two."

"Roger, Fortune. Thank you."

"Where's the Old Man? He taking a late lunch or something?"

"Who knows, Leon. We are almost back on board the transport and that's all I give a shit about. After seeing what that black crap did to those poor colonists I want to get away from this place as fast as I can."

"What do you think that stuff was? I ain't never seen anything like that before."

"That's because if you had seen it you'd be dead. Now go see if our passengers have pissed themselves or died of fright. We'll be docked in under ten minutes."

"Gotcha, boss."

# Chapter 24

## *Flight Deck, Shuttle One*

Ionized gases wrapped the shuttle as it entered the atmosphere and for a brief time it was out of radio contact with the Peggy Sue. After slowing from orbital velocity, Bobby reestablished communications with the ship.

"Peggy Sue, Shuttle One, we have just gone subsonic and are approaching the target area."

"Shuttle One, Peggy Sue. Roger that. Be advised that the transport appears to be making preparations for getting underway. You won't be able to take the colonists to the Fortune. Over."

"Yeah, this keeps getting better and better," Bobby said to Beth. "Roger that, Peggy Sue. We will get you a sitrep in about five minutes."

"Roger, Shuttle One. We are standing by."

The shuttle approached the continent on which New Mecca was located, coming in from the west. This brought it in over a range of mountains followed by rocky hill country. Ahead lay the plains.

"Look, there is still grassland," Beth observed. "They may still be alive."

"I'll swing south of the settlement and we can make a low pass before deciding where to land."

"Right." Beth switched to the comm link. "Ms. Acuna, be advised we are on approach to the settlement. I'll let you know as soon as we pick a landing site."

"Roger, Ma'am," came the Gunny's reply.

Bobby raised his eyebrows and glanced sideways at Beth. "You never call Rosey 'Gunny' like everyone else."

"Not now, Bobby, the curtain is about to go up... Oh bollocks!"

"Shit!" Bobby quickly pulled up, trading forward speed for altitude.

Below the shuttle a black stain was spreading rapidly across the prairie grass. It came from along the river that ran south and east of the settlement.

"It's headed right for the village. Can we get there in time?"

Bobby's experienced pilot's eye gauged the speed of the advancing blackness below. "That stuff is moving at about klicks an hour."

"It will be on them in maybe ten minutes. Can we warn them, could they run?"

"Beth the average human's top speed is between 20 and 25 kph. Besides, they have nowhere to run to."

"Then we're too late." Stony faced, Beth stared at the doomed settlement. "We can't save them."


### Hills Above New Mecca

The flock of sheep was contentedly grazing its way along the edge of the prairie grass, along the boundary line between verdant Earth life and the bare native rock of Paradise. Shadi looked at the rugged foothills, only twenty meters from the end of the settlers' imported greenness. They looked old and worn, like the bones of the planet uncovered from a shallow dug grave. Her morbid thoughts were interrupted by the double sonic boom of an incoming shuttle.

*That's strange. I thought there were to be no more shuttle deliveries.* She looked up and spotted the craft as it passed overhead. It was different from the big delta shaped shuttles that had ferried them from ship to surface. This shuttle was smaller yet it seemed stouter, a blunter projectile.

She followed the path of the strange shuttle as it flew toward the settlement. Her thoughts were interrupted by Dorri's shout.

"Shadi, look at the village. Can you make out what is happening?"

"What?" Peering east toward the settlement, through the shimmering air of a hot prairie day, she saw what looked like a mirage—a black highlight moving across the green grass around New Mecca. "It looks like a mirage, caused by the rising air currents."

"I've never seen a mirage like that, it looks like black ink spilled on a green blotter."

Dorri was right. The darkness didn't act like a mirage, shimmering above the ground at the junction of earth and sky. This was more of a black flood spreading across the grassland. Dorri turned and ran to where her sister was standing.

"What is that? It looks like something is flowing out of the river."

"I don't know, Dorri, but it is about to reach the walls of the village."

As the sisters watched from their vantage point in the hills, people began to emerge from the settlement. The small figures ran their direction, away from the houses. As blackness spread around either side of New Mecca, like an ocean wave closing around a sandcastle in the rising tide, darkness could be seen engulfing the buildings.

A horse ran out of the village, pursued by a breaking wave of surging blackness. The horse galloped past the running townsfolk, who were swept under by the dark torrent. Long fingers of black raced ahead, catching up to the fleeing horse, dragging it down and flowing over it. Horses were now extinct on Paradise—only two humans and a small flock of sheep remained.

"Shadi, what is happening?" asked Dorri fearfully.

"Run," Shadi said in a hoarse whisper.

"What?"

Hiking up her long robe, eyes wide, she turned to her sister.

"Run, Dorri! Run for the bare rock on the hill above us."

"What about the sheep?"

"Leave the sheep! Run, little star, like you've never run before!"

The sisters ran for their lives while the sheep placidly chewed their cuds, unaware of death's approach.

### Bridge, Peggy Sue

"That's right Captain. The contagion has reached the settlement. I'm afraid we're too late. We had no chance to even land."

"Understood, Shuttle One. Do not risk yourselves landing on the surface." Billy Ray sat in the captain's command chair, staring at empty space with hard eyes. The anger and disdain he felt for Fortune's captain boiled within him. "Peggy Sue, you will send a message to the Fortune on the open emergency channel, instructing them to call us back immediately or face the consequences."

"Yes, Captain."

"Mr. Umky. Power up the main railgun battery and get me a firing solution on the Fortune. Mr. Lawson, raise the shields and maneuver to intercept the target."

"Aye, aye, Sir."

"Sound Battle Stations. Bring all weapons online."

The klaxon's rasp sounded throughout the ship as the Peggy Sue moved to intercept the colonization ship floating one hundred and forty thousand kilometers way.

### Bridge, ESS Fortune

On board the Colonization Board ship the Captain and the Navigator were on the bridge, having an argument. The Captain had just ordered the engine room to bring power online so the ship could get underway.

"Captain, what are you doing? We can't leave without making sure that there are no survivors on the surface of the planet!"

"You heard the transmission from the merchant shuttle, the last settlement was overcome by the black death. There is no one here to save except ourselves."

"You can't be sure. We should at least wait for a full surface scan by the observation satellites."

"No! As soon as all of our shuttles are back on board we are returning to home base. We have to tell them not to send anymore ships, any more colonists. They shouldn't have sent us here in the first place!"

"Captain, the survey drone spent six months looking for danger and found none. Hell, the Trading Company types even went to the surface in several locations and found nothing."

"Nothing until they almost lost their ship to that vile blackness!" Sid was becoming more agitated as he ranted on. "That bastard Vincent waited until all the settlers were on the planet, until the grass had been planted and everything was offloaded. Then he starts screaming about death from the dirt beneath the colonists' feet. He must have called it forth, to kill all those people, to ruin my mission!"

"Come on, Captain Chakrabarti. There is no way the merchants caused this catastrophe. It was just the devil's own luck that Paradise wasn't dead after all."

"We need to get back so I can report this atrocity!"

The Captain's ravings were interrupted by the ship's computer.

"Captain, I have received an urgent message on the emergency channel. The captain of the Peggy Sue has ordered us to reply."

"Ordered? How dare he!"

"Captain, my sensors indicate that the Peggy Sue is underway. Her shields have been raised and they are powering up their weapons."

"Oh balls!" said the Navigator. "Captain, if you won't reply I will. I don't know what they are up to but that ship can blow us out of space without trying hard."

"Go ahead and answer then! And don't think that I'm not going to report your insubordination!" The Captain stormed off to his small sea cabin just off the bridge. If it were possible to slam an automatic sliding door he would have. The Navigator moved to the main console and switched on the comm circuit to acknowledge the call from Peggy Sue.

### Shuttle B, ESS Fortune

Frank watched the docking indicator signal final capture with relief. If he never saw the surface of Paradise again it would be a lifetime too soon.

"Leon, we're docked, buddy. You can bring our passengers forward and use the crew airlock to board the ship. No need to drop the cargo ramp this time."

"Roger that, Frank. We'll be up front directly. This damned preacher is driving me crazy."

"Oh? What's he doing? He's not getting violent or anything, is he?"

"No, he's just spewing all short's of crap about God's wrath and Judgment Day and being tried and found wanting. The two acolytes are scared to death. Hell, one of them is crying."

"That's just great." Frank punched in the sequence of commands that opened the crew gangway, lowering the airstair into the airlock chamber leading off the shuttle. "I've opened the crew hatch. You take Brother Nut Job and his followers up to the bridge to see the Captain. I still have to go through the shutdown procedure to secure the shuttle for the trip home."

"Yeah, you always got something to do so's you can avoid dealing with scut work."

"You should have become a pilot, Leon. We get all the breaks."

Frank switched off the intercom and called the bridge.

"Bridge, Shuttle Bravo. We have docked and are disembarking passengers. I'm sending Leon forward with three survivors from Zion."

"Roger that, Shuttle Bravo. Send them forward. The Captain is insisting we get underway for home ASAP."

The voice was that of the Navigator, not the Captain. Frank shrugged—even captains had to hit the head sometimes.

"They are on their way. I will let you know when the shuttle is secure for getting underway."

"I copy, Shuttle Bravo. You might want to check with Chu and Bell. The Captain sent them to secure Shuttle Charlie more than an hour ago."

"They're probably goofing off as usual. When I get done here I'll go over to bay three and give 'em a hand."

"Roger that. Bridge out."

### Shuttle Bay Three, ESS Fortune

"Just what is so important about checking out Shuttle C?" asked the crewman called Bell. "That damn computer is becoming as much of a nag as the Old Man."

"We have to secure it for departure before we can leave for home, and anything that gets us closer to going home I'm all for," replied Chu, one of the shuttle pilots.

"Yeah, yeah. So drop the cargo ramp and let's put this puppy to bed."

Chu punched in his authorization code on the airlock panel. The access light glowed green, indicating that the controls were now live. With a few more finger swipes the shuttle's large rear cargo ramp clanked and unsealed, whining as it lowered into the airlock's interior.

The ramp touched down on the airlock floor and the outer door slid open. As Chu secured the lock controls Bell entered and started up the ramp to the shuttle's cargo hold.

"Shout if you find anything out-of-place," called Chu. "I'll be right up."

# Chapter 25

## Shuttle One, New Mecca

The armored shuttle loitered above the settlement of New Mecca while the black contagion swept over the place. They watched as the few settlers who managed to run from the destruction of the village were pulled down and absorbed. They witnessed the death of the running horse, the last living thing to escape the forsaken settlement.

"You were right, Bobby. The threads managed to pull down that horse—people had no chance to outrun it."

"It's not our fault, Beth. If we had left a half hour earlier we might have been caught on the ground." Bobby shuddered involuntarily.

"It's just that I hate feeling so bloody helpless."

"Hey, the FLIR is showing something in the infrared up ahead."

"Where?"

"There," he said, zooming in with an optical camera on the IR target. On the center part of the shuttle's curved control panel a view of a hillside appeared, half grass covered, half bare rock.

"It looks like a flock of sheep. And, look! There are two people running up the hill!"

"Your right! We may not have missed everyone after all." Bobby slammed the throttle forward and the shuttle lept toward the foothills, racing above the oncoming blackness on the ground.

Bobby angled the shuttle to the north of the two fleeing shepherds, so they would not be harmed by the shuttle's powerful repulsors when he brought it to a hover in front of them.

"Cargo Hold, look alive back there," Beth called to the Marines in the rear of the craft, "we have a couple of survivors."

Without waiting for a response she unstrapped from the copilot's seat, telling Bobby, "I'm going to get into position. When we are on the ground drop the ramp."

"I'm not going to land, that stuff is coming on too fast. I'm going to do a nose up hover and pop the ramp so it just touches the ground."

"Right, I'll tell the others." Beth headed aft at a run.

The shuttle approached the rocky ground at an alarming rate, triggering plaintive warnings from the collision alarms. At the last minute, Bobby pitched the shuttle's nose up to almost forty five degrees and decelerated cruelly. At the same time he slid the massive craft sideways, in front of the running settlers. Dust and lose stones flew from the heavy shuttle's repulsors, but away from the prospective survivors. With the tail less than ten meters from the ground, Bobby dropped the rear cargo ramp. It barely kissed the surface.

Concentrating on holding the shuttle's position, Bobby kept his hand on the main throttle, ready to catapult the vessel away from the surface if necessary. While Bobby fought to keep the shuttle's awkward hover stable the Marines moved down the extended ramp. The Gunny took the lead, moving to the very end of the ramp on the left. Kato hung back on the right side by the ramp's support strut. Between them ran Beth.

### Hills Above New Mecca

Running uphill in Paradise's heavier than Earth-normal gravity quickly had both girls breathing hard. Upon reaching bare rock, Shadi looked back over her shoulder to check on Dorri. Her sister was three meters behind her, laboring up the incline and almost free of the grass.

Looking at the sheep, still near where their shepherds had abandoned them, Shadi gasped. The flock had finally realized that they were in danger and tried to run after their human guardians. Too late. Ropey black sinews whipped around their plump bodies, wrapping them into struggling black bundles. The bundles quickly ceased their struggles and were absorbed into the growing black flood. The threads rushed on, up the slope after the last two humans on the planet.

"Run, Dorri, run!" Shadi urged her sister on. She then resumed her own uphill flight.

Dorri didn't bother to reply, but she did increase her effort, running a bit faster now that she was on bare ground. As they struggled up the rocky slope a low thrumming sound swelled up around them. The sound became louder, to the point where it resonated in their chests, as a huge gray wedge of metal passed them on the left.

It pulled ahead of the running girls, rearing up like a motor cycle doing a wheelie. As it pitched up at a forty five degree angle a ramp opened in the shuttle's rear. As the bottom of the ramp touched the rocky hillside figures moved down it, standing at an odd angle to the planet's gravity. The first figure was a huge gray-black monster. Dorri screamed.

"Djin!" she shrieked, thinking the dark shapes were demons.

"No, Dorri! It's a shuttle. They are trying to rescue us."

Before Dorri could reply a second figure appeared. This one was also large and gray but it was recognizable as some form of space suit. Within its transparent bubble helmet was the head of an African woman. She spoke to them in Arabic.

"Yella, yella! Run and jump onto the ship!"

Shadi turned and yelled to her sister.

"Jump up on the ramp, Dorri!"

The almost exhausted Dorri stumbled past her sister and with a final effort jumped onto the shuttle's extended ramp. The African woman grabbed her, pulled her up the ramp and passed her to another dark figure inside the ship.

Shadi felt an instant of relief as Dorri was whisked to safety. *Allah is merciful, we may live after all.*

Then she looked back and saw black sinews reaching for her.

Shadi screamed.

### Shuttle One, The Hills Above New Mecca

The shuttle's cargo ramp contained deck gravity plates that created a local gravity field normal to its surface. This meant that those standing on the ramp appeared to be standing at a forty five degree angle with respect to the ground. Whether this gave the approaching survivors any pause was not evident as the smaller of the two jumped for the ramp.

The young girl stumbled in the unexpected gravity shift. Beth grabbed her arm and half lifted, half drug her back into the cargo hold. She passed her living burden off to Kashi, waiting just off the ramp inside the hold.

Turning back down the ramp Beth saw the second settler, also a young girl, facing away from the shuttle. The girl was screaming and immobile, frozen in fear. Beth ran, but she knew she was too far up the ramp to reach the girl in time. Beth yelled.

"No, damn it!"

The Gunny was closest to the girl, standing almost on the end of the ramp. The lead Marine quickly sized up the situation—the First Officer was too far up the ramp to help and the black shit was already reaching out for the helpless girl. Rosey swore under her breath.

"Fuck it."

Rosey jumped from the ramp to the rocky hillside below. She landed heavily on her left leg, flexing to absorb the force of the landing. In a single continuous motion, she swung her left arm wide, scooping up the paralyzed girl and throwing her bodily into the shuttle.

Beth was halfway back down the ramp when the second girl came flying on board. She managed to catch the second survivor as she saw with horror that the black threads had reached the Gunny.

Thrown off balance, Rosey rolled on the ground. Under the weight of the heavy armor she struggled awkwardly to her feet. Back upright, she managed a single step in the direction of the ramp.

"Bobby, punch it!" Beth cried, realizing that there was nothing they could do for the Gunny and that the ravenous black threads would be on board the shuttle in another instant.

Bobby, with reflexes faster than a mongoose, rammed the forward thrusters to full even before Beth had finished speaking his name. The shuttle jumped from the ground at the same forty five degree angle it had been hovering at.

Beth held on to the second survivor, hugging the girl close to her armored chest. The view out the back of the shuttle's open cargo door showed the ground rapidly falling away. As the cargo ramp closed, a sea of roiling black threads seethed around the figure of Rosey Acuna.

The shuttle sped safely away, but the last thing Beth saw was burned into her mind—the Gunny's outstretched gauntleted hand, reaching out of the swarming blackness.

### Bridge, Peggy Sue

"Peggy Sue, Shuttle One. We are headed for orbit with two, I repeat, two survivors from New Mecca."

"Copy that, Shuttle One. Interrogative casualty count?"

There was a pause.

"One casualty, Gunny Acuna. She's missing and presumed dead."

*Oh dear God no! Rosey is like family.* The Captain's thoughts raced. *The crew will take this badly, not to mention the surviving Marines.*

"Roger, Shuttle One. Be advised we are moving to intercept the Fortune, though there no longer seems to be any point in delaying them."

"Captain," said Doc White, who had come forward from the sick bay during the rescue operation, "tell them to put the survivors on pure oxygen for an hour or so. They have been under higher than normal atmospheric pressure for an extended period of time. Their tissues are probably saturated with nitrogen."

289

"Right Doc. Shuttle One, the Doc says to put the survivors on pure oxygen, otherwise they might get the bends."

"We copy, Peggy Sue. We will report in when we are in high orbit. Shuttle One, clear."

The Captain stood quietly for a moment, his face unreadable. He squinted momentarily and then sat down in the command chair, evidently having arrived at a decision.

"Helm, Lay in a course to pick up Shuttle One."

"Aye, aye, Captain."

### Cargo Hold, ESS Fortune

Leon was still trying to cajole his wards into the large elevator at the center of the cargo hold. That lift ran up the ship's spine, all the way to the crew quarters just below the bridge. Frank was finished securing the shuttle for the trip home, shutting down its reactor and shifting all onboard systems over to external power from Fortune. He descended the airstair and was standing in the door of the airlock when he heard a scream.

Looking to port, he saw another shuttle pilot, Steve Chu, running along the hold's perimeter. The man screamed again and then shouted.

"It melted him! It fuckin' melted Bell!"

Before Chu could clarify his statement a thin whip of black cord lashed out from behind him and encircled his legs. Chu went down as more threads engulfed him. In an instant he was gone and the threads shot forward, seeking new prey.

"Go!" Frank shouted to the party boarding the elevator. He ducked back inside the airlock hitting the emergency close button on the inside wall. The door slammed shut and Frank bolted up the airstair, retracting it behind him.

\* \* \* \* \*

At the elevator, Leon was having trouble convincing Brother Abraham that he needed to talk with the Captain. Frank's warning cry, followed by the appearance of rapidly moving black threads from the far bulkhead convinced the three ex-colonists where Leon could not. They dove for the inside of the lift, cowering against the far wall of the car. Leon stepped inside and punched the up button.

"Come on you recalcitrant piece of garbage, move," he yelled at the door as it slid shut. The door slid home just in time, though banging and rasping sounds could be heard from outside. After an instant's hesitation, the car rose toward the bow of the ship.

"God please spare me!" Abraham beseeched the almighty. "It is surely Lucifer who thirsts for my soul, who has pursued me even into space from that vile hell below."

"Brother Abraham, what are we to do?" wailed one of the young men who had also escaped death on the planet.

Abraham ignored his followers and continued to beg God's forgiveness for his manifold sins. By the time the elevator deposited the four on the crew level, Leon was regretting not letting the blackness take the craven sycophant.

\* \* \* \* \*

After sealing the shuttle's crew hatch Frank paused for a few moments to don a space suit. He didn't know if a suit would protect him against the ravaging black death but he figured it couldn't hurt. Making his way to the flight deck he began reversing the shutdown sequence he had finished only minutes earlier. Waiting for internal power to be restored, he transmitted a message in the clear over the open emergency channel.

"All personnel on board the ESS Fortune. Be advised that the black contagion that wiped out the planetary settlements is on board the ship. I say again, the contagion is on board the Fortune."

After repeating the warning twice he got a reply from Fortune's bridge.

"Party broadcasting on the emergency frequency, please identify yourself, this is the ESS Fortune. Over."

"Fortune, Shuttle Bravo. This is Frank Hoenig, pilot in charge. That black crap just ate Chu as he was running away from shuttle bay three. I don't know if it got Leon and the three settlers we rescued or not."

"Shuttle Bravo, be advised that Leon and the survivors have made it to the bridge. What is your situation? Over."

"I'm locked inside the shuttle with the airlock doors all sealed."

"Did any of it get inside the shuttle?"

"If it had we wouldn't be having this conversation."

"What would you suggest we do? Can you stay in the shuttle for the trip back to Earth?"

"Plenty of air and water, but scant rations for a month. You're not planning on doing a transit back home with that shit in the hold are you?"

"Affirmative, Shuttle Bravo. It is Captain Chakrabarti's intention to get underway immediately."

"You're crazy! The Fortune is not like a warship, with lots of separate airtight zones, its life support is all interconnected. The black crud will find its way to you before we get home. I suggest you get to the escape pods and abandon ship. I can pick you up in the shuttle later."

"And then what do we do?"

Frank had no answer for the last question so he said nothing.

## Chapter 26

### Shuttle One, Paradise Orbit

Shadi and Dorri sat on uncomfortable canvas jump-seats with breathing masks over their noses and mouths. The African woman who had helped rescue them disappeared right after they left the surface of the planet and none of the others had tried to talk to them except for another African, a man in a bubble helmeted suit like the woman wore. He got them seated and strapped in and pantomimed breathing through the masks they now had on their faces.

Though they were glad to be alive, both sisters were starting to get bored and a little bit angry at being ignored. Then the African woman returned from the front of the shuttle. She stopped in front of them and stared, hands on hips. Then she removed her helmet and spoke to them in understandable Arabic.

"My name is Beth Melaku. I am First Officer on the Peggy Sue, a starship owned by the Orion Arm Trading Company. Who are you?"

"I'm Shadi, and this is my sister Dorri. We were settlers at New Mecca; we belonged to the house of Imam Mustafa Al-Ghazali."

"Was that man, Mustafa Al-Ghazali, your father?"

"No, our family was from Teheran. They died in the great bombardment."

"I'm sorry to hear that, Shadi." The African woman looked at her closely and said in Farsi, "So you are Iranian, not Arabs"?

"Yes, Ma'am," Shadi replied in the same language.

"Hmm," the dark woman said.

"Can I ask you a question?"

"Yes, of course."

"Are you all Africans on this ship?"

"What?" Beth blinked. "Ah, I see. Kashi helped you with your masks and you can't see the faces of the Marines in their heavy armor. Kashi is indeed an African, from Nigeria."

Beth paused for a moment to make sure she had been understood. Her Farsi was not nearly as good as her Arabic. Both girls nodded their comprehension.

"My parents were from Ethiopia, but I was born and raised in Britain. We have people from many nations on board this shuttle and on the Peggy Sue. For example, Kate is German, and Bosco, one of the Marines, is Russian. The others here are Americans."

"We also speak English, Ms. Melaku," said Dorri, speaking for the first time.

Beth smiled at her and again changed languages. "That is good to know, Dorri. It will make talking to the crew much easier."

"What's to happen to us, Ma'am?" asked Shadi in excellent English.

"Right now we are waiting for our Captain to rendezvous with us. Then we will dock with the ship and get the ship's medical doctor to examine you, just to make sure you are alright. Then you will talk to the Captain and he will figure out what to do with you."

Both girls looked somewhat dubious at that last statement. In Farsi Dorri said to Shadi, "We are going to be under the control of another patriarch, sister."

Beth smiled. "Oh, I think you will find that our Captain is a very reasonable man—very fair when it comes to such matters. You see he is from Texas and follows a sort of cowboy code. He believes that everyone should be treated with respect, especially women and children. He is also my husband."

Again Beth smiled at the sisters, whose eyes went wide when the tall British/Ethiopian woman said she was married to a cowboy from Texas.

### Bridge, Peggy Sue

The distance between the Peggy Sue and Shuttle One was under five hundred kilometers when a broadcast on the open emergency channel came through. After listening to the conversation between the shuttle pilot named Frank and Fortune's bridge, Billy Ray leaned back in his chair, forehead wrinkled in thought.

"Shuttle One, Peggy Sue. You about ready to rendezvous pardner?"

"Roger that, Peggy Sue. I'm matching velocity for docking as we speak."

"Good, I think we are not done with this black contagion stuff yet."

"Copy that. We heard the emergency transmission ourselves."

"When you get back on board, drop the survivors in medical and you and Beth come to my sea cabin. We all need to talk."

"Roger, Captain. We're on our way."


### Bridge, ESS Fortune

Leon and his companions arrived on the bridge to find the Captain locked in his sea cabin and the Navigator at the helm. A couple of the other ratings were also present.

"Where's the Captain?" Leon demanded. "We barely escaped with our lives from that black crap down in the cargo hold."

"The Captain is locked inside his sea cabin," replied the Navigator, the ranking officer present. "I have shutdown environmental support for the hold and lower decks to keep that stuff out of the crew space."

"I'm telling you, that is not going to keep that shit out!"

"We trusted you to lead us to a new land of milk and honey," shouted the preacher. "Instead you delivered us to Gehenna. You are in league with the devil and will die at the hands of the angel of death!"

The two young colonists sank to their knees in terror. Leon and the other crewmen drew closer together, baring the raving Brother Abraham's access to the bridge controls. Brother Abraham advanced on the crew.

"The angels will come forth and take out the wicked from among the righteous, and will throw them into the furnace of fire; in that place there will be weeping and gnashing of teeth!"

Behind the ranting preacher the door to the Captain's sea cabin slid silently open. Captain Chakrabarti stepped into the room with a stunner in his hand, one of the few weapons on board. He stunned the preacher from behind.

Brother Abraham sank to his knees and then fell forward, face down on the deck. His two followers tried to rise and come to his aid. Captain Chakrabarti stunned them as well.

"Thank God, Captain," said the Navigator. "That guy totally lost it. We need to drag them to the crew escape pods and abandon ship before that black crap reaches us."

"Nonsense," said the Captain, his eyes wild. "We are going to proceed to the transit point and head back to Earth."

"Sir, respectfully that is not a... Ungh!"

The Navigator crumpled under the beam from the Captain's stunner.

"The rest of you mutineers, stand away from the controls!"

The remaining crewmen backed away from their commanding officer, eyes on the muzzle of his stunner. It was obvious to Leon that the Captain was totally insane. He also realized that if the Captain stunned him he would stand no chance of escaping.

With the path to the control console clear the Captain moved swiftly. Changing the stunner to his left hand he began entering commands with his right. The crew exchanged glances—they knew their only hope was to rush the Captain all at once.

"Computer, verify course selection," the Captain commanded.

"Course for alignment with alter-space transit point plotted. Estimated time until transition four hours and twenty-three minutes," the computer answered.

"Emergency code *Götterdämmerung*. Lock course and execute!"

Leon the other two crewmen rushed the Captain. One rating fell, stunned to insensibility, but the other two managed to overpower Chakrabarti and wrest the stunner from him.

"Code accepted, Captain. Course locked in; execution proceeds," the computer confirmed.

"Too late!" the Captain cackled. "We are headed back to Earth. I'll see you all strung up from the yard arms!"

"He's totally bonkers," said the remaining conscious crewman.

"Yeah," said Leon, "Computer, cancel course. Remain in orbit."

"Course selection can not be canceled without override code."

"Aw shit," Leon said.

Captain Chakrabarti cackled madly.


### Captain's Sea Cabin, Peggy Sue

Beth and Bobby were still wearing their skintight inner pressure suits when they arrived at the Captain's sea cabin. They detailed Kate to take the two survivors to sick bay for a checkup and told the Marines to remain in armor on board the shuttle until the Captain decided on a course of action. They might be called on to board the colonization transport ship. Billy Ray and Mizuki were already seated as the rescuers entered.

"What's the situation, Captain?" asked Beth, looking a bit drawn. Billy Ray could see the pain in his wife's eyes. The loss of the Gunny hit her hard, but there wasn't time to deal with that now.

"As you heard, we have reports that the contagion is on board the Fortune. Evidently it has killed several crewmembers and the rest are locked in the forward section of the ship."

"Is there any way we can kill it?" asked Bobby.

"We have no way to do so with certainty, Bobby," Mizuki replied. "Since it devours anything organic we cannot synthesize a poison."

"What about breaching the hull, depressurizing the ship?" asked Beth. "Could exposure to vacuum kill it?"

"According to the alien recordings, they thought it arrived on a swarm of meteors. If that was the case then it can obviously survive in a vacuum."

"So what can we do to kill it, Mizuki?" asked the Captain.

"The only sure way is to turn it to plasma, which would have a detrimental effect on those left on board the ship."

"To say the least," added Bobby.

The discussion was interrupted by a call from the bridge.

"Captain, Bridge."

"Go Bridge," Billy Ray replied.

"Mr. Umky reports that the Fortune is underway and maneuvering for alter-space transition, Sir."

"Copy, Bridge. Keep me informed of any changes in course."

Billy Ray's face was grim as he looked around the table.

"People, we cannot let that ship go back to Earth. Not with the contagion on board."

"You're right, Captain. It would kill anyone who tried to board the ship, and if it got loose on Farside it could end mankind."

"Exactly, Mizuki."

"There's nothing for it then. We shall have to destroy the Fortune before she can transit."

"Right, Number One. Let's get to our stations."

The Captain and his officers exited the sea cabin and hastened to their posts on the bridge.

\* \* \* \* \*

Bobby took his seat next to Nigel at the helm, Mizuki manned the sensor console, and Beth took the observers seat next to the Captain's command chair. Billy Ray looked around the bridge, checking that everyone was in place and ready for action. He sat down and spoke to Nigel at the helm.

"Mr. Lewis, close to within a thousand kilometers of the Fortune. Smartly, sir, do not spare the engines."

"Aye, aye, Sir!"

Behind the Captain, Umky smiled a faint bearish smile. After all, there was nothing a polar bear liked more than running prey to ground.

298

### ESS Fortune, Underway

Leon looked around the bridge. There were five unconscious people: the three settlers, the Navigator and one crewman. The Captain, his hands bound behind him by a plastic tie wrap, was sitting in a chair rocking forward and back. The only effectives were Leon and the other crewman.

"We are going to have to drag these people to the escape pods," Leon said.

"Why not wait until they recover?" asked the crewman. "They should only be out a half hour or so. We won't be in positing to transit for another four hours."

"You want to just sit around and hope that black crap doesn't find us for a half hour?"

"Oh yeah. I forgot about that."

"Let me call Frank and see if he has any ideas."

Leon went to the console and opened a channel to the shuttle where Frank had taken refuge.

"Shuttle Bravo, Bridge. Come in Frank."

"Go Bridge, you got me."

"Hey Frank, I'm stuck here on the bridge with five unconscious people and the Captain, who's gone round the bend big time. He's restrained and babbling like a crazy man."

"That you Leon? Are you alone up there?"

"No, I got one of the ratings with me."

"Why are we underway?"

"The Captain gave the computer some kind of emergency code and told the ship to take us home. We're getting lined up to make the transition to alter-space."

"That is not good, Leon. You need to get out of there."

"My thoughts exactly, but we can't just leave the others laying here on the deck. It wouldn't be right."

"Can you drag them into the escape pods?"

"Yeah but it will take time. The pods are a deck down and we will have to drag them one at a time to the elevator. Plus, the bridge elevator won't hold them all in one trip. I'm afraid the black crap will find us while we're moving them."

"Lower the deck gravity."

"What?"

"I said, lower the deck gravity. It'll make it easier to move them."

"Great idea, Frank. I knew it was a good idea calling you. Assuming we do get off this rust bucket, what happens next?"

"I'm going to call that merchant captain and ask him to come pick us up."

"You think he will?"

"I'm declaring an emergency. Law of the sea applies. All ships in the area are required to provide assistance."

"OK. We'll get to work moving the others. Bridge out."

## Chapter 27

### Bridge, Peggy Sue

"Captain, I'm getting an SOS beacon from the Fortune," reported Mizuki from her console.

*Now what?* "Peggy Sue, open a channel to the Fortune."

"Captain, the SOS is coming from one of the Fortune's shuttles."

"Well contact the shuttle then."

"Yes, Captain. On your console now."

"Ship signaling an emergency please respond, this is the merchant ship Peggy Sue."

"Peggy Sue, this is the ESS Fortune. We are in trouble here and need assistance."

"Who am I talking to?"

"This is Frank Hoenig, one of the shuttle pilots. I'm locked in my shuttle getting ready to separate from the ship, but there are several people trapped forward."

"We received transmissions that indicated the contagion from the planet was loose on board your ship. Is that correct."

"Yes, it's already wiped out half the crew."

"How do you expect those in the bow to escape, Frank?"

"They are dragging those who were stunned into the escape pods. As soon as everyone is secured they will eject the pods."

"Stunned? Who was stunned and by whom?"

"It's a long story."

"Humor me, Mr. Hoenig."

"The Captain went berserk, came out of his sea cabin with a stunner and started zapping people. He stunned three settlers we rescued from Zion and a couple of crewmen before they managed to overpower him. There are only two effectives left on the Bridge."

"Can the people on the bridge cut the engines? It appears that Fortune is maneuvering for the alter-space transition point to Earth."

"No, according to Leon the Captain gave some kind of code word and locked the helm controls."

"Mr. Hoenig, I cannot let Fortune depart for Earth. Not with the contagion on board."

"I understand, Peggy Sue. You can call the bridge and talk to Leon if you think it will do any good. I'm undocking and getting clear of Fortune. I would greatly appreciate a lift."

"Copy that, Mr. Hoenig. Get clear. I will call Mr. Leon."

### Bridge, ESS Fortune

Leon and the crewman had finished one trip down to the level where the escape pod access was. They managed to fit the two unconscious crewmembers and the two acolytes into the lift. After securing them in two of the escape pods they returned for the Captain and the Preacher. As they arrived a call was coming in on the comm console.

"ESS Fortune, ESS Fortune, Peggy Sue. Please reply."

"Now what?" the crewman asked.

"That would be our ride home once we get out of here." Leon moved to the console to answer the hail.

"Go Peggy Sue, This is the Fortune."

"Is this Mr. Leon?"

"Yes, it is. And it's just Leon."

Pause.

"What is your status, Leon?"

"We got four people secured in the escape pods and we are about to take the last two down. Then we will be getting the hell outta here. Over."

"Copy, Fortune. The clock is running and you need to get off that ship, now."

"We're on it. Give us five more minutes. Fortune out."

Leon turned to the other man and said, "Get the preacher up, I'll go open the elevator door."

The crewman grunted and bent to pick up Brother Abraham's inert form. From his chair the Captain cackled like a mad hen. Leon walked over to the lift entrance and opened the door.

He turned back in time to see the first black thread emerge from the ventilator. Leon's sense of self preservation took over—he lept into the elevator and hit the door close button. He watched terrified as black threads wrapped the other crewman and Brother Abraham. The door slid home as the black sinews reached Captain Chakrabarti, helpless and bound in his chair.

Sid was still cackling as the darkness engulfed him.


### *Shuttle B, ESS Fortune*

Instruments on the control panel finally indicated that the shuttle's reactor was on line. Frank switched the shuttle to internal power and released the docking clamps. With practiced ease he lifted the shuttle from its docking cradle and opened space between the ship and his craft.

"Bridge, Shuttle Bravo. Leon, buddy, are you still on board?"

No answer.

"Peggy Sue, Shuttle Bravo. Come in."

"Go Shuttle Bravo."

"I am free of the ship, what course should I steer for rendezvous?"

"For now just get away from the Fortune. Put as much distance between you and the ship as you can."

"Roger that, Peggy Sue. Break. I have not heard from Leon in several minutes, can you raise the Fortune?"

"That is a negative, Shuttle Bravo."

### Crew Level, ESS Fortune

The elevator door opened on the deserted crew level, one deck down from the bridge. Leon looked out the door and then bolted for the escape pod access hatches. The closest pod was the one with the Navigator and other crewman. As he ran past the entrance to the pod he hit the emergency launch button.

Ten meters away was the entrance to the second pod, the one with the two settlers. Leon dove through the entrance. Tucking into a ball, he grabbed the lip of the pod's hatch, letting his momentum spin him about. For an instant he thought he saw movement at the entrance.

Leon slapped the large red emergency launch button. The pod's hatch slammed shut and a heartbeat later it launched itself into space. There was no deck gravity inside the pod and Leon ended up with both of the acolytes on top of him, his face pressed to the small view port in the access hatch.

As the ship fell away Leon could see the empty hatch where the other escape pod had been ejected. With any luck the five of them made it off the doomed transport alive.

### Bridge, Peggy Sue

"Captain, I am picking up rescue beacon signals from two escape pods that were just ejected from the Fortune."

"Very good, Dr. Ogawa," the Captain replied. "Mr. Umky, target the Fortune with a pair of torpedoes. Antimatter warheads. A two second delay between the launches."

"Aye, aye, Captain," the bear replied.

"We will give the pods and the shuttle enough time to get free of the blast radius before firing."

After a moment's consideration, the Captain called Shuttle B.

"Shuttle Bravo, Peggy Sue."

"Go Peggy Sue."

"You might wish to put as much of the shuttle's mass between you and the Fortune as you can. You are clear of the blast radius but there will be a burst of radiation after the torpedoes detonate."

"Torpedoes? I copy, Peggy Sue."

"The escape pods are at a sufficient distance from the target, Captain," Mizuki reported.

"Very good. You may fire when ready, Umky."

"Aye, aye, Captain."

Two muted thuds, separated by as many seconds, marked the launch of the gravitonic torpedoes. Once free of the ship they accelerated at 1,000 gravities, locked onto the transport ship. Holographic overlays of the torpedo tracks were superimposed on the view forward through the Peggy Sue's transparent nose.

Fourteen seconds later the first torpedo impacted Fortune's shields, traveling at a relative velocity of half a million kilometers per hour. The shields had as much effect as tissue paper. The first warhead detonated.

Peggy Sue's computer automatically darkened the transparent panels in the ship's nose to dampen the star bright flash of antimatter annihilating matter. The first flash was followed by another, two seconds later, when the second warhead detonated inside the expanding cloud of plasma and debris created by the first.

"Sensors show the target is destroyed, Captain," said Umky with a hint of satisfaction in his voice.

"Very good, Mr. Umky. Dr. Ogawa, any indication of solid debris?"

"No, Captain. The Fortune is now just an expanding cloud of plasma."

"Excellent. Peggy Sue, sound secure from battle stations." Billy Ray took a moment to ponder his handiwork. *I sure hope there was no one left alive on that ship.*

"Mr. Lewis, let's go see to the survivors."

"Aye, aye, Captain."

### Sick Bay, Peggy Sue

Shadi and Dorri lay side by side on twin medical beds made up with stiff white linen. They stared in wonder at the multicolored displays that were attached to each bed, showing heartbeat, respiration, and other bodily functions the girls could only guess at.

"How long do you think they will keep us here?" asked Dorri in Farsi.

"I don't know," her sister replied. "Just relax and enjoy the first clean bed you've had since leaving the transport ship."

"I would, if I didn't feel like a specimen in a science experiment."

Their conversation was interrupted by the entrance of the ship's doctor, another African woman—no, an African-American woman. Betty White, MD, paused at the foot of Dorri's bed and consulted her data tablet. She nodded and moved to Shadi's bed, repeating the performance.

"Well, ladies. It looks like your time spent on the colonization ship and the planet's surface has done you no harm. You have some vitamin deficiencies but otherwise you seem to be well nourished and in good health."

Betty smiled brightly at the girls, giving them a chance to ask questions. When they didn't, she continued. "Shadi, you are sixteen, and Dorri, you are thirteen, is that correct?"

Both girls nodded.

"And you have been having regular menstrual cycles?"

Dorri blushed and Shadi answered "yes."

"Dorri?"

"Yes, Doctor."

"Good, stress and the strange environment might have caused you some irregularities. I take it neither of you have been sexually active?"

306

This time both young women blushed.

"That's what my instruments say, but it never hurts to ask." Betty smiled again, trying to make them feel at ease.

"What's going to happen to us now?" asked Shadi.

"Before the blackness came we were about to be married off to older men," Dorri added.

"Really? Well that will not be happening here, not unless you find someone and both of you want to get married. Though I must say, you two are a little young to be getting married to anyone. You especially, Dorri."

The relief on the sisters' faces was obvious. They were half afraid they would be sold into bondage or added to the Captain's harem.

"What are we going to do? I mean to earn our keep," asked Shadi. "On the planet we took care of the sheep, but I doubt you need a couple of shepherds on this ship."

"Oh, you never know. We do have a lot of gardens located around the ship. They grow fresh fruits and vegetables for the people on board. But you are right, we don't keep any livestock. The Captain will be along soon to talk with you about such things."

"Were there any other survivors?" asked Dorri, no longer able to contain herself. "Are we the only ones to make it out alive?"

"I'm not sure. There are several people who made it off the Fortune before the Captain blew it up. I suspect I will know as soon as they bring the survivors on board. They will have to be examined just like you were."

"The Captain blew up the transport ship?"

"Yes, Shadi. It was infested with the same contagion that destroyed your settlement—all three settlements. I'm sorry you lost all of your friends, but at least you two are safe, and you still have each other." Betty's eyes got a faraway look. "I had a sister once, but I lost here during the bombardment."

The two girls looked at each other as the Doctor stood silent, lost in her memories. Then Betty's focus returned, as did her smile.

307

"Alright, that's all for now. I'm going to keep you a bit longer until the last few test results come back from the autolab. The controls on the sides of the beds will let you sit upright and along the left sides there are fold out trays. The trays contain data surfaces that you can use to access the ship's library. While you are waiting you can look things up about the ship and crew, or whatever. The computer will help you if you get stuck. Right, Peggy Sue?"

"Certainly, Doctor White," said a new voice, seemingly from nowhere. The computer then said in Farsi, "it will be good to practice my Farsi with some native speakers."

The girls' eyes went wide when the computer addressed them in Farsi. They then busied themselves adjusting their beds and accessing the data surfaces.

Betty chuckled. "I can see you two will be just fine in here. The Captain will be along shortly to talk with you. Then he will take you to the mess hall for lunch."

# Chapter 28

## Cargo Hold, Peggy Sue

The armored figure of Chief Zackly stood in the middle of the deck, fists on hips, elbows out. To either side stood a Marine in heavy armor, brandishing a large UV cutting laser. After observing the contagion in action during the rescue mission, it was recognized that railguns would not be an effective weapon against it. Consequently, the engineers had devised a new weapon for the Marines—cutting lasers modified to have a wider beam spread. The idea was, if any of the escape pods had black crap hiding on them, the Marines would turn the whole pod into plasma before the contagion could find a way onto the ship.

"All right, Hitch, poke the first one through the cargo door."

Steve Hitch was outside the ship, piloting a space tug—really nothing more than a heavy push plate with surrounding grapples and a cluster of repulsors to move it about. The tug didn't even have a cabin; Hitch was wearing regular space armor, as was Matt Jacobs in the second tug.

"Pushing her in now, Chief," the petty officer replied. Aside from causing trouble and annoying the Marines, Hitch and Jacobs were both qualified to operate most of the small craft on board the Peggy Sue. They could even fly the Captain's pinnace in a pinch, not that the Captain would let them.

The Peggy Sue had been modified to incorporated the T'aafhal's magic permeable hatch material, like that installed over the docks on Farside. Though the starboard cargo door had not been physically opened, it was possible for solid objects to pass through the seemingly intact hull. Of course, the permeability was controllable and had to be switched on, otherwise people and things could accidentally fall overboard into the vacuum of space.

There was another complication, however. An object passing into the ship had an atmosphere on one side and vacuum on the other. The pressure of the air in the ship, though it could not escape through the barrier, still exerted force on the object. An object that stopped part of the way through the barrier would pop

---

back out into space if not held in position by an opposing force. Getting that force right using the tug was Steve Hitch's job.

As the roughly spherical escape pod passed into the ship the force trying to expel it reach its peak half way in. The sailor expertly adjusted the amount of force generated by the tug's repulsors until equilibrium was reached, and the pod was sticking half way through the door.

"All right, hold it right there, Hitch," yelled the grizzled old Chief. They were linked by their suit radios so yelling was not required. Still, habits learned during decades spent on ships at sea died hard.

"Gotcha, Chief," Hitch answered.

The Chief gave the visible portion of the pod the eye. He was not alone. Peggy Sue's computer also examined the pod from all possible angles and at great magnification. Satisfied that there was no contamination on the pod's surface, the ship spoke to the Chief.

"It appears to be clean, Chief Zackly."

"Great." The Chief was not one to hold long conversations with equipment, even a starship.

Leaning in closely, the Chief peered through the transparent viewing port in the middle of the pod's circular hatch. Inside, peering back, were a couple of disheveled crewmen from the Fortune. The Chief snorted.

"All right, yous. Let's get these shipwrecked sailors out of the lifeboat and onto the deck."

An engineer, also suited up, stepped up to the pod and fiddled with the control panel next to the hatch. With a hiss of escaping gas the hatch swung upward, and the passengers tumbled out onto the deck. They quickly scrambled to their feet and found themselves staring at a small man in space armor.

"That all of ya?"

"Uh, yeah. Who are you?"

"I'm Master Chief Zackly, the chief of this ship, you knuckle head. I'll ask the questions here."

Both sailors swallowed hard.

"Hitch, get this piece of garbage off my deck."

The open escape pod quickly melted back through the cargo door as though it never existed. The Chief looked the refuges up and down with a critical eye.

"Sound off! Name and rank. You first, Chatty Cathy."

"Raoul Mendez, ship's navigator," the man said.

"Not anymore." Zackly shifted his gaze to the second man. "And you?"

"Ethan Jones, Sir. Able Spacer."

"Do not sir me, sonny, I work for a living."

Jones stared at the cargo hold wall, eyes focused on a spot two feet above the Chief's head, doing his best to remember how to stand at attention.

"All right, Sheffield! Get these two sorry sailors outta here. Take 'em to the showers and get 'em new jumpsuits."

"Aye, aye, Chief," Lou replied, motioning for the still disoriented survivors to follow him forward.

"Jacobs! Push the other piece of jetsam into the hold."

"Aye, Chief," Matt replied from outside the ship. In less than a minute another escape pod appeared, as though it was being extruded through the solid cargo bay door. As with the first pod it stopped halfway in. The inspection sequence and door opening was repeated, only this time the passengers did not tumble out onto the deck. From inside the spherical pod a voice called out.

"Permission to come aboard, Sir?"

"Permission granted. You may come aboard." the Chief replied with a crooked smile.

Leon ushered his two charges out the hatch and lined them up facing the Chief before joining them in line himself. He saluted the Chief and spoke.

"Petty Officer Second Class Leon Delaney, late of the ESS Fortune, reporting with a party of two ex-colonists," then, catching the rank insignia on the Chief's armor, added, "Chief."

The Chief returned his salute before addressing the man.

"I ain't really the OOD, but then this ain't a normal way to come aboard. I do appreciate yer upholding Navy tradition though. Welcome aboard, Mr. Delaney."

"Thank you, Chief."

"And who are these two?"

"Malachi and Hezekiah, two colonists from the late Brother Abraham's congregation."

The parties mentioned smiled meekly at the Chief but did not speak.

"Just what I need, a couple of Bible thumpers who don't know a sheet from a halyard. Well, take 'em forward for showers and a change of clothes, this one looks like he pissed himself. The Captain will sort them all out."

"Aye, aye, thank you Chief."

Outside the ship, Matt Jacobs gave the second pod a final push, setting it drifting away from the ship. His partner Steve Hitch had already disposed of the first pod in a similar fashion. Pulling close enough to Matt's tug to talk on suit-to-suit, Hitch spoke.

"What was the Chief talking about? To my knowledge we ain't never had a sheet or a halyard on the Peggy Sue."

"I believe the Chief was speaking metaphorically, Stevie. We need to talk to this Leon guy, it sounds like he may know his ass from a hole in the ground."

"Right."


### Pinnace Two

Frank finished putting Shuttle B on a course that would eventually spiral into the red star at the center of the system. He hated to see the end of the shuttle, she had been a good ship. But the Peggy Sue's Captain wanted nothing left floating around this star system that might harbor remnants of the black contagion.

"Adios, old girl," he said, locking the controls and moving aft to the airlock.

Depressurizing the compartment between the flight deck and the cargo hold, the pilot peered out the small transparent porthole on the crew entrance door. There, hanging in space next to his soon to be former command was another, much smaller shuttle.

The smaller craft was Peggy Sue's second pinnace, a small boat used to transfer crew between ships in space or to and from a planet's surface. A side hatch was open and a figure in a space suit could be seen waving. Frank stepped back and opened the door.

The pilot was at ease flying a shuttle, landing on a planet or docking with a starship, but stepping out into inky black nothingness gave him the willies. He took a deep breath and carefully launched himself in the direction of the pinnace.

The float over seem to take forever, though less than a minute elapsed between leap and arrival. His aim was good, coming close enough for the man in the side hatch to lean out and clasp hands. Pulling the last refugee from the Fortune inside, the crewman secured the hatch and started repressurizing the small shuttle.

The man spoke to him over suit-to-suit comm.

"All right, mate. You're safe and sound now." The man's accent was Australian. He called out to the pilot. "Mr. Lewis. It's grouse, the bloke is on board."

"Roger that, Jay. We're headed for home."

Outside the pinnace's panoramic windows the stars pinwheeled as the small shuttle changed course for its mother ship. Frank looked around the well appointed interior of the craft and wondered.

*Now what? At least I'm alive and not stuck inside a shuttle eating rat bars for a month, hoping that black crud doesn't find a way in. I hope the Peggy Sue's Captain doesn't hold a grudge, old Chakrabarti must have pissed him off pretty good. These guys seem OK though, and the merchant ship can't be more messed up than the Fortune. That's it, think positive thoughts, Frank, positive thoughts.*


## Main Lounge, Peggy Sue

The Captain had Mizuki fetch the two female survivors from sick bay and bring them to the main lounge while he oversaw the recovery of the survivors from the Fortune. The sisters looked around the lounge with great interest—there was nothing this opulent on board the Fortune. In fact, they had seen nothing to compare with the rich wood and polished metal surfaces of the lounge since they had been rescued from Earth years ago.

Their lives had been spent in utilitarian refugee apartments on the Moon, seldom getting to venture out to the enclosed base. In over a year living at Farside they never saw the lunar surface or the Moon's stricken but still beautiful mother planet. The journey to Paradise was no better, traveling in the hold of the Colonization Board transport.

Paradise had been a welcome change, right up until they were told they had to marry men they did not know. Of course, they got out of the forced nuptials when the planet decided to kill everyone in all three settlements. Given past events, Shadi and Dorri could not be blamed for being a bit leery regarding their new circumstances.

"Please, sit down," said Mizuki, motioning to a table near the large eye-shaped viewport on the starboard side of the lounge. "What would you like to drink?"

Dorri looked shyly at the oriental woman and asked, "do you have Parsi or Zam Zam?"

"I'm not sure I know what those are," said Mizuki with a quizzical look on her face.

"Sorry," added Shadi, "they are both cola flavored soft drinks, like Pepsi or Coca-cola. Either of those would do fine. We haven't had a soda in years."

"I'm sure that Jimmy has something like that behind the bar." Mizuki turned and signaled to the Jamaican bartender, motioning him over to the table.

"Ah, you be bringin' I new customers," he said with a white toothy smile and thick Jamaican accent. "What is your pleasure, ladies?"

"Jimmy, this is Shadi and Dorri, both new to the Peggy Sue. Ladies, this is Jimmy Tosh, our head chef and bartender."

The girls mumbled polite hellos, still a bit self-conscience being without headscarfs in the presence of men. Mizuki ordered for the party.

"The young ladies will have a cola if you please, and I will have mineral water."

"No problem, mon, comin' right up. Will you be having someting to eat? I have a very nice curried conch salad with saffron rice today."

"That sounds wonderful, Jimmy. Girls, what would you like?"

After a moment's hesitation Shadi asked, "Could we have cheese burgers? And fries?"

"For you beautiful ladies, anyting."

Humming a happy tune, Jimmy went back to the kitchen behind the bar. From the kitchen, he could be heard singing and banging pots around. Of all the people on board the Peggy Sue, Jimmy was the most consistently upbeat. Some said it was his Rastafarian beliefs, others the plants he had growing in a back corner of one of the hydroponic gardens on deck three.

"Where is he from?" asked Shadi. "I've never heard anyone talk like he talks."

"He is from Jamaica, an island in the Caribbean Sea. He was the bartender at a restaurant back on the Moon—its owner is a friend of the Captain's. Jimmy got into a bit of trouble and needed to disappear for a while, so we brought him along on the voyage."

"Really, why?"

"You will find that most of us on board the Peggy Sue are old friends, almost like a big family. We help each other out when we can. When you meet Billy Ray—Captain Vincent—you will see what I mean."

"What do you do on the ship?" asked Dorri.

"I am the Science Officer. I am in charge of the other scientists who are on the expedition. That and I also have a station on the bridge where I operate the ship's telescopes if we are exploring a new system, or get into a fight."

"You are also a scientist?"

"Yes, I am an astrophysicist. And since we do not have an astronomer aboard I also help navigate the ship."

"There seem to be so many women in important positions on this ship," Shadi observed. "Is this normal?"

"Yes, Shadi. On this ship and many others men and women are equals, judged only by their ability. Women even fight beside the men when we go into battle. We practice martial arts together in the cargo hold when we are underway. Once you feel more at home you might want to join us, it is a very good way to stay in shape."

While they were waiting on their food, a flock of small flying creatures emerged from a companionway at the rear of the lounge. They swarmed out of the opening and up to the ceiling, tumbling across the open space to swirl around the table the women were sitting at.

"Butterflies!" squealed Dorri, clapping her hands together. The fluttering insects flashed blue and green and turquoise as they surrounded the diners.

"You keep butterflies on your ship, Dr. Ogawa?" asked Shadi.

Mizuki said something in Japanese to the flying creatures, which seemed to quiet them down. She smiled at the girls and explained.

"They are not really butterflies. They are an alien species I found on a distant space station. Actually they found me."

"Really?"

"Yes, they seem to share a single consciousness, and to act at times as a single being. You can tell their mood by the colors they display—right now they are happy because they have found me."

"Do they just fly loose around the ship?" Dorri asked, holding out a finger for one of the flying creatures to alight on.

"No, usually they stay in our quarters. My partner, Bobby, must have let them out. Sometimes they get out by accident, and sometimes on purpose. Bobby, the sailing master, was flying the shuttle that picked you up from the surface."

"We did not get to meet him yet, or the Marines," said Shadi.

"They were all enclosed in their armor, but we would like to thank them all," added her sister.

"Yes, especially the Marine who threw me onto the ship, do you know him?"

Mizuki hesitated.

"That Marine was a she, Shadi. Gunnery Sergeant Rosey Acuna."

The butterflies became less animated, clustering around the table. Their colors changed to indigo and dark purples, some landed on Mizuki's hair and shoulders."

"What's wrong? Why did the butterflies change?"

"I think we should wait for the Captain to answer that question."

The sisters looked at each other, obviously brimming over with a million more questions. Before they could continue cross examining the lady scientist Jimmy arrived with the food. With squeals of delight the girls attacked their meals—delicacies they never thought to taste again.

As quickly as they had changed to dark somber colors the butterflies regained their happier coloration. Reflecting the girls' excitement the butterflies added yellow to their palate.

\* \* \* \* \*

The sisters were finishing up their french fries and sipping at refilled drinks when a tall man in a black and navy blue jumpsuit entered the lounge. Tall and trim, with piercing eyes and dark curly

317

hair, he could only be the Captain. He approached the table and introduced himself.

"Good afternoon, ladies. I am Captain Vincent, master and commander of the Peggy Sue. I trust that Dr. Ogawa has been taking good care of you?"

"Yes, Sir," Shadi and Dorri replied together.

"I want to talk with you about your future. Specifically your near term future."

The sisters nodded in response.

"Though I would like to take you, and the other survivors of this debacle, back to Farside right now that is not my mission. Ours is a commercial venture and we have creditors to pay off back home."

"Sir," interrupted Shadi. "We have no one to return to. On the Moon, Earth or anywhere."

"Hmm," Billy Ray said, as he searched for the proper words to say. "I am very sorry for your loss, but the fact that there is no one back home waiting for your return actually simplifies things a bit."

"How so, Captain?" asked Mizuki.

"It means these young ladies are now the captains of their own destinies, so to speak. By that I mean, if they decide to pursue a future while on this voyage the decision will not be rescinded when they get back home."

"Oh?" said Shadi cautiously.

"Yes, Shadi. We are scheduled to visit several other star systems before returning to Earth. We will be in space for at least a year. It is not my policy to carry supernumerary passengers, who contribute nothing to the mission or the running of the ship. What this means is that you and your sister will have to work for your passage back home. The Chief will assign you to assist various members of the crew in their normal duties, until we can find out what you are best at."

The sisters looked at each other, concern on their faces.

"It's not that bad, ladies. I think you will like most of the things you'll learn. After all, how many young women get to help sail a starship?"

"We'd be part of the crew?" asked Dorri.

The Captain nodded.

"What about their education, Captain?" Mizuki asked, slipping into an advocate's role for the two girls.

"Thank you for mentioning that, Dr. Ogawa. We will need to ascertain where you are in your basic schooling. Then Dr. Ogawa and her staff will create courses of study for each of you."

"I know that they are both fluent in English, Arabic, and Farsi. I do not know about science or general literacy," Mizuki replied.

"We both can read quite well, Sir." said Dorri, who was staying uncharacteristically quiet.

"But we don't have a lot of schooling in science or mathematics." Shadi looked embarrassed.

"Well, your language skills speak well of your capacity to learn. I'm sure that you will pick up math and science skills quickly. You will have the personal attention of a number of scientific experts, right Dr. Ogawa?"

"That is correct, Captain. In fact, the problem will be keeping my scientists from trying to turn Shadi and Dorri into full-time lab assistants." Mizuki smiled to show that her statement was in jest, mostly.

"So there you have it, ladies. You will be given a cabin together in the Goat Locker—I'm sorry, the senior enlisted quarters—and take your meals here in the main mess. I'll have one of the female crewmembers come and get you settled.

"If you have any questions just ask anyone, or the ship's computer. Just say 'Peggy Sue' out loud and the ship will answer, right Peggy Sue?"

"That is correct, Captain. I have already been introduced to Shadi and Dorri."

"Captain, can I ask a question?" said Shadi.

"Of course."

"Dr. Ogawa told me that the Marine who saved my life was a woman, named Gunnery Sergeant Rosey Acuna. Could I meet her? I would like to thank her for what she did."

The Captain glanced in Mizuki's direction and then back at the young girl. His face grew serious.

"I'm afraid that is not possible, Shadi. You see, Rosey didn't make it back off the planet."

"She got taken by the blackness? She died?"

"We don't know for sure—she was wearing heavy armor—but it is probable."

"Oh!" Shadi held her hands over her mouth and tears welled in her eyes. "Why would she do that, she didn't even know me?"

"It's what Marine's do, protect the innocent. Now that we have all the survivors from the Fortune on board we will return to orbit and scan for her, but the chances of her surviving are not good. I'm sorry."

Dorri took her sister's hand and gave it a squeeze. Sensing their sadness the butterflies turned nearly black, fluttering down to land on the girls. A few even landed on the Captain's wide shoulders.

"Thank you," said Shadi, in a quiet voice, "for not lying to us."

"I try not to lie to my crew. It tends only to make things worse in the long run."

After an awkward silence, Billy Ray spoke again.

"If you have any problems or you think someone is trying to take advantage of you tell Chief Zackly or the First Officer. The First Officer is the woman who brought you on board from the shuttle."

"The tall African woman?" asked Shadi.

"British actually, but yes."

"Is she really your wife?" asked Dorri.

"Yes indeed. She is most definitely my wife, Dorri." Billy Ray smiled as he said that, but his thoughts were more serious. *Now I need to go and talk to my wife about the loss of the Gunny.* "Anything else?"

Receiving no further questions, the Captain nodded and left, headed for the lower deck and a rendezvous with his wife.

## Chapter 29

### *Captain's Quarters, Peggy Sue*

Billy Ray found Beth sitting on the edge of their bed, head down, her hands clasped before her. She did not look up as he approached.

"You OK, hon?"

Beth shook her head no. Billy Ray eased himself onto the bed next to her.

"You want to tell me what's eatin' at you?"

Again she shook her head no.

"I can guess. Yer tore up about losing the Gunny."

"Is it that obvious?" Beth looked up and turned her head to face him.

"To me. Honey, we've lived together for more than a couple of years. I'd be a poor husband if I couldn't tell when something was on yer mind."

"I lost her, Billy Ray. It was my mission. I was responsible and I lost her."

"This is a dangerous business we're in, Beth. We've lost people every time we've left Earth. We lost people on the Space Mushroom..." Billy Ray hesitated for an instant, as emotional pain griped his heart. He remembered a woman with honey blond hair and cornflower blue eyes; the first woman he ever loved; the woman the ship he now captained was named after. Forcing his renegade emotions into the background he continued. "...we lost people in the Bug Queen's Palace. Several people were horribly wounded on Ring Station, and we lost whole ships full of people during the battle for the solar system."

Beth stared at her hands again and nodded yes, almost imperceptibly.

"You lost people when you commanded the corvette squadron, entire crews. Sweetheart, everyone knows the risks, and they choose to do it anyway."

"It's not just that. I treated Rosey badly... and she didn't deserve it. I should have shown her more respect. Now she's gone, and I cannot make amends." Silent tears ran down Beth's cheeks.

"I knew you had a burr under your saddle about her, but I figured it would work itself out over time."

"I think I disliked her because of her past, it reminded me too much of my own. Flitting from man to man, morale be damned."

"Yeah, well yer flitting days are over, lady. Besides, I don't think Rosey held it against you, you givin' her the cold shoulder. She was a Marine Gunnery Sergeant, she expected her officers to be hard-cases."

"I was still in the wrong."

"Sweetheart, I watched the video feed from your mission. Rosey chose to do what she did. She could have stayed on the ramp and let the black threads take the girl, but she didn't. She was a Marine, and she did what Marines do. She put herself in harm's way for the sake of others, in this case an innocent young girl."

"I still don't think I can forgive myself." Beth leaned against her husband's shoulder. "Just hold me."

Billy Ray put his arm around her and did just that. Her sobs slowly grew more pronounced until they wracked her body.

*Most of the crew thinks you are a stone cold bitch, my love. They don't know how much you care for your people, deep down inside. A good officer has to be strong, can't let emotion cloud their decisions, even if it hurts like hell afterward.*

The tears passed. Beth sniffled and looked up at Billy Ray, her eyes red from crying. "I do so wish I could make it up to her, somehow."

As Billy Ray searched for something to say to ease his wife's pain his comm pip chirped—a priority message for the Captain from the CIC.

### Hills Above New Mecca

The flexibot descended the rocky hillside in a controlled tumble. Its sensors registered significant change in the area since it last passed that way. Gone was the Earth vegetation, the flock of sheep, and the colonists. This area now looked much like any other on the surface of the planet; dun-colored and sterile.

Optically scanning the surrounding terrain as it bounced and rolled, the survey robot detected a dark patch ahead. Drawing closer to the anomaly, it resolved into a roughly humanoid form—a large humanoid form. The object's surface looked worn and weathered, like the dark, lava encased figures found in the ruins of Pompeii.

The robot edged closer, intent on taking a sample of the object's material. It detected a signal. A signal that invoked a new set of command protocols, instructions with overriding priority. The signal was an emergency beacon, weak and thready, that said there might be something alive inside the black figure sprawled on the barren hillside.

Rods and cables shifted, extending upward. The flexibot quickly identified the nearest satellite and began retransmitting the emergency signal. High overhead the signal was received, recognized and passed on, broadcast to any Earth ships in the star system. It eventually made its way to the attention of those on duty in the Peggy Sue's CIC, and from them to the ship's captain.

### Crew Lounge, Lower Deck, Peggy Sue

The survivors from the Fortune were gathered in the crew lounge adjacent to the enlisted quarters. They had been interviewed by the grizzled old Chief who had extracted them from the escape pods, and several officers. As a result, they all were assigned duties under the supervision of existing crewmembers. This did not sit particularly well with all the survivors.

"Man, what is with these people?" griped Raoul Mendez, the former navigator.

"You really don't know who these people are?" asked Leon. "The Captain, First Officer and Sailing Master were all high ranking Navy officers during the war. Before that they were part of the original crew of the Peggy Sue, the starship we're on."

"Like I'm supposed to know who all these people are," Mendez muttered.

"They are some of the most famous explorers in all the Orion Arm. How I wish I had landed a berth on this ship instead of that bucket-of-bolts livestock transport we came here on."

"Yeah, yeah. They got me working for some Jap broad as a junior navtec."

Frank Hoenig, the shuttle pilot, was the last man retrieved from space. He just finished talking with the Sailing Master and had drawn some different conclusions than his former shipmates.

"I'd be careful with that mouth of yours, Mendez. That Japanese lady is Dr. Mizuki Ogawa."

"Huh? So what?"

"She is one of the most respected astrophysicists of our time, and she was also on this ship's second voyage—the second voyage to the stars ever made by Earthlings. She has seen more strange worlds and fought more aliens than you have ever dreamed of. That's so what."

"Hey, I've heard of her," Leon exclaimed. "She's like a samurai warrior physics chick. If she had a rock band she'd be a female Buckaroo Bonsai."

"I would keep a civil tongue in my head if I were you, Raoul. She could kick your sorry ass without breaking a sweat," Frank added. Raoul scowled.

"I'm looking at this as a net positive," Leon said, ignoring the disgruntled navigator. "I'm alive and I've already found new employment."

"Well my friend, play your cards right and you just might work your way into a permanent position." In an almost conspiratorial tone, Frank added, "The crew gets a piece of the action from any discoveries made during the voyage."

"I don't care, I just want to go home," Ethan Jones opined.

"Hey," said Leon, "what happened to those two settler boys?"

Mendez snorted. "Who gives a shit? I hate to say it but I'm with Jones, I just want to go home."

"You guys got no imagination," countered Leon. "This could be the opportunity of a lifetime."

"I'll give yous the opportunity of a lifetime," said a gruff voice from the aft doorway. "Hoenig, Delaney, haul your asses aft to the armory and get fitted for some armor. Yer gonna make one last visit to Paradise."

"Aye, aye, Chief," the two men responded as they hurried aft.

"The rest of yous scupper turds, grab yer data pads. I ain't done orientating yous yet."


### Shuttle One, Descending

Bobby was once again at the controls of the heavy armored shuttle, making a return trip he never thought he'd make. Next to him was Fred, the new shuttle pilot from the Fortune. The Captain wanted him to get a little on the job training, and to see how he handled himself under stress.

Sitting in the port side jump-seat, Beth seemed on edge. Bobby and Beth had been friends from the time she started dating Billy Ray—he knew she had taken the Gunny's loss hard, he just hoped she didn't have her expectations too high. Just because a survey drone found an emergency beacon didn't mean there was somebody alive down there.

In the other jump seat was Doc White, just in case there was a survivor. She seldom left the ship and was excited to see the dead planet up close.

"This is the area that the holotank displayed earlier? The little town in the middle of green prairie land?"

"Yes, Betty," Bobby answered. "The area just ahead had been seeded and was expanding rapidly before the contagion took it out."

"And we're sure it's gone, right? The contagion I mean."

"That's what Mizuki and the science dweebs said. As long as we are all encased in space armor we shouldn't reawaken the stuff."

"Look! Down there." Beth pointed excitedly to something on the surface off the port side.

"Yeah, the locator shows that as the drone location. We'll swing around and land pointed uphill. Frank, you bring her around."

"Roger."

"Just remember, she flies like a brick, an overpowered brick, but still a brick."

* * * * *

Frank managed to set the shuttle down ten meters beyond the flexibot. The robot drone stood like a beacon tower next to the prostrate figure on the rocky hillside. Betty and Beth headed for the rear of the craft, Beth in the lead.

"OK. I'm going to the back to keep an eye on things," Bobby said to Frank. "If I start yelling get us into the air quickly."

"Roger that. I've been through that drill once already."

"There might be hope for you yet, Frank." Bobby clapped his co-pilot on the shoulder and followed after the women.

The scene at the rear ramp was crowded, with the three Marines, Beth, and Dr. White all trying to get a look at the dark object laying next to the rod and wire tower formed by the flexibot. Behind them Kashi and the new crewman, Leon, stood by with a portable medical capsule, an emergency stretcher on repulsors with full medical sensors. The capsule could be sealed, providing air and oxygen to a wounded patient even in vacuum.

"Let's see what we have, people," Beth said.

"Bosco, Vinny, lead off," ordered Kato. "I'm right behind you."

The Marines were armed as they had been in the ship's hold when the escape pods were recovered, with UV lasers. The plan was for the Marines to be the only personnel to dismount from the shuttle. If the black contagion did make an appearance the hope was that the lasers could hold it off long enough for them to get back on board and get the shuttle into the air.

328

As the Marines neared the figure, the flexibot shrank downward and tumbled away from the site. Bosco reached the dark figure first.

"It looks like one of our armor suits all right."

"Is it intact?" asked Beth.

Kneeling down, Bosco ran a gauntleted hand along the side of the battered suit. The outer layers of armor flaked and crumbled under his touch.

"The armor is badly degraded, but the suit seems intact."

Vinny called out, "I'm getting telemetry readings that show an internal atmosphere. The power levels are low but there's still active life support."

"What do you want us to do, Commander?" asked Kato, scanning the area for any movement, any indication of a threat.

"Try to stand the suit up."

Bosco and Vinny obeyed, gently lifting the top of the suit, levering it into an upright position. The suit arms stayed frozen in the same positions they had on the ground: the left arm bent, hand next to the helmet; the right arm out stretched, reaching for the sky.

"What now, Ma'am?"

"Bring the suit onto the ramp." As the Marines complied with Beth's orders, she turned to Bobby. "When they are all standing on the ramp I want it raised until it's level with the cargo floor. Then liftoff into a hover so nothing can get to us."

"Right. Frank, did you copy that?"

"Roger, standing by."

Moving the massive, damaged suit was no problem for the augmented musculature of the Marines' armor. The figure was soon standing on the cargo ramp and the shuttle hovering a hundred meters above the ground.

"OK, Kashi and Leon, hose it down with distilled water, just in case." Though Beth was dying to open the battered suit of armor, she forced herself to methodically follow the plan drawn up with

329

the science section on the trip down. Water and crud sluiced off the end of the ramp, falling to the dead world below.

During the wash down the supporting Marines rotated the suit until it was facing out the open cargo hatch. This put the suit's back to those inside. Entry to a suit of heavy armor was from the back, where the back mounted equipment and ammunition storage opened like a clam-shell. The sailors secured the water hose and stood back, expectantly.

Beth nodded to Kato. "Crack it open, Sergeant Kwan."

Equipment and chunks of armor fell off as Kato pried the back of the suit open. Inside was a body, in a skintight pressure suit. Doc White and Kashi rushed forward to pull the limp form from its armor shell. The head lolled back and the face could be clearly seen—it was Rosey Acuna.

*Thank God!* Beth started toward the Gunny's slack body but stopped herself.

Working quickly Doc White and Kashi stripped the sergeant's body and, with Leon's help, got her into the medical capsule. Betty moved purposefully about the fallen Marine, palpating extremities and attaching IV lines. Finally she slid the clear cover shut, providing an oxygen enriched atmosphere for her patient to breath.

"Doc?" Beth asked, a hint of anxiety in her voice.

"She's alive. Pulse is week and she's a bit dehydrated, but she should be OK."

It was as though a great weight was lifted from Beth's shoulders. There were smiles all around among the crew. The Marines' expressions were not visible within their armored helmets but the change in body language indicated their elation.

"Ma'am, what do we do with the suit?" asked Kato.

"There might still be some contamination on it, throw it off the ramp."

"Aye, aye, Ma'am." Kato motioned to the Marines still supporting the empty suit. They took a step and heaved the ruined husk out of the shuttle. It fell to the surface, out of sight of those in the cargo bay.

330

"Frank, close the ramp and let's get underway for orbit. I'll be forward in a minute."

"Roger that, Commander Danner."

Inside the clear covering of the medical capsule Rosey stirred. Given hydration fluids and oxygen, her medical nanites kicked into overdrive. With effort she managed to focused and look around at her assembled rescuers.

"If this is heaven I'm real disappointed," she mumbled. "And if it's hell, it looks just like the place I came from."

Beth leaned over the stretcher beaming.

"Welcome back, Gunny."

## Chapter 30

### Sick Bay, Peggy Sue

The Gunny had a steady stream of visitors, to the point where Dr. White was becoming annoyed. She made a comment to that effect to Rosey, who was an old friend and shipmate.

"Yeah, you'd think I owed them all money or something," the Marine said from her hospital bed. "Doc, how long are you going to keep me on my backside?"

"Until I'm sure I'm not missing something," Betty shot back. "After all the uproar, I'll be damned if I'm gonna take the blame for you dropping dead because some microbe was overlooked."

"Well, when you put it that way."

A new set of visitors entered the ward—the two rescued girls and the First Officer. The sisters stood shyly at the foot of the bed, with Beth standing behind them, smiling. The First Officer was doing a lot of smiling since they brought Rosey back from the surface.

"Gunny," Beth began, "meet Dorri and Shadi, the two young ladies we retrieved from the last settlement."

Rosey smiled and moved the bed to a more upright position. "Hello, ladies. It's good to see you."

"It is wonderful to see you, Gunnery Sergeant Rosy Acuna," said Dorri. "If not for you I would no longer have a sister."

"Yes, you saved my life," added Shadi, "and for a time we were all afraid that your kindness had cost you yours."

Rosey actually blushed. "Just call me Gunny. Like I said, it's good to see you both alive and kicking. All my friends should have known, it takes more than a deadly planet wide contagion to take out a Marine."

"And the Gunny is a true Marine," Beth said. "The best on the ship and an example for Marines everywhere."

The Gunny's eyes got a bit wider at the First Officer's effusive praise. "Thank you, Ma'am. Just doing the job."

"Can I ask you a question, Gunny?" asked Shadi.

"Certainly."

"Dr. Ogawa said she would teach us kendo, but she said that you were the best person to learn self defense from. Would you teach my sister and me how to fight?"

A smile spread slowly across the Gunny's face. "I would be happy to have you join the Marines' daily class. But you will need to participate in the daily run and PT—physical training—each morning before hand-to-hand combat instruction. Is that OK?"

Both girls nodded yes enthusiastically.

"We start at 0500 in the cargo hold. Though it will take me another day or two to get out of this hospital bed."

"We'll be there, Gunny. Thank you!"

"Thanks, Gunny," added the First Officer. "Let me know when you are ready to return to duty."

"Yes, Ma'am."

With that, Beth herded her young charges out of the room, thanking Betty on the way out. Betty returned to Rosey's bedside.

"They seem like a couple of nice kids, and Beth was being awfully nice herself. If she's not careful she'll damage her reputation."

"Don't be snarky, Doc. The First Officer has a tough job, this being a new crew and all."

"Yeah, well she took your accident hard, Rosey. Enjoy her shift in attitude while you can. By the way, I think I have two other new recruits for you."

"Oh? Not some of those lava creatures."

"No, a couple of farm boys from the Fortune. I think they were followers of that Brother Abraham guy."

"That is just what I need."

"According to Hank Zackly, when he informed them that you survived your unexpected stay on the surface they started babbling all sorts of stuff about you being 'the chosen of God' and having 'defeated the angel of death'."

"Great, now I'm Joan of Arc. I always wanted my own cult." Rosey shook her head. "If I recall, things didn't work out so well for Saint Joan."

"Well they're big and beefy and not overly bright. I'd think they're perfect for the Marines." Betty smiled a wicked smile to show Rosey she was just giving her a hard time. At one time Betty had been a Navy Medical Corpsman attached to the Marines.

"Well, we'll see. If I can't turn 'em into Marines by the time we make home port we can always leave 'em on the shore. Besides, it will give me something challenging to do."

"If you are looking forward to conducting basic training I'd say you are ready to get out of that bed. I'll bring you a new jump suit and booties."

"Outstanding, thanks Doc."


### Officer's Quarters, Peggy Sue

Will Krenshaw was having a crisis of conscience. He had been less than fully candid when he signed on for the voyage, claiming that he had been affiliated with a university back on Earth that had been destroyed during the alien bombardment and was left unemployed. He was a qualified microbiologist, and he had worked at a university, but he neglected to mention that he was in the pay of Fleet intelligence.

His mission was to watch the officers and crew of the Peggy Sue, and report any questionable activities or unlawful acts they might commit during the voyage. The Intel section was convinced that Captain Vincent and his merry band were no better than buccaneers and pirates, out to plunder any planet they happened upon.

At first he suspected that the Fleet officers were right, the crew certainly seemed filled with questionable characters. The Captain all but blasted his way out of the solar system, ignoring orders from Navy vessels to stop. But then, after arriving in this system, Will began to have doubts.

The merchants were cautious to the point of paranoia about contaminating the targeted planet, or risking the lives of the Marines and scientists sent to the surface. The officers all acted professionally and Dr. Ogawa insisted on maintaining the highest professional standards. They left Paradise intact for the arriving colonists and headed farther out into the system. That's when Will really began to suspect he was on the wrong side.

The explorers went to great lengths, at no small personal risk, to make contact with the lava creatures. They actually made friends with the sentient boulders and exchanged items with them— possibly mankind's first act of friendly interstellar trade. Will suspected that the Fleet would have either ignored the fascinating silicon life form or simply blasted their little moon to bits and been done with it.

Then came that horrible business with Joe Rogers. Granted Joe was a bit of a loose cannon, but what a ghastly way to die! More importantly, the Captain didn't just cut and run. He raced back to Paradise to warn the colonists. The crew of the Peggy Sue risked their own lives trying to rescue those poor settlers while the Colonization Board people stood by and watched. The Captain and crew of the Peggy Sue were looking more and more like the good guys here, and not the avaricious plunderers the Navy had described.

In the end, he wrote a fairly neutral report, which was hidden inside a seemingly innocuous letter to a colleague back at Farside. That letter was included in the electronic mail to be sent back on the survey drone. True, several hundred people died and the Peggy Sue did destroy the transport ship, but he'd be damned if he didn't think they'd done the right thing. Oh well. Perhaps the merchants would commit an unspeakable atrocity or two at their next port of call.

### Cargo Hold, Peggy Sue

The Captain and Sailing Master were examining a large cylindrical container, which lay on its side near the starboard cargo door. It had been built by Engineer Baldursson's artificers to fit into a bay on the planetary survey drone. The bay used to contain disposable survey probes that had been expended during its mission to Paradise. The drone itself floated in space just outside the cargo door.

"So we can fit a half a ton of jewels and a sample of the alien tech from Paradise into this thing?" asked Billy Ray.

"Aye, Captain," replied Arin. "Plus a beacon tuned to company frequencies and all the encrypted video."

"Both the alien recordings and our own records of what happened here?"

"Ja, that and the survey drone's data."

"Good. Let's get this installed in the probe and send it on its way. If there was a way to send some of the survivors I would send them as well."

"You should have thought of that before you vaporized the transport ship," said Bobby, teasing his friend.

"Did you want to round up that black stuff that was in her hold, pardner?" Billy Ray shot back. "Besides, the controls had been locked, sending Fortune back to Earth."

"Yeah, there wouldn't have been anyone left on arrival. Nothing but ghosts."

"Yer right, and there's already an awful lot of ghosts in the Orion Arm."

The engineers finished closing up the capsule and two of them wearing space suits pushed the cylinder through the cargo door. Following the cylinder, the men disappeared through the door into the vacuum outside.

"You think the authorities will shit doughnuts back at Farside when they find out almost all the settlers are dead and we blew up the Colonization Board ship?"

"I don't know, Bobby. We included statements from the surviving settlers and crewmembers. The new pilot, Frank, and his buddy Leon were quite explicit about Captain Chakrabarti freaking out after the settlers were all slaughtered. I hope they understand why we had to do what we did. Hell, we almost lost one of our own

337

rescuing those two girls after Chakrabarti refused to try and rescue anyone from the surface."

"Yeah, but you know politicians and bureaucrats, they only see things from their own selfish point of view. If it doesn't benefit them personally they don't much care. Hopefully the beacon will attract a company ship first."

"Either way, its gonna tight beam the recorded material to company HQ after emergence. That should give TK and the board enough ammunition to fend off the jackals."

"Still, it would just be a shame for some ass-hat from the Fleet to get all that alien poo." Bobby looked at his friend and grinned.

"We got several more tons of the stuff right over there." Billy Ray motioned at several sealed containers farther aft in the hold. "But you're right, they don't deserve a thing. Come on, let's go to the bridge and watch the probe head back home."

"Right there with ya, Billy Ray."


### Bridge, Peggy Sue

"The Captain is on the bridge," announced Nigel Lawson, acting OOD.

"I have the deck and the conn, Mr. Lewis," Billy Ray answered. With increasing tension and threat levels more Navy formality had crept into the crew's interactions. Certainly the entire crew was deadly serious when the Fortune was destroyed and its survivors rescued.

Bobby took his seat next to Nigel at the helm, while Beth and Mizuki occupied their usual positions behind the Captain. With the bridge fully manned the ship was ready to sail.

"Put the survey drone on the forward screen, Dr. Ogawa."

"Hai, Captain." Mizuki focused the ship's largest telescope on the survey drone as it approached the alter-space transit point back to Earth. A holographic projection replaced the normal view forward through the Peggy Sue's transparent bow.

"Less than two minutes to transit, Captain," reported Nigel.

The bridge fell silent as all hands watched the drone. Just large enough to house the necessary shields and gravitonic drives, the drone was as small an alter-space capable object as Earthly technology could build. The seconds to transit ticked down.

The slender drone shimmered and vanished.

"Very well," Billy Ray said, "that particular die is cast."

"I wonder what the reaction will be back home," Beth mused.

"An honest tale speeds best, being plainly told."

"Shakespeare, Richard the Third, Sir," called out Nigel from the helm, causing the Captain to smile. Identifying his quotations had become a popular game among the bridge crew.

"Whatever the reaction is, we won't find out for another year or so, plenty of time for any ruckus to die down. What they decide to do with the next colonization effort remains to be seen."

"I hope they do a more thorough survey next time, it might save innocent lives."

"Not our call, Number One." Billy Ray remained pensively silent for half a minute before issuing new orders to the crew.

"Alright people, we have new stars to see and new aliens to meet! Helm, align us for transit to Gliese 667's primary stars. From there we're headin' out into unknown territory."

The crew's spirits rose as the ship left the ill-fated planet named Paradise and the ghosts of Orion in her wake. The prospects of greater, and more profitable, adventures lay before them as the Peggy Sue headed for unexplored space.

# Epilogue

## Board Room, Orion Arm Trading Company

TK Parker sat at the head of the boardroom table, an ostentatious slab of polished hardwood worth a fortune on the Moon. There were seven board members present, including the former Texas Oilman, all wealthy and successful before they were forced to flee Earth. They came from many countries and were of different ethnic and religious backgrounds. What they had in common was wealth and the overwhelming desire to acquire more.

"Let's come to order, people. We got a lot of things to discuss today, including more fallout from the Peggy Sue's actions at the Paradise colony."

"So have we heard back from the follow-up science expedition sent to GJ667Cc?" asked Indu Nadar, a former Indian manufacturing magnate and the board's only female member. "It has been almost eight months."

"We have, Indu. I have a short recorded message from Dr. von Langsdorf, the expedition leader. If no one objects I'd like to play it."

No objections were raised and TK called up the holovid recording on the table's center projector. The image of an erect older man appeared. He seemed to be facing each of the attendees, regardless of their position at the table. The man's image began to speak.

"This is to inform the board that we have made great progress in analyzing and controlling the contagion that infects planet Paradise." The man paused as though he anticipated the murmurs that circulated around the table. The lead scientist continued.

"We have come to the conclusion that the organism itself is an artificial life form, or ALF, an engineered creation smaller than a nanite with its own metabolic pathways, genome, and life cycle. It's genetic material is simple and unlike any found in known warm life."

The man's figure was replaced by a scene from the planet which showed a field of growing plants, presumably Earth life, being overcome by the black pestilence.

"It is simple, rugged, and effectively immortal. Without intervention it will keep its host planet clean of life as we know it forever."

TK paused the playback.

"Now here's where it gets interesting, people."

The recording resumed with a different field of grass as the scientist's voice-over continued.

"We have made a number of advances with respect to controlling or eradicating the contagion. The presence of organic molecules stimulate the ALF, causing it to emerge from hibernation and enter its active state. Using robotic devices and teleoperated laboratory equipment we have identified a number of exogenous antagonists that prevent the ALF from reproducing and from absorbing other living organisms, which provide energy for its growth."

Again the black strands began to ravage the growing plants, dissolving all they came in contact with. But then the spread of the contagion stopped. It rebounded from a strip of plants that formed a boarder around the field. This effectively contained the outbreak, which soon withered and vanished back into the sandy soil.

"As you can see, the contagion is unable to infest fields of specially modified Earth plants. The plants are genetically modified to host symbiotic micro organisms which secrete the antagonists that halt the contagion. While this gives some protection against the contagion, it is not a cure for the planet's infestation.

"We are now working on a constellation of micro organisms that, when applied to an infested planet, will actively deny the spread of the contagion and eventually destroy it in its dormant spoor state. Once this is done we will be able to disinfect Paradise, making it safe for colonization by Earth life."

The hologram faded from view, leaving the board members sitting in contemplative silence. Henri Bouchard, a former Swiss banker, was first to break the silence.

"So this means we can claim the planet and colonize it ourselves? I'm not sure I would want to be among the early settlers."

"I think we'll need to terraform the plant over a period of years to prove that the contagion won't come back, Henri. But yes, those dim bulbs over at the Colonization Board have given up their claim to Paradise."

"Initially, they seemed quite upset about the destruction of their ship," remarked Indu Nadar, "and the slaughter of their colonists."

"Not really. Oh, they'll miss the ship, but the colonists? Not so much. Their real, long-term goal is getting as many human beings living on as many planets as possible. To the CB the settlers themselves were just livestock, additional gene pools to draw on if needed."

"I still don't understand why they sent those three sets of religious fanatics."

"First time out, send some expendables. Those poor people were not exactly highly sought after types. Under educated and mostly useless here on the Moon, or any other closed environment installation inside the solar system. They would always remain dependent on the state, a permanent lower class. Their presence would have eventually caused problems, so the CB decided to send 'em off to be farmers on a far away planet. Got 'em off of the Moon and they weren't gonna be missed if the colony failed."

"That's horrible, TK." Indu shuddered involuntarily.

TK shrugged. "Not much compassion over there at the CB. Still, it worked out for us—we got the planet after all."

"Imagine," said Liong Tan, an Indonesian of Chinese descent, "controlling the wealth of an entire planet, one with much more land area than Earth. This certainly makes the company a profitable one, even if the return on investment will take some time to realize."

"It ain't just a planet, people. It could be dozens of planets."

"What? What do you mean TK?"

343

"Think about it, Liong. We know of scores of planets, and a lot of them have indigenous life. This life may or may not be compatible with Earth life. Either way it can be a problem."

TK had everyone's attention now. After looking around the table at his fellow board members he pushed ahead.

"Incompatible means we have to displace the native ecosystem and replace it with a more benign one. Compatible means there is a chance of infection, cross breading with native organisms, and other complications. Regardless, the best way to establish an Earth colony on an exoplanet is to remove any native life and replant the place with Earth organisms."

"And the contagion, if it can be controlled, can help do precisely that," said Indu Nadar, as full realization dawned on her.

"Right you are, darlin'. What we have here is a way to make spreading humanity, and all Earth life, across the Galaxy much simpler."

"But what about the military, won't they be wanting to classify this discovery and turn it into a weapon?" asked Norm Philips, a former Australian mining magnate.

"Norm, there's some things too dangerous to trust the military with, and this is one of 'em. In fact, we need to keep this thing top secret."

"Why would you say that, mate?"

"This can be our ace in the hole. Before we all left Earth we only had a single world for everybody. With this we can have a whole passel of worlds for people to live on."

"And we will be in a position to develop those worlds and to promote trade between them," added Liong Tan.

"Right you are, my friend, but only if we keep this quiet. We will proceed like we have been: building new ships, sending out exploratory missions, finding new aliens and habitable planets. Except now, when we find an Earth-like world with no indigenous sentient life, we sterilize it and plant a new ecosystem. We get perfectly inhabitable new planets with nobody the wiser."

"Do we know who made this contagion? Was this their intended purpose for creating it?"

"We may never know. Whoever they were they weren't very considerate of others. They effectively committed genocide—or is it ecocide—on Paradise."

"They were obviously advanced, will we run into them somewhere in the wider galaxy? Will we have to fight them?" asked Liong Tan.

"Don't know. After 10,000 years maybe they killed themselves off, or maybe the Dark Lords got 'em. For now, let's not borrow trouble."

TK looked around the room and saw the others were already tallying the wealth to be gained from such a scheme. In truth, Parker saw this as a way to help mankind spread to the stars, a goal he shared with the Colonization Board. To survive, humanity needed to grow strong enough to resist the Dark Lords and their minions, who were sure to return one day. If the greed of his fellow board members helped him accomplish his goal, so be it.

"So what do y'all say? Are we in agreement?"

The sly old Texan raised his hand, signaling a vote of the board. Around the table all the hands went up.

"It's unanimous," he said with a smile. "I say we seal the records of this meeting and get back to work."

www.ingramcontent.com/pod-product-compliance
Lightning Source LLC
Chambersburg PA
CBHW071230250626
47163CB00001B/112